Alistair MacLean

Alistair MacLean

Where Eagles Dare

Ice Station Zebra

CHANCELLOR
PRESS

Where Eagles Dare was first published in Great Britain
in 1967 by William Collins Sons & Co Ltd

Ice Station Zebra was first published in Great Britain
in 1963 by William Collins Sons & Co Ltd

This edition first published in Great Britain in 1984 by

Chancellor Press
an imprint of the Octopus Publishing Group p.l.c.
59 Grosvenor Street
London, W1

ISBN: 0 907486 75 4

Printed in Great Britain at The Pitman Press, Bath

Alistair MacLean

Contents

Where Eagles Dare

Ice Station Zebra

Alistair MacLean

Where Eagles Dare

Where Eagles Dare

To Geoff and Gina

Chapter One

The vibrating clangour from the four great piston engines set teeth on edge and made an intolerable assault on cringing eardrums. The decibel-level, Smith calculated, must have been about that found in a boiler factory, and one, moreover, that was working on overtime rates, while the shaking cold in that cramped, instrument-crowded flight-deck was positively Siberian. On balance, he reflected, he would have gone for the Siberian boiler factory any time because, whatever its drawbacks, it wasn't liable to fall out of the sky or crash into a mountain-side which, in its present circumstances, seemed a likely enough, if not imminent contingency for all that the pilot of their Lancaster bomber appeared to care to the contrary. Smith looked away from the darkly opaque world beyond the windscreens where the wipers fought a useless battle with the driving snow and looked again at the man in the left-hand captain's seat.

Wing Commander Cecil Carpenter was as completely at home in his environment as the most contented oyster in his shell in Whitstable Bay. Any comparison with a Siberian boiler factory he would have regarded as the ravings of an unhinged mind. Quite clearly, he found the shuddering vibration as soothing as the ministrations of the gentlest of masseurs, the roar of the engines positively soporific and the ambient temperature just right for a man of his leisured literary tastes. Before him, at a comfortable reading distance, a book rested on a hinged contraption which he had swung out from the cabin's side. From what little Smith could occasionally see of the lurid cover, depicting a blood-stained knife plunged into the back of a girl who didn't seem to have any clothes on, the Wing Commander held the more serious contemporary novelists in a fine contempt. He turned a page.

'Magnificent,' he said admiringly. He puffed deeply on an ancient briar that smelt like a fumigating plant. 'By heavens, this feller can write. Banned, of course, young Tremayne' – this to the fresh-faced youngster in the co-pilot's seat – 'so I can't let you have it till you grow up.' He broke off, fanned the smoke-laden air to improve the visibility, and peered accusingly at his co-pilot. 'Flying Officer Tremayne, you have that look of pained apprehension on your face again.'

'Yes, sir. That's to say, no, sir.'

'Part of the malaise of our time,' Carpenter said sorrowfully. 'The young lack so many things, like appreciation of a fine pipe tobacco or faith in their commanding officers.' He sighed heavily, carefully marked the place in his book, folded the rest away and straightened in his seat. 'You'd think a man would be entitled to some peace and quiet on his own flight-deck.'

He slid open his side screen. An icy gust of snow-laden wind blew into the flight-deck, carrying with it the suddenly deepened roar from the engines.

Carpenter grimaced and thrust his head outside, shielding his eyes with a gauntleted right hand. Five seconds later he shook his head dispiritedly, screwed his eyes shut as he winced in what appeared to be considerable pain, withdrew his head, closed the screen, brushed the snow away from his flaming red hair and magnificent handlebar moustache, and twisted round to look at Smith.

'It is no small thing, Major, to be lost in a blizzard in the night skies over war-torn Europe.'

'Not again, sir,' Tremayne said protestingly.

'No man is infallible, my son.'

Smith smiled politely. 'You mean you don't know where we are, sir?'

'How should I?' Carpenter slid down in his seat, half-closed his eyes and yawned vastly. 'I'm only the driver. We have a navigator and the navigator has a radar set and I've no faith in either of them.'

'Well, well.' Smith shook his head. 'To think that they lied to me at the Air Ministry. They told me you'd flown some three hundred missions and knew the continent better than any taxi driver knows his London.'

'A foul *canard* put about by unfriendly elements who are trying to prevent me from getting a nice safe job behind a desk in London.' Carpenter glanced at his watch. 'I'll give you exactly thirty minutes' warning before we shove you out over the dropping zone.' A second glance at his watch and a heavy frown. 'Flying Officer Tremayne, your gross dereliction of duty is endangering the entire mission.'

'Sir?' An even deeper apprehension in Tremayne's face.

'I should have had my coffee exactly three minutes ago.'

'Yes, sir. Right away, sir.'

Smith smiled again, straightened from his cramped position behind the pilots' seats, left the flight-deck and moved aft into the Lancaster's fuselage. Here in this cold, bleak and forbidding compartment, which resembled nothing so much as an iron tomb, the impression of the Siberian boiler factory was redoubled. The noise level was so high as to be almost intolerable, the cold was intense and metal-ribbed metal walls, dripping with condensation, made no concessions whatsoever to creature comfort. Nor did the six metal-framed canvas seats bolted to the floor, functionalism gone mad. Any attempt to introduce those sadistically designed instruments of torture in HM penitentiaries would have caused a national outcry.

Huddled in those six chairs sat six men, probably, Smith reflected, the six most miserable men he'd ever seen. Like himself, each of the six was dressed in the uniform of the German Alpine Corps. Like himself, each man wore two parachutes. All were shivering constantly, stamping their feet and beating their arms, and their frozen breath hung heavy in the ice-chill air. Facing them, along the upper starboard side of the fuselage, ran a taut metal wire which passed over the top of the doorway. On to this wire were clipped snap-catches, wires from which led down to folded parachutes resting on top of an assortment of variously shaped bundles, the contents of only one of which could be identified by the protruding ends of several pairs of skis.

The nearest parachutist, a dark intense man with Latin features, looked up at Smith's arrival. He had never, Smith thought, seen Edward Carraciola look quite so unhappy.

'Well?' Carraciola's voice was just as unhappy as his face. 'I'll bet he's no more bloody idea where we are than I have.'

'He does seem to navigate his way across Europe by opening his window and sniffing the air from time to time,' Smith admitted. 'But I wouldn't worry—'

He broke off as a sergeant air-gunner entered from the rear, carrying a can of steaming coffee and enamel mugs.

'Neither would I, sir.' The sergeant smiled tolerantly. 'The Wing Commander has his little ways. Coffee, gentlemen? Back at the base he claims that he reads detective novels all the time and depends upon one of the gunners telling him from time to time where we are.'

Smith cradled frozen hands round the coffee mug. 'Do *you* know where we are?'

'Of course, sir.' He seemed genuinely surprised, then nodded to the metal rungs leading to the upper machine-gun turret. 'Just nip up there, sir, and look down to your right.'

Smith lifted an enquiring eyebrow, handed over his mug, climbed the ladder and peered down to his right through the Perspex dome of the turret cupola. For a few seconds only the darkness filled his eyes then gradually, far below and seen dimly through the driving snow, he could make out a ghostly luminescence in the night, a luminescence which gradually resolved itself into a criss-cross pattern of illuminated streets. For a brief moment only Smith's face registered total disbelief then quickly returned to its normal dark stillness.

'Well, well.' He retrieved his coffee. 'Somebody should tell them down there. The lights are supposed to be out all over Europe.'

'Not in Switzerland, sir,' the sergeant explained patiently. 'That's Basle.'

'Basle?' Smith stared at him. 'Basle! Good God, he's gone seventy or eighty miles off course. The flight plan routed us north of Strasbourg.'

'Yes, sir.' The sergeant air-gunner was unabashed. 'The Wing Commander says he doesn't understand flight plans.' He grinned, half apologetically. 'To tell the truth, sir, this is our milk-run into the Vorarlberg. We fly east along the Swiss frontier, then south of Schaffhausen—'

'But that's over Swiss territory!'

'Is it? On a clear night you can see the lights of Zurich. They say Wing Commander Carpenter has a room permanently reserved for him there in the Baur-au-Lac.'

'What?'

'He says if it's a choice between a prisoner-of-war camp in Germany and internment in Switzerland he knows which side of the frontier he's coming down on . . . After that we fly down the Swiss side of Lake Constance, turn east at Lindau, climb to eight thousand to clear the mountains and it's only a hop, skip and jump to the Weissspitze.'

'I see,' Smith said weakly. 'But – don't the Swiss object?'

'Frequently, sir. Their complaints always seem to coincide with the nights we're around those parts. Wing Commander Carpenter claims it's some ill-intentioned Luftwaffe pilot trying to discredit him.'

'What else?' Smith asked, but the sergeant was already on his way to the flight-deck. The Lancaster lurched as it hit an infrequent air pocket, Smith grabbed a rail to steady himself and Lieutenant Morris Schaffer, of the American Office of Strategic Services and Smith's second-in-command, cursed fluently as the better part of a cup of scalding coffee emptied itself over his thigh.

'That's all I need,' he said bitterly. 'I've no morale left. I wish to God we *would* crash-land in Switzerland. Think of all those lovely Wienerschnitzels and Apfelstrudels. After a couple of years living among you Limeys, Spam and powdered eggs and an ounce of margarine a day, that's what Mama Schaffer's little boy requires. Building up.'

'You'd also live a damn' sight longer, friend,' Carraciola observed morosely. He transferred his gaze to Smith, gave him a long considering look. 'The whole set-up stinks, Major.'

'I don't think I understand,' Smith said quietly.

'Suicidal, is what I mean. What a bunch. Just look at us.' He gestured to the three men sitting nearest to him on his left: Olaf Christiansen, a flaxen-haired first cousin of Leif Ericsson, Lee Thomas, a short dark Welshman – both those men seemed slightly amused – and Torrance-Smythe, as languidly aristocratic-looking as any ci-devant French count that ever rode a tumbrel, a doleful ex-Oxford don who clearly wished he were back among the University cloisters. 'Christiansen, Thomas, old Smithy and myself. We're just a bunch of civil servants, filing clerks—'

'I know very well what you are,' Smith said quietly.

'Or yourself.' In the de-synchronized thunder of the engines the soft-voiced interruption had gone unnoticed. 'A major in the Black Watch. No doubt you cut quite a dash playing the bagpipes at El Alamein, but why the hell *you* to command us? No offence. But this is no more in your line than it is ours. Or Lieutenant Schaffer here. An airborne cowboy—'

'I hate horses,' Schaffer said loudly. 'That's why I had to leave Montana.'

'Or take George here.' Carraciola jerked a thumb in the direction of the last member of the party, George Harrod, a stocky army sergeant radio-operator with an expression of profound resignation on his face. 'I'll bet he's never as much as made a parachute jump in his life before.'

'I have news for you,' Harrod said stoically. 'I've never even been in a plane before.'

'He's never even been in a plane before,' Carraciola said despairingly. 'My God, what a bunch of no-hopers! All we need is a team composed of specialist Alpinists, Commandos, mountaineeers and safe-breakers and what do we have?' He shook his head slowly. 'We have us.'

Smith said gently: 'We were all the Colonel could get. Be fair. He told us yesterday that the one thing in the world that he didn't have was time.'

Carraciola made no reply, none of the others spoke, but Smith didn't have to be any clairvoyant to know what was in the minds of all of them. They were thinking what he was thinking, like himself they were back several hours in time and several hundred miles in space in that Admiralty Operations Room in London where Vice-Admiral Rolland, ostensibly Assistant Director of Naval Operations but in fact the long-serving head of MI6, the counter-espionage branch of the British Secret Service, and his deputy, Colonel Wyatt-Turner, had gravely and reluctantly briefed them on what they had as gravely and reluctantly admitted to be a mission born from the sheerest desperation.

'Deucedly sorry and all that, chaps, but time is of the essence.' Wyatt-Turner, a big, red-faced, heavily moustached colonel, tapped his cane against a wall-map of Germany, pointing to a spot just north of the Austrian border and a little west of Garmisch-Partenkirchen. 'Our man was brought down here at 2 a.m. this morning but SHAEF, in their all-knowing wisdom, didn't let us know until 10 a.m. Damned idiots! Damned idiots for not letting us know until so late and double-damned idiots for ignoring our advice in the first place. Gad, will they never learn to listen to us?' He shook his head in anger, tapped the map again. 'Anyway, he's here. Schloss Adler. The castle of the eagle. Believe me, it's well named, only an eagle could get there. Our job—'

Smith said: 'How are you so sure he's there, sir?'

'We're sure. Mosquito he was in crash-landed only ten miles away. The pilot got off a radio message just before a German patrol closed in.' He paused, smiled grimly, continued: 'Schloss Adler, Major Smith, is the combined HQ of the German Secret Service and the Gestapo in South Germany. Where else would they take him?'

'Where indeed? How was he brought down, sir?'

'Through the most damnable ill-luck. We carried out a saturation raid on Nürnberg last night and there shouldn't have been a German fighter within a hundred miles of the Austrian border. But a wandering Messerschmidtt patrol got him. That's unimportant. What's important is getting him out before he talks.'

'He'll talk,' Thomas said sombrely. 'They all do. *Why* did they disregard our advice, sir? We told them two days ago.'

'The whys don't matter,' Wyatt-Turner said tiredly. 'Not any more. The fact that he'll talk does. So we get him out. *You* get him out.'

Torrance-Smythe cleared his throat delicately. 'There are paratroops, sir.'

'Scared, Smithy?'

'Naturally, sir.'

'The Schloss Adler is inaccessible and impregnable. It would require a battalion of paratroops to take it.'

'Of course,' Christiansen said, 'the fact that there's no time to mount a massed paratroop attack has no bearing on the matter.' Christiansen appeared positively cheerful, the proposed operation obviously appealed vastly to him.

Wyatt-Turner gave him the benefit of his icy blue stare then decided to ignore him.

'Secrecy and stealth are the only hope,' he went on. 'And you gentlemen are – I trust – secretive and stealthy. You are experts at that and experts at survival behind enemy lines where all of you have spent considerable periods of time, Major Smith, Lieutenant Schaffer and Sergeant Harrod here in their professional capacities, the rest of you in – um – other duties. With the—'

'That was a damned long time ago, sir,' Carraciola interrupted. 'At least for Smithy, Thomas, Christiansen and myself. We're out of touch now. We don't know the latest developments in weapons and combat techniques. And God only knows we're out of training. After a couple of years behind a desk it takes me all my time to run fifty yards after a bus.'

'You'll have to get fit fast, won't you?' Wyatt-Turner said coldly. 'Besides, what matters most is, that with the exception of Major Smith, you all have an extensive knowledge of Western Europe. You all speak fluent German. You'll find your combat training – on the level you'll be engaged in – as relevant today as it was five years ago. You are men with exceptional records of resourcefulness, ability and ingenuity. If anyone has a chance, you have. You're all volunteers, of course.'

'Of course,' Carraciola echoed, his face carefully deadpan. Then he looked speculatively at Wyatt-Turner. 'There is, of course, another way, sir.' He paused, then went on very quietly indeed. 'A way with a hundred per cent guarantee of success.'

'Neither Admiral Rolland nor I claim to be infallible,' Wyatt-Turner said slowly. 'We have missed an alternative? You have the answer to our problems?'

'Yes. Whistle up a Pathfinder squadron of Lancasters with 10-ton block-buster bombs. Do *you* think *anyone* in the Schloss Adler would ever talk again?'

'I don't think so.' Admiral Rolland spoke gently and for the first time, moving from the wall-map to join the group. Admiral Rolland always spoke gently. When you wielded the almost incredible range of power that he did, you didn't have to talk loudly to make yourself heard. He was a short, grey-haired man, with a deeply trenched face and an air of immense authority. 'No,' he repeated, 'I don't think so. Nor do I think that your grasp of the realities of the situation is any match for your total ruthlessness. The captured man, Lieutenant General Carnaby, is an American. If we were to destroy him General Eisenhower would probably launch his Second Front against us instead of against the Germans.' He smiled deprecatingly, as though to remove rebuke from his voice. 'There are certain – um – niceties to be observed in our relationship with our Allies. Wouldn't you agree?'

Carraciola didn't agree or disagree. He had, apparently, nothing to say. Neither did anyone else. Colonel Wyatt-Turner cleared his throat.

'That's it then, gentlemen. Ten o'clock tonight at the airfield. No more questions, I take it?'

'Yes, sir, there bloody well is, begging the Colonel's pardon, sir.' Sergeant George Harrod not only sounded heated, he looked it, too. 'What's all this about? Why's this geezer so bloody important? Why the hell do we have to risk our necks—'

'That'll do, Sergeant.' Wyatt-Turner's voice was sharp, authoritative. 'You know all you require to know—'

'If we're sending a man to what may be his death, Colonel, I think he has the right to know why,' Admiral Rolland interrupted gently, almost apologetically. 'The rest know. He should too. It's painfully simple, Sergeant. General Carnaby is the overall co-ordinator of planning for the exercise known as Operation Overlord – the Second Front. It would be absolutely true to say that he knows more about the Allied preparations for the Second Front than any man alive.

'He set off last night to meet his opposite numbers in the Middle East, Russia and the Italian Front to co-ordinate final plans for the invasion of Europe. The rendezvous was in Crete – the only meeting point the Russians would accept. They haven't a plane fast enough to out-run the German fighters. The British Mosquito can – but it didn't last night.'

Silence lay heavy in the austere operations room. Harrod rubbed his hand across his eyes, then shook his head slowly, as if to clear it. When he spoke again all the truculence, all the anger had vanished from his voice. His words came very slowly.

'And if the General talks—'

'He'll talk,' Rolland said. The voice was soft, but it carried total conviction.

'As Mr Thomas has just said, they all talk. He won't be able to help himself. A mixture of mescalin and scopolamine.'

'And he'll tell them all the plans for the Second Front.' The words came as from a man in a dream. 'When, where, how – Good God, sir, we'll have to call the whole thing off!'

'Precisely. We call it off. No Second Front this year. Another nine months on the war, another million lives needlessly lost. You understand the urgency, Sergeant, the sheer desperate urgency of it all?'

'I understand, sir. Now I understand.' Harrod turned to Wyatt-Turner. 'Sorry I spoke like that, sir. I'm afraid – well, I'm a bit edgy, sir.'

'We're all a bit edgy, Sergeant. Well, the airfield at ten o'clock and we'll check the equipment.' He smiled without humour. 'I'm afraid the uniforms may not fit too well. This is early closing day in Savile Row.'

Sergeant Harrod huddled more closely into his bucket seat, beat freezing hands against freezing shoulders, morosely surveyed his uniform, wrinkled like an elephant's legs and about three sizes too big for him, then raised his voice above the clamour of the Lancaster's engines.

'Well,' he said bitterly, 'he was right about the bloody uniforms, anyway.'

'And wrong about everything else,' Carraciola said heavily. 'I still say we should have sent in the Lancasters.'

Smith, still standing against the starboard fuselage, lit a cigarette and eyed him speculatively. He opened his mouth to speak when it occurred to him that he had seen men in more receptive mood. He looked away without saying anything.

In the flight-deck, now slid so impossibly far forward in his seat that the back of his head rested on the back of his seat, Wing Commander Carpenter was still deeply and contentedly preoccupied with pipe, coffee and literature. Beside him, Flying Officer Tremayne was obviously failing to share his mood of pleasurable relaxation. He was, in fact, keeping a most anxious watch, his eyes constantly shifting from the instrument panel to the opaque darkness beyond the windscreen to the recumbent figure of his superior officer who appeared to be in danger of dropping off to sleep at any moment. Suddenly Tremayne sat far forward in his seat, stared for long seconds through the windscreen ahead of him then turned excitedly to Carpenter.

'There's Schaffhausen down there, sir!'

Carpenter groaned heavily, closed his book, swung back the hinged book-rest, finished his coffee, levered himself upright with another groan, slid open his side-screen and made an elaborate pretence of examining the loom of light far below, without, however, actually going to the lengths of exposing his face to the wind and the driving snow outside. He closed the screen and looked at Tremayne.

'By heavens,' he said admiringly, 'I believe you're right. It's a great comfort to have you along, my boy, a great comfort.' He switched on the intercom while Tremayne looked suitably abashed. 'Major Smith? Yes. Thirty minutes to go.' He switched off and turned again to Tremayne. 'Right. South-east down the old Bodensee. And for God's sake keep to the Swiss side.

Smith hung up the headphones and looked quizzically at the six seated men.

'That's it, then. Half an hour. Let's hope it's warmer down there than it is up here.'

No one had any comment to make on that. No one seemed to have any hope either. Soundlessly, wordlessly, they looked without expression at one another, then pulled themselves stiffly to their frozen feet. Then very slowly, very awkwardly, their numbed hands and cramped conditions making things almost impossibly awkward for them, they prepared themselves for the drop. They helped each other strap loads on their backs, beneath the high-mounted parachutes, then struggled into their white waterproof snow trousers. Sergeant Harrod went one better. He pulled a voluminous snow-smock over his head, zipped it up with difficulty and drew the hood over his head. He turned round questioningly as a hand tapped the hummocked outline below his white smock.

'I hardly like to say this,' Schaffer said diffidently, 'but I really don't reckon your radio is going to stand the shock of landing, Sergeant.'

'Why not?' Harrod looked more lugubrious than ever. 'It's been done before.'

'Not by you, it hasn't. By my reckoning you're going to hit the ground with a terminal velocity of a hundred and eighty miles an hour. Not to put too fine a point on it, I think you're going to experience some difficulty in opening your chute.'

Harrod looked at him, looked at his other five smockless companions, then nodded slowly and touched his own smock.

'You mean I put this on *after* we reach the ground?'

'Well,' Schaffer said consideringly, 'I really think it would help.' He grinned at Harrod, who grinned back almost cheerfully. Even Carraciola's lips twitched in the beginnings of a smile. The release of tension within that frozen fuselage was almost palpable.

'Well, well, time I earned my wing-commander's pay while you stripling pilots sit and gaze in rapt admiration.' Carpenter studied his watch. 'Two fifteen. Time we changed places.'

Both men unhooked their safety belts and awkwardly changed over. Carpenter fastidiously adjusted the right-hand seat's back rest until it was exactly right for him, manoeuvred his parachute to its position of maximum comfort, fastened his seat-belt, unhooked and adjusted on his head a combined earphones and microphone set and made a switch.

'Sergeant Johnson?' Carpenter never bothered with the regulation call-up formalities. 'Are you awake?'

Back in the navigator's tiny and extremely uncomfortable recess, Sergeant Johnson was very much awake. He had been awake for hours. He was bent over a glowing greenish radar screen, his eyes leaving it only to make rapid reference to the charts, an Ordnance map, a picture and a duplicate compass, altimeter and air-speed indicator. He reached for the switch by his side.

'I'm awake, sir.'

'If you fly us into the side of the Weissspitze,' Carpenter said threateningly, 'I'll have you reduced to aircraftman. Aircraftman second class, Johnson.'

'I wouldn't like that. I make it nine minutes, sir.'

'For once we're agreed on something. So do I.' Carpenter switched off, slid open the starboard screen and peered out. Although there was just the faintest wash of moonlight in the night sky, visibility might as well have been zero. It was a greyly opaque world, a blind world, with nothing to be seen but the thinly driving snow. He withdrew his head, brushed away the snow from his huge moustache, closed the screen, looked regretfully at his pipe and carefully put it away in his pocket.

For Tremayne, the stowage of the pipe was the final proof that the Wing Commander was clearing the decks for action. He said unhappily: 'A bit dicey, isn't it, sir? Locating the Weissspitze in this lot, I mean?'

'Dicey?' Carpenter sounded almost jovial. 'Dicey? I don't see why? It's as big as a mountain. In fact, it *is* a mountain. We can't miss it, my dear boy.'

'That's what I mean.' He paused, a pause with more meaning in it. 'And this plateau on the Weissspitze that we have to drop them on. Only three hundred yards wide, sir. Mountain above it, cliff below it. And those adiabatic mountain winds, or whatever you call them, blowing in any old unpredictable direction. A fraction to the south and we'll hit the mountain, a fraction to the north and they'll fall down that whacking great cliff and like as not all break their necks. Three hundred yards!'

'What do you want?' Carpenter demanded expansively. 'Heathrow Airport? Three hundred yards? All the room in the world, my boy. We land this old crate on runways a tenth of that width.'

'Yes, sir. I've always found runway landing lights a great help, sir. At seven thousand feet up the side of the Weissspitze—'

He broke off as a buzzer rang. Carpenter made a switch.

'Johnson?'

'Yes, sir.' Johnson was huddled more closely than ever over his radar screen where the revolving scanner-line had picked up a white spot immediately to the right of centre of the screen. 'I have it, sir. Right where it should be.' He looked away from the screen and made a quick check on the compass. 'Course oh-nine-three, sir.'

'Good lad.' Carpenter smiled at Tremayne, made a tiny course alteration and began to whistle softly to himself. 'Have a look out your window, laddie. My moustache is beginning to get all waterlogged.'

Tremayne opened his window, strained his head as far as possible, but still there was only this grey and featureless opacity. He withdrew his head, silently shook it.

'No matter. It must be there somewhere,' Carpenter said reasonably. He spoke into the intercom. 'Sergeant? Five minutes. Hook up.'

'Hook up!' The sergeant air-gunner repeated the order to the seven men standing in a line along the starboard side of the fuselage. 'Five minutes.'

Silently they clipped their parachute snap catches on to the overhead wire, the sergeant air-gunner carefully checking each catch. Nearest the door and first man to jump was Sergeant Harrod. Behind him stood Lieutenant Schaffer whose experience with the OSS had made him by far the most experienced parachutist of the group and whose unenviable task it was to keep an eye on Harrod. He was followed by Carraciola, then Smith – as leader he preferred to be in the middle of the group – then Christiansen, Thomas and Torrance-Smythe. Behind Torrance-Smythe two young air-craftmen stood ready to slide packaged equipment and parachutes along the wire and heave them out as swiftly as possible after the last man had jumped. The sergeant air-gunner took up position by the door. The tension was back in the air again.

Twenty-five feet forward of where they were standing, Carpenter slid open his side screen for the fifth time in as many minutes. The now downward drooping moustache had lost much of its splendid panache but the Wing Commander had obviously decided that there were more urgent considerations in life than waterlogged moustaches. He was wearing goggles now, continuously brushing away snow and moisture with a chamois leather, but the view ahead – or lack of view – remained obstinately the same, still that greyly driving snow looming out of and vanishing into that greyly impenetrable opacity, still nothingness. He closed the screen.

A call-up buzzer rang. Carpenter made a switch, listened, nodded.

'Three minutes,' he said to Tremayne. 'Oh-nine-two.'

Tremayne made the necessary minute course adjustment. He no longer looked through the side-screen, he no longer even looked at the screen ahead of him. His whole being was concentrated upon flying that big bomber, his all-exclusive attention, his total concentration, on three things only: the compass, the altimeter, and Carpenter. A degree too far to the south and the Lancaster would crash into the side of the Weissspitze: a couple of hundred feet too low and the same thing would happen: a missed signal from Carpenter and the mission was over before it had begun. The young, the absurdly young face was expressionless, the body immobile as he piloted the Lancaster with a hair-trigger precision that he had never before achieved. Only his eyes moved, in a regular, rhythmic, unvarying pattern: the compass, the altimeter, Carpenter, the compass, the altimeter, Carpenter: and never longer than a second on each.

Again Carpenter slid open his side-screen and peered out. Again he had the same reward, the opacity, the grey nothingness. With his head still outside he lifted his left hand, palm downwards, and made a forward motion. Instantly Tremayne's hand fell on the throttle levers and eased them forward. The roar of the big engines died away to a more muted thunder.

Carpenter withdrew his head. If he was concerned, no trace of it showed in his face. He resumed his soft whistling, calmly, almost leisurely, scanned the instrument panel, then turned his head to Tremayne. He said conversationally:

'When you were in flying school, ever hear tell of a strange phenomenon known as stalling speed?'

Tremayne started, glanced hurriedly at the instrument panel and quickly gave a fraction more power to the engines. Carpenter smiled, looked at his watch and pressed a buzzer twice.

The bell rang above the head of the sergeant air-gunner standing by the fuselage door. He looked at the tense, expectant faces before him and nodded.

'Two minutes, gentlemen.'

He eased the door a few inches to test whether it was moving freely. With the door only fractionally open the suddenly deepened roar from the engines was startling but nowhere nearly as dismaying as the snow-laden gust of icy wind that whistled into the fuselage. The parachutists exchanged carefully expressionless glances, glances correctly interpreted by the sergeant who closed the door and nodded again.

'I agree, gentlemen. No night for man nor beast.'

Wing Commander Carpenter, his head once again poked through the side-screen, didn't think so either. Five seconds' exposure to that arctic wind and driving snow and your face was full of porcupine quills: fifteen seconds and the totally numbed skin conveyed no sensation at all, it was when you withdrew your head and waited for the exquisite pain of returning circulation that the fun really started: but this time Carpenter was determined not to withdraw his head until he had complete justification for doing so: and the only justification would be the sighting of the Weissspitze. Mechanically, industriously, he rubbed the chamois leather across his goggles, stared unblinkingly into the greyly swirling gloom and hoped that he saw the Weissspitze before the Weissspitze saw him.

Inside, Tremayne's eyes continued on their rhythmic, unvarying pattern of movement: the compass, the altimeter, Carpenter, the compass, the altimeter, Carpenter. But now his gaze was resting fractionally longer on Carpenter each time, waiting for the sudden signal that would galvanize him into throwing the big Lancaster into a violent bank to port, the only avoiding action they could possibly take. Carpenter's left hand was moving, but he wasn't giving any signal, the fingers of his left hand were drumming gently on his knee. This, Tremayne suddenly and incredulously realized, was probably the highest state of excitement that Carpenter was capable of achieving.

Ten seconds passed. Five. And another five. Tremayne was conscious that, even in that ice-cold cabin, the sweat was pouring down his face. The urge to pull the bomber away to the left, to avoid the shattering, annihilating collision that could be only seconds away now, was almost overpowering. He was aware of a fear, a fear bordering on a reason-abdicating panic, such as he had never previously guessed at, let alone experienced. And then he became aware of something else. The drumming of Carpenter's left fingers had abruptly ceased.

Carpenter had it now. It was more imagined than real, more guessed at than seen, but he had it now. Then gradually, almost imperceptibly, ahead and a little to the right of the direction of flight, he became aware of something more solidly tangible than wishful thinking beginning to materialize out of the nothingness. And then, suddenly, it wasn't materializing any more, it was solidly, unmistakably there, the smooth, unbroken side of an almost vertically towering mountain soaring up at a dizzy 80° until it vanished in the grey darkness above. Carpenter withdrew his head, leaving the screen open this time, and pressed his head-switch.

'Sergeant Johnson?' The words came out stiffly, mechanically, not because of any crisis of emotion that the Wing Commander was passing through but because his entire face, lips included, was so frozen that he could no longer articulate properly.

'Sir?' Johnson's voice over the intercom was disembodied, empty, but even the metallic impersonality of that single word could not disguise the bow-taut tension behind it.

Carpenter said: 'I think Flying Officer Johnson a much nicer name.'

'Sir?'

'Relax. I have it. You can go back to sleep.' He switched off, took a quick look through the side-screen, reached up and touched an overhead switch.

Above the starboard door in the fuselage, a red light came on. The sergeant air-gunner laid his hand on the door.

'One minute, gentlemen.' He jerked the door wide open, securing it on its

standing latch, and a miniature blizzard howled into the belly of the
Lancaster. 'When the red light turns green—'

He left the sentence unfinished, partly because those few words were
crystal clear in themselves, partly because he had to shout so loudly to make
himself heard over the combined roar of wind and engines that any superfluity
of words was only that much wasted effort.

No one else said anything, mainly because of the near impossibility of
making oneself heard. In any event, the parachutists' silently exchanged
glances conveyed more eloquently than words the very obvious thought that
was in the minds of all of them: if it was like that inside, what the hell was
it like outside? At a gesture from the sergeant, they moved up in line to the
open door. Sergeant Harrod in the lead. On his face was the expression of
a Christian martyr meeting his first and last lion.

The Lancaster, like some great black pterodactyl from out of the primeval
past, roared on through the driving snow alongside the smoothly precipitous
side of the Weissspitze. That sheer wall of ice-encrusted rock seemed very
close indeed. Tremayne was convinced that it was impossibly close. He
stared through the still open screen by Carpenter's head and would have
sworn that the starboard wing-tip must be brushing the side of the mountain.
Tremayne could still feel the sweat that bathed his face but his lips were as
dry as ashes. He licked them, surreptitiously, so that Carpenter would not
see him, but it didn't do any good at all: as dry as ashes they remained.

Sergeant Harrod's lips weren't dry, but that was only because his face
was taking the full brunt of the horizontally driving snowstorm that lashed
along the bomber's fuselage. Otherwise, he shared Tremayne's sentiments
and apprehensions to a very marked degree. He stood in the doorway,
gripping the fuselage on each side to hold him in position against the gale
of wind, his storm-lashed face showing no fear, just a peculiarly resigned
expression. His eyes were turned to the left, looking forward with an almost
hypnotized fixity at that point in space where it seemed that at any second
now the starboard wing-tip must strike against the Weissspitze.

Inside the fuselage, the red lamp still burned. The sergeant air-gunner's
hand fell on Harrod's shoulder in an encouraging gesture. It took Harrod
all of three seconds to free himself from his thrall-like fixation with that
starboard wing-tip and take a half step back inside. He reached up and
firmly removed the sergeant's hand.

'Don't shove, mate.' He had to shout to make himself heard. 'If I'm to
commit suicide, let me do it in the old-fashioned way. By my own hand.' He
again took up position by the open door.

At the same instant Carpenter took a last quick look through the side-
screen and made the gesture that Tremayne had been waiting for, been
praying for, a slight turning motion of the left hand. Quickly Tremayne
banked the big bomber, as quickly straightened up again.

Slowly, the mountain-side fell away. The mountain-brushing episode had
been no mere bravado or folly, Carpenter had been deliberately lining up
for his pre-determined course across the narrow plateau. Once again, and
for the last time, he had his head outside, while his left hand slowly –
interminably slowly, it seemed to Tremayne – reached up for the button on
the bulkhead above the screen, located it, paused, then pressed it.

Sergeant Harrod, head craned back at a neck-straining angle, saw the red
light turn to green, brought his head down, screwed shut his eyes and, with

a convulsive jerk of his arms, launched himself out into the snow and the darkness, not a very expert launching, for instead of jumping out he had stepped out and was already twisting in mid-air as the parachute opened. Schaffer was the next to go, smoothly, cleanly, feet and knees together, then Carraciola followed by Smith.

Smith glanced down below him and his lips tightened. Just dimly visible in the greyness beneath, Harrod, a very erratic human pendulum, was swinging wildly across the sky. The parachute cords were already badly twisted and his clumsily desperate attempts to untwist them resulted only in their becoming more entangled than ever. His left-hand cords were pulled too far down, air was spilling from the parachute, and, still swaying madly, he was side-slipping to his left faster than any man Smith had ever seen side-slip a parachute before. Smith stared after the rapidly disappearing figure and hoped to God that he didn't side-slip his way right over the edge of the precipice.

Grim-faced, he stared upwards to see how the others had fared. Thank God, there was no worry there. Christiansen, Thomas and Smithy all there, so close as to be almost touching, all making perfectly normal descents.

Even before the last of the parachutists, Torrance-Smythe, had cleared the doorway, the sergeant air-gunner was running towards the after end of the fuselage. Swiftly he flung aside a packing-case, dragging a tarpaulin away, reached down and pulled a huddled figure upright. A girl, quite small, with wide dark eyes and delicate features. One would have looked for the figure below to be as petite as the features, but it was enveloped in bulky clothes over which had been drawn a snow-suit. Over the snow-suit she wore a parachute. She was almost numb with cold and cramp but the sergeant had his orders.

'Come on, Miss Ellison.' His arm round her waist, he moved quickly towards the doorway. 'Not a second to lose.'

He half led, half carried her there, where an aircraftman was just heaving the second last parachute and container through the doorway. The sergeant snapped the parachute catch on to the wire. Mary Ellison half-turned as if to speak to him, then turned away abruptly and dropped into the darkness. The last parachute and container followed at once.

For a long moment the sergeant stared down into the darkness. Then he rubbed his chin with the palm of his hand, shook his head in disbelief, stepped back and pulled the heavy door to. The Lancaster, its four engines still on reduced power, droned on into the snow and the night. Almost immediately, it was lost to sight and, bare seconds later, the last faint throb of its engines died away in the darkness.

Chapter Two

Smith reached his hands far up into the parachute shrouds, hauled himself sharply upwards and made a perfect knees-bent, feet-together landing in about two feet of snow. The wind tugged fiercely at his parachute. He struck the quick release harness clasp, collapsed the parachute, pulled it in, rolled it up and pressed it deeply into the snow, using for weight the pack he had just shrugged off his shoulders.

Down there at ground level – if seven thousand feet up on the Weissspitze could be called ground level – the snowfall was comparatively slight compared to that blizzard they'd experienced jumping from the Lancaster but, even so, visibility was almost as bad as it had been up above, for there was a twenty-knot wind blowing and the dry powdery snow was drifting quite heavily. Smith made a swift 360° sweep of his horizon but there was nothing to be seen, nobody to be seen.

With fumbling frozen hands he clumsily extracted a torch and whistle from his tunic. Facing alternately east and west, he bleeped on the whistle and flashed his torch. The first to appear was Thomas, then Schaffer, then, within two minutes altogether, all of the others with the exception of Sergeant Harrod.

'Pile your chutes there and weight them,' Smith ordered. 'Yes, bed them deep. Anyone seen Sergeant Harrod?' A shaking of heads. 'Nobody? No sight of him at all?'

'Last I saw of him,' Schaffer said, 'he was going across my bows like a destroyer in a heavy sea.'

'I saw a bit of that,' Smith nodded. 'The shrouds were twisted?'

'Put a corkscrew to shame. But I'd have said there was no danger of the chute collapsing. Not enough time. We were almost on the ground before I lost sight of him.'

'Any idea where he landed, then?'

'Roughly. He'll be all right, Major. A twisted ankle, a bump on the head. Not to worry.'

'Use your torches,' Smith said abruptly. 'Spread out. Find him.'

With two men on one side of him, three on the other, all within interlocking distance of their torch beams, Smith searched through the snow, his flash-light raking the ground ahead of him. If he shared Schaffer's optimism about Harrod, his face didn't show it. It was set and grim. Three minutes passed and then came a faint shout from the right. Smith broke into a run.

Carraciola it was who had called and was now standing at the farther edge of a wind-swept outcrop of bare rock, his torch shining downwards and slightly ahead. Beyond the rock the ground fell away abruptly to a depth of several feet and in this lee a deep drift had formed. Half-buried in its white depths, Sergeant Harrod lay spread-eagled on his back, his feet almost touching the rock, his face upturned to the falling snow, his eyes open. He did not seem to notice the snow falling on his eyes.

They were all there now, staring down at the motionless man. Smith jumped down into the drift, dropped to his knees, slid an arm under Harrod's shoulders and began to lift him to a sitting position. Harrod's head lolled back like that of a broken rag doll. Smith lowered him back into the snow and felt for the pulse in the throat. Still kneeling, Smith straightened, paused for a moment with bent head then climbed wearily to his feet.

'Dead?' Carraciola asked.

'He's dead. His neck is broken.' Smith's face was without expression. 'He must have got caught up in the shrouds and made a bad landing.'

'It happens,' Schaffer said. 'I've known it happen.' A long pause, then: 'Shall I take the radio, sir?'

Smith nodded. Schaffer dropped to his knees and began to fumble for the buckle of the strap securing the radio to Harrod's back.

Smith said: 'Sorry, no, not that way. There's a key around his neck, under his tunic. It fits the lock under the flap of the breast buckle.'

Schaffer located the key, unlocked the buckle after some difficulty, eased the straps off the dead man's shoulders and finally managed to work the radio clear. He rose to his feet, the radio dangling from his hand, and looked at Smith.

'Second thoughts, what's the point. Any fall hard enough to break his neck wouldn't have done the innards of this radio any good.'

Wordlessly, Smith took the radio, set it on the rock, extended the antenna, set the switch to 'Transmit', and cranked the call-up handle. The red tell-tale glowed, showing the transmission circuit to be in order. Smith turned the switch to receive, turned up the volume, moved the tuning knob, listened briefly to some static-laden music, closed up the radio set and handed it back to Schaffer.

'It made a better landing than Sergeant Harrod,' Smith said briefly. 'Come on.'

'We bury him, Major?' Carraciola asked.

'No need.' Smith shook his head and gestured with his torch at the drifting snow. 'He'll be buried within the hour. Let's find the supplies.'

'Now, for God's sake don't lose your grip!' Thomas said urgently.

'That's the trouble with you Celts,' Schaffer said reprovingly. 'No faith in anyone. There is no cause for alarm. Your life is in the safe hands of Schaffer and Christiansen. Not to worry.'

'What else do you think I'm worrying about?'

'If we all start sliding,' Schaffer said encouragingly, 'we won't let you go until the last possible minute.'

Thomas gave a last baleful glance over his shoulder and then began to edge himself out over the black lip of the precipice. Schaffer and Christiansen had an ankle apiece, and they in turn were anchored by the others. As far as the beam of Thomas's torch could reach, the cliff stretching down into the darkness was absolutely vertical, black naked rock with the only fissures in sight blocked with ice and with otherwise never a hand- or foot-hold.

'I've seen all I want to,' he said over his shoulder. They pulled him back and he edged his way carefully up to their supply pile before getting to his feet. He prodded the pack with the skis protruding from one end.

'Very handy,' he said morosely. 'Oh, very handy for this lot indeed.'
'As steep as that?' Smith asked.
'Vertical. Smooth as glass and you can't see the bottom. How deep do you reckon it is, Major?'
'Who knows?' Smith shrugged. 'We're seven thousand feet up. Maps never give details at this altitude. Break out that nylon.'

The proper supply pack was located and the nylon produced, one thousand feet of it coiled inside a canvas bag as it had come from the makers. It had very little more diameter than a clothes line but its wire core made it immensely strong and every yard of it had been fully tested to its rated breaking strain – its actual breaking strain was much higher – before leaving the factory. Smith tied a hammer to one end, and with two of the men holding him securely, paid it out over the edge, counting his arm spans as he let it go. Several times the hammer snagged on some unseen obstruction but each time Smith managed to swing it free. Finally the rope went completely slack and, despite all Smith's efforts, it remained that way.

'Well.' Smith moved back from the edge. 'That seems to be about it.'
'And if it isn't, hey?' Christiansen asked. 'If it's caught on a teensy-weensy ledge a thousand feet above damn all?'
'I'll let you know,' Smith said shortly.
'You measured it off,' Carraciola said. 'How deep?'
'Two hundred feet.'
'Eight hundred feet left, eh?' Thomas grinned. 'We'll need it all to tie up the garrison of the Schloss Adler.'
No one was amused. Smith said: 'I'll need a piton and two walkie-talkies.'
Fifteen feet back from the edge of the cliff they cleared away the snow and hammered an angled piton securely into the bare rock. Smith made a double bowline at one end of the nylon, slipped his legs through the loops, unclasped his belt then fastened it tightly round both himself and the rope and slipped a walkie-talkie over his shoulder. The rope was then passed round the piton and three men, backs to the cliff, wrapped it round their hands and prepared to take the weight. Schaffer stood by with the other walkie-talkie.

Smith checked that there were no sharp or abrasive edges on the cliff-top, wriggled cautiously over and gave the signal to be lowered. The descent itself was simple. As Thomas had said, it was a vertical drop and all he had to do was to fend himself off from the face as the men above paid out the rope. Once only, passing an overhang, he spun wildly in space, but within ten seconds regained contact with the rock face again. Mountaineering made easy, Smith thought. Or it seemed easy: perhaps, he thought wryly, it was as well that he couldn't see what stretched beneath him.

His feet passed through eighteen inches of snow and rested on solid ground. He flashed his torch in a semi-circle, from cliff wall to cliff wall. If it was a ledge, it was a very big one for, as far as his eye and torch could reach, it appeared to be a smooth plateau sloping gently outwards from the cliff. The cliff wall itself was smooth, unbroken, except for one shallow fissure, a few feet wide, close by to where he stood. He climbed out of the double bowline and made the switch on the walkie-talkie.

'OK so far. Haul up the rope. Supplies first, then yourselves.'
The rope snaked upwards into the darkness. Within five minutes all the

equipment had been lowered in two separate loads. Christiansen appeared soon afterwards.

'What's all the fuss about this Alpine stuff, then?' he asked cheerfully. 'My grandmother could do it.'

'Maybe we should have brought your grandmother along instead,' Smith said sourly. 'We're not down yet. Take your torch and find out how big this ledge is and the best way down and for God's sake don't go falling over any precipices.'

Christiansen grinned and moved off. Life was for the living and Christiansen gave the impression of a man thoroughly enjoying himself. While he was away reconnoitring, all the others came down in turn until only Schaffer was left. His plaintive voice came over the walkie-talkie.

'And how am I supposed to get down? Hand over hand for two hundred feet? Frozen hand over frozen hand for two hundred feet on a rope this size? You'd better stand clear. Somebody should have thought of this.'

'Somebody did,' Smith said patiently. 'Make sure the rope is still round the piton then kick the other eight hundred feet over the edge.'

'There's always an answer.' Schaffer sounded relieved.

They had just lowered him to the ground when Christiansen returned.

'It's not so bad,' he reported. 'There's another cliff ahead of us, maybe fifty yards away, curving around to the east. At least I think it's a cliff. I didn't try to find out how deep or how steep. I'm married. But the plateau falls away gently to the west there. Seems it might go on a fair way. Trees, too. I followed the line of them for two hundred yards.'

'Trees? At this altitude?'

'Well, no masts for a tall ship. Scrub pine. They'll give shelter, hiding.'

'Fair enough,' Smith nodded. 'We'll bivouac there.'

'So close?' The surprised tone in Schaffer's voice showed that he didn't think much of the idea. 'Shouldn't we get as far down this mountain as possible tonight, Major?'

'No need. If we start at first light we'll be well below the main tree line by dawn.'

'I agree with Schaffer,' Carraciola said reasonably. 'Let's get as much as we can behind us. What do you think, Olaf?' This to Christiansen.

'It doesn't matter what Christiansen thinks.' Smith's voice was quiet but cold as the mountain air itself. 'Nor you, Carraciola. This isn't a round-table seminar, it's a military operation. Military operations have leaders. Like it or not, Admiral Rolland put me in charge. We stay here tonight. Get the stuff across.'

The five men looked speculatively at one another, then stooped to lift the supplies. There was no longer any question as to who was in charge.

'We pitch the tents right away, boss?' Schaffer asked.

'Yes.' In Schaffer's book, Smith reflected, 'boss' was probably a higher mark of respect than either 'Major' or 'sir'. 'Then hot food, hot coffee and a try for London on the radio. Haul that rope down, Christiansen. Come the dawn, we don't want to start giving heart attacks to any binocular-toting characters in the Schloss Adler.'

Christiansen nodded, began to haul on the rope. As the free end rose into the air, Smith gave a shout, jumped towards Christiansen and caught his arm. Christiansen, startled, stopped pulling and looked round.

'Jesus!' Smith drew the back of his hand across his forehead. 'That was a close one.'

'What's up?' Schaffer asked quickly.

'Two of you. Hoist me up. Quickly! Before that damn rope disappears.'

Two of them hoisted him into the air. Smith reached up and caught the dangling end of the rope, dropped to earth, taking the rope with him and then very carefully, very securely, tied it to the other end of the rope.

'Now that you've *quite* finished—' Torrance-Smythe said politely.

'The radio.' Smith let out a long sigh of relief. 'There's only one list of frequencies, call signs and code. Security. And that one list is inside Sergeant Harrod's tunic.'

'Mind if I mop my brow, too, boss?' Schaffer enquired.

'I'll go get it for you if you like,' Christiansen enquired.

'Thanks. But it's my fault and I'll get it. Besides, I'm the only person here who's done any climbing – or so I believe from Colonel Wyatt-Turner – and I think you'd find that cliff rather more awkward to climb than descend. No hurry. Let's bivouac and eat first.'

'If you can't do better than this, Smithy,' Schaffer said to Torrance-Smythe, 'you can have a week's notice. Starting from a week ago.' He scraped the bottom of his metal plate and shuddered. 'I was brought up in a Christian home, so I won't tell you what this reminds me of.'

'It's not my fault,' Torrance-Smythe complained. 'They packed the wrong size tin-openers.' He stirred the indeterminate-looking goulash in the pot on top of the butane stove and looked hopefully at the men seated in a rough semi-circle in the dimly-lit tent. 'Anyone for any more?'

'That's not funny,' Schaffer said severely.

'Wait till you try his coffee,' Smith advised, 'and you'll be wondering what you were complaining about.' He rose, poked his head through the door to take a look at the weather, looked inside again. 'May take me an hour. But if it's been drifting up there . . .'

The seated men, suddenly serious, nodded. If it had been drifting up there it might take Smith a very long time indeed to locate Sergeant Harrod.

'It's a bad night,' Schaffer said. 'I'll come and give you a hand.'

'Thanks. No need. I'll haul myself up and lower myself down. A rope round a piton is no elevator, but it'll get me there and back and two are no better than one for that job. But I'll tell you what you can do.' He moved out and reappeared shortly afterwards carrying the radio which he placed in front of Schaffer. 'I don't want to go all the way up there to get the codebook just to find that some hob-nailed idiot has fallen over this and given it a heart attack. Guard it with your life, Lieutenant Schaffer.'

'Aye, aye, sir,' Schaffer said solemnly.

With a hammer and a couple of spare pitons hanging from his waist, Smith secured himself to the rope, with double bowline and belt as before, grabbed the free end of the rope and began to haul himself up. Smith's statement to the others that this was a job for a mountaineer seemed hardly accurate for the amount of mountaineering skill required was minimal. It was gruelling physical labour, no more. Most of the time, with his legs almost at right angles to his body, he walked up the vertical cliff face: on the stretch of the overhang, with no assistance for his arms, he twice had to take a turn of the free end of the rope and rest until the strength came back to aching shoulder and forearm muscles: and by the time he finally dragged himself, gasping painfully and sweating like a man in a sauna bath, over the edge of the cliff, exhaustion was very close indeed. He had overlooked the crippling effect of altitude to a man unaccustomed to it.

He lay face down for several minutes until breathing and pulse returned to something like normal – or what was normal for seven thousand feet – rose and examined the piton round which the nylon passed. It seemed firm enough but, for good measure, he gave it another few heavy blows with the hammer, undid the double bowline round his legs and secured the end of the rope to the piton with a round turn and two half-hitches, hauling on the rope until the knot locked tight.

He moved a few feet farther away from the cliff edge, cleared away the snow and lightly hammered in one of the spare pitons he had brought with him. He tested it with his hand to see if it broke clear easily. It did. He tapped it in lightly a second time and led round it the part of the rope that was secured to the firmly anchored first piton. Then he walked away, moving up the gently sloping plateau, whistling 'Lorelei'. It was, as Smith himself would have been the first to admit, a far from tuneful whistle, but recognizable for all that. A figure appeared out of the night and came running towards him, stumbling and slipping in the deep snow. It was Mary Ellison. She stopped short a yard away and put her hands on her hips.

'Well!' He could hear her teeth chattering uncontrollably with the cold. 'You took your time about it, didn't you?'

'Never wasted a minute,' Smith said defensively. 'I had to have a hot meal and coffee first.'

'You had to have – you beast, you selfish beast!' She took a quick step forward and flung her arms around his neck. 'I hate you.'

'I know.' He pulled off a gauntlet and gently touched her disengaged cheek. 'You're frozen.'

'You're frozen, he says! Of course I'm frozen. I almost *died* in that plane. Why couldn't you have supplied some hot water bottles – or – or an electrically heated suit or – or something? I thought you loved me!'

'I can't help what you think,' Smith said kindly, patting her on the back. 'Where's your gear?'

'Fifty yards. And *stop* patting me in that – that avuncular fashion.'

'Language, language,' Smith said. 'Come on, let's fetch it.'

They trudged upwards through the deep snow, Mary holding his arm tightly. She said curiously: 'What on earth excuse did you give for coming back up here? Lost a cuff-link?'

'There was something I had to come for, something apart from you, although I gave a song-and-dance act of having forgotten about it until the last moment, until it was almost too late. The radio code-book inside Sergeant Harrod's tunic.'

'He – he lost it? He dropped it? How – how could he have been so criminally careless!' She stopped, puzzled. 'Besides, it's chained—'

'It's still inside Sergeant Harrod's tunic,' Smith said sombrely. 'He's up here, dead.'

'Dead?' She stopped and clutched him by the arms. After a long pause, she repeated: 'He's dead! That – that nice man. I heard him saying he'd never jumped before. A bad landing?'

'So it seems.'

They located the kit-bag in silence and Smith carried it back to the edge of the cliff. Mary said: 'And now? The code-book?'

'Let's wait a minute. I want to watch this rope.'

'Why the rope?'

'Why not?'

'Don't tell me,' Mary said resignedly. 'I'm only a little girl. I suppose you know what you're doing.'

'I wish to God I did,' Smith said feelingly.

They waited, again in silence, side by side on the kit-bag. Both stared at the rope in solemn concentration as if nylon ropes at seven thousand feet had taken on a special meaningfulness denied nylon ropes elsewhere. Twice Smith tried to light a cigarette and twice it sputtered to extinction in the drifting snow. The minutes passed, three, maybe four: they felt more like thirty or forty. He became conscious that the girl beside him was shivering violently – he guessed that she had her teeth clamped tight to prevent their chattering – and was even more acutely conscious that his entire left side – he was trying to shelter her from the wind and snow – was becoming numb. He rose to leave when suddenly the rope gave a violent jerk and the piton farther from the cliff edge was torn free. The loop of the rope slid quickly down past the piton to which it was anchored and kept on going till it was brought up short by its anchor. Whatever pressure was on the rope increased until the nylon bit deeply into the fresh snow on the cliff-edge. Smith moved across and tested the pressure on the rope, at first gingerly and tentatively then with all his strength. The rope was bar-taut and remained bar-taut. But the piton held.

'What – what on earth—' Mary began, then broke off. Her voice was an unconscious whisper.

'Charming, charming,' Smith murmured. 'Someone down there doesn't like me. Surprised?'

'If – if that spike hadn't held we'd never have got down again.' The tremor in her voice wasn't all due to the cold.

'It's a fair old jump,' Smith conceded.

He took her arm and they moved off. The snow was heavier now and even with the aid of their torches visibility was no more than six feet, but, by using the rocky out-crop as a bearing, it took Smith no more than two minutes to locate Sergeant Harrod, now no more than a featureless mound buried in the depths of the snow-drift. Smith brushed aside the covering shroud of white, undid the dead man's tunic, recovered the code-book, hung the chain round his neck and buttoned the book securely inside his own Alpenkorps uniform.

Then came the task of turning Sergeant Harrod over on his side. Unpleasant Smith had expected it to be, and it was: impossible he hadn't expected it to be, and it wasn't – not quite. But the effort all but defeated him, the dead man was stiff as a board, literally frozen solid into the arms outflung position into which he had fallen. For a second time that night Smith could feel the sweat mingling with the melted snow on his face. But by and by he had him over, the frozen right arm pointing up into the snow-filled sky. Smith knelt, brought his torch close and carefully examined the back of the dead man's head.

'What are you trying to do?' Mary asked. 'What are you looking for?' Again her voice was a whisper.

'His neck is broken. I want to find out just *how* it was broken.' He glanced up at the girl. 'You don't have to look.'

'Don't worry.' She turned away. 'I'm not going to.'

The clothes, like the man, were frozen stiff. The hood covering Harrod's head crackled and splintered in Smith's gauntleted hands as he pulled it down, exposing the back of the head and neck. Finally, just below the collar of the snow smock, Smith found what he was searching for – a red mark at the base of the neck where the skin was broken. He rose, caught the dead man's ankles and dragged him a foot or two down the slope.

'What now?' In spite of herself Mary was watching again, in reluctant and horrified fascination. 'What are you looking for now?'

'A rock,' Smith said briefly. There was a cold edge to the words and although Mary knew it wasn't intended for her, it was an effective discouragement to any further questioning.

Smith cleared the snow for two feet around where Harrod's head had lain. With hand and eyes he examined the ground with meticulous care, rose slowly to his feet, took Mary's arm and began to walk away. After a few steps he hesitated, stopped, turned back to the dead man and turned him over again so that the right arm was no longer pointing towards the sky.

Half-way back to the cliff-edge, Smith said abruptly:

'Something struck Harrod on the back of the neck. I thought it might have been a rock. But there was no rock where he lay, only turf.'

'There was a rocky outcrop near by.'

'You don't break your neck on a rocky outcrop, then stand up and jump out into a snow-drift. Even had he rolled over into the drift, he could never have finished with his head seven feet out from the rock. He was struck by some hard metallic object, either the butt of a gun or the haft of a knife. The skin is broken but there is no bruising for the neck was broken immediately afterwards. When he was unconscious. To make us think it was an accident. It must have happened on the rock – there was no disturbance in the snow round Harrod – and it must have happened while he was upright. A tap on the neck, a quick neck-twist, then he fell or was pushed over the edge of the outcrop. Wonderful stuff, stone,' Smith finished bitterly. 'It leaves no footprints.'

Mary stopped and stared at him.

'Do you realize what you're saying?' She caught his speculative and very old-fashioned look, took his arm and went on quickly: 'No, I mean the implications. I'm sorry, I'm sorry, of course you do. John, I – I'm scared. Even all those months with you in Italy – well you know, nothing like this—' She broke off, then continued: 'Couldn't there – couldn't there be some other explanation?'

'Like he hit himself on the back of the head or the abominable snowman got him?'

She looked at him steadily, her dark eyes far too large in what could be seen of her hooded face. 'I don't deserve that, John. I *am* frightened.'

'Me, too.'

'I don't believe you.'

'Well, if I'm not, it's damn well time I started to be.'

Smith checked his descent when he estimated he was about forty feet from the base of the cliff. He took two turns of the nylon round his left leg, clamped it with his right, took a turn round his left arm, pulled off his right gauntlet with his teeth, stuffed it inside his tunic, eased out his Luger, slid the safety catch and went on his way again, checking his speed of descent with his gauntleted left hand. It was a reasonable enough expectation that whoever had tried to pull down the rope would be waiting there to finish off the job.

But there was no reception committee waiting, not, at least, at the spot where he touched down. He traversed a quick circle with his torch. There was nobody there and nothing there and the footprints that must have been there were long obscured by the drifting snow. Gun in one hand, torch in the other, he moved along the cliff face for thirty yards then moved out in a semi-circle until he arrived back at the cliff face. The rope-puller had evidently opted for discretion. Smith returned to the rope and jerked it. In two minutes he had Mary's kit-bag down and, a few minutes later, Mary herself. As soon as she had stepped out of the double bowline, Smith undid the knot, pulled the rope down from the top of the cliff and coiled it. So numbed and frozen were his hands by this time that the operation took him nearly fifteen minutes.

Rope over one shoulder, her kit-bag on the other, Smith led Mary to the fissure in the cliff side.

'Don't pitch the tent,' Smith said. 'Unroll it, put your sleeping bag on one half, get into it and pull the other half of the tent over you. Half an hour and you'll be covered with drifting snow. The snow will not only keep you warm, it'll hide you from any somnambulists. I'll be along in the morning before we leave.'

He walked away, stopped, looked back. Mary was still standing where he had left her, looking after him. There was no sag to her shoulders, no particular expression to her face, but for all that she looked oddly defenceless, lonely and forlorn, a quality as undefinable as it was unmistakable. Smith hesitated, then went back to her, unrolled her tent and sleeping bag, waited till she had climbed in, zipped up the bag and pulled the other half of the tent up to her chin. She smiled at him. He fixed the sleeping bag hood, pulled a corner of the tent over it and left, all without saying a word.

Locating his own tent was simple enough, a steady light burnt inside it. Smith beat the snow from his clothes, stooped and entered. Christiansen, Thomas and Carraciola were in their sleeping bags and were asleep or appeared to be. Torrance-Smythe was checking over their store of plastic explosives, fuses, detonators and grenades, while Schaffer was reading a paperback – in German – smoking a cigarette – also German – and faithfully guarding the radio. He put down the book and looked at Smith.

'OK?'

'OK.' Smith produced the code-book from his tunic. 'Sorry I was so long, but I thought I'd never find him. Drifting pretty badly up there.'

'We've arranged to take turns on watch,' Schaffer said. 'Half an hour each. It'll be dawn in three hours.'

Smith smiled. 'What are you guarding against in these parts?'

'The abominable snowman.'

The smile left Smith's face as quickly as it had come. He turned his attention to Harrod's code-book and spent about ten minutes in memorizing call-up signals and wave-frequencies and writing a message out in code. Before he had finished Schaffer had turned into his sleeping bag, leaving Torrance-Smythe on watch. Smith folded the message, tucked it in a pocket, rose, took the radio and a rubber ground-sheet to protect it from the snow.

'I'm going to move out a bit,' he said to Torrance-Smythe. 'Reception is lousy among trees. Besides, I don't want to wake everybody up. Won't be long.'

Two hundred yards from the tent, after having stopped twice and changed direction twice, Smith knelt with his back – and the rubber ground-sheet – to the drifting snow. He extended a fourteen feet telescopic aerial, adjusted a pre-selected call-up and cranked a handle. Four times he cranked the handle and on the fifth he got results. Someone was keeping a very close radio watch indeed.

'This is Danny Boy,' the set speaker crackled. The signal was faint and intermittent, but just comprehensible. 'Danny Boy replying to you. Over.'

Smith spoke into the mouth microphone. 'This is Broadsword. Can I speak to Father Machree or Mother Machree? Over.'

'Sorry. Unavailable. Over.'

'Code,' Smith said. 'Over.'

'Ready.'

Smith extracted the paper from his pocket and shone his torch on it. There were two lines containing meaningless jumbles of letters and, below that, the plain language translation, which read: 'SAFE LANDING HARROD DEAD WEATHER FINE PLEASE AWAIT MESSAGE 0800 GMT'. Smith read off the corresponding code figures and finished off: 'Have that delivered to Father Machree by 0700. Without fail.'

Torrance-Smythe looked up at Smith's return.

'Back already?' Surprise in his voice. 'You got through?'

'Not a chance,' Smith said disgustedly. 'Too many bloody mountains around.'

'Didn't try for very long, did you?'

'Two and a half minutes.' It was Smith's turn to look surprised. 'Surely you know that's the safe maximum?'

'You think there may be radio monitoring stations hereabouts?'

'Oh, no, not at all.' Smith's voice was heavy with sarcasm. 'You wouldn't expect to find radio monitors in the Schloss Adler, would you now?'

'Well, now.' Torrance-Smythe smiled tiredly. 'I believe someone did mention it was the southern HQ of the German Secret Service. Sorry, Major. It's not that I'm growing old, though there's that, too. It's just that what passes for my mind is so gummed up by cold and lack of sleep that I think it's stopped altogether.'

Smith pulled off his boots and snow-suit, climbed into his sleeping bag and pulled the radio close to him.

'Then it's time you had some sleep. My explosives expert is going to be no good to me if he can't tell a detonator from a door-knob. Go on. Turn in. I'll keep watch.'

'But we had arranged—'

'Arguments, arguments,' Smith sighed. 'Insubordination on every hand.' He smiled. 'Straight up, Smithy, I'm wide awake. I know I won't sleep tonight.'

One downright lie, Smith thought, and one statement of incontrovertible truth. He wasn't wide awake, he was physically and mentally exhausted and on the slightest relaxation of willpower oblivion would have overtaken him in seconds. But that he wouldn't sleep that night was beyond doubt: no power on earth would have let him sleep that night but, in the circumstances, it was perhaps wiser not to say so to Torrance-Smythe.

Chapter Three

The pre-dawn greyness was in the sky. Smith and his men had broken camp. Tent and sleeping bags were stored away and the cooking utensils – after a very sketchy breakfast scarcely deserving of the name – were being thrust into haversacks. There was no conversation, none at all: it wasn't a morning for speaking. All of them, Smith thought, looked more drawn, more exhausted, than they had done three hours ago: he wondered how he himself, who had had no sleep at all, must look. It was as well, he reflected, that mirrors were not part of their commando equipment. He looked at his watch.

'We'll leave in ten minutes,' he announced. 'Should give us plenty of time to be down in the tree line before sun-up. Assuming there are no more cliffs. Back in a moment. Visibility is improving and I think I'll go recce along the cliff edge. With any luck, maybe I can see the best way down.'

'And if you haven't any luck?' Carraciola asked sourly.

'We've still that thousand feet of nylon rope,' Smith said shortly.

He pulled on his snow-suit and left, angling off in the direction of the cliff. As soon as he was beyond the belt of the scrub pines and out of sight of the camp he changed direction uphill and broke into a run.

A single eye appeared under a lifted corner of snow-covered canvas as Mary Ellison heard the soft crunch of running footsteps in the snow. She heard the first two bars of a tuneless whistling of 'Lorelei', unzipped her sleeping bag and sat up. Smith was standing above her.

'Not already!' she said protestingly.

'Yes already. Come on. Up!'

'I haven't slept a wink.'

'Neither have I. I've been watching that damned radio all night – and watching to check that no somnambulists took a stroll in this direction.'

'You kept awake. You did that for me?'

'I kept awake. We're off. Start in five minutes. Leave your tent and kit-bag here, you won't be requiring them again. Take some food, something to drink, that's all. And for God's sake, don't get too close to us.' He glanced at his watch. 'We'll stop at 7 a.m. Check your watch. Exactly 7 a.m. And *don't* bump into us.'

'What do you think I am?' But Smith didn't tell her what he thought she was. He had already gone.

A thousand feet farther down the side of the Weissspitze the trees were something worth calling trees, towering conifers that soared sixty and seventy feet up into the sky. Into the clear sky, for the snow had stopped falling now. It was dawn.

The slope of the Weissspitze was still very steep, perhaps one in four or five. Smith, with his five men strung out behind him in single file, slipped and stumbled almost constantly: but the deep snow, Smith reflected, at least cushioned their frequent falls and as a mode of progress it was a damn sight preferable to shinning down vertical cliff-faces, on an impossible thin clothes-line. The curses of his bruised companions were almost continuous but serious complaints were marked by their total absence: there was no danger, they were making excellent time and they were now completely hidden in the deep belt of pines.

Two hundred yards behind them Mary Ellison carefully picked her way down the tracks made by the men below her. She slipped and fell only very occasionally for, unlike the men, she was carrying no over-balancing gear on her back. Nor had she any fear of being observed, of coming too close to Smith and the others: in still, frosty air on a mountain sound carries with a preternatural clarity and from the sound of the voices farther down the slope she could judge her distance from them to a nicety. For the twentieth time she looked at her watch: it was twenty minutes to seven.

Some time later, for much more than the twentieth time, Smith checked his watch again. It was exactly 7 o'clock. The dawn had gone and the light of full day-time filtered down through the snow-bent boughs of the conifers. Smith stopped and held up his hand, waiting until the other five had caught up with him.

'We must be half-way down now.' He shrugged off the heavy pack on his back and lowered it gratefully into the snow. 'I think it's time we had a look at the scenery.'

They piled their gear and moved off to the right. Within a minute the pines started to thin out and at a signal from Smith they all dropped to hands and knees and crawled forward the last few yards towards the edge of the belt of pines. Smith carried a telescope in his hand: Christiansen and Thomas both wore binoculars. Zeiss binoculars. Admiral Rolland had left nothing to chance. Beyond the last of the pines a mound of snow obstructed their view of the valley below. Shrouded from top to toe, in the all enveloping white of their snow-smocks, they completed the last few feet on their elbows and knees.

What lay below them was something out of a fairy tale, an impossibly beautiful scene from an impossibly beautiful fairy tale, a fairy tale set aeons back in the never-never land of the age of dreams, a kindlier land, a nobler land than man had ever known since first he had set his hand against his brother. A land that never was, Smith thought, a land that never was: but there it lay before them, the golden land that never was, the home of that most dreaded organization in the entire world, the German Gestapo. The impeccable incongruity of it all, Smith reflected, passed all belief.

The valley was bowl-shaped, open to the north, hemmed in by steeply rising hills to the east and west, closed off by the towering bulk of the Weissspitze to the south.

A scene of fantastic beauty. Nine thousand, seven hundred and ten feet in height, the second highest mountain in Germany, the Weissspitze soared up menacingly like another north wall of the Eiger, its dazzling whiteness caught in the morning sun, its starkly lovely outline sharply etched against the now cloudless blue of the sky. High up near the cone-shaped summit could be seen the line of black rock marking the cliff Smith and his men had descended during the night with, just below it, a much greater cliff-face on the plateau above which they had spent the night.

Directly opposite where they lay, and almost exactly on the same level, was the Schloss Adler itself. The castle of the eagle had been aptly named, an impregnable fortress, an inaccessible eyrie set between mountain and sky.

Just below the spot where the steep-sided slopes of the Weissspitze began to flatten out northwards into the head of the valley, a geological freak, known as a volcanic plug, jutted two hundred vertical feet up into the sparkling, ice-cold air. It was on this that the Schloss Adler had been built. The northern, western and eastern sides of this volcanic plug were sheer, perpendicular walls of rock, walls that swept up smoothly, without intermission or break into the structure of the castle itself: from where they lay, it was impossible to say where the one ended and the other began. To the south, a steeply-sloping ridgeback connected the plug to the equally sloping ramparts of the Weissspitze.

The castle itself was another dream, the dream of the apotheosis of medievalism. This dream, Smith was aware, was as illusory as the golden age of its setting. It wasn't medieval at all, it had been built as late as the mid-nineteenth century to the express order of one of the madder of the Bavarian monarchs who had suffered from a comprehensive list of delusions, of which grandeur had not been the least. But, delusions or not, he had had, as the deluded so often have – to the dismay and consternation of their allegedly saner brethren – impeccable taste. The castle was perfect for the valley, the valley for the castle. Any other combination would have been inconceivable.

The Schloss Adler was built in the form of a hollow square. It was towered, battlemented and crenellated, its most imposing aspects, two perfectly circular towers, the one to the east higher than that to the west, facing down the valley towards the north. Two smaller, but still magnificent towers, lay at the southern corners, facing the looming bulk of the Weissspitze. From where Smith lay, at some slight level above that of the castle, he could just see into the open square in its middle, outside access to which was obtained by a pair of huge iron gates at the rear. The sun had not yet climbed sufficiently high above the eastern hills for its rays to strike the castle directly, but, for all that, its incredibly white walls gleamed and glittered as if made of the most iridescent marble.

Below the soaring northern ramparts of the castle the valley fell away steeply to the Blau See, beautiful pine-fringed jewel of a lake of the deepest and most sparkling blue, a colour which with the green of the pines, the white dazzle of the snow and the brilliant, lighter blue of the sky above formed a combination of breath-taking loveliness. Impossibly lovely, Smith thought, a completely faithful colour reproduction of the scene would have had everybody shouting 'fake'.

From where they lay they could see that the belt of pines in which they lay hidden extended almost all the way down to the lake. Getting down there unobserved would be no problem at all. An almost exactly matching line of pines swept down the opposite – the eastern – side of the valley.

From the lake those two long sweeps of pines, climbing steadily upwards as they marched to the south, must have appeared like a pair of great curving horns almost meeting at the top of the lower of the two cliff-faces on the Weissspitze.

A small village lay at the head of the lake. Basically it consisted of a single wide street, perhaps two hundred yards in length, a railway station, two inevitable churches perched on two inevitable knolls and a thin scattering of houses climbing up the steep slopes on either side of the village. From the southern end of the village a road curved up the far side of the valley till it reached the ridge-back to the south of the castle: this ridge-back it ascended by a series of hairpin bends, the last of which led to the great doors guarding the forecourt at the back of the castle. The road, just then, was completely blocked by snow and sole access to the castle was obviously by means of the *Luftseilbahn*, an aerial cableway. Two cables stretched from the village straight up to the castle, crossing three supporting pylons en route. Even as they watched, a cable-car was completing the last section of its journey up to the castle. At a distance of not much more than a hundred feet from the glittering walls of the Schloss Adler it appeared to be climbing almost vertically.

On the Blau See, about a mile beyond the village, lay a very large group of regularly spaced huts, arranged in rectangular patterns. It bore an uncommonly close resemblance to a military encampment.

'Well, I'll be damned!' With an almost physical effort of will, Schaffer forced himself to look away and Smith could see the wonder reflected in his eyes. 'Is this for real, boss?'

It wasn't a question that called for an answer. Schaffer had summed up their collective feeling pretty well and there was nothing that anyone could add that wouldn't seem and sound superfluous. Prone in the snow, they watched in silence as the cable-car climbed agonizingly slowly up the last fifty feet towards the castle. It seemed as if it would never make it and Smith could almost palpably sense the empathy of his companions and himself as they willed that little car on the last few feet of its journey. But make it it did and it disappeared from sight under the roof of the cable header station that has been built into the western foot of the castle. The tension relaxed and Schaffer cleared his throat.

'Boss,' he said diffidently, 'there are a couple of minor points that occur to me. Requiring elucidation, one might say. First of all, if I didn't know better I'd say that was a military barracks down by that little old lake there.'

'You don't know better. That *is* a military barracks down by that little old lake there. And no ordinary military barracks either, I might say. That's the training HQ of the Jäger battalions of the Wehrmacht's Alpenkorps.'

'Oh, my gosh! The Alpine Corps! If I'd known this I'd never have come along. The Alpine Corps! Why didn't someone tell Ma Schaffer's nearest and dearest?'

'I thought you knew,' Smith said mildly. 'Why do you think we're not dressed as German sailors or Red Cross nurses?'

Schaffer unzipped his snow-smock, minutely examined his Alpenkorps uniform as if seeing it for the first time, then zipped it up again. He said carefully: 'You mean to say we're going to mingle, careless like, with the German Army.' He paused, looked wide-eyed at Smith's smiling nod, then went on incredulously: 'But – but we'll be recognized as strangers!'

'Training troops come and go all the time,' Smith said off-handedly. 'What's six new faces among six hundred new faces?'

'This is terrible,' Schaffer said gloomily.

'Worse than horses?' Smith smiled. 'After all, the Alpenkorps don't buck and trample all over you.'

'Horses don't carry machine-guns,' Schaffer said morosely.

'And your second point?'

'Ah, yes. The second point. There's the little matter of the old Schloss itself. Kinda forgotten our helicopter, haven't we? How do we get in?'

'A good point,' Smith conceded. 'We'll have to think about it. But I'll tell you this. If Colonel Wyatt-Turner can penetrate the German High Command and, more important, get away again, this should be a piece of cake for us.'

'He did what?' Schaffer demanded.

'Didn't you know?'

'How should I know?' Schaffer was irritated. 'Never met the guy till yesterday.'

'He spent the years '40 to '43 inside Germany. Served in the Wehrmacht for part of the time. Ended up in the GHQ in Berlin. Says he knows Hitler quite well.'

'Well, I'll be damned.' Schaffer paused for a long moment, finally arrived at a conclusion. 'The guy,' he said moodily, 'must be nuts.'

'Maybe. But if he can do it, we can. We'll figure a way. Let's get back among the trees.'

They inched their way back into cover, leaving Christiansen behind with Smith's telescope to keep watch. After they'd made a temporary camp, heated and drunk some coffee, Smith announced his intention of trying to contact London again.

He unpacked the radio and sat down on a kit-bag a few feet distant from the others. The switch that cut in the transmitter circuit was on the left hand side of the radio, the side remote from where the other four men were sitting. Smith switched on with a loud positive click, cranked the call-up handle with his left hand. With the very first crank his left hand moved the transmitting switch from 'On' to 'Off', the whirring of the call-up blanketing the sound. Smith cranked away diligently at intervals, stopping from time to time to make minute adjustments to the controls, then finally gave up and sat back, shaking his head in disgust.

'You'll never make it with all those trees around,' Torrance-Smythe observed.

'That must be it,' Smith agreed. 'I'll try the other side of the wood. Might have better luck there.'

He slung the transmitter over his shoulder and trudged off through the deep snow, cutting straight across to the other side of the belt of pines. When he thought he was safely out of eyeshot of the men at the camp, he checked with a quick look over his shoulder. They were out of sight. He turned more than ninety degrees left and hurried up the hill until he cut the tracks that he and his men had made on the way down. He followed the tracks uphill, whistling 'Lorelei', but whistling softly: in that frosty air, sound travelled dangerously far. He stopped whistling when Mary appeared from where she had been hiding behind a fallen pine.

'Hallo, darling,' she said brightly.

'We'll have less of the "darlings",' Smith said briskly. 'It's 8 a.m. Father Machree awaits. And keep your voice down.'

He sat on the fallen tree, cranked the handle and established contact almost immediately. The transmission from London was still very faint but clearer than it had been in the earlier hours of the morning.

'Father Machree is waiting,' the radio crackled. 'Hold. Hold.'

Smith held and the unmistakable voice of Admiral Rolland took over from the London operator.

'Position please, Broadsword.'

Smith consulted the piece of paper in his hand, again in code and plain language. The message read: WOODS DUE WEST CASTLE DESCENDING W.H. THIS EVENING. Smith read out the corresponding code letters.

There was a pause, presumably while Rolland was having the message decoded, then his voice came again.

'Understood. Proceed. Harrod killed accidentally?'

'No. Over.'

'By the enemy? Over.'

'No. What is the weather report? Over.'

'Deteriorating. Freshening winds, strong later. Snow. Over.'

Smith looked up at the still and cloudless sky above. He assumed that Rolland hadn't got his forecasts mixed up. He said: 'Time of next broadcast uncertain. Can you stand by? Over.'

'Am remaining HQ until operation complete,' Rolland said. 'Good luck. Goodbye.'

Smith closed up the radio and said thoughtfully to Mary: 'I didn't much care for the way he said goodbye there.'

In the naval Operations room in Whitehall, Admiral Rolland and Colonel Wyatt-Turner, one on either side of the radio operator manning a huge transceiver, looked at each other with heavy faces.

'So the poor devil was murdered,' Wyatt-Turner said flatly.

'A high price to pay for confirmation that we were right,' Rolland said sombrely. 'Poor devil, as you say. The moment we gave him that radio to carry we signed a death-warrant. I wonder who's next. Smith himself?'

'Not Smith.' Wyatt-Turner shook his head positively. 'Some people have a sixth sense. Smith has a seventh, eighth and ninth and a built-in radar set for danger. Smith can survive under any circumstances I can conceive of. I didn't pick him with a pin, sir. He's the best agent in Europe.'

'Except possibly yourself. And don't forget, Colonel, there may possibly be circumstances that even you can't conceive of.'

'Yes, that's so.' He looked directly at Rolland. 'What do you reckon his chances are, sir?'

'Chances?' Rolland's eyes were remote, unseeing. 'What do you mean, chances? He doesn't have any.'

Almost precisely the same thought was in Smith's mind as he lit a cigarette and looked at the girl beside him, careful not to let his thoughts show in his face. Not until that first sight he'd just had of the castle had the full realization of the apparent impossibility of their task struck him. Had he known what the precise physical situation had been, he doubted very much whether he would have come. Deep in the furthest recesses of his mind, he knew, although he would not admit it to himself, that there really was no room for the element of doubt. He wouldn't have come. But he had come. He was here and he had better do something about it.

He said to Mary: 'Have you had a squint at the old Schloss yet?'

'It's a fantastic place. How on earth do we ever get General Carnaby out of there?'

'Easy. We'll take a walk up there tonight, get inside and take him away.'

Mary stared at him in disbelief and waited for him to amplify his statement. He didn't. Finally, she said: 'That's all?'

'That's all.'

'The simplicity of true genius. You must have spent a lot of time working that one out.' When he still didn't reply, she went on, elaborately sarcastic: 'In the first place, of course, there'll be no trouble about getting in. You just go up to the main door and knock.'

'More or less. Then the door – or window – opens, I smile at you, say thank you and pass inside.'

'You what.'

'I smile and say thank you. Even in wartime, there's no reason why the little courtesies—'

'Please!' She was thoroughly exasperated now. 'If you can't talk sense—'

'*You* are going to open the door for *me*,' Smith explained patiently.

'Are you feeling all right?'

'The staff shortage in Germany is acute. The Schloss Adler is no exception. You're just the type they're looking for. Young, intelligent, good-looking, you can cook, polish, sew on Colonel Kramer's buttons—'

'Who's Colonel Kramer?' Her tone as much as her face showed the bewilderment in her mind.

'Deputy Chief of the German Secret Service.'

Mary said with conviction: 'You must be mad.'

'If I wasn't I wouldn't be doing this job.' He glanced at his watch. 'I've been gone too long and I fear that I'm surrounded by the odd suspicious mind. We move off at five. Exactly five. Down in the village there's a *Gasthaus* on the east side of the main street called "Zum Wilden Hirsch." "The Wild Deer." Remember it, "Zum Wilden Hirsch." We don't want you wandering into the wrong pub. Behind it there's a shed used as a beer cellar. It's always kept locked but there will be a key in the door tonight. I'll meet you there at exactly eight o'clock.'

He turned to go, but she caught him by the arm.

'How do you know all this?' she asked tensely. 'About the *Gasthaus* and the bottle store and the key being there and about Colonel Kramer and—'

'Ah, ah!' Smith shook his head admonishingly and touched her lips with his forefinger.

'Hand-book for spies, golden rule number one.' She drew away from him and stared down at the snow-covered ground, her voice low and bitter. 'Never ever tell anyone anything unless you have to.' She paused and looked up. 'Not even me?'

'Especially not you, poppet.' He patted her lightly on the cheek. 'Don't be late.'

He walked away down the slope leaving her looking after him with an expressionless face.

Lieutenant Schaffer lay stretched out and almost buried in the deep snow, half-hidden behind the bole of a pine, with a telescope to his eye. He twisted as he heard the soft crunch of snow behind him and saw Smith approaching on his hands and knees.

'Couldn't you knock or something?' Schaffer asked irritably.

'Sorry. Something you wanted to show me, so the boys say.'

'Yeah.' Schaffer handed Smith the telescope. 'Take a gander at this lot. Thought it might interest you.'

Smith took the telescope and fingered the very precise adjustment until he achieved maximum definition.

'Lower down,' Schaffer said. 'At the foot of the rock.'

Smith traversed the telescope down the sides of the Schloss Adler and the sheer walls of the volcanic plug until the fine cross-hairs came to rest on the snow-covered slopes at the foot. Moving across the slope he could see two soldiers with slung machine-carbines and, not on leashes, four dogs.

'My, my,' Smith murmured thoughtfully. 'I see what you mean.'

'Those are Dobermann pinschers, boss.'

'Well, they aren't toy poodles and that's a fact,' Smith agreed. He moved the telescope a little way up the walls of the volcanic plug, held it there.

'*And* floodlights.' he added softly.

He lowered the telescope again, past the patrolling soldiers and dogs, till it came to rest on a high wire fence that appeared to go all the way around the base of the volcanic plug.

'*And* a dinky little fence.'

'Fences,' Schaffer said pontifically, 'are made to be cut or climbed.'

'You try cutting or climbing this one, laddie, and you'll be cooked to a turn in nothing flat. A standard design, using a standard current of 2300 volt, single-phase, 60 cycle AC. All the best electric chairs have it.'

Schaffer shook his head. 'Amazing the lengths some folks will go to protect their privacy.'

'Fences, floods and Dobermanns,' Smith said. 'I don't think that combination will stop us, do you, Lieutenant?'

'Of course not. Stop us? Of course not!' He paused for some moments, then burst out: 'How in God's name do you propose—'

'We'll decide when the time comes,' Smith said easily.

'You mean you'll decide,' Schaffer said complainingly. 'Play it pretty close to the cuff, don't you?'

'That's because I'm too young to die.'

'Why me, for God's sake?' Schaffer demanded after a long pause. 'Why pick me for this job? This isn't my line of country, Major.'

'God knows,' Smith said frankly. 'Come to that, why me?'

Schaffer was in the middle of giving him a long and pointedly disbelieving look when he suddenly stiffened and cocked his head up to the sky in the direction of the unmistakably rackety whirr of a helicopter engine. Both men picked it up at once. It was coming from the north, over the Blau See, and heading directly towards them. It was a big military version and, even at that distance, the swastika markings were clearly distinguishable. Schaffer started to move backwards towards the line of pines.

'Exit Schaffer,' he announced hurriedly. 'The bloodhounds are out for us.'

'I don't think so,' Smith said. 'Stay where you are and pull your smock over your head.'

Quickly they pulled their white smocks over their heads until only their eyes, and Smith's telescope, partly buried in the snow, could be seen. From thirty yards in any direction, including straight up, they must have been quite invisible.

The helicopter swept up the valley still maintaining a course directly towards the spot where the two men lay hidden. When it was only a few hundred yards away even Smith began to feel uneasy and wondered if by some evil mischance the enemy knew or suspected their presence. They were bound to have heard the engines of the Lancaster, muted though they had been, during the night. Had some suspicious and intelligent character – and there would be no lack of those in the Schloss Adler – come up with the right answer to the question of the presence of this errant bomber in one of the most unlikely places in all Germany? Could picked members of the Alpenkorps be combing the pine woods even at that moment – and he, Smith, had been so confident that he hadn't even bothered to post a guard. Then, abruptly, when the helicopter was almost directly overhead, it side-slipped sharply to its left, sank down over the castle courtyard, hovered for a few moments and slowly descended. Smith surreptitiously mopped his forehead and applied his eye to the telescope.

The helicopter had landed. The rotor stopped, steps descended and a man climbed down to the courtyard floor. From his uniform, Smith decided, a very senior officer. Then he suddenly realized that it was a very very senior officer indeed. His face tightened as he pushed the telescope across to Schaffer. 'Take a good look,' he advised.

Schaffer took a good look, lowered the telescope as the man passed through a doorway. 'Pal of yours, boss?'

'I know him. Reichsmarschall Julius Rosemeyer. The Wehrmacht Chief of Staff.'

'My very first Reichsmarschall and me without my telescopic rifle,' Schaffer said regretfully. 'I wonder what his highness wants.'

'Same as us,' Smith said briefly.

'General Carnaby?'

'When you're going to ask the Allies' overall co-ordinator of planning a few questions about the Second Front you don't send just the corporal of the guard to interview him.'

'You don't think they might have come to take old Carnaby away?' Schaffer asked anxiously.

'Not a chance. The Gestapo never gives up its prisoners. In this country the Wehrmacht does what the Gestapo says.'

'Or else?'

'Or else. Off you go – they've more coffee on the brew back there. Send someone to relieve me in an hour.'

Admiral Rolland's weather forecast for the Sea turned out to be perfectly correct. As the endless shivering hours dragged slowly by the weather steadily deteriorated. By noon the sun was gone and a keen wind sprung up from the east. By early afternoon snow had begun to fall from the darkened sky, slowly at first then with increasing severity as the east wind steadily increased in strength and became bitingly cold. It looked like being a bad night, Smith thought. But a bad night that reduced visibility to near-zero and kept people indoors was what they wanted: it would have been difficult for them to saunter up to the Schloss Adler bathed in the warm light of a harvest moon. Smith checked his watch.

'Time to go.' He climbed stiffly to his feet and beat his arms to restore circulation. 'Call Thomas, will you.'

Rucksacks and kit-bags were slung and shouldered. Thomas, who had been keeping watch, appeared carrying Smith's telescope. Thomas was very far from being his usual cheerful self, and it wasn't just the fact that he'd spent the last hour exposed to the full force of wind and snow that had left him in such ill-humour.

'Is that damned radio working yet?' he asked Smith.

'Not a hope. Six tries, six failures. Why?'

'I'll tell you why,' Thomas said bitterly. 'Pity we couldn't get the Admiral to change his mind about the paratroops. A full troop train just got in, that's all.'

'Well, that's fine,' Smith said equably. 'The old hands will think we're new boys and the new boys will think we're old hands. Very convenient.'

Thomas looked thoughtfully at Smith.

'Very, *very* convenient.' He hesitated, then went on: 'How about loosening up a bit, Major?'

'What do you mean?'

'Come off it,' Carraciola said roughly. 'You know damn well what he means. It's our lives. Why do we have to go down into that damned village? And how do you intend to get Carnaby out? If we're to commit suicide, tell us why. You owe us that.'

'I owe you nothing,' Smith said flatly. 'I'll tell you nothing. And if you know nothing you can't talk. You'll be told when the time comes.'

'You, Smith,' Torrance-Smythe said precisely, 'are a cold-blooded devil.'

'It's been said before,' Smith said indifferently.

The village railway station was a small, two-track, end-of-the-line depot. Like all end-of-the-line depots it was characterized by rust, dilapidation, the barest functionalism of design and an odd pessimistically-expectant air of waiting for someone to come along and finish it off properly. At any time, its air of desolation was total. That night, completely deserted, with a high, gusting wind driving snow through pools of light cast by dim and swaying electric lamps, the ghostly impression of a place abandoned by man and by the world was almost overwhelming. It suited Smith's purpose perfectly.

He led his five snow-smock clad men quickly across the tracks and into the comparative shelter of the station buildings. They filed silently past the closed bookstall, the freight office, the booking office, flitted quickly into the shadows beyond and stopped.

Smith lowered the radio, shrugged off his rucksack, removed snow-smock and trousers and sauntered casually alongside the tracks – the thrifty Bavarians regarded platforms as a wasteful luxury. He stopped outside a door next to a bolted hatch which bore above it the legend GEPACK ANNAHME. He tried the door. It was locked. He made a quick survey to check that he was unobserved, stooped, examined the keyhole with a pencil flash, took a bunch of oddly shaped keys from his pockets and had the door opened in seconds. He whistled softly and was almost at once joined by the others, who filed quickly inside, already slipping off their packs as they went. Schaffer, bringing up the rear, paused and glanced up at the sign above the hatch.

'My God!' He shook his head. 'The left luggage office!'

'Where else?' Smith asked reasonably. He ushered Schaffer in, closed and locked the door behind him. Hooding his pencil torch until only a finger-width beam emerged, he passed by the luggage racks till he came to the far end of the room where a bay window was set in the wall. It was a perfectly ordinary sash window and he examined it very minutely, careful that at no time the pinpoint of light touched the glass to shine through to the street beyond. He turned his attention to the vertical wooden planking at the side of the window, took out his sheath knife and levered a plank away to expose a length of twin-cored flex stapled vertically to the wall. He split the cores, sliced through each in turn, replaced the plank and tested the lower sash of the window. It moved easily up and down.

'An interesting performance,' Schaffer observed. 'What was all that in aid of?'

'It's not always convenient to enter by the front door. Or, come to that, leave by it either.'

'A youth mis-spent in philandering or burgling,' Schaffer said sadly. 'How did you know it was wired for sound?'

'Even a small country station will have valuables stored in its left luggage office from time to time,' Smith said patiently. 'But it will *not* have a full-time baggage attendant. The attendant, booking clerk, ticket-collector, porter and station-master are probably all one man. So it's kept locked. But there's no point in barring the front door if your bag-snatcher can climb in through the back window. So your back window is grilled or wired. No grille – and a badly-fitting plank. Obvious.'

'Obvious to you, maybe,' Carraciola said sourly. 'All this – ah – expertise with skeleton keys and burglar alarms. The Black Watch you said you were in?'

'That's right.'

'Very odd training they give you in those Scottish regiments. Very odd indeed.'

' "Thorough" is the word you're searching for,' Smith said kindly. 'Let's go and have a drink.'

'Let's do that,' Carraciola said heavily. 'Remind me to get mine down in one go or ten gets you one that I'll never live to finish it.'

'It would be a shame to waste good beer,' Smith agreed. He waited until the last man was out, locked the door behind him and rejoined them as they walked out of the main station entrance under the 'Bahnhof' sign. They were now no longer carrying rucksacks or wearing snow-smocks. All were dressed in the uniforms of soldiers of a Jäger battalion, Smith as a major, Schaffer as a lieutenant and the other four as sergeants. Their uniforms were no longer as immaculately crease-free as they might have been nor for that matter, as Sergeant Harrod had observed, did they fit as well as they might have done. But in a village street or crowded bar, at night-time, they should pass muster. Or so Smith devoutly hoped.

It was a typical main street in a typical high alpine village. The buildings lining either side of the street, solid, rugged, four-square buildings, looked as if they had been defying the bitter Bavarian winters for a long long time and intended going on doing so for as long again. Nearly all the houses were of the wooden chalet type, with great sweeping eaves and balconies running the full width of the front of the houses. A few were of comparatively modern construction, with shingled walls, large double-glazed windows and fancy wrought-iron grille-work, but most were very old and low, planked with rough adze-cut wood, and having the interlocking wall-beams projecting at the corners.

There were no street lamps but neither was there any attempt at a blackout. Elongated rectangles of light from uncurtained windows patterned the snow-packed streets. Beyond the far or southern end of the street, intermittently seen through the sweeping curtains of snow, a cluster of bright lights seemed to hang suspended in the sky. Instinctively, almost, Smith stopped to gaze at this distant constellation and his men stopped with him. The lights of the Schloss Adler, the castle of the eagle, seemed impossibly remote, as unattainable as the mountains of the moon. Wordlessly, the men looked at them in long silence, then at one another, then, by mutual and still silent consent, moved on their way again, their boots crunching crisply in the beaten snow, their frozen breaths wisping away in the chill night wind.

The main street – the only street – was deserted, quite empty of life. Inevitably so, on so bitter a night. But if the street was deserted, the village was anything but: the sounds of laughter and singing and the babel of voices filled the night air and the nose-to-tail row of parked German trucks along one side of the street showed clearly enough just who was responsible for the singing and the laughter. For the training troops in the military barracks on the Blau See there was only one centre of entertainment for twenty miles around and this village was it: the *Gasthaüser* and *Weinstuben* were jammed to the doors with soldiers of the Alpenkorps, probably the most highly trained combat troops in Europe.

Schaffer said plaintively: 'I don't really feel like a drink, boss.'

'Nonsense,' Smith said encouragingly. 'You're just shy at the thought of meeting strangers.' He stopped in front of a *Gasthaus* with the legend 'Drei Könige' above the door. 'Here's a likely looking place, now. Hang on a minute.'

He climbed the steps, opened the door and looked inside. Down in the street the other five looked at one another, the same mingled apprehension and expectancy mirrored in every eye. Austrian *Schrammel* music, hauntingly and nostalgically evocative of a kindlier and happier age, flooded through the open doorway. The expressions on the faces of the men below didn't change. There was a time and a place for *Schrammel* music and this wasn't it.

Smith shook his head, closed the door and rejoined his men.

'Packed,' he said. 'Not even standing room.' He nodded across the street to another hostelry, the 'Eichhof,' a small, squat, beetle-browed building with adze-cut corner beams and an air of advanced dilapidation. 'Let's see what this has to offer.'

But the 'Eichhof' had nothing to offer. Regretfully but firmly Smith closed its front door and turned away.

'Jammed,' he announced. 'Besides, a low-class dump unsuitable for officers and NCOs of the Wehrmacht. But this next place looks more promising, don't you think?'

From the pointed silence it was apparent that the other five didn't think anything of the kind, and, in fact, apart from the factor of size, the third

Weinstube looked remarkably like the ones Smith had just passed up. 'Zum Wilden Hirsch', it was called, and above the sign was a snow-shrouded wooden carving of a wild deer.

Smith walked up the half-dozen steps to the front door and opened it. He winced as the blast of sound reached him, an almost physical assault upon the eardrums. Heaven knew the last two *Weinstuben* had been clamorous enough but compared to this place they now seemed, in retrospect, to have been invested in a cathedral silence. To the blaring accompaniment of a battery of discordant accordions what appeared, from the sheer volume of sound, to be an entire regiment were giving 'Lili Marlene' all they had. Smith glanced at his men, nodded and passed inside.

As the others followed, Schaffer paused in the doorway as Christiansen took his arm and said wonderingly: 'You think he thinks this *isn't* packed?'

'They must,' Schaffer conceded, 'have had them packed six deep in the other joints.'

Chapter Four

They weren't exactly stacked six deep inside 'Zum Wilden Hirsch' but they might well have been if the music-swaying crowd of elbow-jostling customers had assumed the horizontal instead of the perpendicular. He had never, Smith thought, seen so many people in one bar before. There must have been at least four hundred of them. To accommodate a number of that order called for a room of no ordinary dimensions, and this one wasn't. It was a very big room indeed. It was also a very very old room.

The floor of knotted pine sagged, the walls sagged and the massive smoke-blackened beams on the roof seemed to be about ready to fall down at any moment. In the middle of the room stood a huge black wood-burning stove, a stove stoked with such ferocious purpose that the cast-iron top cover glowed dull red. From just below the cover two six-inch twenty-foot long black-enamelled stove pipes led off to points high up on opposite sides of the room – a primitive but extremely efficient form of central heating. The three-sided settees – half booths – lining three walls of the room were of oak darkened by age and smoke and unknown centuries of customers, each booth having recessed holes for stowing newspapers rolled round slats of wood. The twenty or so tables scattered across the floor had hand-cut wooden tops of not less than three inches in thickness with chairs to match. Most of the back of the room was taken up by a solid oaken bar with a coffee-machine at one end, and, behind the bar, swing doors that presumably led to the kitchen. What little illumination there was in the room came from ceiling-suspended and very sooty oil lamps, each one with its generations-old patch of coal-black charred wood in the roof above.

Smith transferred his attention from the room to the customers in the room, a clientele of a composition such as one might expect to find in a high Alpine village with a military encampment at its back door. In one corner were a group of obvious locals, men with still, lean, aquiline, weather-beaten faces, unmistakably men of the mountains, many of them in intricately embroidered leather jackets and Tyrolean hats. They spoke little and drank quietly, as did another small group at the back of the room, perhaps a dozen or so nondescript civilians, clearly not locals, who drank sparingly from small Schnapps glasses. But ninety per cent of the customers were soldiers of the German Alpenkorps, some seated, many more standing, but all giving of their very best with 'Lili Marlene', and nearly all of them enthusiastically waving their pewter-capped litre Steinbechers in the air, happily oblivious, in that moment of tearfully nostalgic romanticism, of the fact that the amount of beer finding its way to comrades' uniforms and the floor was about the equivalent of a moderately heavy rainstorm.

Behind the bar was the obvious proprietor, a gargantuan three-hundred pounder with an impressive moon-like face and several girls busy filling trays with Steinbechers. Several others moved about the room, collecting or serving beer-mugs. One of them approaching in his direction caught Smith's eye.

It would have been surprising if she hadn't. It would have been surprising if she hadn't caught the attention of every man there. But there was no surprise. She did. She would have won any Miss Europe contest hands down if she had had a face other than her own which, though pleasant and plump, was rather plain. But any possible lack of attraction in that cheerfully smiling face was more than over-compensated for elsewhere. She was dressed in a gaily-patterned dirndl and Tyrolean blouse, had a hand-span waist, an hour-and-a-half-glass figure and an obvious predilection for low-cut blouses, that in terms of attracting local custom, must have been worth a fortune to the gigantic proprietor behind the bar. She drew a great deal of attention from the assembled soldiery, not all of it just consisting of admiring glances: if she weren't wearing armour-plating, Smith reflected, she must be permanently black and blue. She approached Smith, brushed back her blonde hair and smiled, the gesture as provocative as the smile.

'Can I help you, sir?'

'Dark beer, please,' Smith said politely. 'Six.'

'With pleasure, sir.' Again the provocative smile, this time accompanied by a half-appraising, half-lingering look from cornflower blue eyes, then she turned and walked away, if her method of locomotion could strictly be described as walking. Schaffer, a slightly dazed expression on his face, stared after her, then caught Smith by the arm.

'*Now* I know why I left Montana, boss.' His voice held something of the dazed quality on his face. 'It wasn't because of the horses after all.'

'Your mind on the job if you don't mind, Lieutenant.' Smith looked thoughtfully after the girl, rubbed his chin and said slowly: 'Barmaids know more about what's going on in their own manor than any chief of police – and that one looks as if she might know more than most. Yes, I'll do that.'

'Do what?' Schaffer asked suspiciously.

'Try to get next to her.'

'I saw her first,' Schaffer said plaintively.

'You can have the next dance,' Smith promised. The levity of the words were belied by the cool watchful expression on his face as his eyes constantly

travelled the room. 'When you get your drinks, circulate. See if you can hear
any mention of Carnaby or Reichsmarschall Rosemeyer.'

He caught sight of an empty chair by a corner table, moved across and
sat in it, nodding politely to a rather bleary-eyed Alpenkorps captain deep
in what appeared to be rather patronizing conversation with two lieutenants.
The captain showed no more than a brief recognition of his presence and,
as far as Smith could tell, no other person present was showing the slightest
interest in either himself or his companions. The accordion band finished its
stint more or less on the same note and at the same time and the singing of
'Lili Marlene' died away. For long seconds there was a profound and
nostalgic silence, four hundred men alone with Lili Marlene under the
barrack gate lantern, then, as if on cue, a babel of voices broke out all over
the room: four hundred men with unfinished litre mugs do not remain
sentimental for overly long.

He caught sight of the girl returning with six Steinbechers on a tray,
pushing her way through the crowd and fending off admirers with a practised
hand. She gave drinks to Smith's men who immediately but unostentatiously
broke up and began to wander away into different parts of the room. The
girl looked around, located Smith, smiled brightly, crossed to his table, and
put the Steinbecher on it. Before she could straighten, Smith put his arm
around her waist and pulled her on to his knee. The Jäger captain across
the table broke off his conversation, stared across in startled disapproval,
opened his mouth as if to speak, caught Smith's discouraging glance, decided
to mind his own business and resumed his conversation. Smith, in his turn,
looked away, squeezed the girl's waist, patted her knee and smiled what he
hoped was a winning smile.

'And what might your name be, my Alpine rose?' His voice had a slightly
slurred edge to it.

'Heidi.' She struggled to rise, but didn't really put her heart into it.
'Please, Major. I have work to do.'

'There is no more important work than entertaining soldiers of the
Fatherland,' Smith said loudly. Holding Heidi firmly to forestall any attempt
at escape, he took a long pull at his beer, then continued, quietly now, the
mug still in front of his face: 'Shall I sing you a song?'

'What song?' Heidi asked warily. 'I hear too much singing.'

'I whistle better than I sing. Listen.' He whistled, very softly the first two
bars of 'Lorelei'. 'Do you like that?'

Heidi stiffened and stared but immediately relaxed and smiled at him
coquettishly.

'It's very nice, Major. And I'm sure you have a beautiful singing voice,
too.'

Smith put his Steinbecher down with an unsteady bang that brought more
disapproval from the other side of the table then lifted his hand to wipe the
froth from his lips. Heidi smiled down at him, but the wary eyes weren't
smiling.

Smith said from behind his hand: 'The men at the bar? The civilians?
Don't turn round.'

'Gestapo.' She made another apparently futile attempt to free herself.
'From the castle.'

'One's a lip-reader.' Smith had the Steinbecher in front of his face again.

'I can tell. They're watching. Your room in five minutes. Hit me good and hard.'

Heidi stared at him in bewilderment, then yelped in pain as he pinched her, far from gently. She drew back, her right hand came over in a round-house swing and the sound of the slap could be heard clear across the crowded room, cutting sharply through the deep buzz of conversation. The voices died away, Steinbechers remained poised half-way towards lips, and every eye in the room turned until it was focused on the scene of the disturbance. Smith now had the exclusive and undivided attention of close on four hundred German soldiers which was exactly how he wanted it: no man anxious to avoid attention at all costs would ever do anything to incur the slightest risk of drawing that unwanted attention.

Heidi pushed herself to her feet, rubbed herself tenderly, snatched up the note which Smith had earlier placed on the table and stalked haughtily away. Smith, his already reddening face discomfited and tight in anger, rose, made to leave the table then halted when confronted by the Jäger captain who had already risen from his side of the table. He was a spruce, erect youngster, very much of the Hitler Jügend type, punctilious and correct but at that moment rather suffering from the effect of too many Steinbechers. Beneath the redly-dulled eyes lay a gleam which bespoke the not uncommon combination of self-importance and officious self-righteousness.

'Your conduct does not become an officer of the Wehrmacht,' he said loudly.

Smith did not reply at once. The embarrassed anger faded from his face to be replaced by an expressionlessly penetrating stare. He gazed unwinkingly into the captain's eyes for so long that the other finally looked away. When Smith's voice came it was too quiet to be heard even at the next table.

'*Herr* Major, when you talk to me, little man.' The tone was glacial: so now were also the eyes. 'Major Bernd Himmler. You may have heard of me?'

He paused significantly and the young captain seemed to shrink perceptibly before his eyes. Himmler, head of the Gestapo, was the most feared man in Germany. Smith could have been any relative of Himmler, possibly even his son.

'Report to me at 8 a.m. tomorrow morning,' Smith said curtly. He swung away without waiting for an answer. The Alpenkorps captain, suddenly very sober indeed, nodded wordlessly and sank wearily into his chair. As Smith strode towards the door the hubbub of conversation resumed. For the soldiers stationed in that remote military outpost, drinking beer, very large quantities of beer, was the only pastime: such incidents were no sooner seen than forgotten.

On his way to the door Smith stopped briefly by Schaffer and said: 'Well, I fouled that one up.'

'You could have handled it differently,' Schaffer conceded, then went on curiously: 'What did you say to him? The young Alpine Corps captain, I mean.'

'I gave him to understand that I was Himmler's son.'

'The Gestapo boss?' Schaffer asked incredulously. 'God above, you took a chance.'

'I couldn't afford to take a chance,' Smith said cryptically. 'I'll go try the "Eichhof". Better luck there, maybe. Back in ten minutes. Less.'

He left Schaffer looking uncertainly after him, made an urgent negative move of his hand towards Carraciola, who was approaching him, and passed outside. He moved a few paces along the wooden boardwalk, stopped and glanced briefly up and down the snow-filled street. It was deserted in both directions. He turned and walked quickly up a narrow alleyway which paralleled the side of 'Zum Wilden Hirsch'. At the rear stood a small wooden hut. Smith checked again that he was unobserved, opened the door quietly. 'Eight o'clock,' he said into the darkness. 'Come on.'

There was a rustle of clothes and Mary appeared in the doorway. She was shivering violently, her face blue-tinged with the extreme cold. She looked questioningly at Smith but he took her arm without a word and led her quickly to the back door of the *Gasthaus*. They entered a small hallway, dimly lit by an oil lamp, crossed it, climbed a flight of stairs, moved along a corridor and stopped at the second door on the right. They passed swiftly inside, Smith closing the door behind him.

It was a small room, plainly furnished, but from the chintz soft furnishings and toilet articles on a dressing-table, very obviously a feminine room. Mary sat down on the bed, hugging herself tightly to try to restore some warmth and looked up at Smith without any admiration in her face.

'I hope you're enjoying your little game,' she said bitterly. 'Seem to know your way around, don't you?'

'Instinct,' Smith explained. He stooped over the low-burning oil lamp by the bed, turned up the flame, glanced briefly about the room, located a battered leather case in one corner, swung it to the bed and snapped open the lid. The case contained women's clothing. He pulled Mary to her feet and said: 'Don't waste time. Take off your clothes. And when I say that, I mean your clothes. Every last stitch. Then get into that top outfit there. You'll find everything you need.'

Mary stared at him.

'Those clothes? Why on earth must I—'

'Don't *argue*. Now!'

'Now it is,' she said resignedly. 'You might at least turn your back.'

'Relax,' Smith said wearily. 'I have other things on my mind.' He crossed to the window, stood peering out through a crack in the chintz curtains and went on: 'Now, hurry. You're supposed to be coming off the bus from Steingaden that arrives in twenty minutes' time. You'll be carrying that case, which contains the rest of your clothes. Your name is Maria Schenk, you're from Düsseldorf, a cousin of a barmaid that works here, and you've had TB and been forced to give up your factory job and go to the mountains for your health. So you've got this new job, through this barmaid, in the Schloss Adler. And you have identity papers, travel permit, references and letters in appropriately post-marked envelopes to prove all of it. They're in that handbag in the case. Think you got all that?'

'I - I think so,' she said uncertainly. 'But if you'd only tell me—'

'For God's sake!' Smith said impatiently. 'Time, girl, time! Got it or not?'

'Maria Schenk, Düsseldorf, factory, TB, cousin here, Steingaden - yes, I have it.' She broke off to pull a ribbed blue wool dress over her head, smoothed it down and said wonderingly: 'It's a perfect fit! You'd think this dress was made for me!'

'It *was* made for you.' Smith turned round to inspect her. '36–26–36 or whatever. We – um – broke into your flat and borrowed a dress to use as a model. Thorough, that's us.'

'You broke into my flat?' she asked slowly.

'Well, now, you wouldn't want to go around like a refugee from a jumble sale,' Smith said reasonably. He looked at the dress with an approving eye. 'Does something for you.'

'I'd like to do something for you,' she said feelingly. Her eyes mirrored her bafflement, her total lack of understanding. 'But – but it must have taken *weeks* to prepare those clothes – and those papers!'

'Like enough,' Smith agreed. 'Our Forgery Section did a very special job on those papers. Had to, to get you into the lion's den.'

'Weeks,' Mary said incredulously. 'Weeks! But General Carnaby's plane crashed only yesterday morning.' She stared at him, registering successive expressions of confusion, accusation and, finally, downright anger. 'You *knew* it was going to crash!'

'Right first time, my poppet,' Smith said cheerfully. He gave her an affectionate pat. 'We rigged it.'

'*Don't* do that,' she snapped, then went on carefully, her face still tight with anger: 'There really *was* a plane crash?'

'Guaranteed. The plane crash-landed on the airfield HQ of the Bavarian Mountain Rescue pilots. Place called Oberhausen, about five miles from here. The place we'll be leaving from incidentally.'

'The place we'll be leaving—' She broke off, gazed at him a long moment then shook her head almost in despair. 'But – but in the plane I overheard you telling the men that if the mission failed or you had to split up that you were all to make a rendezvous at Frauenfeld, over the Swiss border.'

'Did you now?' There was mild interest in Smith's voice. 'I must be getting confused. Anyway, this Mosquito put down on the Oberhausen airfield riddled with machine-gun bullet holes. British machine-gun bullet holes, but what the hell, holes are holes.'

'And you'd risk the life of an American general – and all the plans for the Second Front—'

'Well, now, that's why I'm in such a hurry to get inside the Schloss Adler.' Smith cleared his throat. 'Not before they get his secrets out of him but before they find out that he's *not* an American general and knows no more about the Second Front than I do about the back of the moon.'

'What! He's a plant?'

'Name of Jones,' Smith nodded. 'Cartwright Jones. American actor. As a Thespian he's pretty second rate but he's a dead ringer for Carnaby.'

She looked at him with something like horror in her eyes.

'You'd risk an innocent—'

'He's getting plenty,' Smith interrupted. 'Twenty-five thousand dollars for a one-night stand. The peak of his professional career.'

There came a soft double knock on the door. A swift sliding movement of Smith's hand and a gun was suddenly there, a Mauser automatic, cocked and ready to go. Another swift movement and he was silently by the door, jerking it open. Smith put his gun away. Heidi came in, Smith shutting the door behind her.

'Well, cousins, here we are,' he announced. 'Mary – now Maria – and Heidi. I'm off.'

'You're off!' Mary said dazedly. 'But – but what am I supposed to *do*?'

'Heidi will tell you.'

Mary looked uncertainly at the other girl. 'Heidi?'

'Heidi. Our top secret agent in Bavaria since 1941.'

'Our – top—' Mary shook her head. 'I don't believe it!'

'Nobody would.' Smith surveyed Heidi's opulent charms with an admiring eye. 'Brother, what a disguise!'

Smith opened the back door of the *Gasthaus* with a cautious hand, moved swiftly outside and remained stock-still in the almost total darkness, waiting for his eyes to become accustomed to the change of light. The snow, he thought, was heavier than when they had first entered 'Zum Wilden Hirsch' and the wind had certainly freshened. It was bitingly cold.

Satisfied that he was unobserved, Smith turned to the left, took two steps and bit off an exclamation as he tripped over some unseen object and fell his length in the snow. He rolled over three times in the snow just in case any bystander might have a knife or gun and homicidal ideas about using them, then got to his feet with cat-like speed, his Mauser in one hand, his pencil-flash in the other. He snapped on the torch and swung round in a 360° turn. He was alone.

Alone, that was, but for the crumpled form over which he had tripped, an Alpenkorps sergeant lying face-down in the snow, a form lying still and curiously relaxed in that huddled shapelessness of death.

Smith stooped and rolled the figure over to expose the great red stain in the snow where the body had been lying. The pencil-flash rested briefly on the front of the tunic, a tunic gashed and soaked in blood. The beam of the torch moved up to the face. No more cloisters for this don, Smith thought in irrational emptiness, no more honey still for tea, and the fault is all mine and I can see it in his face. The already dulled and faded eyes of Torrance-Smythe stared up at him in the sightless reproach of death.

Smith straightened to his feet, his face remote and withdrawn, and quartered the immediate ground area with his light. There were no signs of a struggle but struggle there must have been, for some tunic buttons had been ripped off and the high collar torn open. Smithy had not died easily. Flash still in hand, Smith walked slowly along to the mouth of the narrow alleyway, then stopped. A confusion of footprints, dark smears of blood in the trodden snow, dark bare patches on the wooden walls of the *Gasthaus* where struggling men had staggered heavily against it – here was where the struggle had been. Smith switched off the light, returned both torch and gun to their hiding-places and stepped out into the street. On the one side was 'Zum Wilden Hirsch' with the sound of singing once again emanating from it, on the other side a brightly-lit telephone kiosk outside a Post Office. In the kiosk, talking animatedly on the telephone, was a uniformed figure, a soldier Smith had never seen before. The street itself was deserted.

Schaffer leaned negligently against the bar, the picture of complete and careless relaxation. His face belied him. It was grim and shocked and he was savagely shedding a cigarette between his fingers.

'Smithy!' Schaffer's voice was a low and vicious whisper. 'Not Smithy! You *sure*, boss?'

'I'm sure.' Smith's face still held the same remote and withdrawn expression, almost as if all feeling had been drained from him. 'You say he left in a hurry three minutes after I'd gone. So he wasn't after me. Who else left?'

'No idea.' Schaffer snapped the cigarette in half, dropped it to the floor. 'The place is packed. And there's another door. I *can't* believe it. Why old Smithy? *Why* Torrance-Smythe. He was the cleverest of us all.'

'That's why he's dead,' Smith said somberly. 'Now listen carefully. It's time you knew the score.'

Schaffer looked at him steadily and said: 'It's more than time.'

Smith began to speak in a very low voice, in fluent completely idiomatic German, careful that his back was turned to the Gestapo officers at the far end of the bar. After a minute or two he saw Heidi returning to the room through the doorway behind the bar but ignored her as she ignored him. Almost immediately afterwards a gradual diminution in the babel of talk, followed by an almost complete silence, made him fall quiet himself and follow the direction of the gaze of hundreds of soldiers all of whom were looking towards the door.

There was a reason for the silence, especially good reason, Smith thought, for soldiers almost totally cut off from womankind. Mary Ellison, clad in a belted rain-coat, with a scarf over her head and a battered suitcase in her hand, was standing in the doorway. The silence seemed to deepen. Women are rare at any time in a high Alpine *Gasthaus*, unaccompanied young women even rarer and beautiful young women on their own virtually unknown. For some moments Mary stood there uncertainly, as if unsure of her welcome or not knowing what to do. Then she dropped her bag, and her face lit up as she caught sight of Heidi, a face transformed with joy. Marlene Dietrich in *The Blue Angel*, Smith thought inconsequentially. With a face and a figure and an acting talent like that, she could have had Hollywood tramping a path of beaten gold to her doorstep . . . Through the silent room she and Heidi ran toward one another and embraced.

'My dear Maria! My dear Maria!' There was a break in Heidi's voice that made Smith reflect that Hollywood might have been well advised to tramp out two paths of beaten gold. 'So you came after all!'

'After all these years!' Mary hugged the other girl and kissed her again. 'It's wonderful to see you again, Cousin Heidi! Wonderful, wonderful, wonderful! Of *course* I came. Why ever not?'

'Well!' Heidi made no effort to lower her voice as she looked around significantly. 'They're a pretty rough lot, hereabouts. You should carry a gun, always. Hunter battalion, they call themselves. They're well named!'

The soldiers broke out into a roar of laughter and the normal hubbub of sound resumed almost at once. Arm in arm, Heidi led Mary across to the small group of civilians standing at the far end of the bar. She stopped in front of the man in the centre of the group, a dark, wiry, intelligent-faced man who looked very very tough indeed, and performed the introductions.

'Maria, this is Captain von Brauchitsch. He – um – works in the Schloss Adler. Captain, my cousin, Maria Schenk.'

Von Brauchitsch bowed slightly.

'You are fortunate in your cousins, Heidi. We were expecting you, Miss Schenk.' He smiled. 'But not someone as beautiful as this.'

Mary smiled in turn, her face puzzled. 'You were expecting—'

'He was expecting,' Heidi said dryly. 'It is the captain's business to know what is going on.'

'Don't make me sound so sinister, Heidi. You'll frighten Miss Schenk.'
He glanced at his watch. 'The next cable-car leaves in ten minutes. If I
might escort the young lady—'

'The young lady is going to my room first,' Heidi said firmly. 'For a
wash-up and a Kaffee-Schnapps. Can't you see that she's half-dead with
cold?'

'I do believe her teeth are chattering,' von Brauchitsch said with a smile.
'I thought it might have been me. Well, the cable-car after the next one,
then.'

'And I'm going with her,' Heidi announced.

'Both of you?' Von Brauchitsch shook his head and smiled again. Von
Brauchitsch was always smiling. 'My lucky night.'

'Permits, travel documents, identity cards and letters you have,' Heidi said.
She fished up some papers from the recesses of her Tyrolean blouse and
handed them to Mary who was sitting across from her on the bed in her
room. 'Plan of the castle and instructions. Do your homework well then give
them back to me. I'll take them up. You might be searched – they're a
suspicious bunch up there. And drink up that Schnapps – first thing von
Brauchitsch will do is to smell your breath. Just to check. He checks
everything. He's the most suspicious of the lot.'

'He seemed a very pleasant man to me,' Mary said mildly.

'He's a very unpleasant Gestapo officer,' Heidi said dryly.

When Heidi returned to the bar, Smith and Schaffer had been rejoined by
Carraciola, Thomas and Christiansen. All five appeared to be carefree in
their drinking and chatting inconsequentially, but their low and urgent
voices were evidence enough of the desperate worry in their minds. Or in
the minds of some of them.

'You haven't seen old Smithy, then?' Smith asked quietly. 'None of you
saw him go? Then where in hell has he got to?'

There was no reply, but the shrugs and worried frowns were reply
enough. Christiansen said: 'Shall I go and have a look?'

'I don't think so,' Smith said. 'I'm afraid it's too late to go anywhere now.'

Both doors of 'Zum Wilden Hirsch' had suddenly burst open and half a
dozen soldiers were coming quickly in through either door. All had slung
machine-carbines, Schmeissers, at the ready. They fanned out along the
walls and waited, machine-carbines horizontal, fingers on triggers, their eyes
very calm, very watchful.

'Well, well,' Christiansen murmured. 'It was a nice war.'

The sudden and total silence was emphasized rather than broken by the
crisp footfalls on the wooden floor as a full colonel of the Wehrmacht came
striding into the room and looked coldly around him. The gargantuan
proprietor of the *Gasthaus* came hurrying round from the back of the bar,
tripping over chairs in the anxiety and fear limned so unmistakably clearly
in his pumpkin of a face.

'Colonel Weissner!' It required no acute ear to catch the shake in the
proprietor's voice. 'What in God's name—'

'No fault of yours, mein Herr.' The colonel's words were reassuring
which was more than the tone of his voice was. 'But you harbour enemies
of the state.'

'Enemies of the state.' In a matter of seconds the proprietor's complexion had changed from a most unbecoming puce to an even more unbecoming washed-out grey while his voice now quavered like a high-C tuning fork. 'What? I?. I Josef Wartmann—'

'Please.' The colonel held up his hand for silence. 'We are looking for four or five Alpenkorps deserters from the Stuttgart military prison. To escape, they killed two officers and a guardroom sergeant. They were known to be heading this way.'

Smith nodded and said in Schaffer's ear: 'Very clever. Very clever indeed.'

'Now then,' Weissner continued briskly. 'If they're here, we'll soon have them. I want the senior officers present of drafts thirteen, fourteen and fifteen to come forward.' He waited until two majors and a captain came forward and stood at attention before him. 'You know all your officers and men by sight?'

The three officers nodded.

'Good. I wish you—'

'No need, Colonel.' Heidi had come round from behind the bar and now stood before Weissner, hands clasped respectfully behind her back. 'I know the man you're after. The ringleader.'

'Ah!' Colonel Weissner smiled. 'The charming—'

'Heidi, Herr Colonel. I have waited table on you up in the Schloss Adler.'

Weissner bowed gallantly. 'As if one could ever forget.'

'That one.' Her face full of a combination of righteous indignation and devotion to duty, Heidi pointed a dramatically accusing finger at Smith. 'That's the one, Herr Colonel. He – he pinched me!'

'My dear Heidi!' Colonel Weissner smiled indulgently. 'If we were to convict every man who ever harboured thoughts of—'

'Not that, Herr Colonel. He asked me what I knew or had heard about a man called General Cannabee – I think.'

'General Carnaby!' Colonel Weissner was no longer smiling. He glanced at Smith, motioned guards to close in on him, then glanced back at Heidi. 'What did you tell him?'

'Herr Colonel!' Heidi was stiff with outraged dignity. 'I hope I am a good German. *And* I value my engagements at the Schloss Adler.' She half-turned and pointed across the room. 'Captain von Brauchitsch of the Gestapo will vouch for me.'

'No need. We will not forget this, my dear child.' He patted her affectionately on the cheek, then turned to Smith, the temperature of his voice dropping from warm to sub-zero. 'Your accomplices, sir, and at once.'

'At once, my dear Colonel?' The look he gave Heidi was as glacial as the Colonel's voice. 'Surely not. Let's get our priorities straight. First, her thirty pieces of silver. Then us.'

'You talk like a fool,' Colonel Weissner said contemptuously. 'Heidi is a true patriot.'

'I'm sure she is,' Smith said bitterly.

Mary, her face still and shocked, stared down from the uncurtained crack in Heidi's dark room as Smith and the four others were led out of the front door of 'Zum Wilden Hirsch' and marched off down the road under heavy escort to where several command cars were parked on the far side of the street. Brusquely, efficiently, the prisoners were bundled into two of the cars, engines started up and within a minute both cars were lost to sight round a bend in the road. For almost a minute afterwards Mary stood there, staring out unseeingly on the swirling snow, then pulled the curtains together and turned back towards the darkened room.

She said in a whisper: 'How did it happen?'

A match scratched as Heidi lit and turned up the flame of the oil lamp.

'I can't guess.' Heidi shrugged. 'Someone, I don't know who, must have tipped Colonel Weissner off. But I put the finger on him.'

'Mary stared at her. 'You – you—'

'He'd have been found out in another minute anyway. They were strangers. But it strengthens our hand. I – and you – are now above suspicion.'

'Above suspicion!' Mary looked at her in disbelief then went on, almost wildly: 'But there's no point in going ahead now!'

'Is there not?' Heidi said thoughtfully. 'Somehow, I feel sorrier for Colonel Weissner than I do for Major Smith. Is not our Major Smith a man of resource? Or do our employers in Whitehall lie to us? When they told me he was coming here, they told me not to worry, to trust him implicitly. A man of infinite resource – those were their exact words – who can extricate himself from positions of utmost difficulty. They have a funny way of talking in Whitehall. But already I trust him. Don't you?'

There was no reply. Mary stared at the floor, her eyes bright with unshed tears. Heidi touched her arm and said softly. 'You love him as much as that?'

Mary nodded in silence.

'And does he love you?'

'I don't know. I just don't know. He's been too long in this business – even if he did know,' she said bitterly, 'he probably wouldn't tell himself.'

Heidi looked at her for a moment, shook her head and said: 'They should never have sent you. How can you hope to—' She broke off, shook her head again, and went on: 'It's too late now. Come on. We mustn't keep von Brauchitsch waiting.'

'But – but if he doesn't come? If he can't escape – and how *can* he escape?' She gestured despairingly at the papers lying on the bed. 'They're bound to check with Düsseldorf first thing in the morning about those forged references.'

Heidi said without any particular expression in her voice: 'I don't think he'd let *you* down, Mary.'

'No,' Mary said dolefully. 'I don't suppose he would.'

The big black Mercedes command car swept along the snow-packed road that paralleled the Blau See, the windscreen wipers just coping with the thickly-swirling snow that rushed greyly back at the windscreen through powerful headlight beams. It was an expensive car and a very comfortable one, but neither Schaffer up front nor Smith in the rear seat experienced any degree of comfort whatsoever, either mental or physical. On the mental side there was the bitter prospect of the inevitable firing squad and the knowledge that their mission was over even before it had properly begun: on the physical side they were cramped in the middle of their seats, Schaffer flanked by driver and guard, Smith by Colonel Weissner and guard, and both Smith and Schaffer were suffering from pain in the lower ribs: the owners of the Schmeisser machine-pistols, the muzzles of which were grinding into the captives' sides, had no compunction about letting their presence be known.

They were now, Smith estimated, half-way between village and barracks. Another thirty seconds and they would be through the barrack gates. Thirty seconds. No more.

'Stop this car!' Smith's voice was cold, authoritative with an odd undertone of menace. 'Immediately, do you hear? I must think.'

Colonel Weissner, startled, turned and stared at him. Smith ignored him completely. His face reflected an intensely frowning concentration, a thin-lipped anger barely under control, the face of a man to whom the thought of disobedience of his curt instruction was unthinkable: most certainly not the face of a man going to captivity and death. Weissner hesitated, but only fractionally. He gave an order and the big car began to slow.

'You oaf! You utter idiot!' Smith's tone, shaking with anger, was low and vicious, so low that only Weissner could hear it. 'You've almost certainly ruined everything and, by God, if you have, Weissner, you'll be without a regiment tomorrow!'

The car pulled into the roadside and stopped. Ahead, the red tail lights of the command car in front vanished into a snow-filled darkness. Weissner said brusquely, but with a barely perceptible tremor of agitation in his voice: 'What the devil are you talking about?'

'You knew about this American general, Carnaby?' Smith's face, eyes narrowed and teeth bared in anger, was within six inches of Weissner's. 'How?' He almost spat the word out.

'I dined in the Schloss Adler last night. I—'

Smith looked at him in total incredulity.

'Colonel Paul Kramer told you? He actually talked to you about him?' Weissner nodded wordlessly. 'Admiral Canaris' Chief of Staff! And now everybody knows. God in heaven, heads will roll for this.' He screwed the heels of his palms into his eyes, lowered his hands wearily to his thighs, gazed ahead unseeingly and shook his head, very slowly. 'This is too big, even for me.' He fished out his pass and handed it to Weissner, who examined it in the beam of a none too steady torch. 'Back to the barracks at once! I must get through to Berlin immediately. My uncle will know what to do.'

'Your uncle?' By what seemed a great effort of will Weissner looked up from the pass he held in his hand: his voice was no steadier than the torch. '*Heinrich* Himmler?'

'Who do you think?' Smith snarled. 'Mickey Mouse?' He dropped his voice to a low murmur. 'I trust you never have the privilege of meeting him, Colonel Weissner.' He gave Weissner the benefit of a long and speculative look singularly lacking in any encouragement, then turned away and prodded the driver, none too lightly, in the back. 'The barracks – and make it quick!'

The car moved off. Anything that the nephew of the dreaded Heinrich Himmler, Chief of the Gestapo, said was good enough for the driver.

Smith turned to the guard by his side. 'Take that damned thing out of my ribs!'

Angrily, he snatched the gun away. The guard, who had also heard of Himmler, meekly yielded up the machine-pistol. One second later he was doubled up in helpless retching agony as the butt of the Schmeisser smashed into his stomach and another second later Colonel Weissner was pinned against the window of his Mercedes as the muzzle of the Schmeisser ground into his right ear.

Smith said: 'If your men move, you die.'

'Okay.' Schaffer's calm voice from the front seat. 'I have their guns.'

'Stop the car,' Smith ordered.

The car came to a halt. Through the windscreen Smith could see the lights of the barracks guard-room, now less than two hundred yards away. He gave Weissner a prod with the Schmeisser muzzle.

'Out!'

Weissner's face was a mask of chagrined rage but he was too experienced a soldier even to hesitate. He got out.

'Three paces from the car,' Smith said. 'Face down on the snow. Hands clasped behind your head. Schaffer, your gun on your guard. Out beside the General, you.' This with his gun muzzle in the driver's neck.

Twenty seconds later, Schaffer at the wheel, they were on their way, leaving three men face downwards in the snow and the fourth, Smith's erstwhile guard, still doubled up in agony by the roadside.

'A creditable effort, young Himmler,' Schaffer said approvingly.

'I'll never be that lucky again,' Smith said soberly. 'Take your time passing the barracks. We don't want any of the sentries getting the wrong idea.'

At a steady twenty miles an hour they passed the main gates and then the secondary gates, apparently, as far as Smith could see, without exciting any comment. Just behind the three-pointed star on the car's radiator flew a small triangular pennant, the Camp Commandant's personal standard, and no one, it was safe to assume, would question the comings and goings of Colonel Weissner.

For half a mile or so beyond the secondary gates the road ran northwards in a straight line with, on the left, a sheer hundred-foot cliff dropping down into the waters of the Blau See, and, to the right, a line of pines, not more than fifty yards wide, backing up against another vertical cliff-face which soared up until lost in the snow and the darkness.

At the end of the half-mile straight, the road ahead swept sharply to the right to follow an indentation in the Blau See's shore-line, a dangerous corner marked by white fencing which would normally have been conspicuous enough by night-time but which was at the moment all but invisible against the all-enveloping background of snow. Schaffer braked for the corner. A thoughtful expression crossed his face and he applied still heavier pressure to the brake pedal and glanced at Smith.

'An excellent idea.' It was Smith's turn to be approving. 'We'll make an agent out of you yet.'

The Mercedes stopped. Smith gathered up the Schmeissers and pistols they had taken from Weissner and his men and got out. Schaffer wound down the driver's window, released the hand-brake, engaged gear and jumped out as the car began to move. With his right arm through the window Schaffer walked and then, as the car began to gather speed, ran along beside the Mercedes, his hand on the steering wheel. Twenty feet from the cliff edge he gave a last steering correction, jerked the quadrant hand throttle wide open and leapt aside as the car accelerated. The wooden fence never had a chance. With a splintering crash barely audible above the roaring of the engine at maximum revs in first gear, the Mercedes went through the barrier as if it had been made of cardboard, shot out over the edge of the cliff and disappeared from sight.

Smith and Schaffer reached the safety of an unbroken stretch of fencing and peered down just in time to see the car, upside down now and its headlamps still blazing, strike the surface of the lake with an oddly flat explosive sound, like distant gun fire. A column of water and weirdly phosphorescent spray reached half-way up the cliff side. When it subsided, they could at once locate from an underwater luminescence the position of the sinking car: the headlamps were still burning. Smith and Schaffer looked at each other then Smith thoughtfully removed his peaked cap and sent it sailing over the edge. The strong gusting wind blew the cap in against the cliff face, but it tumbled on down and landed, inside up, on still surfacing bubbles iridescently glittering from the light now far below. Then the light went out.

'So who cares?' Schaffer straightened up from the fencing and shrugged his shoulders. 'Wasn't our car. Back to the village, hey?'

'Not on your life,' Smith said emphatically. 'And I mean that – literally. Come on. Other way.'

Clutching their recently acquired weapons, they ran round the corner in the direction in which the car had been travelling. They had covered less than seventy yards when they heard the sound of car engines and saw wavering beams lighting up the splintered fence. Seconds later Smith and Schaffer were off the road, hidden in the pines and moving slowly back in the direction of a command car and two armoured cars that had now pulled up at the broken barrier.

'That's it, then, Herr Colonel.' An Alpenkorps sergeant with shoulder-slung gun peered gingerly over the edge of the cliff. 'Going too fast, saw it too late – or never saw it at all. The Blau See is over a hundred metres deep here, Herr Colonel. They're gone.'

'Maybe they're gone and maybe they're not. I wouldn't trust that lot as far as my front door.' Colonel Weissner's voice carried clearly and sounded bitter. 'They may have faked it and doubled back. Send one party of men straight into the pines there as far as the cliff wall. Five metre spacing. Let them use their torches. Then another party of men five hundred metres in the car back towards the camp. You go with them, Sergeant. Again spread out to the cliff-face. Let them come together. And be quick.'

Schaffer, from his hiding-place behind the bole of a pine, looked thoughtfully at Smith.

'I have to concede a point, boss, it's perhaps as well we didn't go straight back to the village. Cunning old devil, isn't he?'

'And what does that make me?' Smith murmured.

'Okay, okay. I'll concede that point, too.'

Five minutes passed. Comparatively little of the falling snow penetrated the thickly-matted branches of the pines and the two men could clearly see the occasional flicker of torches as the line of men nearest them moved away to the south, their lights probing behind tree-trunks and under windfalls as they searched for the two escaped prisoners. Colonel Wiessner paced up and down, slowly, beside his command car, his head bowed as if immersed in thought. From time to time he consulted his watch. As Smith watched, he moved out to the unbroken fencing and remained there, peering down towards the surface of the Blau See.

By and by Smith and Schaffer could hear the distant sound of muffled voices and within a minute the sergeant moved into the beam of the command car headlamps, approached Colonel Weissner and saluted.

'Not even a footprint, Herr Colonel.'

Weissner straightened and turned.

'There wouldn't be,' he said sombrely. 'I've just seen a hat floating in the water. A squalid end for such brave men, Sergeant. A squalid end.'

Chapter Five

The cable-car moved slowly out of the lower station at the beginning of its long climb up to the castle. An impossible climb, Mary thought, a dangerous and impossible climb. Peering through the front windows she could just distinguish the outline of the first pylon through the thinly-driving snow. The second and third pylons were invisible, but the intermittently shining cluster of lights suspended impossibly high in the sky showed clearly enough where they had to go. People have made it before, she thought dully, we'll probably make it, too. The way she felt then, with the bottom gone from her world, she didn't particularly care whether she made it or not.

The cable-car was a twelve-passenger vehicle, painted bright red outside, well-lit inside. There were no seats, only grab-rails along the two sides. That the grab-rails were very necessary became immediately and alarmingly obvious. The wind was now very strong and the car began to sway alarmingly only seconds after clearing the shelter of the lower station.

Apart from two soldiers and an apparent civilian, the only other passengers consisted of von Brauchitsch, Mary and Heidi, the last now with a heavy woollen coat and cossack fur hat over her ordinary clothes. Von Brauchitsch, holding on to the grab-rail with one hand, had his free arm round Mary's shoulders. He gave them a reassuring squeeze and smiled down at her.

'Scared?' he asked.

'No.' And she wasn't, she hadn't enough emotion left to be scared, but even with no hope left she was supposed to be a professional. 'No, I'm not scared. I'm terrified. I feel sea-sick already. Does – does this cable ever break?'

'Never.' Von Brauchitsch was reassurance itself. 'Just hang on to me and you'll be all right.'

'That's what he used to say to me,' Heidi said coldly.

'Fräulein,' von Brauchitsch explained patiently, 'I am gifted beyond the average, but I haven't yet managed to grow a third arm. Guests first.'

With a cupped cigarette in his hand, Schaffer leaned against the base of an unmistakable telephone pole and gazed thoughtfully into the middle distance.

There was reason both for the hooded cigarette and the thoughtful expression. Less than a hundred yards away from where he stood at the edge of the pines bordering the road running alongside the shore of the Blau See he could see guards, clearly illuminated by over-head lights, moving briskly to and fro in the vicinity of the barrack gates. Dimly seen behind them were the outline of the barracks themselves.

Schaffer shifted his stance and gazed upwards. The snow was almost gone now, the moon was threatening to break through, and he had no difficulty at all in distinguishing the form of Smith, his legs straddled across the lowest cross-bar.

Smith was busily employed with a knife, a specially designed commando knife which, among other advanced features, had a built-in wire cutter. Carefully, methodically, he brought the wire-cutter to bear. With eight consecutive snips eight consecutive telephone wires fell to the ground. Smith closed and pocketed his knife, disentangled his legs from the cross-bar, wrapped his arms round the pole and slid down to the ground. He grinned at Schaffer.

'Every little helps,' he said.

'Should hold them for a while,' Schaffer agreed. Once more they gathered up their guns and moved off to the east, vanishing into the pine woods which bordered the rear of the barracks.

The cable-car swayed more alarmingly than ever. It had now entered upon the last near-vertical lap of its journey. With von Brauchitsch's arm still around her shoulders, with her face still pressed against the front windows of the car, Mary stared up at the towering battlements, white as the driving snow, and thought that they reached up almost to the clouds themselves. As she watched, a break came in the wisping clouds and the whole fairy-tale castle was bathed in bright moonlight. Fear touched her eyes, she moistened her lips and gave an involuntary shiver. Nothing escaped von Brauchitsch's acute perception. He gave her shoulders another reassuring squeeze, perhaps the twentieth in that brief journey.

'Not to worry, Fräulein. It will be all right.'

'I hope so.' Her voice was the ghost of a whisper.

The same unexpected moonlight almost caught Smith and Schaffer. They had just crossed the station tracks and were moving stealthily along towards the left luggage office when the moon broke through. But they were still in the shadows of the over-hanging station roof. They pressed back into those shadows and peered along the tracks, past the hydraulic bumpers which marked the end of the line. Clearly now, sharply-limned as if in full daylight, red etched against the white, they could see one cable-car approaching the lower station, the other climbing the last few vertical feet towards the header station and, above that, the dazzling outline of the Schloss Adler glittering under the bright moon.

'That helps,' Schaffer said bitterly. 'That helps a lot.'

'Sky's still full of clouds,' Smith said mildly. He bent to the keyhole of the left luggage office, used his skeleton keys and moved inside. Schaffer followed, closing the door.

Smith located their rucksacks, cut a length of rope from the nylon, wrapped it round his waist and began stuffing some hand grenades and plastic explosives into a canvas bag. He raised his head as Schaffer diffidently cleared his throat.

'Boss?' This with an apprehensive glance through the window.

'Uh-huh?'

'Boss, has it occurred to you that Colonel Weissner probably knows all about this cache by this time? What I mean is, we may have company soon.'

'We may indeed,' Smith admitted. 'Surprised if we don't have. That's why I've cut this itsy-bitsy piece of rope off the big coil and why I'm taking the explosives and grenades only from my rucksack and yours. It's a very big coil – and no one knows what's inside our rucksacks. So it's unlikely that anything will be missed.'

'But the radio—'

'If we broadcast from here we might be caught in the act. If we take it away and they find it gone they'll know that that car at the bottom of the Blau See is empty. Is that it?'

'More or less.'

'So we compromise. We remove it, but we return it here after we've broadcast from a safe place.'

'What do you mean "safe place",' Schaffer demanded plaintively. The darkly saturnine face was unhappy. 'There isn't a safe place in Bavaria.'

'There's one not twenty yards away. Last place they'd look.' He tossed Schaffer a bunch of skeleton keys. 'Ever been inside a Bavarian ladies' cloakroom?'

Schaffer fielded the keys, stared at Smith, shook his head and left. Quickly he moved down the tracks, his torch flashing briefly on and off. Finally his torch settled on a doorway with, above it, the legend DAMEN.

Schaffer looked at it, pursed his lips, shrugged his shoulders and got to work on the lock.

Slowly, with apparently infinite labour, the cable-car completed the last few feet of its ascent and passed in under the roof of the Schloss Adler header station. It juddered to a halt, the front door opened and the passengers disembarked. They moved from the header station – built into the north-west base of the castle – up through a steeply-climbing twenty-five foot tunnel which had heavy iron doors and guards at either end. Passing the top gateway, they emerged into the courtyard, the entrance of which was sealed off by a massively-barred iron gate guarded by heavily armed soldiers and Dobermann pinschers. The courtyard itself was brightly illuminated by the light of dozens of uncurtained interior windows. In the very centre of the courtyard stood the helicopter which had that morning brought Reichsmar-schall Rosemeyer to the Schloss Adler. Under the cover of a heavy tarpaulin – momentarily unnecessary because of the cessation of the snow – a dungareed figure, possibly the pilot, worked on the helicopter engine with the aid of a small but powerful arc-lamp.

Mary turned to von Brauchitsch, still holding a proprietary grip on her arm, and smiled ruefully.

'So many soldiers. So many men – and, I'm sure, so few women. What happens if I want to escape from the licentious soldiery?'

'Easy.' Von Brauchitsch really did have, Mary thought dully, a most charming smile. 'Just jump from your bedroom window. One hundred metres straight down and there you are. Free!'

The ladies' cloakroom in the station was a superlatively nondescript place, bleakly furnished with hard-backed benches, chairs, deal tables and a sagging wooden floor. The Spartans would have turned up their noses at it, in its sheer lack of decorative inspiration it could have been surpassed only by its counterpart in England. The expiring remains of a fire burnt dully in a black enamel stove.

Smith was seated by the central table, radio beside him, consulting a small book by the light of a hooded pencil-flash and writing on a slip of paper. He checked what he had written, straightened and handed the book to Schaffer.

'Burn it. Page by page.'

'Page by page? All?' Surprise in the saturnine face. 'You won't be requiring this any more?'

Smith shook his head and began to crank the radio handle.

There was a very much better fire in the Operations Room in Whitehall, a pine-log fire with a healthy crackle and flames of a respectable size. But the two men sitting on either side of the fire were a great deal less alert than the two men sitting by the dying embers of the fire in the Bavarian Alps. Admiral Rolland and Colonel Wyatt-Turner were frankly dozing, eyes shut, more asleep than awake. But they came to full wakefulness, jerking upright, almost instantly, when the long-awaited call-sign came through on the big transceiver manned by the civilian operator at the far end of the room. They glanced at each other, heaved themselves out of their deep arm-chairs.

'Broadsword calling Danny Boy.' The voice on the radio was faint but clear. 'Broadsword calling Danny Boy. You hear me? Over.'

The civilian operator spoke into his microphone, 'We hear you. Over.'

'Code. Ready? Over.'

'Ready. Over.'

Rolland and Wyatt-Turner were by the operator's shoulder now, his eyes fixed on his pencil as he began to make an instantaneous transcription of the meaningless jumble of letters beginning to come over the radio. Swiftly the message was spelt out: TORRANCE-SMYTHE MURDERED. THOMAS CHRISTIANSEN AND CARRACIOLA CAPTURED.

As if triggered by an unheard signal, the eyes of Rolland and Wyatt-Turner lifted and met. Their faces were strained and grim. Their eyes returned to the flickering pencil.

ENEMY BELIEVE SCHAFFER AND SELF DEAD, the message continued. EFFECTING ENTRY INSIDE THE HOUR. PLEASE HAVE TRANSPORT STANDING BY NINETY MINUTES. OVER.

Admiral Rolland seized the microphone from the operator.

'Broadsword! Broadsword! Do you know who I am, Broadsword?'

'I know who you are, sir. Over.'

'Pull out, Broadsword. Pull out now. Save yourselves. Over.'

'You – must – be – joking.' The words were spoken in slow motion, a perceptible pause between each pair. 'Over.'

'You heard me.' Rolland's voice was almost as slow and distinct. 'You *heard* me. That was an order, Broadsword.'

'Mary is already inside. Over and out.'

The transceiver went dead.

'He's gone, sir,' the operator said quietly.

'He's gone,' Rolland repeated mechanically. 'Dear God, he's gone.'

Colonel Wyatt-Turner moved away and sat down heavily in his chair by the fire. For such a big, burly man he appeared curiously huddled and shrunken. He looked up dully as Admiral Rolland sank into the opposite chair.

'It's all my fault.' The Colonel's voice was barely distinguishable. 'All my fault.'

'We did what we had to do. All *our* fault, Colonel. It was my idea.' He gazed into the fire. 'Now this – this on top of everything else.'

'Our worst day,' Wyatt-Turner agreed heavily. 'Our worst day ever. Maybe I'm too old.'

'Maybe we're all too old.' With his right forefinger Rolland began to tick off the fingers of his left hand. 'HQ Commander-in-Chief, Portsmouth. Secret alarm triggered. Nothing missing.'

'Nothing taken,' Wyatt-Turner agreed wearily. 'But the vigil emulsion plates show photostatic copies taken.'

'Two. Southampton. Barge-movement duplicates missing. Three, Plymouth. Time-lock in the naval HQ inoperative. We don't know what this means.'

'We can guess.'

'We can guess. Dover. Copy of a section of the Mulberry Harbour plans missing. An error? Carelessness? We'll never know. Five, Bradley's HQ guard sergeant missing. Could mean anything.'

'Could mean everything. All the troop movements for Overlord's Omaha beach are there.'

'Lastly, seven OS reports today. France, Belgium, Netherlands. Four demonstrably false. Other three unverifiable.'

For long moments there was a heavy, a defeated silence, finally broken by Wyatt-Turner.

'If there was ever any doubt, there's none now.' He spoke without looking up, his eyes gazing emptily into the fire. 'The Germans have almost total penetration here – and we have almost none on the continent. And now this – Smith and his men, I mean.'

'Smith and his men,' Rolland echoed. 'Smith and his men. We can write them off.'

Wyatt-Turner dropped his voice, speaking so softly that the radio operator couldn't overhear.

'And Operation Overlord, sir?'

'Operation Overlord,' Rolland murmured. 'Yes, we can write that off, too.'

'Intelligence is the first arm of modern warfare,' Wyatt-Turner said bitterly. 'Or has someone said that before?'

'No intelligence, no war.' Admiral Rolland pressed an intercom button. 'Have my car brought round. Coming, Colonel? To the airfield?'

'And a lot farther than that. If I have your permission, sir.'

'We've discussed it.' Admiral Rolland shrugged. 'I understand how you feel. Kill yourself if you must.'

'I've no intention.' Wyatt-Turner crossed to a cupboard and took out a Sten gun, turned to Rolland and smiled: 'We may encounter hostiles, sir.'

'You may indeed.' There was no answering smile on the Admiral's face.

'You heard what the man said?' Smith switched off the transmitter, telescoped the aerial and glanced across at Schaffer. 'We can pull out now.'

'Pull out now? Pull out now?' Schaffer was outraged. 'Don't you realize that if we do they'll get to Mary inside twelve hours.' He paused significantly, making sure he had all Smith's attention. 'And if they get to her they're bound to get to Heidi ten minutes later.'

'Come off it, Lieutenant,' Smith said protestingly. 'You've only seen her once, for five minutes.'

'So?' Schaffer was looking positively belligerent. 'How often did Paris see Helen of Troy? How often did Antony see Cleopatra. How often did Romeo—' He broke off then went on defiantly: 'And I don't care if she is a traitor spying on her own people.'

'She was born and brought up in Birmingham,' Smith said wearily.

'So who cares? I draw the line at nothing. Even if she is a Limey—' He paused. 'English?'

'Come on,' Smith said. 'Let's return this radio. We may have callers soon.'

'We mustn't be raising too many eyebrows,' Schaffer agreed.

They returned the radio, locked the left luggage office and were just moving towards the station exit when they were halted by the sound of truck engines and a siren's ululation. They pressed back against a wall as headlights lit up the station entrance. The leading truck came to a skidding halt not ten yards away.

Schaffer looked at Smith. 'Discretion, I think?'

'Discretion, indeed. Behind the booking office.'

The two men moved swiftly alongside the tracks and hid in the deep shadows behind the booking office. A sergeant, the one who had organized the search along the Blau See, came running through the entrance, followed by four soldiers, located the left luggage office, tried the door handle, reversed his machine-pistol and hammered the lock without effect, reversed his gun again, shot away the lock and passed inside, torch in hand. He appeared at the doorway almost at once.

'Tell the captain. They didn't lie. The Engländers' gear is here!' One of the soldiers left and the sergeant said to the three remaining men: 'Right. Get their stuff out and load it up.'

'There goes my last pair of cotton socks,' Schaffer murmured mournfully as their rucksacks were taken away. 'Not to mention my toothbrush and—'

He broke off as Smith caught his arm. The sergeant had stopped the man carrying the radio, taken it from him, placed his hand on it and stood quite still. He was directly under one of the small swinging electric lights and the expression on his face could clearly be seen to change from puzzlement to disbelief to complete and shocked understanding.

'Kapitan!' the sergeant shouted. 'Kapitan.'

An officer came hurrying through the station entrance.

'The radio, Kapitan! It's warm, very warm! It's been in use inside the last five minutes.'

'In the last five minutes? Impossible!' He stared at the sergeant. 'Unless—'

'Yes, Herr Kapitan. Unless.'

'Surround the station,' the officer shouted. 'Search every room.'

'Oh God!' Schaffer moaned. 'Why can't they leave us alone?'

'Quickly,' Smith said softly. He took Schaffer's arm and they moved through the dark shadows till they reached the ladies' cloakroom. Careful not to rattle his skeleton keys, Smith had the door open in seconds. They passed inside and locked the door behind them.

'This won't look so good in my obituary,' Schaffer said dolefully. There was a perceptible edge of strain under the lightly-spoken words.

'What won't?'

'Gave his life for his country in a ladies' lavatory in Upper Bavaria. How can a man RIP with that on his mind? . . . What's our friend outside saying?'

'If you shut up we might hear.'

'And when I say everywhere, I mean everywhere.' The German captain was barking out his commands in the best parade-ground fashion. 'If a door is locked, break it open. If you can't break it open, shoot the lock away. And if you don't want to die in the next five minutes, never forget that these are violent and extremely dangerous men almost certainly armed with stolen Schmeisser machine-pistols, apart from their own weapons. Make no attempt to capture them. Shoot on sight and shoot to kill.'

'You heard?' Smith said.

'I'm afraid I did.' There was a perceptible click as Schaffer cocked his machine-pistol.

They stood side-by-side in the darkness listening to the sounds of the search, the calling of voices, the hammering of rifle butts on wood, the splintering of yielding doors, the occasional short burst of machine-gun fire where a door, presumably, had failed to yield to more conventional methods of persuasion. The sounds of the approaching search grew very close.

'They're getting warm,' Schaffer murmured.

Schaffer had underestimated the temperature. Just as he finished speaking an unseen hand closed on the outer door handle and rattled the door furiously. Smith and Schaffer moved silently and took up position pressed close against the wall, one on either side of the door.

The rattling ceased. A heavy crashing impact from the outside shook the door on its hinges. A second such impact and the woodwork in the jamb by the lock began to splinter. Two more would do it, Smith thought, two more.

But there were no more.

'*Gott in Himmel*, Hans!' The voice beyond the door held – or appeared to hold – a mixture of consternation and outrage. 'What are you thinking of? Can't you read?'

'Can't I—' The second voice broke off abruptly and when it came again it was in tones of defensive apology. 'DAMEN! *Mein Gott!* DAMEN!' A pause. 'If you had spent as many years on the Russian Front as I have—' His voice faded as the two men moved away.

'God bless our common Anglo-Saxon heritage,' Schaffer murmured fervently.

'What are you talking about?' Smith demanded. He had released his tense grip on the Schmeisser and realized that the palms of his hands were damp.

'This misplaced sense of decency,' Schaffer explained.

'A far from misplaced and highly developed sense of self-preservation,' Smith said dryly. 'Would *you* like to come searching for a couple of reputed killers, like us, knowing that the first man to find us would probably be cut in half by a burst of machine-gun fire? Put yourself in their position. How do you think those men feel. How would you feel?'

'I'd feel very unhappy,' Schaffer said candidly.

'And so do they. And so they seize on any reasonable excuse not to investigate. Our two friends who have just left have no idea whatsoever whether we're in here or not and, what's more, the last thing they want to do is to find out.'

'Stop making with the old psychology. All that matters is that Schaffer is saved. Saved!'

'If you believe that,' Smith said curtly, 'you deserve to end up with a blindfold round your eyes.'

'How's that again?' Schaffer asked apprehensively.

'You and I,' Smith explained patiently, 'are not the only people who can put ourselves in the places of the searchers. You can bet your life that the captain can and more than likely the sergeant, too – you saw how quickly he caught on to the damn' radio. By and by one or other is going to come by, see this closed and undamaged door, blow his top and insist on a few of his men being offered the chance to earn a posthumous Iron Cross. What I mean is, Schaffer is not yet saved.'

'What do we do, boss?' Schaffer said quietly. 'I don't feel so funny any more.'

'We create a diversion. Here are the keys – this one. Put it in the lock and hold it ready to turn. We'll be leaving in a hurry – troops of this calibre can't be fooled for long.'

He dug into his knapsack, fished out a hand-grenade, crossed the cloakroom into the washroom and, in almost total darkness, felt his way across it to where the window at the back should have been, finally located it from the source of a faint wash of light. He pressed his nose against the glass but could see nothing, cursed softly as he realized a washroom window would always certainly be frosted, located the latch and slowly swung the window wide. With infinite caution, a fraction of an inch at a time, he thrust his head slowly through the window.

Nobody blew his head off. There were soldiers immediately to be seen, it was true, soldiers armed and at the ready, but they weren't looking in his direction: there were five of them, spread out in an arc of a circle, perhaps fifteen yards from the station entrance, and every machine-pistol was trained on that entrance. Waiting for the rabbits to bolt, Smith thought.

What was of much more interest was the empty truck parked only feet away from the window where he was: it was the reflected light from its side-lights that had enabled him to locate the window. Hoping that the truck was built along conventional lines, Smith armed the grenade, counted three, lobbed it under the back wheels of the truck and ducked behind the shelter of the washroom wall.

The two explosions – grenade and petrol tank – went off so almost simultaneously as to be indistinguishable in time. Shattered glass from the window above showered down on his head and his ear-drums hurt fiercely both from the roar of sound and the proximity to the explosive shock-wave. Smith made no attempt to inspect the damage he had done, less from the urgent need for haste to leave there than from the very obvious fact that the remains of the truck outside had burst into flames and to have lifted his head above that window-sill would have been a swift form of illuminated suicide: not that he could have done so in any event for the wind-driven flames from the truck were already beginning to lick through the shattered washroom window. On hands and knees Smith scuttled across the washroom floor, not rising till he had reached the cloakroom. Schaffer, who had his hand on the key and the door already open a fraction of an inch turned at Smith's approach.

'To the hills, boss?' he enquired.

'To the hills.'

The track-side of the station was, predictably, deserted: those who had not automatically run to investigate the source of the explosion would have as automatically assumed that the explosion was in some way connected with an escape attempt or resistance on the part of the hunted men. However it was, the result was the satisfactory same.

They ran along the tracks till they came to the bumpers at the end of the line, skirted these and continued running until they were safely among the scatter of houses that rose steeply up the hill-side on the eastern side of the village. They stopped to take breath and looked back the way they had come.

The station was on fire, not yet heavily on fire, but, with flames rising six to eight feet and black smoke billowing into the night sky, obviously already beyond any hope of extinction.

Schaffer said: 'They're not going to be very pleased.'

'I shouldn't think so.'

'What I mean is, they're really going to go after us now. With everything they have. They've Dobermann pinschers up at the castle and I've no doubt they have them at the camp too. They've only to bring them to the station, sniff our gear, have them circle the station, pick up our scent and that's it. Smith and Schaffer torn to shreds. I'll take on the Alpenkorps by numbers, but I draw the line at Dobermann pinschers, boss.'

'I thought it was horses you were scared of?' Smith said mildly.

'Horses, Dobermann pinschers, you name it, I'm scared of it. All it's got to have is four feet.' He looked gloomily at the burning station. 'I'd make a rotten vet.'

'No worry,' Smith assured him. 'We won't be here long enough for any of your four-footed pals to come bothering you.'

'No?' Schaffer looked at him suspiciously.

'The castle,' Smith said patiently. 'That's what we're here for. Remember?'

'I hadn't forgotten.' The flames from the blazing station were now licking thirty, forty feet up in the air. 'You gone and ruined a perfectly good station, you know that?'

'As you would say yourself,' Smith reminded him, 'it wasn't our station to start with. Come on. We've a call to make then we'll go see what kind of reception awaits us at the Schloss Adler.'

Mary Ellison was just at that moment discovering what the reception in the Schloss Adler was like. In her case it was none too pleasant. Von Brauchitsch and Heidi beside her, she was gazing around the great hall of the castle, stone walls, stone flags, a dark oaken roof, when a door at the end of the hall opened and a girl came towards them. There was an arrogance, a crisp authority about her: she marched, rather than walked.

But a very beautiful girl, Mary had to admit to herself, big, blonde, blue-eyed and beautiful. She could have been a pin-up girl for the Third Reich. At the moment, the blue eyes were very cold.

'Good-evening, Anne-Marie,' von Brauchitsch said. There was a marked lack of cordiality in his voice. 'This is the new girl, Fräulein Maria Schenk. Maria, this is the Colonel's secretary, in charge of all female staff.'

'Took your time about getting here, didn't you, Schenk?' If Anne-Marie had a soft, lilting, mellifluous voice she wasn't bothering to use it just then. She turned to Heidi and gave her an icy up-and-down. 'And why you? Just because we let you wait table when the Colonel has company—'

'Heidi is this girl's cousin,' von Brauchitsch interrupted brusquely. '*And she has my permission.*' The cold implication that she should confine herself to her duties was unmistakable.

Anne-Marie glared at him but made no attempt to press the point. Very few people would have done. Von Brauchitsch was just that sort of person.

'In here, Schenk.' Anne-Marie nodded to a side door. 'I have a few questions to ask.'

Mary looked at Heidi, then at von Brauchitsch, who shrugged and said: 'Routine investigation, Fräulein. I'm afraid you must.'

Mary preceded Anne-Marie through the doorway. The door was firmly closed behind them. Heidi and von Brauchitsch looked at each other. Heidi compressed her lips and the expression that momentarily flitted over her face about matched the one Anne-Marie had been wearing: von Brauchitsch made the age-old helpless gesture of lifting his shoulders high, palms of the hands turned up.

Within half a minute the reason for von Brauchitsch's helpless gesture became obvious. Through the door there came first the sound of a raised voice, a brief scuffle then a sharp cry of pain. Von Brauchitsch exchanged another resigned glance with Heidi, then turned as he heard heavy footsteps behind him. The man approaching was burly, weather-beaten, middle-aged and in civilian clothes: but although not in uniform he could never have been mistaken for anything other than an army officer. The heavy blue-shaven jowls, bull-neck, close-cropped hair and piercing blue eyes made him almost a caricature of the World War I Prussian Uhlan cavalry officer. That he was by no means as fossilized as he appeared was quite evident from the distinctly respectful manner in which von Brauchitsch addressed him.

'Good evening, Colonel Kramer.'

'Evening, Captain. Evening, Fräulein.' He had an unexpectedly gentle and courteous voice. 'You wear an air of expectancy?'

Before either could answer, the door opened and Anne-Marie and Mary entered: Mary gave the impression of having been pushed into the room. Anne-Marie was slightly flushed and breathing rather heavily, but otherwise her beautiful Aryan self. Mary's clothes were disordered, her hair dishevelled and it was obvious that she had been crying. Her cheeks were still tear-stained.

'We'll have no more trouble with *her*,' Anne-Marie announced with satisfaction. She caught sight of Kramer and the change in her tone was perceptible. 'Interviewing new staff, Colonel.'

'In your usual competent fashion, I see,' Colonel Kramer said dryly. He shook his head. 'When will you learn that respectable young girls do not like being forcibly searched and having their underclothes examined to see if they were made in Piccadilly or Gorki Street?'

'Security regulations,' Anne-Marie said defensively.

'Yes, yes.' Kramer's voice was brusque. 'But there are other ways.' He turned away impatiently. The engaging of female staff was not the problem of the deputy chief of the German Secret Service. While Heidi was helping

Mary to straighten her clothes, he went on, to von Brauchitsch: 'A little excitement in the village tonight?'

'Nothing for us.' Von Brauchitsch shrugged. 'Deserters.'

Kramer smiled.

'That's what I told Colonel Weissner to say. I think our friends are British agents.'

'What!'

'After General Carnaby, I shouldn't wonder,' Kramer said carelessly. 'Relax, Captain. It's over. Three of them are coming up for interrogation within the hour. I'd like you to be present later on. I think you'll find it most entertaining and – ah – instructive.'

'There were five of them, sir. I saw them myself when they were rounded up in "Zum Wilden Hirsch".'

'There *were* five,' Colonel Kramer corrected. 'Not now. Two of them – the leader and one other – are in the Blau See. They commandeered a car and went over a cliff.'

Mary, her back to the men and Anne-Marie, smoothed down her dress and slowly straightened. Her face was stricken. Anne-Marie turned, saw Mary's curiously immobile position and was moving curiously towards her when Heidi took Mary's arm and said quickly: 'My cousin looks ill. May I take her to her room?'

'All right.' Anne-Marie waved her hand in curt dismissal. 'The one you use when you are here.'

The room was bleak, monastic, linoleum-covered, with a made-up iron bed, chair, tiny dressing-table, a hanging cupboard and nothing else. Heidi locked the door behind them.

'You heard?' Mary said emptily. Her face was as drained of life as her voice.

'I heard – and I don't believe it.'

'Why should they lie?'

They believe it.' Heidi's tone was impatient, almost rough. 'It's time you stopped loving and started thinking. The Major Smiths of this world don't drive over cliff edges.'

'Talk is easy, Heidi.'

'So is giving up. *I* believe he is alive. And if he is, and if he comes here and you're gone or not there to help him, you know what he'll be then?' Mary made no reply, just gazed emptily into Heidi's face. 'He'll be dead. He'll be dead because you let him down. Would *he* let *you* down?'

Mary shook her head dumbly.

'Now then,' Heidi went on briskly. She reached first under her skirt then down the front of her blouse and laid seven objects on the table. 'Here we are. Lilliput .21 automatic, two spare magazines, ball of string, lead weight, plan of the castle and the instructions.' She crossed to a corner of the room, raised a loose floor-board, placed the articles beneath it and replaced the board. 'They'll be safe enough there.'

Mary looked at her for a long moment and showed her first spark of interest in an hour.

'You *knew* that board was loose,' she said slowly.

'Of course. I loosened it myself, a fortnight ago.'

'You – you knew about this as far back as then?'

'Whatever else?' Heidi smiled. 'Good luck, cousin.'

Mary sank on to the bed and sat there motionless for ten minutes after Heidi had gone, then rose wearily to her feet and crossed to her window. Her window faced to the north and she could see the line of pylons, the lights of the village and, beyond that, the darkened waters of the Blau See. But what dominated the entire scene were the redly-towering flames and billowing clouds of black smoke reaching up from some burning building at the far end of the village. For a hundred yards around it night had been turned into day and even if there had been a local fire brigade to hand it would have been clearly impossible for them to approach anywhere near the flames. When that first fire went out all that would be left would be smoking ashes. Mary wondered vaguely what it might mean.

She opened her window and leaned out, but cautiously. Even for a person as depressed as she was, there was no temptation to lean too far: castle walls and volcanic plug stretched vertically downwards for almost three hundred feet. She felt slightly dizzy.

To the left and below a cable-car left the castle header station and started to move down to the valley below. Heidi was in that car, leaning out a partially opened window and hopefully waving but Mary's eyes had again blurred with tears and she did not see her. She closed the window, turned away, lay down heavily on the bed and wondered again about John Smith, whether he were alive or dead. And she wondered again about the significance of that fire in the valley below.

Smith and Schaffer skirted the backs of the houses, shops and *Weinstuben* on the east side of the street, keeping to the dark shadows as far as it was possible. Their precautions, Smith realized, were largely superfluous: the undoubted centre of attraction that night was the blazing station and the street leading to it was jammed with hundreds of soldiers and villagers. It must, Smith thought, be a conflagration of quite some note, for although they could no longer see the fire itself, only the red glow in the sky above it, they could clearly hear the roaring crackle of the flames, flames three hundred yards away and with the wind blowing in the wrong direction. As a diversion, it was a roaring success.

They came to one of the few stone buildings in the village, a large barn-like affair with double doors at the back. The yard abutting the rear doors looked like an automobile scrap-yard. There were half-a-dozen old cars lying around, most of them without tyres, some rusted engines, dozens of small useless engine and body parts and a small mountain of empty oil drums. They picked their way carefully through the debris and came to the doors.

Schaffer used skeleton keys to effect and they were inside, doors closed and both torches on, inside fifteen seconds.

One side of the garage was given over to lathes or machine tools of one kind or another, but the rest of the floor space was occupied by a variety of vehicles, mostly elderly. What caught and held Smith's immediate attention, however, was a big yellow bus parked just inside the double front doors. It was a typically Alpine post-bus, with a very long overhang at the back to help negotiate mountain hairpin bends: the rear wheels were so far forward as to be almost in the middle of the bus. As was also common with Alpine post-buses in winter, it had a huge angled snow-plough bolted on to the front of the chasis. Smith looked at Schaffer.

'Promising, you think?'

'If I were optimistic enough to think we'd ever get back to this place,' Schaffer said sourly, 'I'd say it was very promising. You knew about this?'

'What do you think I am? A bus-diviner? Of course I knew about it.' Smith climbed into the driver's seat. The keys were in the ignition. Smith switched on and watched the fuel gauge climb up to the half-full mark. He located the headlamps switch and turned it on. They worked. He pressed the starter button and the engine caught at once. Smith killed it immediately. Schaffer watched the performance with interest.

'I suppose you know you need a PSV licence to drive one of those, boss?'

'I have one around somewhere. Leave half the explosives in the back of the bus. And hurry. Heidi might be down with the next car.'

Smith climbed down from the driver's seat, went to the front doors, unbolted both, top and bottom, and pushed gently. The doors gave an inch, then stopped.

'Padlocked,' Smith said briefly.

Schaffer surveyed the massive steel plough on the front of the bus and shook his head sorrowfully.

'Poor old padlock,' he said.

The snow had stopped but the wind from the west was now very strong. The cold was intense. Masses of ragged dark cloud hurried across the sky and the entire valley was alternately cast into the deepest shadow or bathed in contrastingly dazzling light as the moon was alternately obscured by the clouds or shone through the shifting gaps between them. But there was no alternating light and shade at the far end of the village: the station still burnt furiously enough to render the moon's best efforts pretty ineffectual.

A cable-car was coming slowly down the valley, less than a hundred yards now from the lower station. Impelled by the powerfully gusting wind, it swung wildly, terrifyingly, across the night sky. But as it approached the end of its journey the motion quickly dampened down and disappeared altogether as it approached the station.

The cable-car jerked to a stop. Heidi, the only passenger, climbed out: understandably enough, she was looking rather pale. She walked down the steps at the back of the station, reached ground level then stopped dead as she heard the softly-whistled first few notes of 'Lorelei', She whirled round, then slowly approached two shapes, clad all in white, huddled by the side of the station.

'The Major Smiths of this world *don't* drive off cliff-tops,' she said calmly. She paused, then stepped forward suddenly and gave each man a quick hug and kiss on the cheek. 'But you had me a little worried there.'

'You just keep on worrying like that,' Schaffer said. 'No need to worry about him, though.'

Heidi waved a hand in the direction of the other end of the village. From the cable-car station on the lower slopes they had an excellent if distant view of the fire. 'Are you responsible for this?' she asked.

'It was a mistake,' Smith explained.

'Yeah. His hand slipped,' Schaffer added.

'You two should audition for a turn on vaudeville,' Heidi said dryly. Suddenly serious she said: 'Mary thinks you're both gone.'

'Weissner doesn't,' Smith said. 'The car that went over the cliff went without us. They're on to us.'

'Hardly surprising,' she murmured. 'Or hadn't you noticed the size of the fire.' She paused, then went on bleakly: 'They're not the only ones who are on to you. Kramer knows you're British agents after General Carnaby.'

'Well, well, well,' Smith said thoughtfully. 'I wonder what little bird has been whispering in Kramer's shell-like ear. One with a very long-range voice, methinks.'

'What *are* you talking about?'

'Nothing. It's not important.'

'It's not important! But don't you *see*?' Her voice was imploring, almost despairing. 'They *know* – or will any minute – that you're alive. They *know* who you are. They'll be expecting you up there.'

'Ah, but you overlook the subtleties, my dear Heidi,' Schaffer put in. 'What they *don't* know is that *we* are expecting *them* to be expecting *us*. At least, that's what I think I mean.'

'You're whistling in the dark, Lieutenant. And one last thing: your friends are being brought up to the castle any time now.'

'For interrogation?' Smith asked.

'I don't expect they've been asked up for tea,' she said acidly.

'Fair enough,' Smith nodded. 'We'll go up with them.'

'In the same car?' The words didn't question Smith's sanity, but the tone and expression did.

'Not "in". With.' Smith peered at his watch. 'The post-bus in Sulz's garage. Be there in eighty minutes. And oh! – bring a couple of crates of empty beer bottles.'

'Bring a couple of – oh, all right.' She shook her head in conviction. 'You're both mad.'

'Shines through in our every word and gesture,' Schaffer agreed, then, suddenly serious, added: 'Say a prayer for us, honey. And if you don't know any prayers, keep your fingers crossed till they ache.'

'Please come back,' she said. There was a catch in her voice. She hesitated, made to say more, turned and walked quickly away. Schaffer looked after her admiringly as she walked down the street.

'There goes the future Mrs Schaffer,' he announced. 'Bit tetchy and snappy, perhaps.' He pondered. 'But funny, I thought she was near crying at the end there.'

'Maybe you'd be tetchy and snappy and tearful if you'd been through what she's been in the past two and a half years,' Smith said sourly.

'Maybe she'd be less tetchy and tearful if she knew a bit more about what's going on.'

'I haven't the time to explain everything to everybody.'

'You can say that again. Devious, boss. That's the word for you.'

'Like enough.' Smith glanced at his watch. 'I wish to God they'd hurry up.'

'Speak for yourself.' Schaffer paused. 'When we – well, if we – get away, is she coming with us?'

'Is who coming with us?'

'Heidi, of course!'

'Heidi, of course. If we make it – and we can only do it through Mary, and Mary was introduced by—'

'Say no more.' He stared after the retreating figure and shook his head. 'She'll be a sensation in the Savoy Grill,' he said dreamily.

Chapter Six

The seconds crawled by and became minutes, and the minutes in turn piled up with agonizing slowness until almost quarter of an hour had passed. Brilliant moonshine and a contrastingly almost total darkness had alternated a score of times as the low, tattered, black clouds scudded across the valley, and the cold deepened until it reached down into the bones of the two watchers in the shadows. And still they waited. They waited because they had to: they couldn't reach the Schloss Adler without company and company was a long time in coming.

And they waited in silence, each man alone with his own thoughts. What was in Schaffer's mind Smith couldn't guess. Probably he was blissfully envisaging himself as the instigator of a series of uncontrollable stampedes in a selection of the better known hostelries in the West End of London. Smith's own thoughts were much more pragmatic and concerned solely with the immediate future. He was becoming concerned, and seriously concerned, about the intense cold and how it would affect their chances of making the trip up to the castle intact. Stamp their feet and flail their arms as they might, that numbing cold tightened its grip on them with every minute that passed. What they were about to do needed both physical strength and quick reactions in full measure, and that glacial cold was swiftly draining them of both. Briefly and bleakly he wondered what odds any reasonable bookmaker would have given against their chances of reaching the castle but dismissed the thought still-born. When no other option offered there was no point in figuring the percentages, and, besides, they were due to find out immediately: the long-awaited company was at hand.

Two Alpenkorps command cars, the leading one with wailing siren and flashing headlamps, swept up the village street just as the moon broke through the cloud-wrack once again, flooding the valley with light. Smith and Schaffer looked up at the moon, then at each other and then, wordlessly, moved back and pressed more deeply into the shadows on the west side of the lower station. The two metallic clicks seemed unnaturally loud as they eased forward the safety catches of their Schmeisser machine-pistols.

Engines stopped and headlamps faded and died almost on the same instant as the two cars pulled up beneath the steps. Men hurried out and lined up briefly before advancing single file up the station steps. A dozen altogether, Smith counted, an officer, eight guards and Carraciola, Thomas and Christiansen. All eight guards had their guns at the ready, which seemed a rather superfluous precaution as the three prisoners had their hands manacled behind their backs. Ergo, the guns weren't there to guard the prisoners but against any rescue attempt by Smith and Schaffer. He and Schaffer, Smith thought wryly, must be acquiring quite a reputation for themselves. But, nonetheless, a reassuring spectacle: if the Germans had known the true reason for his, Smith's, presence in Bavaria, they would also have known that they could have taken the three prisoners up with only a pea-shooter for protection and still have remained free from molestation.

The last of the twelve men passed inside the lower station. Smith touched Schaffer's arm. They slung their Schmeissers, scrambled quickly but quietly on to the ice-covered and steeply-sloping roof of the station and silently and with no little difficulty crawled forwards and upwards to the front edge of the roof under which the cable-car would appear as it moved out at the beginning of its long haul towards the castle. They were, Smith knew, terribly exposed: snow-suits or not, a casual passer-by in the street below had only to glance upwards and their detection was certain. Fortunately, there appeared to be no casual passers-by: the free entertainment provided by the burning station was drawing a full house. And then, as the cable began to move, the moon disappeared behind clouds.

They waited, tensely, till the leading edge of the cable-car appeared, swung their legs over the lip of the roof, waited till the suspension bracket passed beneath them, reached down for the cable, allowed themselves to be pulled off the roof, fell across the cable and lowered themselves gently until their feet touched the roof of the cable-car.

Mary walked softly along the dimly-lit, stone-flagged passage, counting off doors as she went. Outside the fifth she stopped, put her ear to it, stooped, glanced through the key-hole, knocked quietly and waited for a response. There was none. She knocked again, more loudly, with the same result. She turned the handle and found the door locked. From her small handbag she produced a set of skeleton keys. When the door yielded, she slipped quickly inside, closed the door and switched on the light.

The room was a considerable improvement on the one she had been given, although furnished with the same regulation iron bedstead. It was close-carpeted, boasted a couple of arm-chairs, and had a small chair with an Oberleutnant's uniform on it, a large wardrobe and a chest of drawers with a holstered belt, gun and binoculars resting on its glass top.

Mary locked the door, withdrew the key, crossed the room, lifted the lower sash window and looked down. She was, she saw, directly above the roof of the cable-car header station, a very steeply downward sloping roof the upper edge of which was built into the castle wall itself. She withdrew her head, removed from her handbag a ball of string with a heavy bolt attached to one end, laid it on the bed, picked up the binoculars and took up station by the window. Shivering in the bitter night wind, she adjusted the focus of the field-glasses, then traversed down the line of the aerial cables. And then she had it, dimly seen but unmistakable, the squat black outline of the cable-car, now half-way between the bottom and middle pylons, swaying madly, frighteningly, across the sky in the high and gusting wind.

Smith and Schaffer lay stretched out on the roof, clutching desperately to the suspension bracket, the only anchorage available. The roof was solidly coated with white-sheeted ice, they could find no purchase anywhere for their feet, and their bodies slid uncontrollably in all directions with the violent buffeting of the car beneath them. The sheer physical strain on hands and arms and shoulders was even worse than Smith had feared: and the worst was yet to come.

Schaffer twisted his head and peered downwards. It was a dizzy, vertiginous and frankly terrifying spectacle. The entire valley below seemed to be swinging through a forty-five degree arc. One second he was looking at the line of pines that bordered the western slope of the valley, then the floor of the valley rushed by beneath them and seconds later he was staring at the line of pines that swept up the eastern side of the valley. He twisted his head upwards, but that was no improvement; the lights of the Schloss Adler careened wildly through the same dizzy arc: it was like being on a combination of a roller-coaster, big dipper and runaway Ferris wheel with the notable exception, Schaffer thought bleakly, that the coaster, dipper and Ferris wheel were provided with safety belts and other securing devices designed to prevent the occupant from parting company with his machine. The wind howled its high and lonely threnody through the cables and the suspension bracket. Schaffer looked away, screwed his eyes shut, lowered his head between his outstretched arms and moaned.

'Still think the horse the world's worst form of transport?' Smith asked. His lips were close to Schaffer's ear.

'Give me my boots and saddle,' Schaffer said, then, even more despairingly, 'Oh, no! Not again!'

Once more, without any warning, the moon had broken through, flooding the two men in its pale cold light. Gauging the time when the strain on their arms was least, they pulled the snow hoods far over their heads and tried to flatten themselves even more closely on to the roof.

In the Schloss Adler two people were watching the wild upward progress of the cable-car, now brilliantly illuminated by the moon. Through Mary's field-glasses two clearly distinguishable shapes of men could be seen stretched out on the cable-car roof. For half a minute she kept the glasses trained on them, then slowly turned away, her eyes wide, almost staring, her face empty of expression. Fifty feet above her head a sentry with slung gun patrolling the battlements stopped and gazed down at the cable-car crawling up the valley. But he didn't gaze for long. Although booted, gauntleted and muffled to the ears, he shook with the cold. It was no night for idle spectating. He looked away indifferently and resumed his brisk sentry-go.

Indifference was a quality that was conspicuously lacking on top of the cable-car. The cable-car was on the last lap now, the section between the last pylon and the castle header station. Soon the moment of truth. A minute from then, Smith thought, and they could both well be lying broken and lifeless on the rocks two hundred feet below.

He twisted his head upwards. The cold moon still sailed across a clear gap in the sky but was closing rapidly towards another bank of cloud. The castle battlements, with the header station at the base, seemed almost vertically above his head. So steeply was the car rising on this last section that the volcanic plug itself was now less than fourteen yards away. His gaze followed the volcanic plug downwards till it reached its base: down there, on the slopes below, patrolling guards and their Dobermann pinschers were barely the size of beetles.

'Suits her, doesn't it?' Schaffer said suddenly. Harsh edges of strain burried in his voice and his face was tight and desperate. 'A lovely name.'

'What are you talking about?' Smith demanded.

'Heidi.'

'Oh, my God!' Smith stared up at the rapidly closing header station. 'Her name is Ethel.'

'You didn't have to tell me.' Schaffer tried to sound aggrieved but it didn't quite come off. He followed Smith's upward gaze and, after a long pause, said very slowly: 'Jesus! Look at the slope of that goddamned roof!'

'I've been looking.' Smith eased his knife from its sheath and made a quick grab at the suspension bracket as a particularly violent swing almost broke his grip with his other hand. 'Get your knife ready. And for God's sake don't lose it.'

The moon slid behind a black patch of cloud and the valley was flooded with darkness. Slowly, carefully, as the cable-car approached the header station and the swaying motion dampened down, Smith and Schaffer eased their way to the after end of the car, rose gingerly but swiftly to their feet and grabbed the cable with their free hands while their feet tried to find what precarious hold they could on the treacherously ice-sheathed roof.

The front of the car passed under the lip of the header station roof. A moment later the suspension bracket followed and Smith lunged forward and upwards, flinging himself bodily on to the roof. His right arm struck downwards and the knife blade pierced the coating of ice and imbedded itself firmly in the wood beneath. Less than a second later Schaffer had landed beside him, the downward arcing knife making contact at exactly the same instant as himself.

The blade broke off at the hilt. Schaffer opened his hand, dropped the haft and clawed desperately at the ice. The dragging nails ripped through the encrusting ice, quite failing to hold him. He reached his left hand to his mouth, tore off the gauntlet and dug both hands in with all the strength that was in him. He slowed, but not enough. His scrabbling toes failed to find any more purchase and he knew he was sliding out over the edge – and that when he went the first thing to halt his fall would be the rock-pile two hundred and fifty feet beneath at the base of the volcanic plug.

Smith had been badly winded by his fall. Several seconds elapsed before he realized that Schaffer wasn't where he should have been – lying on the roof beside him. He twisted round, saw the white blur of Schaffer's strained and desperate face, had a vague impression of Schaffer's eight finger-nails scoring their way through the ice as his body, already up to mid-thigh, slid inexorably over the edge and brought his left hand flashing down with a speed and power that, even in those circumstances, made Schaffer grunt in pain as the vice-like grip clamped over his right wrist.

For some seconds they lay like that, spreadeagled and motionless on the sloping roof, the lives of both dependent on the slim imbedded blade of Smith's knife; then Schaffer, urged by Smith's quivering left arm, began to inch his way slowly upwards. Thirty seconds later and he was level with Smith.

'This is a knife I have, not an ice-axe,' Smith said hoarsely. 'Won't take much more of this. Have you another knife?'

Schaffer shook his head. Momentarily, speech was beyond him.

'Piton?'

The same shake of the head.
'Your torch?'
Schaffer nodded, reached under the cumbersome snow-smock with his left hand and eventually managed to wriggle his torch free.
'Unscrew the bottom,' Smith said. 'Throw it away – and the battery.' Schaffer brought his left hand across to where his right was pinioned by Smith, removed base and battery, flattened the now empty cylinder base a little, reversed his grip and gouged the torch into the ice, downwards and towards himself. He moved his right hand and Smith released his grip. Schaffer remained where he was. Smith smiled and said: 'Try holding me.'
Schaffer caught Smith's left wrist. Tentatively, his hand still hooked in readiness, Smith removed his hand from the haft of the knife. Schaffer's imbedded torch held firm. Cautiously at first, then with increasing confidence as the sharp blade cut through the protective sheathing of ice, Smith carved out a secure handhold in the wooden roof of the station, passed his knife to Schaffer, wriggled out of his snow-smock, undid a few turns of the knotted rope round his waist and secured the free end to Schaffer's belt. He said: 'With the knife and torch, think you can make it?'
'Can I make it?' Schaffer tested both knife and and torch and smiled, a pretty strained effort, but his first for some time. 'After what I've been through – well, ever seen a monkey go up a coconut palm tree?'

Fifty feet above their heads, Mary withdrew from the window and laid the binoculars on the chest of drawers. Her hands shook and the metal of the binoculars rattled like castanets against the glass top. She returned to the window and began to pay out the weighted string.

Smith came up the last few feet of the sloping roof at the end of the rope, caught Schaffer's hand, stood upright on the flat inner section of the roof and at once began to unwind the rest of the knotted rope from his waist. Schaffer, although the temperature was far below freezing, wiped his brow like a man in a heat-wave.
'Brother!' He mopped his brow some more. 'If I can ever do you a favour, like lending you a car-fare—'
Smith grinned, clapped his shoulder, reached up into the gloom, caught the weighted end of the suspended string and quickly bent the nylon on to it. He gave two gentle tugs and the rope began to move upwards as Mary hauled it in through the window. Smith waited until two more gentle return tugs indicated that the rope was securely fastened and began to climb.
He was half-way up to the window when the moon broke through. In his Alpenkorps uniform he was perfectly silhouetted against the gleaming white of the castle walls. He hung there motionless, not daring to move, not so much as even daring to glance upwards or downwards lest the movement attract some hostile attention.
Twenty-five feet below him Schaffer peered cautiously over the edge of the header station roof. The guards and dogs were still patrolling the area round the roof of the volcanic plug. They had only to give one casual upwards glance and Smith's discovery was inevitable. Then some hair-prickling sixth sense made Schaffer look sharply upwards and he became very still indeed. The sentry, another circuit of the battlements completed, was standing with hands splayed out on the parapet, gazing out over the

valley, perhaps watching the now dying flames from the burnt-out station: he had to lower his eyes only a fraction and that was that. Slowly, with his right hand, Schaffer brought up the Luger with the long perforated silencer screwed to its muzzle and laid it, in the best police fashion, across his left wrist. He had no doubt he could kill his man with one shot, the only question was when best to do it, how to weigh the balance of possibilities. If he waited until the man sighted them, he might give a warning shout or thrust himself back into cover before Schaffer could kill him. If he shot the sentry before he sighted them, then there would be no question of either escape or warning. But there was the possibility that the man might pitch forward over the battlements, crash off the roof of the header station and fall into the valley below, close by the patrolling men and dogs. A possibility only, Schaffer decided, not a probability: the slamming effect of the Luger shell would almost certainly knock him backwards off his feet. Schaffer had never before gunned down an unsuspecting man, but he coldly prepared to do so now. He lined up the luminous sight on the man's breast-bone and began to squeeze the trigger.

The moon went behind a cloud.

Slowly, stiffly, Schaffer lowered his gun. Schaffer, once again, wiped sweat from his forehead. He had the feeling that he wasn't through with brow-mopping for the night.

Smith reached the window, clambered over the sill, gave the rope two tugs as a signal for Schaffer to start climbing and passed into the room. It was almost totally dark inside, he'd just time to make out the iron bedstead which had been dragged to the window as anchorage for the rope when a pair of arms wound tightly round his neck and someone started murmuring incoherently in his ear.

'Easy on, easy on,' Smith protested. He was still breathing heavily and needed all the air he could get, but summoned enough energy to bend and kiss her. 'Unprofessional conduct, what's more. But I won't report it this time.'

She was still clinging to him, silent now, when Lieutenant Schaffer made his appearance, dragging himself wearily over the sill and collapsing on the iron bedstead. He was breathing very heavily indeed and had about him the air of one who has suffered much.

'Have they no elevators in this dump?' he demanded. It took him two breaths to get the words out.

'Out of training,' Smith said unsympathetically. He crossed to the door and switched on the light, hurriedly switched it off again. 'Damn. Get the rope in then pull the curtains.'

'This is the way they treated them in the Roman galleys,' Schaffer said bitterly. But he had the rope inside and the curtains closed in ten seconds. As Smith was manoeuvring the bed back into its original position, Schaffer was stuffing the nylon into their canvas bag, a bag, which, in addition to snowsuits and Schmeissers, contained some hand grenades and a stock of plastic explosives. He had just finished tying the neck of the bag when a key scraped in the lock.

Smith motioned Mary to stay where she was as he moved quickly to take up position behind the door: Schaffer, for all his alleged exhaustion, had dropped flat to the floor behind the bed with all the speed and silence of a cat. The door opened and a young Oberleutnant strode into the room, stopping short as he saw Mary, her hand to her mouth. His face registered astonishment, an astonishment almost immediately replaced by an anticipatory half-smile as he stepped forward beyond the opened door. Smith's arm came down and the young officer's eyes turned up in his head.

Smith studied the plans of the castle given him by Mary while Schaffer trussed up the Oberleutnant with the nylon, gagged him with tape and shoved him, jack-knifed, into the bottom of the cupboard. For good measure he pulled the top of the bed against the door.

'Ready when you are, boss.'

'That's now. I have my bearings. First left, down the stairs, third left. The gold drawing-room. Where Colonel Kramer holds court. Complete with minstrels' gallery.'

'What's a minstrel's gallery?' Schaffer enquired.

'A gallery for minstrels. Then the next right-hander takes us to the east wing. Down again, second left. Telephone exchange.'

'Why there?' Schaffer asked. 'We've already cut the lines.'

'Not the ones between here and the barracks, we haven't. Want them to whistle up a regiment of Alpenkorps?' He turned to Mary. 'Helicopter still here?'

'It was when I arrived.'

'The helicopter?' Schaffer showed his puzzlement. 'What gives with the whirlybird, then?'

'This gives with the whirlybird. They could use it either to whip Carnaby out of here – they *might* just be nervous if they think we're on the loose – or they might use it to block our getaway.'

'*If* we get away.'

'There's that. How are you on immobilizing helicopters, Lieutenant Schaffer? Your report states that you were an up-and-coming racing driver and a very competent mechanic before they scraped the bottom of the barrel and dragged you in.'

'I volunteered,' Schaffer said with dignity. 'About the competence, I dunno. But give me a four-pound hammer and I'll sure as little fishes immobilize anything from a bull-dozer to a bicycle.'

'And without the four-pounder? This is not a boiler-makers' convention.'

'I have been known to use finesse.'

Smith said to Mary: 'How can we get a sight of this machine?'

'Just five paces that way.' She pointed to the door. 'Every passage window in the Schloss Adler opens on to the courtyard.'

Smith opened the door, glanced up and down the passage and crossed to an opposite window. Schaffer was by his side.

The comings and goings of the moon made no difference to the state of illumination in the Schloss Adler courtyard. Two big overhead arc lamps burned by the heavily-barred entrance gates. A third burned at the opposite end of the courtyard, over the main doorway leading into the castle itself. At a height of about ten feet, four waterproof storm lamps were fastened to the east and west walls of the courtyard. Lights burned from a dozen windows on the east and northern sides. And the brightest light of all came from an arc-lamp that had been rigged above the helicopter and under the temporary protection of a stretched tarpaulin. A figure in green overalls and a high-peaked cap was working on the helicopter's engine. Smith touched

Schaffer's arm and they moved back into the room where Mary was waiting, closing the door behind them.

'Seems a straightforward operation,' Schaffer said. 'Fixing it so that the chopper doesn't fly again, I mean. I cross to the main gates, overpower the four men on guard, strangle the four Dobermann pinschers, knock off two or three other characters – armed characters – who appear to be patrolling the place all the time, overpower about twenty soldiers who appear to be drinking beer in some sort of canteen across the way, dispose of the guy who's working on the engine and *then* immobilize the chopper. I mean, just immobilizing the chopper itself wouldn't be anything, really, would it?'

'We'll think of something,' Smith said soothingly.

'I'll bet *you* think of something,' Schaffer said moodily. 'That's what I'm afraid of.'

'Time's a-wasting. We won't need those any more.'

Smith folded the plan, handed it to Mary, then frowned as she put it in her bag. 'You know better than that. The Lilliput: it should be on your person, not in the bag. Here.' He handed her the Mauser he'd taken from Colonel Weissner. 'This in your bag. Hide the Lilliput on you.'

'When I get to my room I will,' she said primly.

'All those leering Yankee lieutenants around,' Schaffer said sadly. 'Thank heavens I'm a changed man.'

'His mind is set on higher things,' Smith explained. He glanced at his watch. 'Give us thirty minutes.'

They slipped cautiously through the doorway then strode briskly and confidently along the passage, making no attempt to conceal their presence. The bag with the Schmeissers, rope, grenades and explosives Smith swung carelessly from one hand. They passed a bespectacled soldier carrying a sheaf of papers and a girl carrying a laden tray, neither of whom paid any attention to them. They turned right at the end of the passage, reached a circular flight of stairs and went down three floors until they came to the level of the courtyard. A short broad passage, with two doors on either side, took them to the main door leading out to the courtyard.

Smith opened the door and looked out. The scene was very much as Schaffer had feelingly described it, with far too many armed guards and police dogs around for anyone's peace of mind. The overalled mechanic was still at work on the helicopter's engine. Smith quietly closed the door and turned his attention to the nearest right-hand door in the passage. It was locked. He said to Schaffer: 'Keep an eye open at the end of the passage there.'

Schaffer went. As soon as he was in position, Smith brought out skeleton keys. The third key fitted and the door gave under his hand. He signalled Schaffer to return.

With the door closed and locked behind them, they looked around the room, a room faintly but for their purposes adequately lit by the backwash of light shining through the unshuttered window from the courtyard. It was, quite apparently, the fire-fighting HQ of the castle. The walls were hung with drums of rolled hoses, asbestos suits, helmets and fire-axes: wheeled handpumps, CO_2 cylinders and a variety of smaller cylinders for fighting oil and electrical fires took up much of the floor space.

'Ideal,' Smith murmured.

'Couldn't be better,' Schaffer agreed. 'What are you talking about?'

'If we leave anyone in here,' Smith explained, 'he's unlikely to be discovered unless there's an actual outbreak of fire. Agreed? So.' He took Schaffer by the arm and led him to the window. 'The lad working on the chopper there. About your size, wouldn't you say?'

'I wouldn't know,' Schaffer said. 'And if you've got in mind what I think you have in mind, then I don't want to know, either.'

Smith drew the shutters, crossed to the door and switched on the overhead light.

'You got any better ideas?'

'Give me time,' he complained.

'I can't give you what we haven't got. Take your jacket off and keep your Luger lined up on that door. I'll be back in a minute.'

Smith left, closing but not locking the door behind him. He passed through the outer doorway, walked a few paces across the courtyard, halted at the base of a set of steps leading up to the helicopter and looked up at the man working above him, a tall rangy man with a thin intelligent face and a lugubrious expression on it. If he'd been working bare-handed with metal tools in that freezing temperature, Smith thought, he'd have had a lugubrious expression on his face, too.

'You the pilot?' Smith asked.

'You wouldn't think so, would you?' the overalled man said bitterly. He laid down a spanner and blew on his hands. 'Back in Tempelhof I have two mechanics for this machine, one a farm-hand from Swabia, the other a blacksmith's assistant from the Harz. If I want to keep alive I do my own mechanics. What do you want?'

'Not me. Reichsmarschall Rosemeyer. The phone.'

'The Reichsmarschall?' The pilot was puzzled. 'I was speaking to him less than fifteen minutes ago.'

'A call just came through from the Chancellory in Berlin. It seems urgent.' Smith let a slight note of impatience creep into his voice. 'You better hurry. Through the main door there, then the first on the right.'

Smith stood aside as the pilot clambered down, looked casually around him. A guard with a leashed Dobermann was no more than twenty feet away, but paying no attention to them: with his pinched bluish face sunk deep in his upturned collar, his hands thrust down into his great-coat pockets and his frozen breath hanging heavily in the air, he was too busy concentrating on his own miseries to have time to spare for ridiculous suspicions. Smith turned to follow the pilot through the main door, unobtrusively unholstering his Luger and gripping it by the barrel.

Smith hadn't intended chopping down the pilot with his gun butt but was left with no option. As soon as the pilot had passed through the side door and seen Schaffer's Luger pointing at his chest from a distance of four feet his shoulders lifted – the preliminary, Smith knew, not to violence or resistance but to a shout for help. Schaffer caught him as he pitched forward and lowered him to the floor.

Quickly they unzipped the overall from the unconscious man, bound and gagged him and left him lying in a corner. The overall was hardly a perfect fit for Schaffer, but, then, overalls are rarely a perfect fit for anybody. Schaffer switched the pilot's hat for his own, pulled the peak low over his eyes and left.

Smith switched off the light, unshuttered the window, raised the lower sash and stood, Luger in hand, just far enough back from the window so as not to be seen from outside. Schaffer was already climbing the steps up to the helicopter. The guard was now only feet from the base of the ladder. He'd his hands out of his pockets now and was flailing his arms across his shoulders in an attempt to keep warm.

Thirty seconds later Schaffer climbed down the ladder again, carrying some pieces of equipment in his left hand. He reached the ground, lifted the piece of equipment for a closer inspection, shook his head in disgust, lifted his right hand in a vague half-greeting to the uncaring German guard and headed for the main door again. By the time he reached the fire-fighting room, Smith had the window shuttered again and the light on.

'That was quick,' Smith said approvingly.

'Fear lent him wings, as the saying goes,' Schaffer said sourly. 'I'm always quick when I'm nervous. Did you see the size of the teeth in that great slavering monster out there?' He held up the piece of equipment for inspection, dropped it to the floor and brought his heel down on it. 'Distributor cap. I'll bet they haven't another in Bavaria. Not for that engine. And now, I suppose, you want me to go and impersonate the telephone operator.'

'No. We don't want to exhaust all your Thespian stamina.'

'My what?' Schaffer asked suspiciously. 'That sounds kinda like a nasty crack to me.'

'Your acting resources. The only other impersonation you'll be called to make tonight is that of Lieutenant Schaffer, OSS, the innocent American abroad.'

'That shouldn't be too difficult,' Schaffer said bitterly. He draped the overalls he'd just removed over the unconscious pilot. 'A cold night. Anyway, the telephone exchange.'

'Soon. But I'd like to check first how far they've got with old Carnaby-Jones. Let's take a look.

Two floors higher up and midway along the central passage Smith stopped outside a doorway. At a nod from him, Schaffer reached for a light switch. Except for a faint glow of light at either end, the passage was now completely dark. Smith laid a gentle hand on the door-knob and quietly eased the door open. Fifteen inches, no more. Both men swiftly slid through the narrow gap, Smith quickly and softly closing the door to again.

The room, if so enormous a chamber could be called a room, must have been at least seventy feet long by thirty wide. The farther end of the room was brightly and warmly lit by three large chandeliers: comparatively, the end of the room where Smith and Schaffer stood was shrouded in near darkness.

They stood, not on the floor, but on a platform some dozen feet above the floor. It was a massive and grotesquely carved oaken minstrels' gallery which completely spanned the thirty-foot width of that end and ran perhaps a quarter of the way down both the longer sides of the room. There were rows of wooden benches, an organ on one side of the door through which they had just passed, a battery of organ pipes on the other. Whoever had built that place had obviously liked the organ and choir-singing: or maybe he just thought he did. From the centre of the front of the gallery, opposite the rear door, a flight of steps with intricately scrolled wooden banisters led down to what was very obviously the gold drawing-room.

It was aptly named, Smith thought. Everything in it was gold or golden or gilt. The enormous wall-to-wall carpet was deep gold in colour, the thickness of the pile would have turned a polar bear green with envy. The heavy baroque furniture, all twisted snakes and gargoyles' heads, was gilt, the huge couches and chairs covered in a dusty gold lamé. The chandeliers were gilded and, above the enormous white and gilt-plated fireplace, in which a crackling pine log fire burned, hung an almost equally enormous white and gilt-plated mirror. The great heavy curtains could have been made from beaten gold. The ceiling-high oak panelling, was a mistake, it continued to look obstinately like oak panelling, maybe the original covering gold paint had worn off. All in all, Smith reflected, it was a room only a mad Bavarian monarch could have conceived of, far less lived in.

Three men were seated comfortably round the great fire, to all appearances having an amicable discussion over after-dinner coffee and brandy, which was being served to them from – almost inevitably – a golden trolley by Anne-Marie. Anne-Marie, like the panelling was a disappointment: instead of a gold lamé dress she wore a long white silk sheath gown which, admittedly, went very well with her blonde colouring and snowtan. She looked as if she were about to leave for the opera.

The man with his back to him Smith had never seen before but, because he immediately recognized who the other men were, knew who this man must be: Colonel Paul Kramer, Deputy Chief of the German Secret Service, regarded by MI6 as having the most brilliant and formidable brain in German Intelligence. The man to watch, Smith knew, the man to fear. It was said of Kramer that he never made the same mistake twice – and that no one could remember when he'd last made a mistake for the first time.

As Smith watched, Colonel Kramer stirred, poured some more brandy from a Napoleon bottle by his side and looked first at the man on his left, a tall, ageing, but still good-looking man in the uniform of a Reichsmarschall of the Wehrmacht – at that moment, wearing a very glum expression on his face – then at the man seated opposite, an iron-grey-haired and very distinguished looking character in the uniform of a lieutenant general of the US Army. Without a comptometer to hand, it was difficult to say which of the two generals was wearing the more decorations.

Kramer sipped his brandy and said wearily: 'You make things very difficult for me, General Carnaby. Very, very difficult indeed.'

'The difficulties are of your own making, my dear Kramer,' Cartwright Jones said easily. 'Yours and General Rosemeyer's here . . . There *is* no difficulty.' He turned to Anne-Marie and smiled. 'If I might have some more of that excellent brandy, my dear. My word, we've nothing like this in SHAEF. Marooned in your Alpine redoubt or not, you people know how to look after yourselves.

In the gloom at the back of the minstrels' gallery, Schaffer nudged Smith with his elbow.

'What gives with old Carnaby-Jones knocking back the Napoleon, then?' he asked in a low indignant murmur. 'Why isn't he being turned on a spit or having the French fits coming out of scopolamine?'

'Ssh!' Smith's nudge carried a great deal more weight and authority than Schaffer's had done.

Jones smiled his thanks as Anne-Marie poured him some more brandy, sipped from the glass, sighed in satisfaction and continued: 'Or have you forgotten, General Rosemeyer, that Germany is also a signatory to The Hague conventions?'

'I haven't forgotten,' Rosemeyer said uncomfortably. 'And if I had my way . . . General, my hands are tied. I have my orders from Berlin.'

'And you can tell Berlin all they're entitled to know,' Jones said easily. 'I am General – Lieutenant General – George Carnaby, United States Army.'

'And Chief Co-ordinator of Planning for the Second Front,' Rosemeyer added morosely.

'The Second Front?' Jones asked with interest. 'What's that?'

Rosemeyer said heavily and with earnest gravity: 'General, I've done all I can. You must believe me. For thirty-six hours now, I've held off Berlin. I've persuaded – I've *tried* to persuade the High Command that the mere *fact* of your capture will compel the Allies to alter all their invasion plans. But this, it seems, is not enough. For the last time, may I request—'

'General George Carnaby,' Jones said calmly. 'United States Army.'

'I expected nothing else,' Rosemeyer admitted tiredly. 'How could I expect anything else from a senior army officer? I'm afraid the matter is now in Colonel Kramer's hands.'

Jones sipped some more brandy and eyed Kramer thoughtfully. 'The Colonel doesn't seem very happy about it either.'

'I'm not,' Kramer said. 'But the matter is out of my hands, too. I also have my orders. Anne-Marie will attend to the rest of it.'

'*This* charming young lady?' Jones was politely incredulous. 'A maestro of the thumb-screw?'

'Of the hypodermic syringe,' Kramer said shortly. 'She used to be a trained nurse.' A bell rang and Kramer picked up a phone by his side. 'Yes? Ah! They have, of course, been searched? Very good. Now.' He looked across at Jones. 'Well, well, well. Some interesting company coming up, General. Very interesting indeed. Parachutists. A rescue team – for you. I'm sure you'll be delighted to meet one another.'

'I really can't imagine what you're talking about,' Jones said idly.

'The rescue team we've seen before,' Smith murmured to Schaffer. 'And no doubt we'll be renewing old acquaintances before long. Come on.'

'What? Now?' Schaffer jerked an urgent thumb in the direction of Jones. 'Just when they're going to get to work on him?'

'Out of your social depth, Lieutenant,' Smith whispered. 'They're civilized. First, they finish the brandy. *Then* the works.'

'It's like I said,' Schaffer said mournfully. 'I'm from Montana.'

The two men left as quietly as they had come and as quietly closed the door behind them. Against the loom of light at either end of the corridor, they could see that the passage-way was clear. Smith switched on the light. They walked briskly along the passage, dropped down a flight of stairs, turned left and halted outside a doorway which bore above it the legend TELEFON ZENTRALE.

'Telephone exchange,' Schaffer said.

Smith shook his head in admiration, put his ear to the door, dropped to one knee, peered through the keyhole and, while still in that position, softly tried the handle. Whatever slight sound he made was masked by the muffled sound of a voice speaking over a telephone. The door was locked. Smith slowly released the handle, straightened and shook his head.

'Suspicious bunch of devils,' Schaffer said sourly. 'The skeletons.'

'The operator would hear us. Next door.'

Next door wasn't locked. The door gave before Smith's pressure on the handle. The room beyond was in total darkness and appeared to be empty.

'*Moment, bitte!*' a cold voice said behind them.

Quickly, but not too quickly, Smith and Schaffer turned round. A few feet away stood a soldier, levelled carbine in his hand, his eyes moving in active suspicion from the two men to the kit-bag in Smith's hands. Smith glared at the man, raised an imperative forefinger to his lips.

'*Dummkopf!*' Smith's voice was a low furious whisper through clenched teeth. '*Silenz! Engländer!*'

He turned away impatiently and peered tensely through the partly-opened doorway. Again he held up an imperious hand that commanded silence. After a few more seconds he straightened, lips compressed, looked significantly at Schaffer and moved slightly to one side. Schaffer took his position and started peering in turn. Curiosity, Smith could see, was replacing suspicion in the soldier's face. Schaffer straightened and said softly: 'What in God's name do we do?'

'I don't know,' Smith said in a worried whisper. 'Colonel Kramer told me he wanted them alive. But—'

'What is it?' the soldier demanded in a voice as low as their own. With the mention of Colonel Kramer the last of his suspicions had gone. 'Who is it?'

'You still here,' Smith said irritably. 'All right, go on. Have a look. But be quick!'

The soldier, his face and eyes now alight with intense curiosity and what might have been dreams of rapid promotion, moved forward on tiptoe as Schaffer courteously stepped to one side to let him see. A pair of Lugers grinding simultaneously into both temples effectively put an end to any idea of rapid military advancement that he might briefly have entertained. He was propelled, stumbling, into the room and, by the time he'd picked himself up and turned round, the door was closed, the light on and both pistols lined at his head.

'Those are silencers you see on our guns,' Smith said quietly. 'No heroics, no shooting. Dying for the Fatherland is one thing, dying uselessly for no reason at all is another and very stupid thing. Don't you agree?'

The soldier looked at them, calculated his chances, accepted the fact that he had none and nodded. Schaffer produced a length of rope and said: 'You may be over-eager, son, but you're no fool. Lie down with your hands behind your back.'

The room, Smith saw, was small and lined with metal shelves and filing cabinets. Some sort of storage room for office records. The chances of anyone coming along weren't high and it was, anyway, a chance they had to take. He waited till Schaffer had bound and gagged the prisoner, put his Luger away, helped Schaffer to bind the man to two of the metal poles supporting the shelves, turned to the window, slid up the lower sash and peered out.

The valley to the north stretched out before him, the lights of the village and the smouldering embers of the railway station visible through very gently falling snow. Smith looked to his right. The lighted window of the telephone exchange was only a few feet away. From the window a heavy lead-sheathed cable attached to a wire almost equally as heavy stretched down the castle wall into the darkness.

'That the one?' Schaffer was by his side now.

'That's the one. Let's have the rope.'

Smith eased his legs into a double bowline, wriggled over the window-sill and cautiously lowered himself to the full extent of his arms while Schaffer, standing by the window with the rope belayed round one of the stanchions of the shelving, took the strain. Smith released his grip on the sill and was lowered jerkily by Schaffer till he was about ten or twelve feet down. Then, using a free hand and both feet to fend himself off from the wall he began to swing himself in a pendulum arc across the face of the castle, an assist from Schaffer up above adding momentum to his swing. On the fifth swing the fingers of his left hand hooked round the lead cable and wire. As Schaffer eased off tension on the rope Smith got both hands round the cable and quickly climbed up the few feet to the window above. He was almost certain that the lead cable he had in his hands *was* the telephone outlet, but only almost: he had no desire to slice the blade of his knife through high-powered electricity supply lines.

He hitched a wary eye over the window-sill, saw that the telephone operator, his back almost directly to him, was talking animatedly on the phone, lifted himself another six inches, observed a cable of what appeared to be exactly similar dimensions to the one he was holding running along the skirting-board to some point behind the exchange and then not reappearing again. He lowered himself a couple of feet, grasped cable and wire firmly with his left hand, inserted the point of his knife between cable and wire a few inches below that and started sawing. A dozen powerful saw-cuts and he was through.

He replaced the knife in its sheath, hoisted himself up again and had another look through the window. The operator was still animated, but this time not with his voice but with a hand which he was using furiously to crank a handle at the side of the exchange. After a few seconds of this profitless exercise he gave up and just sat there staring at the switchboard and shaking his head in bafflement. Smith made a signal to Schaffer, released his grip on the cable and swung back across the castle wall.

Mary glanced at her watch for the tenth time in less than as many minutes, stubbed out the half-cigarette she'd been nervously smoking, rose from her chair, opened her hand-bag, checked that the safety catch of the Mauser inside was in the off position, closed the bag and crossed the room. She had just turned the handle and begun to open the door when knuckles rapped on the outside. She hesitated, glanced at the bag in her hand and looked round almost wildly to see where she could dispose of it. But it was too late to dispose of anything. The door opened and a cheerfully smiling von Brauchitsch stood framed in the doorway.

'Ah, Fräulein!' He glanced at the bag and smiled again. 'Lucky me! Just in time to escort you wherever you're going.'

'To escort me—' She broke off and smiled. 'My business is of no consequence. It can wait. You wanted to see me, Captain?'

'Naturally.'

'What about?'

'What about, she says! About nothing, that's what. Unless you call yourself
nothing. Just to see you. Is that a crime? The prettiest girl we've seen—'
He smiled again, this man who was always smiling, and took her arm.
'Come, a little Bavarian hospitality. Coffee. We have an armoury that's been
converted into the finest *Kaffeestube*—'

'But – but my duties?' Mary said uncertainly. 'I must see the Colonel's
secretary—'

'That one! Let her wait!' There was a marked lack of cordiality in von
Brauchitsch's voice. 'You and I have a lot to talk about.'

'We have?' It was impossible to resist the infectious smile, not to reply in
kind. 'Such as?'

'Düsseldorf.'

'Düsseldorf?'

'Of course! That's my home town, too.'

'Your home town, too!' She smiled again and gave his arm the briefest of
squeezes. 'How small a world. That *will* be nice.'

She wondered vaguely, as she walked along, how one could smile and
smile and, inside, feel as chilled as the tomb.

Chapter Seven

For the second time in fifteen minutes Smith and Schaffer stopped at the
doorway outside the gold room's minstrels' gallery, switched out the passage
light, paused, listened, then passed silently inside. This time, however, Smith
reached through the crack of the almost closed door and switched the light
back on again. He did not expect to be using that door again, that night or
any night, and he had no wish to raise any eyebrows, however millimetric
the raising: survival was a matter of the infinitely careful consideration of
all possible dangers, no matter how remote that possibility might at times
appear.

This time, Smith and Schaffer did not remain at the back of the minstrels'
gallery. They moved slowly to the front, till they had come to the head of
the broad flight of stairs leading down to the floor of the gold room and then
sat down on the front oaken benches, one on each side of the gallery's
passageway. They were still shrouded in deep gloom, completely invisible
from below.

Colonel Kramer's stock of VSOP Napoleon brandy was certainly taking
a beating that night, Smith reflected. The Colonel, Reichsmarschall Rosemeyer, Jones and Anne-Marie had been joined by three others – Carraciola,
Thomas and Christiansen. Those last three were no longer manacled and
under heavy guard. On the contrary there was no sign of any guard, and the
three men were sitting deeply relaxed and side by side on one of the massive
gold lamé-covered couches, glasses of brandy, and no small ones at that, in

their hands. Even Anne-Marie now held a glass in her hand. It appeared to be an occasion for a celebration of some note.

Kramer lifted his glass towards the three men seated in the couch.

'Your health, gentlemen. Your very good health.' He turned to the Reichsmarschall. 'Three of the best in Europe, sir.'

'I suppose they are necessary,' Rosemeyer said in resigned distaste. 'At least, their courage is beyond dispute. Your health, gentlemen.'

'Your health, gentlemen,' Jones said bitterly. He sat forward in his chair and hurled his glass into the fire. The glass shattered and there was a momentary tongue of flame as the brandy ignited. '*That's* how I drink the health of double agents.'

Schaffer leaned across the passage-way and whispered: 'I thought you said he couldn't act?'

'Nobody's ever paid him twenty-five thousand bucks a night before,' Smith said sardonically.

'Tut, Tut, General. Best Venetian glass.' Kramer shook his head deprecatingly then smiled. 'But an understandable fit of pique. When your heroic rescuers turn out to be, well, birds of a different feather—'

'Double agents!' In his contempt, Jones almost spat out the words.

Kramer smiled again, tolerantly, and turned to the three men on the couch.

'And the return trip, gentlemen? As well organized as your outward journey?'

'That's about the one thing the close-mouthed so-and-so told us,' Carraciola said with some bitterness. 'A Mosquito bomber is to come to pick us up. Salen, a little village north of Frauenfeld in Switzerland. There's a little civilian airfield just to the north of Salen.'

Schaffer bent across the passage again and said in an admiring whisper: 'You really are a fearful liar.'

'So Salen it is,' Kramer was saying. 'We know all about it. The Swiss are very good at looking the wrong way when it suits them: but for reasons of our own we find it convenient not to protest too much. Odd things happen at Salen ... However, a little message to London. Arrange pick-up times and so forth. Then a helicopter to the border – so much easier than walking, gentlemen – a rubber dinghy for the Rhine and then a short walk. You'll be back in Whitehall, reporting General Carnaby's transfer to Berlin, before you know it.'

'Back in London?' Thomas shook his head in slow emphasis. 'Not on your nelly, Colonel. With Smith and that Yank still at large? What happens if they find out what's really happening? What happens if they remain at large? What happens if they get a message through to London—'

'What do you take us for?' Kramer said tiredly. 'You will also, of course, be reporting the unfortunate demise of your leader. As soon as we located that still-warm radio set in the left luggage office we put on bloodhounds from the barracks. Your precious Major Smith was the last man to handle that set and he left a pretty clear trail. The hounds traced him along the east side of the village as far as a garage and then up to the lower station of the *Luftseilbahn*.'

'The cable-car?' Thomas was frankly disbelieving.

'The cable-car. Our Major Smith is either a very foolhardy or a very dangerous man – I must confess I know nothing of him. And there, at the

lower station, the hounds completely lost the scent. The handlers circled the
station with the hounds and then brought them into the cable-car itself. But
the trail was cold. Our quarry appeared to have vanished into thin air.

'It was then that one of the searchers had the original idea of examining
the thin air, so to speak. He climbed up and examined the roof of the lower
station. Surprise, surprise, unmistakable signs in the snow and ice that two
men had been up there before him. From that it was only a logical step to
examine the roof of the cable-car itself, and sure enough—'

'They're inside!' Christiansen exclaimed.

'And won't get out again.' Colonel Kramer leaned back comfortably in
his chair. 'Have no fear, gentlemen. Every exit is blocked – including the
header station. We've doubled the guards outside and the rest have just
begun to carry out a floor to floor search.'

In the gloom of the minstrels' gallery Smith and Schaffer exchanged
thoughtful glances.

'I don't know,' Thomas said uneasily. 'He's a resourceful devil—'

Kramer held up a hand.

'Fifteen minutes. I guarantee it.' He shifted his glance to Jones. 'I don't
pretend to look forward to this, General, but shall we get on with your – ah
– medication?'

Jones glared at Carraciola, Christiansen and Thomas and said, very
slowly and distinctly: 'You – bloody – swine!'

'Against all my principles, General Carnaby,' Rosemeyer said uncomfortably. 'But if we could only dispense with force—'

'Principles? You make me sick!' Jones stood up and made a strangled
noise in his throat. 'The hell with you all! The Hague Conventions!
Principles! Officers and gentlemen of the Third bloody Reich!' He stripped
off his uniform jacket, rolled up a sleeve and sat down again.

There was a brief and uncomfortable silence, then Kramer nodded to
Anne-Marie who put down her glass and moved off to a side door leading
off the gold drawing-room. It was obvious to everyone that Anne-Marie
wasn't feeling in the least uncomfortable: the half-smile on her face was as
near to that of pleasurable anticipation as she could permit herself in the
presence of Rosemeyer and Kramer.

Again Smith and Schaffer exchanged glances, no longer thoughtful glances,
but the glances of men who know what they have to do and are committed
to doing it. Carefully, silently, they eased themselves up from the choir-stalls,
adjusted the straps of their shoulder-slung Schmeissers until the machine-
pistols were in the horizontal position then started slowly down the stairs,
well apart and as close as possible to their respective banisters, to minimize
the danger of creaking treads.

They were half-way down, just beginning to emerge from the dark gloom
of the gallery, when Anne-Marie re-entered the room. She was carrying a
small stainless steel tray: on the tray were a glass beaker, a phial containing
some colourless liquid and a hypodermic syringe. She set the tray down on
an occasional table close to Jones and broke the phial into the narrow beaker.

Smith and Schaffer had reached the foot of the stairs and were now
advancing towards the group round the fire-place. They had now completely
emerged from the shadows, and were in full view of anyone who cared to
turn his head. But no one cared to turn his head. Every seated person in the
drawing-room was engrossed in the scene before him, watching in varying

degrees of willing or unwilling fascination as Anne-Marie carefully filled the hypodermic syringe and held it up to the light to examine it. Smith and Schaffer continued to advance, their footfalls soundless on the luxuriously deep pile of the gold carpet.

Carefully, professionally, but with the trace of the smile still on her lips, Anne-Marie swabbed an area of Jones's forearm with cotton wool soaked in alcohol and then, as the watchers unconsciously bent forward in their seats, picked up Jones's wrist in one hand and the hypodermic in the other. The hypodermic hovered over the swabbed area as she located the vein she wanted.

'Just a waste of good scopolamine, my dear,' Smith said. 'You won't get anything out of him.'

There was a moment's frozen and incredulous stillness, the hypodermic syringe fell soundlessly to the floor, then everyone whirled round to stare at the two advancing figures, carbines moving gently from side to side. Predictably, Colonel Kramer was the first to recover and react. Almost imperceptibly, his hand began to drift to a button on a panel beside his chair.

'That button, Colonel,' Smith said conversationally.

Slowly, reluctantly, Kramer's hand retreated from the button.

'On the other hand,' Smith went on cordially, 'why not? By all means, if you wish.'

Kramer glanced at him in narrow-eyed and puzzled suspicion.

'You will notice, Colonel,' Smith continued by way of explanation, 'that my gun is not pointing at you. It is pointed at him' – he swung his gun to cover Carraciola – 'at him,' – the gun moved to Thomas – 'at him,' – it covered Christiansen – 'and at him!' Smith swung round abruptly and ground the muzzle of the Schmeisser into Schaffer's ribs. 'Drop that gun! Now!'

'Drop the gun?' Schaffer stared at him in shock and baffled consternation. 'What in the name of God—'

Smith stepped swiftly forward and, without altering his grip on his gun, ifted the barrel sharply upwards and drove the butt of the Schmeisser into Schaffer's stomach. Schaffer grunted in agony, doubled forward with both hands clutched over his midriff, then, seconds later, obviously in great pain, began to straighten slowly. Glaring at Smith, the dark eyes mad in his face, he slipped the shoulder strap and the Schmeisser fell to the carpet.

'Sit there.' With the muzzle of his gun Smith gestured to a chair half-way between Rosemeyer's and the couch where the three men were sitting.

Schaffer said slowly, painfully: 'You goddamned lousy, dirty, double-crossing—'

'That's what they all say. You're not even original.' The contempt in Smith's voice gave way to menace. 'That chair, Schaffer.'

Schaffer lowered himself with difficulty into his chair, rubbed his solar plexus and said, 'You —. If I live to be a hundred—'

'If you live to be a hundred you'll do nothing,' Smith said contemptuously. 'In your own idiom, Schaffer, you're a punk and a pretty second-rate one at that.' He settled himself comfortably in a chair beside Colonel Kramer. 'A simple-minded American,' he explained carelessly. 'Had him along for local colour.'

'I see,' Kramer said. It was obvious that he did not see. He went on uncertainly: 'If we might have an explanation—'

Smith waved him negligently to silence.

'All in good time, my dear Kramer, all in good time. As I was saying, my dear Anne-Marie—'

'How did you know her name was Anne-Marie?' Kramer asked sharply.

Smith smiled enigmatically, ignored him completely, and continued: 'As I was saying, scopolamine is a waste of time. All scopolamine will do, as you're all aware, is to reveal the truth about our friend here, which is that he is not Lieutenant General George Carnaby, Chief Co-ordinator of Planning for the Second Front, but a certain Cartwright-Jones, an American actor being paid precisely twenty-five thousand dollars to impersonate General Carnaby.' He looked over to Jones and bowed. 'My congratulations, Mr Jones. A very creditable performance. Pity you'll have to spend the rest of the war in a concentration camp.'

Kramer and Rosemeyer were on their feet, the others leaning far forward on the couch, an almost exactly identical expression of disbelief showing in every face. If Cartwright Jones had been earth's first visitor from outer space he couldn't possibly have been the object of more incredulous consternation.

'Well, well, well,' Smith said with interest. 'Surprise, surprise, surprise.' He tapped Kramer on the arm and gestured in the direction of Carraciola, Thomas and Christiansen. 'Odd, wouldn't you say, Kramer? They seem just as astonished as you are?'

'Is this true?' Rosemeyer demanded hoarsely of Jones. 'What he says? Do you deny—'

In a voice that was no more than a whisper, Jones said: 'How – how in God's name – who *are* you, sir?'

'A stranger in the night.' Smith waved a hand. 'Dropped in in the passing, you might say. Maybe the Allies will let you have that twenty-five thousand after the war. I wouldn't bank on it though. If international law allows you to shoot a captured enemy soldier dressed as a civilian, maybe the opposite holds good too.' Smith stretched and politely patted a yawn to extinction. 'And now, Anne-Marie, if I could – with your permission, my dear Kramer – have a glass of that excellent Napoleon. Clinging to the roofs of cable-cars works the devil with my circulation.'

The girl hesitated, looked at Kramer and Rosemeyer, found neither encouragement nor discouragement, shrugged, poured a glass and handed it to Smith, who sniffed the bouquet approvingly, drank a little and bowed again to Jones.

'My congratulations, sir. You are a connoisseur.' He sipped again, turned to Kramer and said sadly: 'To think you have been wasting such excellent liquor on enemies of the Third Reich.'

'Don't listen to him, Colonel Kramer, don't listen to him!' Carraciola shouted wildly. 'It's a bluff! He's just trying—'

Smith lined up his gun on Carraciola's chest and said softly: 'Keep quiet or I'll make you quiet, you damned traitor. You'll have your chance – *and* we'll see who's bluffing.' He lowered his gun to his knees and went on tiredly: 'Colonel Kramer, I don't fancy talking and having to keep a gun on this unlovely trio all the time. Have you a guard you can trust? A man who won't talk afterwards, I mean?'

He sat back in his chair, sipped his brandy and ignored the malevolent stares from his four erstwhile colleagues. Kramer looked at him for a very long moment, then nodded thoughtfully and reached for a phone.

The armoury – now converted into a *Kaffeestube* – of the Schloss Adler was very much in keeping with the remainder of the castle, something out of a medieval dream or nightmare, according to how individual tastes and inclinations lay. It was a large, darkly-panelled, stone-flagged room with enormous adzecut smoke-blackened beams and walls behung with ancient and rusty suits of armour, ancient and rusty weapons of all kinds and scores of armorial bearings, some of which could have been genuine. Three-sided half-booths lined the walls and half-a-dozen slab-topped monastery refectory tables, flanked by massive oak benches, paralleled the shorter axis of the room. The oil lamps, suspended by iron chains from the ceiling, were turned low, lending the atmosphere in the armoury an air of intimacy or brooding menace, according to one's original mood on entering. There was no doubt in Mary's mind as to its effect upon her. Her gaze followed half-a-dozen heavily armed and jack-booted men who were just leaving the armoury, then came back reluctantly to the man sitting close beside her in the corner booth.

'Well, what did I tell you?' von Brauchitsch said expansively. 'Coffee to match the surroundings!'

Coffee to match the surroundings, Mary thought, would have tasted of hemlock. She said: 'What did those men want? They seemed to be looking for someone.'

'Forget them. Concentrate on von Brauchitsch.'

'But you spoke to them. What did they *want*?'

'They say there are spies in the castle!' Von Brauchitsch threw his head back, laughed, and spread his hands palms up. 'Imagine! Spies in the Schloss Adler! The Gestapo HQ! They must have flown in on their broom-sticks. The military commandant is an old woman. He has spies in about once a week. Now what was I saying about Düsseldorf?' He broke off, glancing at her empty coffee cup. 'My apologies, my dear Fräulein. Come, more coffee.'

'No, really. I must go.'

Von Brauchitsch laughed again and put his hand on hers.

'Go where? There *is* nowhere to go inside the Schloss Adler. Nonsense, nonsense.' He turned in his seat and called: 'Fräulein! Two more coffees. And with Schnapps, this time.'

While he was ordering, Mary glanced quickly at her watch and a momentary expression of desperation crossed her face, but by the time von Brauchitsch turned back she was smiling sweetly at him. She said: 'You were saying about Düsseldorf—'

The company in the gold drawing-room had now been increased by one, a tall, cold-faced and hard-eyed sergeant who held a carbine cradled in a pair of strong and very capable looking hands. He was standing behind the couch on which Carraciola, Thomas and Christiansen were seated, and he was giving them his entire attention, apart from a frequent sideways glance at Schaffer. He had about him a reassuring air of competence.

'A very much more civilized arrangement,' Smith said approvingly. He rose, leaving his Schmeisser lying on the floor, crossed to the brandy decanter on the sideboard, poured himself another drink and made his way back to the fireplace where he placed his glass on the mantelpiece.

'This will take but minutes, only,' Smith said in a soft and ominous voice.

'Anne-Marie, bring in three more capsules of scopolamine.' He smiled at her. 'And I needn't remind *you* to bring the hypodermics.'

'Colonel Kramer!' Carraciola said desperately. 'This is madness! Are you going to allow—'

'Guard!' Smith's voice was harsh. 'If that man talks again, silence him!' The guard jabbed his carbine muzzle none too lightly into Carraciola's back. Carraciola subsided, fuming, his fists clenched till the ivory showed.

'What do you take Reichsmarschall Rosemeyer and Colonel Kramer for?' Smith demanded cuttingly. 'Credulous fools? Little children? Imbeciles of your own calibre, who imagine you can get away with a cretinous masquerade of this nature? The scopolamine will be used *after* I have established my own bona-fides and *after* I have disproved yours. Anne-Marie?'

Anne-Marie smiled and marched away. It was not every night that she got the chance to administer three injections of scopolamine. Then she stopped and turned, eyebrows raised in interrogation, as Smith called her name again.

'One moment, Fräulein.' Smith, brandy glass in hand, was staring unseeingly into the middle distance and the watchers could see a slow smile coming to his face, a smile obviously heralding the birth of a new idea and one that pleased him very much. 'Of course, of course,' Smith said softly. 'And bring three note-books will you, my dear?'

'*Three* note-books?' Colonel Kramer's tone was neutral, his eyes watchful. '*Three* capsules? You give the impression that we have *four* enemies of the Reich here.'

'Only three enemies that matter,' Smith said in weary patience. 'The American?' The fact that he neither bothered to glance at Schaffer nor even permit a trace of contempt to creep into his voice showed unmistakably his opinion of the American. 'He doesn't even know what day of the week it is. Now then.' He picked up a cigar from an inlaid marquetry box, lit it and sipped some more brandy. 'Let's be fair and establish my bona-fides first. Pointers first, then proof. In the best judicial fashion.

'First, why did I invite another guard in and lay down my own gun?' He paused and went on sarcastically: 'Of course! Because I wanted to increase the odds against myself. Secondly, why didn't I kill Colonel Weissner and his men when I had them at my mercy – if, that is, I'm an enemy of the Third Reich – earlier this evening? I had some difficulty, I might tell you, in restraining our fire-eating American here from turning himself into a one-man firing squad. Very aggressive, he was.'

'I'll damned well tell you why,' Carraciola said viciously. 'Because you knew the shots would be heard!'

Smith sighed, lifted the flap of his jacket, produced an automatic and fired. The sound of the impact of the bullet thudding into the couch inches from Carraciola's shoulder completely blanketed the soft plop made by the automatic itself. Smith carelessly threw the silenced Luger into a nearby empty chair and smiled quizzically at Carraciola.

'Didn't know I had that, did you? I didn't kill Colonel Weissner because German does not kill German.'

'You are German?' Kramer's eyes were still watchful but the tone perhaps a shade less neutral.

'Johann Schmidt, at your service.' This with a little bow and click of the heels. 'Captain John Smith of the Black Watch.'

'From the Rhineland, by your accent?'

'Heidelberg.'

'But that is *my* home town.'

'Indeed?' Smith smiled his interest. 'Then I think we have a mutual friend.'

Momentarily, a faraway look came to Kramer's eyes and he said softly, apparently apropos of nothing: 'The columns of Charlemagne.'

'Ah, and the fountain in the courtyard of the dear old Friedrichsbau,' Smith said nostalgically. He glanced at Kramer, and the nostalgia gave way to a pseudo-mournful reproof. 'How could you, my dear Colonel? To proceed. Why – third point, I think – why did I stage this elaborate car accident – because I *knew* those three impostors wouldn't dare come into the open until they thought I was dead. Anyway, if I *were* the impostor, would I have come back when I knew the game was up? Anyway, to come back for what?' He smiled wearily and nodded at Jones. 'To rescue *another* impostor?'

Kramer said thoughtfully: 'I must say I'm rather beginning to look forward to hearing what our three friends here have to say.'

'I'll tell you *now* what I've bloody well got to say.' Christiansen was on his feet, ignoring the guard's gun, his voice shaking with fury. 'He's fooling you, he's fooling all of us. He's a damned liar and you're too damned stupid to see the wool over your eyes. A tissue of — lies, from beginning to end—'

'That will do!' Kramer's hand was up, his eyes bleak, his tone icy. 'You condemn yourselves from your own mouths. Every statement made so far by this officer is demonstrably true. Sergeant Hartmann' – this to the guard with the carbine – 'if any of those men speak again, do you think you could silence him without silencing him permanently?'

Hartmann produced a small woven-leather truncheon from his tunic and slipped the looped thong over his wrist.

'You know I can, Herr Colonel.'

'Good. Pray continue, Captain Schmidt.'

'Thank you. I hadn't finished.' Smith felt like pouring himself another brandy, a celebration brandy or, alternatively, pinning a medal on Christiansen for having so unerringly if unwittingly exposed the chink in Kramer's armour, a wounded intellectual vanity, the lacerated professional pride of a brilliant man being reminded of his capacity for being duped by one of those who had already duped him. 'For the same excellent reason I came here by the roof of the cable-car – they'd *never* have come into the open if they'd known I was here – and alive. Incidentally, Kramer, hasn't it occurred to you that it's impossible to enter the Schloss Adler from the roof of the header station without the assistance of a rope and someone inside?'

'Damnation!' Coming so soon after Christiansen's reminder of his fallibility, Smith's question left Kramer's self-confidence badly shaken. 'I never thought—'

'Von Brauchitsch,' Smith said carelessly. 'He had his orders direct from Berlin.' He placed his glass on the mantelpiece, walked across and stood before the three spies. 'Tell me, how did I know Jones was an impostor? Why did you *not* know he was one? And if I'm not what I claim to be then what in God's name am I doing here at all? Perhaps you would like to explain that?'

The three men glanced up at him in baleful silence.

'Perhaps they would indeed,' Kramer said heavily. He came and stood by Smith, staring down at the three men with an oddly expressionless gaze that was more disturbing than any show of anger could ever have been. After another and longer silence he said: 'Captain Schmidt, this has gone far enough.'

'Not yet.'

'I require no more,' Kramer persisted.

'I promised you proof – those were but the pointers. A proof to satisfy the Deputy Chief of the German Secret Service – and that proof is in three parts. A yes or no, Colonel Kramer, if you please. Do you or do you not know the name of our top man in Britain?' Kramer nodded. 'Then suppose we ask them?'

The three men on the couch looked at each other, then at Smith. They looked in silence. Thomas licked dry lips, a movement that did not go unnoticed by Kramer. Smith produced a small red note-book from his tunic pocket, removed a rubber band, tore out the central page, then carefully replaced the band on the book and the book in his pocket. He wrote something on the page and handed it to Kramer, who glanced at it and nodded. Smith took the paper from him, walked across to the fire and burned it.

'Now then,' Smith said. 'You have here, in the Schloss Adler, the most powerful radio transmitter in Central Europe—'

'You are singularly well-informed, Captain Schmidt,' Kramer said wryly.

'Smith. I live Smith. I breathe Smith. I *am* Smith. Put a radio-telephone call through to Field-Marshal Kesselring's HQ in Northern Italy. Ask for his Chief of Military Intelligence.'

Kramer said softly: 'The mutual friend you mentioned?'

'An old alumnus of Heidelberg University,' Smith nodded. 'Colonel Wilhelm Wilner.' He smiled. 'Willi-Willi.'

'You know that? Then it will not be necessary to call him.'

'Admiral Canaris would like you to.'

'And you know my chief, too?' Kramer's voice was even softer.

'My self-esteem urges me to say that I do – but modesty and the truth compels me to admit I don't,' Smith said disarmingly. 'I just work for him.'

'I'm convinced already, convinced beyond all doubt,' Rosemeyer said. 'But do as he says, Colonel.'

Kramer did as he was told. He put a call through to the radio room, hung up and waited patiently. Smith lay back in his armchair, brandy in one hand, cigar in the other, the picture of relaxed confidence. If Schaffer and the three men on the couch beside him were either relaxed or confident they entirely failed to show it. Behind them their guard watched his four charges hopefully, as if eager to show his expertise with a blackjack. If either Rosemeyer or Jones were thinking any thoughts at all, those thoughts didn't break through to the surface. Anne-Marie, not quite knowing what was going on, hovered around indecisively, a tentative smile of anticipation still on her face. She was the only person who moved during the period of waiting and that only because Smith crooked a finger at her and indicated his empty brandy glass: so complete was the ascendancy he had achieved that she obeyed the unspoken command without hesitation and brought back a very generous measure of brandy which she set down on his side-table to the accompaniment of a winning smile. Smith gave her a winning smile in return. But no one spoke, not once, during that seemingly interminable wait.

The phone bell rang.

Kramer lifted it and, after a few preliminary exchanges, presumably with operators, said: 'Colonel Wilhelm Wilner. My dear friend, Willi-Willi. How are you.' After the introductory courtesies were over, Kramer said: 'We have an agent here who claims to know you. A Captain John Smith. Have you ever – ah, so you know him? Good, good!' A pause, then he continued: 'Could you describe him?'

He listened intently, looking at Smith as a voice crackled over the receiver. Suddenly he beckoned to Smith, who rose and crossed over to where Kramer was sitting.

'Your left hand,' Kramer said to Smith, took it in his own, then spoke into the phone. 'Yes, the tip of the little finger is missing . . . and the right forearm has what?' Smith bared his right forearm without being told. 'Yes, yes, two parallel scars, three centimetres apart . . . What's that? . . . Tell him he's a traitor?'

'And tell him he's a renegade.' Smith smiled.

'And you're a renegade,' Kramer said on the phone. 'Chambertin, you say. Ah! Thank you, thank you. Goodbye, my old friend.' He replaced the receiver.

'We both prefer French wine,' Smith said apologetically and by way of explanation.

'Our top double agent in the Mediterranean,' Kramer said wonderingly. 'And I'd never even heard of you.'

'Maybe that's why he is what he is,' Rosemeyer said dryly.

'I've been lucky.' Smith shrugged then said briskly: 'Well, then. My credentials?'

'Impeccable,' Kramer said. 'My God, they're impeccable.'

'So,' Smith said grimly. 'Now for our friends' credentials. As you know, Christiansen, Thomas and Carraciola – the real Christiansen, Thomas and Carraciola – while working for—'

'What in God's name are you talking about?' Christiansen shouted. He was on his feet, his face suffused with uncontrollable anger. 'The real Christiansen—' His eyes turned up as Hartmann's blackjack caught him behind the ear and he sagged to the floor.

'He was warned,' Kramer said grimly. 'You didn't hit him too hard, Sergeant?'

'A two-minute tap,' Hartmann said reassuringly.

'Good. I think you may now proceed without interruption, my dear Schmidt.'

'Smith,' Smith corrected him. 'As I was saying, our real agents while working for the British counter-espionage have not only been responsible for the deep infiltration of the German Secret Service into the British espionage network in France and the Low Countries but have also set up an excellent chain of spies in England – a most successful ring, as Admiral Canaris well knows.'

'It's not my territory,' Kramer said. 'But that, of course, I know.'

Smith said coldly: 'To your feet, you impostors, and sit at the table there. Sergeant, lend a hand to that man on the floor there. He appears to be coming round.'

Their faces baffled and uncomprehending, Carraciola and Thomas made their way towards the table and sat down, where they were shortly joined by a very shaky and sick-looking Christiansen. The sergeant remained by him just long enough to ensure that he didn't fall off his chair, then took three paces back and covered them all with his carbine again.

From the other side of the table Smith flung down in front of the three men the little note-books that Anne-Marie had brought. Then he produced his own elastic-banded note-book from his pocket and laid it on the small table beside Kramer.

'If they are who they claim to be,' Smith said quietly, 'it would be reasonable, would it not, my dear Kramer, to expect them to be able to write the names and the addresses or contacts of our agents in England and of the British agents who have been supplanted on the Continent by our men.' He paused significantly. 'And then compare their lists with the genuine one in my book there.'

'It would indeed,' Kramer said slowly. 'Proof at one stroke. Masterly, my dear Captain Schmidt – Smith, I mean.' He smiled, almost wanly. 'I'm afraid I'm not myself tonight. But tell me, Captain.' He touched the banded note-book by his side. 'This list of agents – I mean, carrying it around on your person. Does this not contravene every rule we have?'

'Of course it does. Rules can only be broken by the man who made them. You think that even I would dare without his authority? Admiral Walter Canaris will be in his Berlin office now.' Smith nodded towards the telephone.

'What do you take me for.' Kramer smiled and turned to the three men at the table. 'Well, you heard.'

'There's something terribly far wrong—' Carraciola began despairingly.

'There is indeed,' Kramer interrupted bleakly.

'I don't *doubt* Smith's bona-fides.' Carraciola was almost in anguish now. 'Not any more. But there's been some ghastly mistake—'

'You are the ones who have made it,' Smith said curtly.

'Write,' Kramer commanded. 'Sergeant Hartmann.'

Sergeant Hartmann stepped forward, his leather-thonged blackjack at the ready. The three men bent their heads and wrote.

Chapter Eight

The armoury was almost deserted now. Some time previously, a couple of sergeants had entered, moved around among the coffee tables and taken at least a score of grumbling men away for unspecified duties. Mary did not have to guess at what those unspecified duties might be. She glanced secretly at her watch for what must have been the twentieth time, rubbed her forehead wearily, rose to her feet and smiled palely at von Brauchitsch.

'I'm so sorry, Captain. I must go. I really must go. A most dreadful headache.'

'I *am* sorry, my dear Maria.' A troubled contrition had replaced his habitual smile. 'You should have told me earlier. You don't look at all well. A long journey from the Rhineland, then all this Schnapps—'

'I'm afraid I'm not used to it,' Mary said ruefully. 'I'll be all right when I've lain down.'

'Of course, of course. Come, my dear, let me escort you to your room.'

'No, no!' Then, realizing she had spoken with uncalled-for vehemence, she smiled again and touched his hand. 'I'll be all right. Really I will.'

'Captain von Brauchitsch knows what's best.' The face was serious but friendly, the voice authoritative but with an underlying tone of humour, and Mary knew there was no answer to it. 'I positively insist. Come along.'

He tucked her arm protectively under his and led her from the armoury.

Arm in arm they walked along the passage-way leading from the armoury-cum-*Kaffeestube* towards the central block of the castle. The passage-way, in contrast to the last time they had walked along there, was completely deserted and Mary commented on the fact.

'It's the witches on their broomsticks,' von Brauchitsch laughed. 'The commandant hasn't caught them yet, but give him another few years and you never know. All those poor souls you saw being hauled out of the armoury are now probably poking about the eaves or climbing up the flagpoles. You never know where spies get to nowadays.'

'You seem to treat the possibility lightly enough,' Mary said.

'I'm a Gestapo officer. I'm paid and trained to use my head, not an overheated imagination,' he said curtly, then squeezed her arm and apologized. 'Sorry, that tone of voice was aimed at someone else, not you.' He halted abruptly, peered out a window into the courtyard and said: 'Now that is strange.'

'What's strange?'

'The helicopter there,' von Brauchitsch said thoughtfully. 'Army regulations state that High Command helicopters must be kept in instant readiness at all times. But that one has part of its engine cover dismantled and a tarpaulin stretched in position over it. Wouldn't call that instant readiness, would you?'

'I suppose helicopters need repairing from time to time the same as any other machine.' Her throat was suddenly dry and she wished von Brauchitsch wouldn't hold her so closely: he was bound to notice her accelerating heartbeat. 'What's so unusual about that?'

'What's so unusual is that there was no one working on that machine almost half an hour ago when we first passed by here,' von Brauchitsch said. 'Unheard of for a Reichsmarschall's personal pilot to walk away and leave a job half done.'

'Would it be unheard of for him to take a piece of mechanism inside and repair it under cover?' Mary asked sweetly. 'Or perhaps you haven't seen a thermometer tonight?'

'I'm getting as bad as the old commandant and his witch-hunts,' von Brauchitsch said sadly. He moved on, shaking his head. 'You see before you a horrible example of the dangers of being too long in my business: the obvious answer is far too obvious for shrewd and cunning intellects like ours. I must remember that later on tonight.'

'You're going to exercise this great mind again tonight?' Mary asked lightly.

'In there, as a matter of fact.' Von Brauchitsch nodded as they passed by an ornate door. 'The gold drawing-room.' He glanced at his watch. 'In twenty minutes! So soon! Your charming company, Fräulein.'

'Thank you, kind sir. You – you have an appointment?' Her heart was back at its old tricks again.

'An evening of musical appreciation. Even the Gestapo has its finer side. We are going to listen to a nightingale sing.' He quickened his pace. 'Sorry, Fräulein, but I've just remembered I've one or two reports to prepare.'

'I'm sorry if I've kept you from your work, Captain,' she said demurely. How much does he know, she thought wildly, how much does he suspect, what action has he suddenly decided to take? The von Brauchitschs of this world didn't just suddenly remember anything for the excellent reason that they never forgot it in the first place. 'It's been most kind of you.'

'The pleasure was one-sided,' von Brauchitsch protested gallantly. 'Mine and mine alone.' He stopped outside her bedroom door, took her hand in his and smiled. 'Goodnight, my dear Maria. You really are the most charming girl.'

'Goodnight.' She returned smile for smile. 'And thank you.'

'We really must get to know each other better,' von Brauchitsch said in farewell. He opened her door, bowed, kissed her hand, gently closed the door behind her and rubbed his chin thoughtfully. 'Very much better, my dear Maria,' he said softly to himself. 'Very much better indeed.'

Carraciola, Thomas and Christiansen bent over their notebooks and scribbled furiously. At least the first two did: Christiansen had not yet recovered from the blow on the head and was making heavy weather of his writing. Kramer, who was standing apart with Smith and talking to him in low tones, looked at them in curiosity and with just a trace of uneasiness.

'They seem to be finding plenty of inspiration from somewhere,' he said carefully.

'The spectacle of an open grave is often thought-provoking,' Smith said cynically.

'I am afraid I don't quite follow.'

'Do you know what those men will be fifteen minutes from now?'

'I'm tired,' Kramer said. He sounded it. 'Please don't play with words, Captain Schmidt.'

'Smith. In fifteen minutes they'll be dead. And they know it. They're fighting desperately for extra minutes to live: when you have as little time as they have, even a minute is a prize snatched from eternity. Or the last despairing fling of the ruined gambler. Call it what you like.'

'You wax lyrical, Captain,' Kramer grumbled. He paced up and down for almost a minute, no longer troubling to watch the men at the table, then stopped and planted himself squarely in front of Smith. 'All right,' he said wearily. 'I've been on the spit long enough. I confess I'm baffled. Out with it. What in God's name is behind all this?'

'The simplicity of true genius, my dear Kramer. Admiral Rolland, the head of MI6. And he *is* a genius, make no mistake.'

'So he's a genius,' Kramer said impatiently. 'Well?'

'Carraciola, Thomas and Christiansen were caught three weeks ago. Now, as you are aware, they were concerned only with north-west Europe and were not known here.'

'By reputation, they were.'

'Yes, yes. But only that. Admiral Rolland reckoned that if three fully-briefed men impersonated our three captured men and were despatched here for a perfectly plausible reason, they would be *persona grata* of some note, honoured guests and completely accepted by you. And, of course, once they were accepted by you, they could operate inside the Schloss Adler with complete security and safety.'

'And?'

'Well, don't you see?' It was Smith's turn to be impatient. 'Rolland knew that if General Carnaby—' he broke off and scowled across the room at Carnaby-Jones — 'or that impostor masquerading as General Carnaby were taken here, his opposite number in the German Army would be sent to interrogate him.' Smith smiled. 'Even in Britain they are aware that the prophet must go to the mountain, not the mountain to the prophet: the Army calls upon the Gestapo, not vice versa.'

'Go on, go on!'

'The Wehrmacht Chief of Staff, Reichsmarschall Julius Rosemeyer, would have been just as priceless to the Allies as General Carnaby to us.'

'The Reichsmarschall!' Kramer spoke in a shocked whisper, his eyes straying across the room to Rosemeyer. 'Kidnap!'

'Your precious trusted agents there,' Smith said savagely. 'And they would have got away with it.'

'My God! God in heaven! It's – it's diabolical!'

'Isn't it?' Smith said. 'Isn't it just?'

Kramer left him abruptly, crossed the room to Rosemeyer and sat down in the chair beside him. For perhaps two minutes they talked together in low tones, occasionally glancing in Smith's direction. Kramer it was, Smith could see, who did most of the talking. Rosemeyer who did all of the reacting. Kramer, Smith reflected, must be putting it across rather well: a printed diagram could have been no clearer than the successive expressions of curiosity, puzzlement, astonishment and, finally, shocked realization that reflected on Rosemeyer's face. After some seconds' silence, both men rose to their feet and walked across to where Smith stood. The Reichsmarschall, Smith saw, was a little paler than normal, and when he spoke it required neither a sensitive ear nor imagination to detect a slight tremor in his voice.

He said: 'This is an incredible story, Captain Smith, incredible. But inevitable. It must be. The only explanation that can cover all the facts, put all the pieces of the jig-saw together.' He attempted a smile. 'To change the metaphor, I must say that it comes as a considerable shock to find that one is the missing key in a baffling code. I am eternally in your debt, Captain Smith.'

'Germany is eternally in your debt,' Kramer said. 'You have done her a great service. We shall not forget this. I am sure the Führer will personally wish to honour you with some mark of his esteem.'

'You are too kind, gentlemen,' Smith murmured. 'To do my duty is reward enough.' He smiled faintly. 'Perhaps our Führer will give me two or three weeks' leave – the way I feel tonight my nerves aren't what they were. But if you gentlemen will excuse me – my present task is not yet completed.'

He moved away and walked slowly up and down, brandy glass in hand, behind the three men bent over the table. From time to time he glanced at one of the note-books and smiled in weary cynicism, neither the smile nor the significance of the smile going unremarked by anyone in the room except the three writing men. He stopped behind Thomas, shook his head in disbelief and said, 'My God!'

'Let's finish it now!' Rosemeyer demanded impatiently.

'If you please, Reichsmarschall, let us play this charade out to the bitter end.'

'You have your reasons?'

'I most certainly have.'

Briskly, but not hurriedly, von Brauchitsch walked away from Mary's room, his footfalls echoing crisply on the stone-flagged corridor. Once round the corner of the corridor he broke into a run.

He reached the courtyard and ran across to the helicopter. There was no one there. Quickly he ran up a few steps and peered through the Perspex cupola of the cockpit. He reached ground again and hailed the nearest guard, who came stumbling across, a leashed Dobermann trailing behind him.

'Quickly,' von Brauchitsch snapped. 'Have you seen the pilot?'

'No, Herr Major,' the guard answered nervously. He was an elderly man, long past front-line service and held the Gestapo in great fear. 'Not for a long time.'

'What do you mean by a long time?' von Brauchitsch demanded.

'I don't know. That's to say,' the guard added hastily, 'half an hour. More. Three-quarters, I would say, Herr Major.'

'Damnation,' von Brauchitsch swore. 'So long. Tell me, when the pilot is carrying out repairs is there a place near here he uses as a work-shop?'

'Yes, sir.' The guard was eager to oblige with some positive information. 'That door there, sir. The old grain store.'

'Is he in there now?'

'I don't know, Herr Major.'

'You should know,' von Brauchitsch said coldly. 'It's your job to keep your eyes open. Well, just don't stand there, oaf! Go and find out!'

The elderly guard trotted away while von Brauchitsch, shaking his head angrily over his impatience with the old soldier, crossed the courtyard and questioned the guards at the gate, three tough, competent, young storm-troopers who, unlike the patrol guard, could be guaranteed not to miss anything. He received the same negative answer there.

He strode back towards the helicopter and intercepted the elderly guard running from the old grain store.

'There's nobody there, Herr Major.' He was slightly out of breath and highly apprehensive at being the bearer of what might be ill news. 'It's empty.'

'It would be,' von Brauchitsch nodded. He patted the old shoulder and smiled. 'No fault of yours, my friend. You keep a good watch.'

Unhurriedly, almost, now, he made for the main entrance door, pulling out a set of master keys as he went. He struck oil with the first door he opened. The pilot lay there, still unconscious, the smashed distributor cap lay beside him, the pair of overalls lying on top of him a mute but entirely sufficient explanation of the way in which the distributor cap had been removed without detection. Von Brauchitsch took a torch from a long rack on the wall, cut the pilot's bonds, freed his gag and left him lying there with the door wide open. The passage outside was a heavily travelled one, and someone was bound to be along soon.

Von Brauchitsch ran up the stairs to the passage leading to the bedrooms, slowed down, walked easily, casually past Mary's bedroom and stopped at the fifth door beyond that. He used his master keys and passed inside, switching on the light as he went in. He crossed the room, lifted the lower sash window and nodded when he saw that nearly all the snow on the sill had been brushed or rubbed away. He leaned farther out, switched on his torch and flashed the beam downwards. The roof of the header station was fifty feet directly below and the markings and footprints in the snow told their own unmistakable story.

Von Brauchitsch straightened, looked at the odd position of the iron bedstead against the wardrobe door and tugged the bed away. He watched the wardrobe door burst open and the bound and gagged figure inside roll to the floor without as much as hoisting an eyebrow. This had been entirely predictable. From the depths of the bound man's groans it was obvious that he was coming round. Von Brauchitsch cut him free, removed his gag and left. There were more urgent matters demanding his attention than holding the hands of young Oberleutnants as they held their heads and groaned their way back to consciousness.

He stopped outside Mary's room, put his ear to the door and listened. No sound. He put his eye to the keyhole and peered. No light. He knocked. No reply. He used his master keys and passed inside. No Mary.

'Well, well, well,' von Brauchitsch murmured. 'Very interesting indeed.'

'Finished?' Smith asked.

Thomas nodded. Christiansen and Carraciola glowered. But all three were sitting back and it was obvious that all three were, in fact, finished. Smith walked along behind them, reaching over their shoulders for the notebooks. He took them across the room and laid them on the little table by Kramer's chair.

'The moment of truth,' Smith said quietly. 'One book should be enough.'

Kramer, reluctantly almost, picked up the top book and began to read. Slowly he began to leaf his way through the pages. Smith drained his glass and sauntered unconcernedly across the room to the decanter on the sideboard. He poured some brandy, carefully recapped the bottle, walked a few aimless steps and halted. He was within two feet of the guard with the carbine.

He sipped his brandy and said to Kramer: 'Enough?'

Kramer nodded.

'Then compare it with my original.'

Kramer nodded. 'As you say, the moment of truth.'

He picked up the note-book, slid off the rubber band and opened the cover. The first page was blank. So was the next. And the next . . . Frowning, baffled, Kramer lifted his eyes to look across the room to Smith.

Smith's brandy glass was falling to the ground as Smith himself, with a whiplash violent movement of his body brought the side of his right hand chopping down on the guard's neck. The guard toppled as if a bridge had fallen on him. Glasses on the sideboard tinkled in the vibration of his fall.

Kramer's moment of utter incomprehension vanished. The bitter chagrin of total understanding flooded his face. His hand stretched out towards the alarm button.

'Uh-uh! Not the buzzer, Mac!' The blow that had struck down the guard had held no more whiplash than the biting urgency in Schaffer's voice. He was stretched his length on the floor where he'd dived to retrieve the Schmeisser now trained, rock steady, on Kramer's heart. For the second time that night, Kramer's hand withdrew from the alarm button.

Smith picked up the guard's carbine, walked across the room and changed it for his silenced Luger. Schaffer, his gun still trained on Kramer, picked himself up from the floor and glared at Smith.

'A second-rate punk,' he said indignantly. 'A simple-minded American. That's what you said. Don't know what goddamned day of the week it is, do I?'

'All I could think of on the spur of the moment,' Smith said apologetically.

'That makes it even worse,' Schaffer complained. 'And did you have to clobber me so goddamned realistically?'

'Local colour. What are you complaining about? It worked.' He walked across to Kramer's table, picked up the three notebooks and buttoned them securely inside his tunic. He said to Schaffer: 'Between them, they shouldn't have missed anything ... Well, time to be gone. Ready, Mr Jones?'

'And hurry about it,' Schaffer added. 'We have a street-car to catch. Well, anyhow, a cable-car.'

'It's a chicken farm in the boondocks for me.' Jones looked completely dazed and he sounded exactly the same way. 'Acting? My God, I don't know anything about it.'

'This is all you want?' Kramer was completely under control again, calm, quiet, the total professional. 'Those books? Just those books?'

'Well, just about. Lots of nice names and addresses. A bedtime story for MI6.'

'I see.' Kramer nodded his understanding. 'Then those men are, of course, what they claim to be?'

'They've been under suspicion for weeks. Classified information of an invaluable nature was going out and false – and totally valueless – information was coming in. It took two months' work to pin-point the leakages and channels of false information to one or more of the departments controlled by those men. But we knew we could never prove it on them – we weren't even sure if there was more than one traitor and had no idea who that one might be – and, in any event, proving it without finding out their contacts at home and abroad would have been useless. So we – um – thought this one up.'

'You mean, *you* thought it up, Captain Smith,' Rosemeyer said.

'What does it matter?' Smith said indifferently.

'True. It doesn't. But something else does.' Rosemeyer smiled faintly. 'When Colonel Kramer asked you if the books were all you wanted, you said "just about". Indicating that there was possibly something else. It is your hope to kill two birds with one stone, to invite me to accompany you?'

'If you can believe that, Reichsmarschall Rosemeyer,' Smith said unkindly, 'it's time you handed your baton over to someone else. I have no intention of binding you hand and foot and carrying you over the Alps on my shoulder. The only way I could take you is at the point of a gun and I very much fear that you are a man of honour, a man to whom the safety of his skin comes a very long way behind his loyalty to his country. If I pointed this gun at you and said to get up and come with us or be gunned down, nobody in this room doubts that you'd just keep on sitting. So we must part.'

'You are as complimentary as you are logical.' Rosemeyer smiled, a little, bitter smile. 'I wish the logic had struck me as forcibly when we were discussing this very subject a few minutes ago.'

'It is perhaps as well it didn't,' Smith admitted.

'But – but Colonel Wilner?' Kramer said. 'Field-Marshal Kesselring's Chief of Intelligence. Surely he's not—'

'Rest easy. Willi-Willi is not on our pay-roll. What he said he believed to be perfectly true. He believes me to be the top double-agent in Italy. I've been feeding him useless, false and out-of-date information for almost two years. Tell him so, will you?'

'Kind of treble agent, see?' Schaffer said in a patient explaining tone. 'That's one better than double.'

'Heidelberg?' Kramer asked.

'Two years at the University. Courtesy of the – um – Foreign Office.'

Kramer shook his head. 'I still don't understand—'

'Sorry. We're going.'

'In fact, we're off,' Schaffer said. 'Read all about it in the post-war memoirs of Pimpernel Schaffer—'

He broke off as the door opened wide. Mary stood framed in the doorway and the Mauser was very steady in her hand. She let it fall to her side with a sigh of relief.

'Took your time about getting here, didn't you?' Smith said severely. 'We were beginning to get a little worried about you.'

'I'm sorry. I just couldn't get away. Von Brauchitsch—'

'No odds, young lady.' Schaffer made a grandiose gesture with his right arm. 'Schaffer was here.'

'The new girl who arrived tonight!' Kramer whispered. He looked slightly dazed. 'The cousin of that girl from the—'

'None else,' Smith said. 'She's the one who has been helping me to keep Willi-Willi happy for a long time past. *And* she's the one who opened the door for us tonight.'

'Boss,' Schaffer said unhappily. 'Far be it for me to rush you—'

'Coming now.' Smith smiled at Rosemeyer. 'You were right, the books weren't all I wanted. You were right, I did want company. But unlike you, Reichsmarschall, those I want have a high regard for their own skins and are entirely without honour. And so they will come.' His gun waved in the direction of Carraciola, Thomas and Christiansen. 'On your feet, you three. You're coming with us.'

'Coming with us?' Schaffer said incredulously. 'To England?'

'To stand trial for treason. It's no part of my duties to act as public executioner ... God alone knows how many hundreds and thousands of lives they've cost already. Not to mention Torrance-Smythe and Sergeant Harrod.' He looked at Carraciola, and his eyes were very cold. 'I'll never know, but I think you were the brains. It was you who killed Harrod back up there on the mountain. If you could have got that radio code-book you could have cracked our network in South Germany. That would have been something, our network here has never been penetrated. The radio code-book was a trap that didn't spring ... And you got old Smithy. You left the pub a couple of minutes after I did tonight and he followed you. But he couldn't cope with a man—'

'Drop those guns.' Von Brauchitsch's voice was quiet and cold and compelling. No one had heard or seen the stealthy opening of the door. He stood just inside, about four feet from Mary and he had a small-calibre automatic in his right hand. Smith whirled round, his Luger lining up on the doorway, hesitated a fatal fraction of a second because Mary was almost directly in line with von Brauchitsch. Von Brauchitsch, his earlier gallantry of the evening yielding to a coldly professional assessment of the situation, had no such inhibitions. There was a sharp flat crack, the bullet passed through Mary's sleeve just above the elbow and Smith exclaimed in pain as he clutched his bleeding hand and heard his flying Luger strike against some unidentified furniture. Mary tried to turn round but von Brauchitsch was too quick and too strong. He jumped forward, hooked his arm round her and caught her wrist with the gun and thrust his own over her shoulder. She tried to struggle free. Von Brauchitsch squeezed her wrist, she cried out in pain, her hand opened and her gun fell to the floor. Von Brauchitsch seemed to notice none of this, his unwinking right eye, the only vulnerable part of him that could be seen behind Mary's gun, was levelled along the barrel of his automatic.

Schaffer dropped his gun.

'You shouldn't have tried it,' von Brauchitsch said to Smith. 'An extremely silly thing to do . . . In your circumstances, I'd have done exactly the same silly thing.' He looked at Kramer. 'Sorry for the delay, Herr Colonel. But I *thought* the young lady was very anxious and restive. *And* she knows precious little about her native Düsseldorf. *And* she doesn't know enough not to let people hold her hand when she's telling lies – as she does most of the time.' He released the girl and half turned her round, smiling down at her. 'A delightful hand, my dear – but what a fascinating variation of pulse rates.'

'I don't know what you're talking about and I don't care.' Kramer gave vent to a long luxurious sigh and drooped with relief. 'Well *done*, my boy, well done. My God! Another minute—' He heaved himself to his feet, crossed over to Schaffer, prudently keeping clear of von Brauchitsch's line of fire, searched him for hidden weapons, found none, did the same to Smith with the same results, looked at Mary and hesitated. 'Well, I don't see how she very well can be, but . . . I wonder. Anne-Marie?'

'Certainly, Herr Colonel. It will be a pleasure. We've met before and she knows my methods. Don't you my dear?' With a smile as nearly wolf-like as any beautiful Aryan could give, Anne-Marie walked across to Mary and struck her viciously across the face. Mary cried in pain, staggered back against the wall and crouched there, eyes too wide in a pale face, palms pressed behind her for support from the wall, a trickle of blood coming from the corner of her mouth. 'Well?' Anne-Marie demanded. 'Have you a gun.'

'Anne-Marie!' There was protest and aversion in Kramer's face. 'Must you—'

'I know how to deal with cheap little spies like her!' She turned to Mary and said: 'I'm afraid they don't like watching how I get results. In there!'

She caught Mary by the hair, pulled her to the side door, opened it and pushed her violently inside. The sound of her body crashing to the floor and another gasp of pain came together. Anne-Marie closed the door behind them.

For the next ten seconds or so there could be clearly heard the sound of blows and muffled cries of pain. Von Brauchitsch waved Smith and Schaffer back with his gun, advanced, hitched a seat on the edge of one of the big arm-chairs, winced as he listened to the sound of the struggle and said to Kramer dryly: 'I somehow think the young lady would have preferred me to search her. There's a limit to the value of false modesty.'

'I'm afraid Anne-Marie sometimes lets her enthusiasm carry her away,' Kramer conceded. His mouth was wrinkled in distaste.

'Sometimes?' Von Brauchitsch winced again as more sounds filtered through the door, the crash of a body against a wall, a shriek of pain, low sobbing moans, then silence. 'Always. When the other girl is as young and beautiful as herself.'

'It's over now,' Kramer sighed. 'It's all over now.' He looked at Smith and Schaffer. 'We'll fix that hand first, then – well, one thing about the Schloss Adler, there is no shortage of dungeons.' He broke off, the fractional widening of his eyes matching a similar slumping of his shoulders, and he said carefully to von Brauchitsch: 'You are far too good a man to lose, Captain. It would seem that we were wasting our sympathy on the wrong person. There's a gun four feet from you pointing at the middle of your back.'

Von Brauchitsch, his gun-hand resting helplessly on his thigh, turned slowly round and looked over his shoulder. There was indeed a gun pointing at the middle of his back, a Lilliput .21 automatic, and the hand that held it was disconcertingly steady, the dark eyes cool and very watchful. Apart from the small trickle of blood from her cut lip and rather dishevelled hair, Mary looked singularly little the worse for wear.

'It's every parent's duty,' Schaffer said pontifically, 'to encourage his daughter to take up Judo.' He took the gun from von Brauchitsch's unresisting hand, retrieved his own Schmeisser, walked across to the main door and locked it. 'Far too many folk coming in here without knocking.' On his way back he looked through the open door of the room, whistled, grinned and said to Mary: 'It's a good job I have my thoughts set on someone else. I wouldn't like to be married to you if you lost your temper. That's a regular sickbay dispensary in there. Fix the major's hand as best you can. I'll watch them.' He hoisted his Schmeisser and smiled almost blissfully: 'Oh, brother, how I'll watch them.'

And he watched them. While Mary attended to Smith's injured hand in the small room where Anne-Marie had so lately met her Waterloo, Schaffer herded his six charges into one of the massive couches, took up position by the mantelpiece, poured himself some brandy, sipped it delicately and gave the prisoners an encouraging smile from time to time. There were no answering smiles. For all Schaffer's nonchalance and light-hearted banter there was about him not only a coldly discouraging competence with the weapon in his hand but also the unmistakable air of one who would, when the need arose and without a second's hesitation, squeeze the trigger and keep on squeezing it. Being at the wrong end of a Schmeisser machine-pistol does not make for an easy cordiality in relationships.

Smith and Mary emerged from the side room, the latter carrying a cloth-covered tray. Smith was pale and had his right hand heavily bandaged. Schaffer looked at the hand then lifted an enquiring eyebrow to Mary.

'Not so good.' She looked a little pale herself. 'Forefinger and thumb are both smashed. I've patched it as best I can but I'm afraid it's a job for a surgeon.'

'If I can survive Mary's first aid,' Smith said philosophically, 'I can survive anything. We have a more immediate little problem here.' He tapped his tunic. 'Those names and addresses here. Might be an hour or two before we get them through to England and then another hour or two before those men can be rounded up.' He looked at the men seated on the couch. '*You* could get through to them in a lot less than that and warn them. So we have to ensure your silence for a few hours.'

'We could ensure it for ever, boss,' Schaffer said carelessly.

'That won't be necessary. As you said yourself, it's a regular little dispensary in there.' He removed the tray cloth to show bottles and hypodermic syringes. He held up a bottle in his left hand. 'Nembutal. You'll hardly feel the prick.'

Kramer stared at him. 'Nembutal? I'll be damned if I do.'

Smith said in a tone of utter conviction: 'You'll be dead if you don't.'

Chapter Nine

Smith halted outside the door marked RADIO RAUM, held up his hand for silence, looked at the three scowling captives and said: 'Don't even *think* of tipping anyone off or raising the alarm. I'm not all that keen on taking you back to England. Lieutenant Schaffer, I think we might immobilize those men a bit more.'

'We might at that,' Schaffer agreed. He went behind each of the three men in turn, ripped open the top buttons on their tunics and pulled the tunics down their backs until their sleeves reached their elbows and said in the same soft voice: 'That'll keep their hands out of trouble for a little.'

'But not their feet. Don't let them come anywhere near you,' Smith said to Mary. 'They've nothing to lose. Right, Lieutenant, when you're ready.'

'Ready now.' Carefully, silently, Schaffer eased open the door of the radio room. It was a large, well-lit, but very bleak room, the two main items of furniture being a massive table by the window on the far wall and, on the table, an almost equally massive transceiver in gleaming metal: apart from two chairs and a filing cabinet the room held nothing else, not even as much as a carpet to cover the floorboards.

Perhaps it was the lack of a carpet that betrayed them. For the first half of Schaffer's stealthy advance across the room the operator, his back to them, sat smoking a cigarette in idle unconcern, listening to soft Austrian *Schrammel* music coming in over his big machine: suddenly, alerted by the faintest whisper of sound from a creaking floorboard or just by some sixth sense, he whirled round and jumped to his feet. And he thought as quickly as he moved. Even as he raised his arms high in apparently eager surrender, he appeared to move slightly to his right, shifting the position of his right foot. There came the sudden strident clamour of an alarm bell ringing in the passage outside, Schaffer leapt forward, his Schmeisser swinging, and the operator staggered back against his transceiver then slid unconscious to the floor. But Schaffer was too late. The bell rang and kept on ringing.

'That's all I need!' Smith swore bitterly. 'That's all I bloody well need.' He ran through the radio room door out into the passage, located the glass-cased alarm bell some feet away and struck it viciously with the butt of his Schmeisser. The shattered glass tinkled to the floor and the clangour abruptly ceased.

'Inside!' Smith gestured to the open doorway of the radio room. 'All of you. Quickly.' He ushered them all inside, looked around, saw a side door leading off to the right and said to Mary: 'Quickly. What's in there? Schaffer!'

'Horatio hold the bridge,' Schaffer murmured. He moved across and took up position at the radio room door. 'We could have done without this, boss.'

'We could do without a lot of things in this world,' Smith said wearily. He glanced at Mary. 'Well?'

'Storage rooms for radio spares, looks like.'

'You and Jones take those three in there. If they breathe, kill them.'

Jones looked down at the gun held gingerly in his hand and said: 'I am not a serviceman, sir.'

'I have news for you,' Smith said. 'Neither am I.'

He crossed hurriedly to the transceiver, sat down and studied the confusing array of dials, knobs and switches. For fully twenty seconds he sat there, just looking.

Schaffer said from the doorway: 'Know how to work it, boss?'

'A fine time to ask me,' Smith said. 'We'll soon find out, won't we?' He switched the machine to 'Send', selected the ultra short wave band and lined up his transmitting frequency. He opened another switch and picked up a microphone.

'Broadsword calling Danny Boy,' he said. 'Broadsword calling Danny Boy. Can you hear me? Can you hear me?'

Nobody heard him or gave indication of hearing him. Smith altered the transmitting frequency fractionally and tried again. And again. And again. After the sixth or seventh repetition, Smith started as a crash of machine-pistol fire came from the doorway. He twisted round. Schaffer was stretched full length on the floor, smoke wisping from the barrel of his Schmeisser.

'We got callers, boss,' Schaffer said apologetically. 'Don't think I got any but I sure as hell started their adrenalin moving around.'

'Broadsword calling Danny Boy,' Smith said urgently, insistently. 'Broadsword calling Danny Boy. For God's sake, why don't they answer?'

'They can't come round the corner of the passage without being sawn in half.' Schaffer spoke comfortably from his uncomfortable horizontal position on the floor. 'I can hold them off to Christmas. So what's the hurry?'

'Broadsword calling Danny Boy. Broadsword calling Danny Boy. How long do you think it's going to be before someone cuts the electricity?'

'For God's sake, Danny Boy,' Schaffer implored. 'Why don't you answer? Why don't you answer?'

'Danny Boy calling Broadsword.' The voice on the radio was calm and loud and clear, so free from interference that it might have come from next door. 'Danny Boy—'

'One hour, Danny Boy,' Smith interrupted. 'One hour. Understood? Over.'

'Understood. You have it, Broadsword?' The voice was unmistakably that of Admiral Rolland's. 'Over.'

'I have it,' Smith said. 'I have it all.'

'All sins are forgiven. Mother Machree coming to meet you. Leaving now.'

There came another staccato crash of sound as Schaffer loosed off another burst from his Schmeisser. Admiral Rolland's voice on the radio said: 'What was that?'

'Static,' Smith said. He didn't bother to switch off. He rose, took three paces back and fired a two-second burst from his machine-pistol, his face twisting in pain as the recoil slammed into his shattered hand. No one would ever use that particular radio again. He glanced briefly at Schaffer, but only briefly: the American's face, though thoughtful, was calm and unworried: there were those who might require helpful words, encouragement and reassurance, but Schaffer was not one of them. Smith moved swiftly across to the window and lifted the lower sash with his left hand.

The moon was almost obscured behind some darkly drifting cloud. A thin weak light filtered down into the half-seen obscurity of the valley below. Once again the snow was beginning to fall, gently. The air was taut, brittle, in the intensity of its coldness, an arctic chill that bit to the bone. The icy wind that gusted through the room could have come off the polar ice-cap.

They were on the east side of the castle, Smith realized, the side remote from the cable-car header station. The base of the volcanic plug was shrouded in a gloom so deep that it was impossible to be sure whether or not the guards and Dobermanns were patrolling down there: and, for the purposes of present survival, it didn't really matter. Smith withdrew from the window, pulled the nylon from the kit-bag, tied one end securely to the metal leg of the radio table, threw the remainder of the rope out into the night then, with his left hand, thoroughly scuffed and rubbed away the frozen encrusted snow on both the window-sill and for two or three feet beneath it: it would, he thought, have to be a hypercritical eye that didn't immediately register the impression that there had been fairly heavy and recent traffic over the sill. He wondered, vaguely, whether the rope reached as far as the ground and dismissed the thought as soon as it had occurred to him: again, it didn't really matter.

He crossed the room to where Schaffer lay spread-eagled in the doorway. The key was in the lock on the inside of the door and the lock, he observed with satisfaction, was on the same massive scale as everything else in the Schloss Adler. He said to Schaffer: 'Time to close the door.'

'Let's wait till they show face again then discourage them some more,' Schaffer suggested. 'It's been a couple of minutes since the last lad peeked his head round the corner there. Another peek, another salvo from Schaffer and it might give us another couple of minutes' grace – enough time to make it feasible for us to have shinned down that little rope there and make our getaway.'

'I should have thought of that.' An icy snow-laden gust of wind blew across the room, from open window through open door, and Smith shivered. 'My God, it's bitter!'

'Loss of blood,' Schaffer said briefly, then added, unsympathetically: 'And all that brandy you guzzled back there. When it comes to opening pores—'

He broke off and lay very still, lowering his head a fraction to sight along the barrel of his Schmeisser. He said softly: 'Give me your torch, boss.'

'What is it?' Smith whispered. He handed Schaffer the torch.

'Discretion,' Schaffer murmured. He switched on the torch and placed it on the floor, pushing it as far away from himself as he could. 'I reckon if I were in their place I'd be discreet, too. There's a stick poking round the corner of the passage and the stick has a mirror tied to it. Only, they haven't got it angled right.'

Smith peered cautiously round the door jamb, just in time to see stick and suspended mirror being withdrawn from sight, presumably to make adjustments. A few seconds later and the stick appeared again, this time with the mirror angled at more or less forty-five degrees. Mirror and stick disintegrated under the flatly staccato hammering of Schaffer's machine-pistol. Schaffer stood up, took careful aim at the single overhead light illuminating the passage and fired one shot. Now the sole light in the passage came from the torch on the floor, the light from which would not only effectively conceal from the Germans at the far end of the passage what was going on at the radio room door but, indeed, make it very difficult to decide whether or not the door itself was open or shut.

Smith and Schaffer moved back into the radio room, soundlessly closed the door behind them and as soundlessly turned the key in the lock. Schaffer used the leverage of his Schmeisser to bend the key so that it remained firmly jammed in the wards of the lock.

They waited. At least two minutes passed, then they heard the sound of excited voices at the far end of the passage followed almost at once by the sound of heavy boots pounding down the passage. They moved away from the door, passed inside the radio spares room, leaving just a sufficient crack in the doorway to allow a faint backwash of light to filter through. Smith said softly: 'Mary, you and Mr Jones for Thomas there. A gun in each temple.' He took Christiansen for himself, forced him to kneel and ground his gun into the back of his neck. Schaffer backed Carraciola against a wall, the muzzle of his Schmeisser pressed hard against his teeth. At the other end of the machine-pistol Schaffer smiled pleasantly, his teeth a pale gleam in the near darkness. The stillness inside the little room was complete.

The half-dozen Germans outside the radio room door bore no resemblance to the elderly guard von Brauchitsch had interrogated in the courtyard. They were elite soldiers of the Alpenkorps, ruthless men who had been ruthlessly trained. No one made any move to approach the door handle or lock: the machine-like efficiency with which they broached that door without risk to themselves was clearly the result of a well-drilled procedure for handling situations of precisely this nature.

At a gesture from the Oberleutnant in charge, a soldier stepped forward and with two diagonal sweeps emptied the magazine of his machine-pistol through the door. A second used his machine-pistol to stitch a neat circle in the wood, reversed his gun and knocked in the wooden circle with the butt. A third armed two grenades and lobbed them accurately through the hole provided while a fourth shot away the lock. The soldiers pressed back on each side of the door. The two flat cracks of the exploding grenades came almost simultaneously and smoke came pouring through the circular hole in the door.

The door was kicked open and the men rushed inside. There was no longer any need to take precautions – any men who had been in the same confined space as those two exploding grenades would be dead men now. For a moment there was confusion and hesitation until the blue acrid smoke was partially cleared away by the powerful cross-draught then the Oberleutnant, locating the source of this draught with the aid of a small hand-torch, ran across to the open window, checked at the sight of the rope disappearing over the sill, leaned out the window, rubbed his now-streaming eyes and peered downwards along the beam of his torch. The beam reached perhaps half-way down the side of the volcanic plug. There was nothing to be seen. He caught the rope in his free hand and jerked it savagely: it was as nearly weightless as made no difference. For a moment he focused his torch on the disturbed snow on the window-ledge then swung back into the room.

'*Gott in Himmel!*' he shouted. 'They've got away. They're down already! Quickly, the nearest phone!'

'Well, now.' Schaffer listened to the fading sound of running footsteps, removed the muzzle of his Schmeisser from Carraciola's teeth and smiled approvingly. 'That was a good boy.' Gun in Carraciola's back, he followed Smith out into the wrecked radio room and said thoughtfully: 'It isn't going to take them too long to find out there are no footprints in the snow down there.'

'It's going to take them even less time to discover that this rope is gone.' Swiftly, ignoring the stabbing pain in his right hand, Smith hauled the nylon in through the window. 'We're going to need it. *And* we're going to need some distractions.'

'I'm distracted enough as it is,' Schaffer said.

'Take four or five plastic explosives, each with different fuse length settings. Chuck them into rooms along the corridor there.'

'Distractions coming up.' Schaffer extracted some plastic explosives from the kit-bag, cut the slow-burning RDX fuses off to varying lengths, crimped on the chemical igniters, said, 'Consider it already done,' and left.

The first three rooms he came to were locked and he wasted neither time nor the precious ammunition of his silenced Luger in trying to open them. But each of the next five rooms was unlocked. In the first three, all bedrooms, he placed charges in a Dresden fruit bowl, under an officer's cap and under a pillow: in the fourth room, a bathroom, he placed it behind a WC and in the fifth, a store-room, high up on a shelf beside some highly inflammable-looking cardboard cartons.

Smith, meanwhile, had ushered the others from the still smoke-filled, eye-watering, throat-irritating atmosphere of the radio room into the comparatively purer air of the passageway beyond, and was waiting the return of Schaffer when his face became suddenly thoughtful at the sight of some fire-fighting gear – a big CO_2 extinguisher, buckets of sand and a fireman's axe – on a low platform by the passage wall.

'You *are* slipping, Major Smith.' Mary's eyes were red-rimmed and her tear-streaked face white as paper, but she could still smile at him. 'Distractions, you said. I've had the same thought myself, and I'm only me.'

Smith gave her a half-smile, the way his hand hurt he felt he couldn't afford the other half, and tried the handle of a door beside the low platform, a door lettered AKTEN RAUM – Records Office. Such a door, inevitably, was locked. He took the Luger in his left hand, placed it against the lock, squeezed the trigger and went inside.

It certainly looked like a Records Office. The room was heavily shelved and piled ceiling-high with files and papers. Smith crossed to the window, opened it wide to increase the draught then scattered large piles of paper on the floor and put a match to them. The paper flared up at once, the flames feet high within seconds.

'Kinda forgot this, didn't you?' Schaffer had returned and was bearing with him the large CO_2 cylinder. He crossed to the window. 'Gardyloo or mind your heads or whatever the saying is.'

The cylinder disappeared through the open window. The room was already so furiously ablaze that Schaffer had difficulty in finding his way back to the door again. As he stumbled out, his clothes and hair singed and face smoke-blackened, a deep-toned bell far down in the depths of the Schloss Adler began to ring with a strident urgency. 'For God's sake, what next,' Schaffer said in despair. 'The fire brigade?'

'Just about,' Smith said bitterly. 'Damn it, why couldn't I have checked first? Now they know where we are.'

'A heat-sensing device linked to an indicator?'

'What else? Come on.'

They ran along the central passage-way, driving the prisoners in front of them, dropped down a central flight of stairs and were making for the next when they heard the shouting of voices and the clattering of feet on treads as soldiers came running up from the castle courtyard.

'Quickly! In behind there!' Smith pointed to a curtained alcove. 'Hurry up! Oh, God – I've forgotten something!' He turned and ran back the way he had come.

'Where the hell has he—' Schaffer broke off as he realized the approaching men were almost upon them, whirled and jabbed the nearest prisoner painfully with the muzzle of his Schmeisser. 'In that alcove. Fast,' In the dim light behind the curtains he changed his machine-pistol for the silenced Luger. 'Don't even think of touching those curtains. With the racket that bell's making, they won't even hear you die.'

Nobody touched the curtains. Jack-booted men, gasping heavily for breath, passed by within feet of them. They clattered furiously up the next flight of stairs, the one Smith and the others had just descended, and then the footsteps stopped abruptly. From the next shouted words it was obvious that they had just caught sight of the fire and had abruptly and for the first time realized the magnitude of the task they had to cope with.

'Emergency! Sergeant, get on that phone!' It was the voice of the Oberleutnant who had led the break-in to the radio room. 'Fire detail at the double! Hoses, more CO_2 cylinders. Where in God's name is Colonel Kramer. Corporal! Find Colonel Kramer at once.'

The corporal didn't answer, the sound of jutting heels striking the treads as he raced down the stairs was answer enough. He ran by the alcove and ran down the next flight of stairs until the sound of his footfalls was lost in the metallic clamour of the alarm bell. Schaffer risked a peep through a crack in the curtains just as Smith came running up on tiptoe.

'Where the hell have you been?' Schaffer's voice was low and fierce.

'Come on, come on! Out of it!' Smith said urgently. 'No, Jones, *not* down that flight of stairs, you want to meet a whole regiment of Alpenkorps coming up it? Along the passage to the west wing. We'll use the side stairs. For God's sake, hurry. This place will be like Piccadilly Circus in a matter of seconds.'

Schaffer pounded along the passage beside Smith and when he spoke again the anxiety-born fierceness of tone had a certain plaintive equality to it. 'Well, where the bloody hell have you been?'

'The man we left tied up in the room beside the telephone exchange. The Records Office is directly above. I just remembered. I cut him free and dragged him out to the passage. He'd have burnt to death.'

'You did that, did you?' Schaffer said wonderingly. 'You do think of the most goddamned unimportant things, don't you?'

'It's a point of view. Our friend lying in the passage back there wouldn't share your sentiments. Right, down those stairs and straight ahead. Mary, you know the door.'

Mary knew the door. Fifteen paces from the foot of the stairs she stopped. Smith spared a glance through the passage window on his left. Already smoke and flame were showing through the windows and embrasures in the north-east tower of the castle. In the courtyard below, dozens of soldiers were running around, most of them without what appeared to be any great sense of purpose or direction. One man there wasn't running. He was the overalled helicopter pilot and he was standing very still indeed, bent low over the engine. As Smith watched he slowly straightened, lifted his right arm and shook his fist in the direction of the burning tower.

Smith turned away and said to Mary: 'Sure this is the room? Two stories below the window we came in?'

Mary nodded. 'No question. This is it.'

Smith tried the door handle: the room was locked. The time for skeleton keys and such-like finesse was gone: he placed the barrel of his Luger against the lock.

The corporal despatched by his Oberleutnant to locate Colonel Kramer was faced by the same problem when he turned the handle of the gold drawing-room, for when Smith and the others had left there for the last time Schaffer had locked the door and thoughtfully thrown the key out a convenient passage window. The corporal first of all knocked respectfully. No reply. He knocked loudly, with the same lack of result. He depressed the handle and used his shoulder and all he did was to hurt his shoulder. He battered at the lock area with the butt of his Schmeisser but the carpenters who had built the Schloss Adler doors had known what they were about. He hesitated, then brought his machine-pistol right way round and fired a burst through the lock, praying to heaven that Colonel Kramer wasn't sleeping in a chair in direct line with the keyhole.

Colonel Kramer was sleeping all right, but nowhere near the direct line of the keyhole. He was stretched out on the gold carpet with a considerately-placed pillow under his head. The corporal advanced slowly into the drawing-room, his eyebrows reaching for his hair and his face almost falling apart in shocked disbelief. Reichsmarschall Rosemeyer was stretched out beside the Colonel. Von Brauchitsch and a sergeant were sprawled in arm-chairs, heads lolling on their shoulders, while Anne-Marie – a very dishevelled and somewhat bruised-looking Anne-Marie – was stretched out on one of the big gold-lamé couches.

Like a man in a daze, still totally uncomprehending, the corporal approached Kramer, knelt by his side and then shook him by the shoulder, with gentle respect at first and then with increasing vigour. After some time it was borne in upon him that he could shake the Colonel's shoulder all night and that would be all he would have for it.

And then, illogically and for the first time, he noticed that all the men were without jackets, and that everyone, including Anne-Marie, had their left sleeves rolled up to the elbow. He looked slowly around the drawing-room and went very still as his gaze rested on a tray with bottles, beakers and hypodermic syringes. Slowly, on the corporal's face, shocked incomprehension was replaced by an equally shocked understanding. He took off through the doorway like the favourite in the Olympics 100 metres final.

Schaffer tied the nylon rope round the head of the iron bedstead, tested the security of the knot, lifted the lower sash window, pushed the rope through and peered unhappily down the valley. At the far end of the village a pulsating red glow marked the smouldering embers of what had once been the railway station. The lights of the village itself twinkled clearly. Immediately below and to the right of where he stood could be seen four patrolling guards with as many dogs – Kramer hadn't spoken idly when he'd said the outside guards had been doubled – and the ease with which he could spot them Schaffer found all too readily understandable when he twisted his head and stared skywards through the thinly driving snow. The moon had just emerged from behind a black bar of cloud and was sailing across a discouragingly large stretch of empty sky. Even the stars could be seen.

'I'm going to feel a mite conspicuous out there, boss,' Schaffer said complainingly. 'And there's a wolf-pack loose down below there.'

'Wouldn't matter if they had a battery of searchlights trained on this window,' Smith said curtly. 'Not now. We've no option. Quickly!'

Schaffer nodded dolefully, eased himself through the window, grasped the rope and halted momentarily as a muffled explosion came from the eastern wing of the castle.

'Number one,' Schaffer said with satisfaction. 'Bang goes a bowl of Dresden fruit – or a Dresden bowl of fruit. I do hope,' he added anxiously, 'that there's nobody using the toilet next door to where that bang just went off.'

Smith opened his mouth to make impatient comment but Schaffer was already gone. Fifteen feet only and he was standing on the roof of the header station. Smith eased himself awkwardly over the sill, wrapped the rope round his right forearm, took the strain with his left hand and looked at Mary. She gave him an encouraging smile, but there was nothing encouraging about her expression when she transferred her gaze back to the three men who were lined up facing a wall, their hands clasped behind their necks.

Carnaby-Jones was also covering them but, in his case, he held the gun as if it might turn and bite him at any moment.

Smith joined Schaffer on the roof of the header station. Both men crouched low to minimize the chances of being spotted from below. For the first ten feet out from the wall the roof was quite flat then dropped away sharply at an angle of thirty degrees. Smith thoughtfully regarded this steep slope and said: 'We don't want a repeat performance of what happened to us last time we were out there. We could do with a good piton to hammer into the castle wall here. Or the roof. Some sort of belay for our rope.'

'Pitons we don't need. Look at this.' With his bare hands Schaffer scraped at the snow-encrusted roof of the header station to reveal a fine wire netting and, below that, iron bars covering a pane of plate glass perhaps two feet by one. 'Skylights, I believe they're called. Those bars look pretty firm to me.'

He laid both hands on one of the bars and tugged firmly. It remained secure. Smith laid his left hand on the same bar and they pulled together. It still remained secure. Schaffer grinned in satisfaction, passed the rope round the bar and made no mistake about the knot he tied. Smith sat down on the roof and put his hand to the rope. Schaffer caught his wrist and firmly broke Smith's grip.

'No, you don't.' Schaffer lifted Smith's right hand: the thick wrapping of bandages were already sodden, saturated with blood. 'You can win your VC next time out. This time, you'd never make it. This one is on me.' He paused and shook his head in wonder. 'My God, Schaffer, you don't know what you're saying.'

He removed the kit-bag he'd been carrying round his neck, crawled to the break in the roof, gripped the rope and slid smoothly down the sloping surface. As he approached the roof edge he turned round with infinite care until he was pointing head downwards. Slowly, inch by almost imperceptible inch, the rope above him caught securely between his feet, he lowered himself still farther until his head was projecting over the edge of the roof. He peered downwards.

He was, he discovered, directly above one of the cables. Two hundred feet below, but to his left, this time, guards and Dobermanns were floundering uphill through the deep snow at the best speed they could make, heading for the main entrance, to the castle courtyard. The word had gone out, Schaffer realized, and every available man was being pulled in either to fight the fire or to help in the search for the men who had started the fire. Which meant, Schaffer concluded, that some of the garrison must have checked the state of the ground beneath the radio room window and found there nothing but virgin and undisturbed snow. . .

He twisted his head and looked upwards. There was no sign of any guard patrolling the battlements, which was what he would have expected: there was no point in keeping a posted lookout for an enemy without when every indication pointed to the fact that the enemy was still within.

Schaffer eased himself downwards another perilous six inches till head and shoulders were over the edge of the roof. Only two things mattered now: was there a winch attendant or guard inside the header station and, if there were, could he, Schaffer, hold on to the rope with one hand while with the other he wriggled his Luger free and shoot the guard? Schaffer doubted it. His OSS training had been wide-ranging and intensive but no one had ever thought it necessary that they should master the techniques of a high-wire circus acrobat. His mouth very dry and his heart pounding so heavily as to threaten to dislodge his precarious hand- and toe-holds, Schaffer craned his head and looked inside.

There was neither guard nor winch attendant inside: or, if there were any such, he was so well concealed that Schaffer couldn't see him. But logic said that no one would be hiding there for there was no conceivable reason why anyone should be hiding: logic also said that any person who might have been there would, like the patrolling guards below and the sentry on the battlements, have been called inside the castle to help fight fire and enemy. All Schaffer could see was a cable-car, heavy winching machinery and heavy banks of lead-acid batteries: he was soon convinced that that was all that there was to see. No cause for concern.

But what he did see, something that did dismay him considerably, was that there was only one way for him to get into the station. There was no possibility of his sliding down the rope on to the floor of the station for the excellent reason that the roof of the station, in typically Alpine eaves fashion, overhung the floor by at least six feet. The only way in was by dropping down on to the *Luftseilbahn's* heavy steel cable then overhanding himself up inside the station. Schaffer wasted no time in considering whether this was physically possible. It *had* to be possible. There was no other way in.

Carefully and with no little difficulty Schaffer inched himself back up the rope and the slope of the roof until he was about three feet clear of the edge. He eased his foot-grip on the rope and swung round through 180° until he was once more facing up the slope with his legs now dangling over the edge. He looked up. The crouched figure of Smith showed tension in every line although the face was as expressionless as ever. Schaffer lifted one hand, made a circle with thumb and forefinger, then eased himself over the edge until his searching feet found the cable.

He eased himself farther until he was sitting astride the cable, transferred his grip to the cable and swung down until he was suspended by hands and feet and looked up towards the moon. As a view, Schaffer reflected, it was vastly preferable to contemplating that two hundred foot drop down into the valley below. He started to climb.

He almost failed to make it. For every six inches he made up the cable, he slid back five. The cable was covered by a diabolically slippery coating of oil and sheath ice and only by clenching his fists till his forearms ached could he make any kind of progress at all and the fact that the cable stretched up at forty-five degrees made the difficult the well-nigh impossible. Such a means of locomotion would have been suicidal for the virtually one-handed Smith and quite impossible for either Mary or Carnaby-Jones. Once, after he had made about twelve feet, Schaffer looked down to gauge his chances if he let go and dropped down to the floor beneath, and rapidly concluded that the chances were either that he would break both legs or, if he landed at all awkwardly, would pitch out two hundred feet down to the valley below. As Schaffer later recounted it, this last possibility combined with the vertiginous view of the long long way to the floor of the valley, did him more good than an extra pair of arms. Ten seconds later, sweating and gasping like a long distance runner and very close to the last stages of exhaustion, he hauled himself on to the roof of the cable-car.

He lay there for a full minute until the trembling in his arms eased and pulse and breathing rates returned to not more than a man in a high fever might expect to have, lowered himself quietly and wearily to the floor, took out his Luger, slid the safety catch and began to make a quick check that the header station really was empty of the enemy, a superfluous precaution, reason told him, any concealed person would have been bound both to see and hear his entry, but instinct and training went deeper than reason. There was no one there. He looked behind winches, electric motors and batteries. He had the place to himself.

The next thing was to ensure that he continued to have the place to himself. At the lower end of the sloping archway leading up to the castle courtyard, the heavy iron door stood wide. He passed through this doorway and padded softly up the cobbled pathway until he came to the courtyard exit. Here, too, was another iron gate, as wide open as the other. Schaffer moved as far forward as the shadowing safety of the tunnel's overhang permitted and looked cautiously around the scene before him.

There was certainly, he had to admit, plenty to be seen and under more auspicious circumstances it would have done his heart good. The courtyard scene was as frenzied as the earlier glimpse they had had from the passage, but this time the action was much more purposive and controlled. Shouting, gesticulating figures were supervising the unrolling of hoses, the coupling-up of hydrants, the relays of men carrying extinguishers and buckets of sand. The main gates stood open and unguarded, even the sentries must have been pressed into action: not that the unguarded doors offered any warmly beckoning escape route. Only a suicide would have tried making his escape through a courtyard crowded with sixty or seventy scurrying Alpenkorps troops.

Over to his left the helicopter still stood forlorn and useless. There was no sign of the pilot. Suddenly a loud flat explosion echoed inside the confining walls of the square. Schaffer lifted his head to locate its source, saw fresh clouds of smoke billowing from an upper window in the east wing and briefly wondered which of his diversionary explosives that might be. But only for a brief moment. Some instinct made him glance to his right and his face went very still. The men he'd seen floundering up the slope outside, guards with the Dobermann pinschers, were coming through the main gate, the clouds of frozen breath trailing in the air behind them evidence enough of their exhausting run uphill through that knee-high snow. Schaffer backed away slowly and silently: German soldiers he could cope with or avoid but Dobermanns were out of his class. He swung the heavy iron door to, careful not to make the least whisper of sound, slid home two heavy bolts, ran quickly down the arched passage-way, closed and padlocked the lower door and put the key in his pocket.

He looked up, startled, at a loud crashing of glass and the subsequent tinkle as the shattered fragments tinkled to the floor. Automatically, the barrel of his Luger followed his glance.

'Put that cannon away,' Smith said irritably. Schaffer could clearly see his face now, pressed close to the iron bars. 'Who do you think is up here – Kramer and company?'

'It's my nerves,' Schaffer explained coldly. 'You haven't been through what Lieutenant Schaffer's just been through. How are things up there?'

'Carraciola and friends are face down on the roof, freezing to death in the snow and Mary has the Schmeisser on them. Jones is still up there. Won't even put his head outside. Says he's no head for heights. I've given up arguing with him. How are things your end?'

'Quiet. If anyone is having any passing thoughts about the cable-car, there are no signs f it. Both doors to the courtyard are locked. They're iron and even if someone does start having suspicious thoughts, they should hold them for a while. And, boss, the way I came in is strictly for the birds. And I mean strictly. What you need is wings. Your hand the way it is you could never make it. Mary and the old boy couldn't try it. Carraciola and the rest – well, who cares about Carraciola and the rest.'

'What winch controls are there?' Smith asked.

'Well, now.' Schaffer approached the winch. 'A small lever marked *"Normal"* and *"Notfall"*—'

'Are there batteries down there?' Smith interrupted.

'Yeah. Any amount.'

'Put the lever to *"Notfall"* – "Emergency." They could cut off the main power from inside the castle.'

'OK, it's done. Then there are Start and Stop buttons, a big mechanical handbrake and a gear lever affair marked "Forwards" and "Backwards". With a neutral position.'

'Start the motor,' Smith ordered. Schaffer pressed the 'Start' button and a generator whined into life, building up to its maximum revolutions after perhaps ten seconds. 'Now release the brake and select forward gear. If it works, stop the car and try the other gear.'

Schaffer released the brake and engaged gear, sliding the gear handle progressively over successive stops. The car moved forward, gently at first, but gathering speed until it was clear of the header station roof. After a few more feet Schaffer stopped the car, engaged reverse gear and brought the car back up into its original position. He looked up at Smith. 'Smooth, huh?'

'Lower it down till it's half-way past the edge of the roof. We'll slide down the rope on to the top of the cable-car then you can bring us up inside.'

'Must be all the fish you eat,' Schaffer said admiringly. He set the car in motion.

'I'm sending Carraciola, Thomas and Christiansen down first,' Smith said. 'I wouldn't care for any of us to be on the top of the same cable-car as that lot. Think you can hold them till we get down?'

'You don't improve morale by being insulting to subordinate officers,' Schaffer said coldly.

'I didn't know you'd any left. While you're doing that I'll have another go at persuading Juliet up there to come and join us.' He prodded Carraciola with a far from gentle toe. 'You first. Down that rope and on to the top of the cable-car.'

Carraciola straightened until he was kneeling, glanced down the slope of the roof to the depths of the valley beyond.

'You're not getting me on that lot. Not ever.' He shook his head in finality, then stared up at Smith, his black eyes implacable in their hate. 'Go on, shoot me. Kill me now.'

'I'll kill you if you ever try to escape,' Smith said. 'Don't you know that, Carraciola?'

'Sure I know it. But you won't kill me in cold blood, just standing here. You're a man of principle, aren't you, Major? Ethics, that's the word. The kind of noble sucker who risks his life to free an enemy soldier who might burn to death. Why don't you shoot, Major?'

'Because I don't have to.' With his left hand Smith grabbed Carraciola's hair and jerked his head back till Carraciola, gasping with the pain of it, was staring skywards, while he reversed the grip on his Luger and raised it high. Nausea and pain flooded through him as the ends of the broken finger-bone grated together, but none of this showed in his face. 'I just knock you out, tie a rope round your waist and lower you down over the edge, maybe eight or ten feet. Schaffer eases out the car till it touches you, then he climbs in the back door, goes to the front door and hauls you inside. You can see my right hand's not too good, maybe I won't be able to tie a secure enough knot round you, maybe I won't be able to hold you, maybe Schaffer might let you go when he's hauling you inside. I don't much care, Carraciola.'

'You double-dealing bastard!' Tears of pain filled Carraciola's eyes and his voice was low and venomous. 'I swear to God I'll live to make you wish you'd never met me.'

'Too late.' Smith thrust him away contemptuously and Carraciola had to grab wildly at the rope to prevent himself from sliding over the break of the roof. 'I've been wishing that ever since I found out who and what you really are. Vermin soil my hands. Move now or I damn well will shoot you. Why the hell should I bother taking you back to England?'

Carraciola believed him. He slid down the rope until first his feet then his hands found the security of the supporting bracket of the cable-car. Smith gestured with his gun towards Thomas. Thomas went without a word. Ten seconds later Christiansen followed him. Smith watched the cable-car begin to move up inside the station, then looked upwards to the window from which the rope dangled.

'Mr Jones?'

'I'm still here.' Carnaby-Jones's voice had a quaver to it and he didn't as much as venture to risk a glance over the windowsill.

'Not for much longer, I hope,' Smith said seriously. 'They'll be coming for you, Mr Jones. They'll be coming any moment now. I hate to say this, but I must. It is my duty to warn you what will happen to you, an enemy spy. You'll be tortured, Mr Jones – not simply everyday tortures like pulling out your teeth and toe-nails, but unspeakable tortures I can't mention with Miss Ellison here – and then you'll finish in the gas chambers. *If* you're still alive.'

Mary clutched his arm. 'Would they – would they really do that?'

'Good God, no!' Smith stared at her in genuine surprise. 'What on earth would they want to do that for?' He raised his voice again: 'You'll die in a screaming agony, Mr Jones, an agony beyond your wildest dreams. And you'll take a long time dying. Hours. Maybe days. And screaming. Screaming all the time.'

'What in God's name am I to do?' The desperate voice from above was no longer quavering, it vibrated like a broken bed-spring. 'What *can* I do?'

'You can slide down that rope,' Smith said brutally. 'Fifteen feet. Fifteen little feet, Mr Jones. My God, you could do that in a pole vault.'

'I can't.' The voice was a wail. 'I simply can't.'

'Yes, you can,' Smith urged. 'Grab the rope now, close your eyes, out over the sill and down. Keep your eyes closed. We can catch you.'

'I can't! I can't!'

'Oh God!' Smith said despairingly. 'Oh, my God! It's too late now.'

'It's too – what in heaven's name do you mean?'

'The lights are going on along the passage,' Smith said, his voice low and tense. 'And that window. And the next. They're coming for you, Mr Jones, they're coming now. Oh God, when they strip you off and strap you down on the torture table—'

Two seconds later Carnaby-Jones was over the sill and sliding down the nylon rope. His eyes were screwed tightly shut. Mary said, admiringly: 'You really are the most fearful liar ever.'

'Schaffer keeps telling me the same thing,' Smith admitted. 'You can't all be wrong.'

The cable-car, with the three men clinging grimly to the suspension bracket, climbed slowly up into the header station and jerked to a halt. One by one the three men, under the persuasion of Schaffer's gently waving Luger, lowered themselves the full length of their arms and dropped the last two or three feet to the floor. The last of them, Thomas, seemed to land awkwardly, exclaimed in muffled pain and fell heavily sideways. As he fell, his hands shot out and grabbed Schaffer by the ankles. Schaffer, immediately off-balance, flung up his arms in an attempt to maintain equilibrium and, before he could even begin to bring his arms down again, was winded by a diving rugby tackle by Christiansen. He toppled backwards, his back smashing into a generator with an impact that drove from his lungs what little breath had been left in them. A second later and Christiansen had his gun, driving the muzzle cruelly into a throat gasping for air.

Carraciola was already at the lower iron door, shaking it fiercely. His eye caught sight of the big padlock in its hasp. He swung round, ran back towards Schaffer, knocked aside the gun in Christiansen's hand and grabbed Schaffer by the throat.

'That padlock. Where's the key to that bloody padlock?' The human voice can't exactly emulate the hiss of a snake, but Carraciola's came pretty close to it then. 'That door has been locked from the inside. You're the only person who could have done it. *Where is that key?*'

Schaffer struggled to a sitting position, feebly pushing aside Carraciola's hand. 'I can't breathe!' The moaning, gasping breathing lent credence to the words. 'I can't breathe. I – I'm going to be sick.'

'Where *is* that damned key?' Carraciola demanded.

'Oh God, I feel ill!' Schaffer hoisted himself slowly to a kneeling position, his head bent, retching sounds coming from his throat. He shook his head from side to side, as if to clear away the muzziness, then slowly raised it, his eyes unfocused. He mumbled: 'What do you want? What did you say?'

'The key!' If the need for silence hadn't been paramount, Carraciola's voice would have been a frustrated scream of rage. Half-a-dozen times, in brutal and rapid succession, he struck Schaffer across the face with the palm and back of his hand. 'Where is that key?'

'Easy on, easy on!' Thomas caught Carraciola's hand. 'Don't be such a damned fool. You want him to talk, don't you?'

'The key. Yes, the key.' Schaffer hoisted himself wearily to his feet and stood there swaying, eyes half-closed, face ashen, blood trickling from both corners of his mouth. 'The batteries there, I think I hid them behind the batteries. I don't know, I can't think. No, wait.' The words came in short, anguished gasps. 'I didn't. I meant to, but I didn't.' He fumbled in his pocket, eventually located the key and brought it out, offering it vaguely in Carraciola's direction. Carraciola, the beginnings of a smile on his face, reached out for the key but, before he could reach it Schaffer abruptly straightened and with a convulsive jerk of his arm sent the key spinning through the open end of the station to land in the valley hundreds of feet below. Carraciola stared after the vanished key in total incredulity then, his suffused and enraged face mute evidence of his complete loss of self-control, stooped, picked up Schaffer's fallen Schmeisser and swung it viciously across the American's head and face. Schaffer fell like a tree.

'Well,' Thomas said acidly. 'Now that we've got that out of our system, we can shoot the lock away.'

'You can commit suicide with ricochets – that door's iron, man.' Carraciola had indeed got it out of his system for he was back on balance again. He paused, then smiled slowly. 'What the hell are we all thinking of? Let's play it clever. If we did get through that door the first thing we'd probably collect would be a chestful of machine-gun bullets. Remember, the only people who know who we really are have bloody great doses of Nembutal inside them and are liable to remain unconscious for a long time. To the rest of the garrison we're unknowns – and to the few who saw us arrive, we're prisoners. In both cases we're automatically enemies.'

'So?' Thomas was impatient.

'So, as I say, we play it clever. We go down in this cable-car and play it clever again. We phone old Weissner. We ask him to phone the Schloss Adler, tell him where Smith is and, in case Smith does manage to get down to the village on the other cable-car after us, we ask him to have a reception committee waiting for him at the lower station. Then we go to the barracks – they're bound to have a radio there – and get in touch with you know who. Flaws?'

'Nary a flaw.' Christiansen grinned. 'And then we all live happily ever afterwards. Come on, what are we waiting for?'

'Into the cable-car, you two.' Carraciola waited until they had boarded, walked across the floor until he was directly under the smashed skylight and called: 'Boss!' Schaffer's silenced Luger was in his hand.

On the roof above Smith stiffened, handed the trembling Carnaby-Jones – his eyes were still screwed shut – over to the care of Mary, took two steps towards the skylight and stopped. It was Wyatt-Turner who had said of Smith that he had a built-in radar set against danger and Carraciola's voice had just started it up into instantaneous operation and had it working with a clarity and precision that would have turned Decca green with envy.

'Schaffer?' Smith called softly. 'Lieutenant Schaffer? Are you there?'

'Right here, boss.' Mid-west accent, Schaffer to the life. Smith's radar-scope went into high and had it been geared to warning bells he'd have been deafened for life. He dropped to hands and knees and crawled soundlessly forward. He could see the floor of the station now. The first thing that came into his vision was a bank of batteries, then an outflung hand, then, gradually the rest of the spread-eagled form of Schaffer. Another few inches forward and he sensed as much as saw a long finger pointing in his direction and flung himself to one side. The wind from the Luger's shell rifled his hair. Down below someone cursed in anger and frustration.

'That's the last chance you'll ever have, Carraciola,' Smith said. From where he lay he could just see Schaffer's face – or the bloody mask that covered his face. It was impossible to tell whether he was alive or dead. He looked dead.

'Wrong again. Merely the postponement of a pleasure. We're leaving now, Smith. I'm going to start the motor. Want Schaffer to get his – Christiansen has the Schmeisser on him. Don't try anything.'

'You make for that control panel,' Smith said, 'and your first step into my line of vision will be your last. I'll cut you down, Carraciola. Schaffer's dead. I can see he's dead.'

'He's damn all of the kind dead. He's just been clobbered by a gun butt.'

'I'll cut you down,' Smith said monotonously.

'Goddam it, I tell you he's not dead!' Carraciola was exasperated now.

'I'm going to kill you,' Smith said quietly. 'If I don't, the first guards through that door surely will. You can see what we've done to their precious Schloss Adler – it's well alight. Can't you guess the orders that have gone out – shoot on sight. Any stranger, shoot on sight – and shoot to kill. You're a stranger, Carraciola.'

'For God's sake, will you listen to me?' There was desperation in the voice now. 'I can prove it. He *is* alive. What can you see from up there?'

The signal strengths of Smith's danger radar set began to fade. He said: 'I can see Schaffer's head.'

'Watch it, then.' There was a thud and a silenced Luger bounced to a stop a few inches from Schaffer's head. A moment later Carraciola himself came into Smith's field of vision. He looked up at Smith and at the Schmeisser muzzle staring down at him and said: 'You won't be needing that.' He stooped over Schaffer, pinched his nose with one hand and clamped his other hand over the mouth. Within seconds the unconscious man, fighting for the air that would not come, began to move his head and to raise feeble hands in the direction of his face. Carraciola took his hands away, looked up at Smith and said: 'Don't forget, Christiansen has still that Schmeisser on him.'

Carraciola walked confidently across to the control panel, made the generator switch, released the mechanical handbrake and engaged gear, pushing the lever all the way across. The cable-car leapt forward with a violent jerk. Carraciola ran for it, jumped inside, turned and slammed the door of the cable-car.

On the roof above, Smith laid down his useless Schmeisser and pushed himself wearily to his feet. His face was bleak and bitter.

'Well, that's it, then,' Mary said. Her voice was unnaturally calm. 'Finish. All finish. Operation Overlord – and us. If that matters.'

'It matters to me.' Smith took out his silenced automatic and held it in his good left hand. 'Keep an eye on Junior here.'

Chapter Ten

'No!' For perhaps two dazed, incredulous seconds that were the longest seconds she had ever known, Mary had quite failed to gather Smith's intention: when shocked understanding did come, her voice rose to a scream. 'No! No! For God's sake, no!'

Smith ignored the heart-broken voice, the desperate clutching hand and walked to the end of the flat section of the roof. At the lower edge of the steeply sloping roof section the leading edge of the cable-car had just come into view: a cable-car with, inside it, three men who were exchanging delighted grins and thumping one another joyously on the back.

Smith ran down the ice-coated pitch of the roof, reached the edge and jumped. The cable-car was already seven or eight feet beyond him and almost as far below. Had the cable-car not been going away from him he must surely have broken both legs. As it was, he landed with a jarring teeth-rattling crash, a crash that caused the cable-car to shudder and sway and his legs to buckle and slide from beneath him on the ice-coated roof. His injured right hand failed to find a purchase on the suspension bracket and in his blindly despairing grab with his left hand he was forced to drop his Luger. It slid to the edge of the roof and fell away into the darkness of the valley below. Smith wrapped both arms round the suspension bracket and fought to draw some whooping gasps of air into his starving lungs: he had been completely winded by the fall.

In their own way, the three men inside the cable-car were as nearly stunned as Smith himself. The smiles had frozen on their faces and Christiansen's arm was still poised in mid-air where it had been arrested by the sound and the shock of Smith's landing on the cable-car roof. Carraciola, predictably, was the first to recover and react. He snatched the Schmeisser from Christiansen and pointed it upwards.

The cable-car was now forty to fifty feet clear of the castle and the high wind was beginning to swing it, pendulum-like, across the sky. Smith, weakened by the impact of the fall, the pain in his hand and the loss of blood, hung on grimly and dizzily to the suspension bracket, his body athwart the roof of the car. He felt sick and exhausted and there seemed to be a mist in front of his eyes.

From shoulder to knee and only inches from his body a venomous burst of machine-pistol fire stitched a pattern of holes in the cable-car roof: the mists cleared away from Smith's eyes more quickly than he would have believed possible. A Schmeisser magazine held far more shells than that. They would wait a second or two to see if a falling body passed any of the side windows – with that violently swinging transverse movement it was virtually impossible for anyone to fall off over the leading or trailing ends of the car – and if none came, then they would fire again. But where? What would be the next area of roof chosen for treatment? Would the gunman fire at random or to a systematic pattern? It was impossible to guess. Perhaps at that very moment the muzzle of the Schmeisser was only two inches from the middle of his spine. The very thought was enough to galvanize Smith into a quick roll that stretched him out over the line of holes that had just been made. It was unlikely that the gunman would fire in exactly the same place again, but even that was a gamble, the gunman might figure just as Smith was doing and traverse the same area again. But he wasn't figuring the same as Smith, the next burst was three feet away towards the trailing end of the car.

Using the suspension bracket as support, Smith pulled himself to his feet until he was quite vertical, hanging on to the cable itself. This way, the possible target area was lessened by eighty per cent. Quickly, soundlessly, sliding his hands along the cable, he moved forward until he was standing at the very front of the car.

The cable-car's angle of arc through the sky was increasing with every swing of the pendulum. The purchase for his feet was minimal, all the strain came on his arms, and by far the greater part of that on his sound left arm. There was nothing smoothly progressive about the cable-car's sideways motion through the sky, it jumped and jerked and jarred and jolted like a Dervish dancer in the last seconds before total collapse. The strain on the left arm was intolerable, it felt as if the shoulder sinews were being torn apart: but shoulder sinews are reparable whereas the effects of a Schmeisser blast at point blank range were not. And it seemed, to Smith, highly unlikely that anybody would waste a burst on the particular spot where he was standing, the obvious position for any roof passenger who didn't want to be shaken off into the valley below was flat out on the roof with his arms wrapped for dear life round one of the suspension arm's support brackets.

His reasoning was correct. There were three more bursts, none of which came within feet of him, and then no more. Smith knew that he would have to return to the comparative security of the suspension arm and return there soon. He was nearly gone. The grip of his left hand on the cable was weakening, this forced him to strengthen the grip of his right hand and the resulting agony that travelled like an electric shock from his hand up his arm clear to the right hand side of his head served only to compound the weakness. He would have to get back, and he would have to get back now. He prayed that the Schmeisser's magazine was empty.

And then, and for another reason, he knew that he had no option but to go now: and he knew his prayer hadn't been answered. The leading door of the cable-car opened and a head and a hand appeared. The head was Carraciola's: the hand held the Schmeisser. Carraciola was looking upwards even as he leaned out and he saw Smith immediately: he leaned farther out still, swung the Schmeisser one-handedly until the stock rested on his shoulder and squeezed the trigger.

Under the circumstances accurate aiming was impossible but at a distance of four feet accurate aiming was the last thing that mattered. Smith had already let go of the cable and was flinging himself convulsively backward when the first of the bullets ripped off his left hand epaulette. The second grazed his left shoulder, a brief burning sensation, but the rest of the burst passed harmlessly over his head. He landed heavily, stretched out blindly, located and grasped one of the suspension arms and scuttled crab-like round the base of the suspension arm until he had it and what little pathetic cover it offered between him and Carraciola.

For Carraciola was coming after him and Carraciola was coming to mak' siccar. He had the gun still in his hand and that gun could have very few shells indeed left in the magazine: it would be no part of Carraciola's plan to waste any of those shells. Even as Smith watched, Carraciola seemed to rise effortlessly three feet into the air – a feat of levitation directly attributable to the powerful boost given him by Thomas and Christiansen – jack-knifed forward at hip level and flattened his body on top of the cable-car roof: his legs still dangled over the leading edge. A suicidal move, Smith thought in brief elation, Carraciola had made a fatal mistake: with neither hand hold nor purchase on that ice-coated roof, he must slide helplessly over the edge at the first jerk or jolt of the cable-car. But the elation was brief indeed for Carraciola had made no mistake. He had known what Smith hadn't: where to find a secure lodgment for his hand on the smooth expanse of that roof. Within seconds his scrabbling fingers had found safety – a gash in the cable-car roof that had been torn open by one of the bursts from the Schmeisser. Carraciola's fingers hooked securely and he pulled himself forward until he was in a kneeling position, his toes hooked over the leading edge.

Smith reached up with his wounded hand and clawed desperately for a grenade in the canvas bag slung over his left shoulder, at the same time pushing himself as far back as his anchoring left hand, clutched round a suspension bracket, would permit: at that range a grenade could do almost as much damage to himself as to Carraciola. His legs slid back until his feet projected over the trailing edge and he cried out in pain as a tremendous pressure, a bone-breaking, skin tearing pressure, was applied to his shins, half-way between knees and feet. someone had him by the ankles and that someone seemed determined to separate his feet from the rest of his body. Smith twisted his head round but all he could see was a pair of hands round his ankles, knuckles bone-white in the faint wash of moonlight. And no one man's weight, Smith realized, could have caused that agonizing pain in his shins. His companion must have had him by the waist, whether to increase the pressure or to ensure his safety if Smith did slide over the end. The reasons were immaterial: the effect was the same. He tried to draw up his legs but with a pinning weight of well over 200 lbs., any movement was quite impossible.

Smith risked a quick glance forward, but Carraciola hadn't moved, the cable-car was now half-way between the header station and the top pylon, the pendulum swing was at its maximum and Carraciola, still in his kneeling position, was hanging on for his life. Smith abandoned his attempt to reach for a grenade which could now serve no purpose whatsoever, unsheathed his knife, clasped the haft in the three good fingers of his right hand, twisted round and tried to strike at those hands that were causing him such excruciating agony. He couldn't get within fifteen inches of them.

His legs were breaking: his left arm was breaking: and his clenched grip on the support was slowly beginning to open. He had only seconds to go, Smith knew, and so he had nothing in the world to lose. He changed his grip on his knife, caught the tip of the blade between his broken thumb and the rest of his fingers, turned and threw the knife as powerfully and as accurately as his smashed hand and pain-dimmed eyes would permit. The stinging pain in his left ankle and the scream of pain from the trailing door were simultaneous: immediately, all the pressure on his ankles vanished: a second later, Christiansen, whom Thomas had managed to drag back inside the cable-car, was staring stupidly at the knife that transfixed his right wrist.

In that one instant Smith had won and he had lost. Or so it most surely seemed, for he was defenceless now: Carraciola had bided his time, calculated his chances and flung himself forward until he had reached the safety of the suspension bracket. Now he pulled himself slowly to his feet, his left arm round the suspension arm itself, his left leg twined securely round one of the brackets. The Schmeisser pointed into Smith's face.

'Only one bullet left.' Carraciola's smile was almost pleasant. 'I had to make sure, you see.'

Perhaps he hadn't lost, Smith thought, perhaps he hadn't lost after all. Because of the pinioning effect of Christiansen's hands on his ankles he'd been unaware, until now, how much less difficult it had become to maintain position on that ice-sheathed roof, unaware how much the pendulum swaying of the cable-car had been reduced. And it seemed that, even now, Carraciola was still unaware of it, or, if the change of motion had registered with him, the reason for it had not. With a conscious effort of will Smith shifted his by now half-hypnotized gaze from the staring muzzle of the Schmeisser to a point just over Carraciola's shoulder. The suspension arm of the first pylon was less than twenty feet away.

'Too bad, Smith.' Carraciola steadied the barrel of his machine pistol. 'Comes to us all. Be seeing you.'

'Look behind you,' Smith said.

Carraciola half-smiled in weary disbelief that anyone should try that ancient one on him. Smith glanced briefly, a second time, over Carraciola's shoulder, winced and looked away. The disbelief vanished from Carraciola's face as if a light had been switched off. Some sixth sense or instantaneous flash of comprehension or just some sudden certainty of knowledge made him twist round and glance over his shoulder. He cried out in terror, the last sound he ever made. The steel suspension arm of the pylon smashed into his back. Both his back and inter-twined leg broke with a simultaneous crack that could have been heard a hundred yards away. One second later he was swept from the roof of the cable-car but by that time Carraciola was already dead. From the open rearward door of the car, Thomas and Christiansen, their shocked faces mirroring their stunned disbelief, watched the broken body tumbling down into the darkness of the valley below.

Shaking like a man with the ague and moving like an old man in a dream, Smith slowly and painfully hauled himself forward until he was in a sitting position with an arm and leg wound round one of the after arms of the supporting bracket. Still in the same dream-like slow motion he lifted his head and gazed down the valley. The other cable-car, moving up-valley on its reciprocal course, had just passed the lower-most of the three pylons. With luck, his own cable-car might be the first to arrive at the central pylon. With luck. Not, of course, that the question of luck entered into it any more: he had no options or alternatives left, he had to do what he had to do and luck was the last factor to be taken into consideration.

From his kit-bag Smith extracted two packets of plastic explosives and wedged them firmly between the roof of the car and the two after arms of the suspension bracket, making sure that the tear strip igniters were exposed and ready to hand. Then he braced himself, sitting upright, against the

suspension bracket, using both arms and legs to anchor himself and prepared
to sit it out once more as the cable-car, approaching mid-section of its second
lap between the first and central pylons, steadily increased its swaying angle
of arc across the night sky.

It was foolish of him, he knew, to sit like that. The snow had momentarily
stopped, and the full moon, riding palely in an empty sky, was flooding the
valley with a wash of ghostly light. Sitting as he was he must, he realized,
be clearly visible from either the castle or the lower station: but apart from
the fact that he doubted whether concealment mattered any longer he knew
there was nothing he could do about it, there wasn't the strength left in his
one good arm to allow him to assume the prone spread-eagled position that
he and Schaffer had used on the way up.

He wondered about Schaffer, wondered about him in a vaguely woolly
detached way for which exhaustion, loss of blood and the bitter cold were
almost equally responsible. He wondered about the others, too, about the
elderly man and the girl perched on top of the header station roof, about the
two men inside the cable-car: but Mary and Carnaby-Jones were helpless
to do anything to help and the chances of the unarmed Thomas and
Christiansen carrying out another roof-top sortie were remote indeed: Carraciola had carried a Schmeisser, and they had seen what had happened to
Carraciola. Schaffer, it was Schaffer who mattered.

Schaffer was feeling even more vague and woolly than Smith, if for different
reasons. He was waking, slowly and painfully, from a very bad dream and
in this dream he could taste salt in his mouth and hear a soft urgent feminine
voice calling his name, calling it over and over again. In normal times
Schaffer would have been all for soft feminine voices, urgent or not, but he
wished that this one would stop for it was all part of the bad dream and in
this bad dream someone had split his head in half and he knew the pain
wouldn't go until he woke up. He moaned, put the palms of his hands on
the floor and tried to prop himself up. It took a long time, it took an eternity,
for someone had laid one of the girders from the Forth bridge across his
back, but at last he managed to straighten both his arms, his head hanging
down between them. His head didn't feel right, it didn't even feel like his
head, for, apart from the fact that there seemed to be a butcher's cleaver
stuck in it, it seemed to be stuffed with cotton wool, grey and fuzzy round
the edges. He shook his head to clear it and this was a mistake for the top
of his head fell off. Or so it felt to Schaffer as the blinding coruscation of
multi-coloured lights before his eyes arranged themselves into oddly kaleidoscopic patterns. He opened his eyes and the patterns dimmed and the
lights began to fade: gradually, beneath his eyes the pattern of floorboards
began to resolve themselves, and, on the board, the outlines of hands. His
own hands.

He was awake, but this was one of those bad dreams which stayed with
you even when you were awake. He could still taste salt – the salt of blood
– his head still felt as if one incautious shake would have it rolling across
the floor and that soft and urgent voice was still calling.

'Lieutenant Schaffer! Lieutenant Schaffer! Wake up, Lieutenant, wake
up! Can you hear me?'

He'd heard that voice before, Schaffer decided, but he couldn't place it.
It must have been a long time ago. He twisted his head to locate the source

of the voice – it seemed to come from above – and the kaleidoscopic whirligig of colours were back in position again, revolving more quickly than ever. Head-shaking and head-twisting, Schaffer decided, were contra-indicated. He returned his head slowly to its original position, managed to get his knees under him, crawled forward in the direction of some dimly-seen piece of machinery and hauled himself shakily to his feet.

'Lieutenant! Lieutenant Schaffer! I'm up here.'

Schaffer turned and lifted his head in an almost grotesque slow motion and this time the whole universe of brightly dancing stars was reduced to the odd constellation or two. He recognized the voice from the distant past now, it was that of Mary Ellison, he even thought he recognized the pale strained face looking down from above, but he couldn't be sure, his eyes weren't focusing as they should. He wondered dizzily what the hell she was doing up there staring down at him through what appeared to be the bars of a shattered sky-light: his mind, he dimly realized, was operating with all the speed and subtle fluency of a man swimming upstream against a river of black molasses.

'Are you – are you all right?' Mary asked.

Schaffer considered this ridiculous question carefully. 'I expect I shall be,' he said with great restraint. 'What happened?'

'They hit you with your own gun.'

'That's right.' Schaffer nodded and immediately wished he hadn't. He gingerly fingered a bruise on the back of his head. 'In the face. I must have struck my head as—' He broke off and turned slowly to face the door. 'What was that?'

'A dog. It sounded like a dog barking.'

'That's what I thought.' His voice slurred and indistinct, he staggered drunkenly across to the lower iron door and put his ear to it. 'Dogs,' he said. 'Lots of dogs. And lots and lots of hammering. Sledge-hammers, like enough.' He left the door and walked back to the centre of the floor, still staggering slightly. 'They're on to us and they're coming for us. Where's the Major?'

'He went after them.' The voice was empty of all feeling. 'He jumped on to the top of the cable-car.'

'He did, eh?' Schaffer received the news as if Smith's action had been the most natural and inevitable thing in the world. 'How did he make out?'

'How did he make—' There was life back in her voice now, a shocked anger at Schaffer's apparent callousness. She checked herself and said: 'There was a fight and I think someone fell off the roof. I don't know who it was.'

'It was one of them,' Schaffer said positively.

'One of – how can you say that?'

'The Major Smiths of this world don't drive over the edge of a cliff. Quotation from the future Mrs Schaffer. The Major Smiths of this world don't fall off the roofs of cable-cars. Quotation from the future Mrs Schaffer's future husband.'

'You're recovering,' Mary said coldly. 'But I think you're right. There's still someone sitting on top of the cable-car and it wouldn't be one of them, would it?'

'How do you know there's someone sitting—'

'Because I can see him,' she said impatiently. 'It's bright moonlight. Look for yourself.'

Schaffer looked for himself, then rubbed a weary forearm across aching eyes. 'I have news for you, love,' he said. 'I can't even see the damn' cable-car.'

The cable-car was ten yards away from the central pylon. Smith, upright now, stooped, tore off the two friction fuses, straightened and, holding the cable in his left hand, took up position just on the inner side of the car roof. At the last moment he released his grip on the cable and stretched both arms out before him to break the impact of his body against the suspension arm. The ascending car on the other cable was now almost as close to the central pylon as his own. It didn't seem possible that he could make it in time.

The impact of the horizontal suspension arm drove the thought from his mind and all the breath from his body; had it not been for the buffering effect of his outstretched arms, Smith was sure, some of his ribs must have gone. As it was, he was almost completely winded but he forced himself to ignore the pain and his heaving lungs' demand for oxygen, swung his feet up till they rested on the lower cross-girder, hooked his hands round the upper girder and made his way quickly across to the other side. At least, his hands and his feet moved quickly, but the steel was so thickly coated in clear smooth ice that his scrabbling feet could find almost no purchase whatsoever on the lower girder. He had reached no farther than the middle when the ascending car began to pass under its suspension arm. For the first time that night Smith blessed the brightness of the moon. He took two more slipping, sliding steps and launched himself towards the ice-coated cable that glittered so brightly in the pale moonlight.

His left hand caught the cable, his right arm hooked over it and the cable itself caught him high up on the chest. He had made no mistake about the location of his hand and arm, but his sliding take-off had caused his body to fall short and the cable slid up under his chin with a jerk that threatened to decapitate him. His legs swung out far beneath him, swung back and touched the roof as he lowered himself to the full extent of his left arm. He released his grip on the cable, dropped on all fours and reached out blindly but successfully for one of the arms of the suspension bracket. For long seconds he knelt there, retching uncontrollably as he was flooded by the nausea and pain from his throat and still winded lungs: then, by and by, the worst of it passed and he lay face down on the floor as the cable-car began to increase its pendulum swing with the increasing distance from the central pylon. He would not have believed that a man could be so totally exhausted and yet still have sufficient residual strength and sufficient self-preservation instinct to hang on to that treacherous and precarious hand-hold on that ice-coated roof.

Long seconds passed and some little measure of strength began to return to his limbs and body. Wearily, he hauled himself up into a sitting position, twisted round and gazed back down the valley.

The cable-car he had so recently abandoned was now hardly more than fifty yards from the lowermost pylon. Thomas and Christiansen sat huddled in the middle, the latter wrapping a makeshift bandage round his injured hand. Both fore and aft doors were still open as they were when the abortive attack on Smith had been made. That neither of the two men had ventured near the extremities of the car to try to close either of the doors was proof enough of the respect, if not fear, in which Smith was now held.

From the roof of the cable-car came a brilliant flash of light, magnesium-blinding in its white intensity: simultaneously there came the sound of two sharp explosions, so close together as to be indistinguishable in time. The two rear supports of the suspension bracket broke and the car, suspended now by only the two front supports, tilted violently, the front going up, the rear down.

Inside, the angle of the floor of the car changed in an instant from the horizontal to at least thirty degrees. Christiansen was flung back towards the still open rear door. He grabbed despairingly at the side – but he grabbed with his wounded hand. Soundlessly, he vanished through the open doorway and as soundlessly fell to the depths of the valley below.

Thomas, with two sound hands and faster reactions, had succeeded in saving himself – for the moment. He glanced up and saw where the roof was beginning to buckle and break as the forward two suspension arm support brackets, now subjected to a wrenching lateral pressure they had never been designed to withstand, began to tear their retaining bolts free. Thomas struggled up the steeply inclined floor till he stood in the front doorway: because of the tilt of the car, now almost 45° as the front supports worked loose, the leading edge of the roof was almost touching the car. Thomas reached up, grabbed the cable with both hands, and had just cleared his legs from the doorway when the two front supports tore free from the roof in a rending screech of metal. The cable-car fell away, slowly turning end over end.

Despite the cable's violent buffeting caused by the sudden release of the weight of the car, Thomas had managed to hang on. He twisted round and saw the suspension arm of the lowest pylon only feet away. The sudden numbing of all physical and mental faculties was accurately and shockingly reflected in the frozen fear of his face, the lips drawn back in a snarling rictus of terror. The knuckles of the hands gleamed like burnished ivory. And then, suddenly, there were no hands there, just the suspension arm and the empty wire and a long fading scream in the night.

As his cable-car approached the header station, Smith edged well forward to clear the lip of the roof. From where he crouched it was impossible to see the east wing of the Schloss Adler but if the columns of dense smoke now drifting across the valley were anything to go by, the fire seemed to have an unshakable hold. Clouds were again moving across the moon and this could be both a good thing and a bad thing: a good thing in that it would afford them cover and help obscure those dense clouds of smoke, a bad thing in that it was bound to highlight the flames from the burning castle. It could only be a matter of time, Smith reflected, before the attention of someone in the village or the barracks beyond was caught by the fire or the smoke. Or, he thought grimly, by the increasing number of muffled explosions coming from the castle itself. He wondered what might be the cause of them: Schaffer hadn't had the time to lay all those distractions.

The roof of the cable-car cleared the level of the floor of the header station and Smith sagged in relief as he saw the figure standing by the controls of the winch. Schaffer. A rather battered and bent Schaffer, it was true, an unsteady Schaffer, a Schaffer with one side of his face masked in blood, a Schaffer who from his peering and screwed-up expression had obviously some difficulty in focusing his gaze. But undoubtedly Schaffer and as nearly a going concern as made no odds. Smith felt energy flow back into him, he hadn't realized just how heavily he had come to depend on the American: with Schaffer by his side it was going to take a great deal to stop them now.

Smith glanced up as the roof of the header station came into view. Mary and Carnaby-Jones were still there, pressed back against the castle wall. He lifted a hand in greeting, but they gave no sign in return. Ghosts returning from the dead, Smith thought wryly, weren't usually greeted by a wave of the hand.

Schaffer, for all the trouble he was having with his eyes and his still obviously dazed condition, seemed to handle the winch controls immaculately. It may have been – and probably was – the veriest fluke, but he put the gear level in neutral and applied the brake to bring the cable-car to rest exactly half-way in under the lip of the roof. First Mary and then Jones came sliding down the nylon rope on to the roof of the car, Jones with his eyes screwed tightly shut. Neither of them spoke a word, not even when Schaffer had brought them up inside and they had slid down on to the floor of the station.

'Hurry! Hurry!' Smith flung open the rear door of the cable-car. 'Inside, all of you!' He retrieved Schaffer's Luger from the floor, then whirled round as he heard the furious barking of dogs followed bv the sound of heavy sledges battering against the iron door leading from the station. The first of the two defences must have been carried away: now the second was under siege.

Mary and a stumbling Schaffer were already inside the cable-car. Jones, however, had made no move to go. He stood there, Smith's Schmeisser in his hand, listening to the furious hammering on the door. His face seemed unconcerned. He said, apologetically: 'I'm not very good at heights, I'm afraid. But this is different.'

'Get inside!' Smith almost hissed the words.

'No.' Jones shook his head. 'You hear. They'll be through any minute. I'll stay.'

'For God's sake!' Smith shouted in exasperation.

'I'm twenty years older than any of you.'

'Well, there's that.' Smith nodded consideringly, held out his right hand, said, 'Mr Jones. Good luck,' brought across his left hand and half-dragged, half-carried the dazed Jones into the cable-car. Smith moved quickly across to the controls, engaged gear all the way, released the handbrake and ran after the moving car.

As they moved out from below the roof of the station, the sound of the assault on the inner door seemed to double in its intensity. In the Schloss Adler, Smith reflected, there would be neither pneumatic chisels nor oxy-acetylene equipment for there could be no conceivable call for either, but, even so, it didn't seem to matter: with all the best will in the world a couple of iron hasps couldn't for long withstand an attack of that nature. Thoughtfully, Smith closed the rear door. Schaffer was seated, his elbows on his knees, his head in his hands. Mary was kneeling on the floor, Jones's head in her lap, looking down at the handsome silvery-haired head. He couldn't see her expression but was dolefully certain that she was even then preparing a homily about the shortcomings of bullies who went around clobbering elderly and defenceless American actors. Almost two minutes passed in complete silence before Carnaby-Jones stirred, and, when he did, Mary herself stirred and looked up at Smith. To his astonishment, she had a half-smile on her face.

'It's all right,' she said. 'I've counted ten. In the circumstances, it was the only argument to use.' She paused and the smile faded. 'I thought you were gone then.'

'You weren't the only one. After this I retire. I've used up a lifetime's luck in the past fifteen minutes. You're not looking so bright yourself.'

'I'm not feeling so bright.' Her face was pale and strained as she braced herself against the wild lurching of the cable-car. 'If you want to know, I'm sea-sick. I don't go much on this form of travel.'

Smith tapped the roof. 'You want to try travelling steerage on one of those,' he said feelingly. 'You'd never complain about first-class travel again. Ah! Pylon number two coming up. Almost half-way.'

'*Only* half-way.' A pause. 'What happens if they break through that door up there?'

'Reverse the gear lever and up we go.'

'Like it or not?'

'Like it or not.'

Carnaby-Jones struggled slowly to a sitting position, gazed uncomprehendingly around him until he realized where he was, rubbed his jaw tenderly and said to Smith: 'That was a dirty trick.'

'It was all of that,' Smith acknowledged. 'I'm sorry.'

'I'm not.' Jones smiled shakily. 'Somehow, I don't really think I'm cut out to be a hero.'

'Neither am I, brother, neither am I,' Schaffer said mournfully. He lifted his head from his hands and looked slowly around. His eyes were still glassy and only partially focusing but a little colour was returning to his right cheek, the one that wasn't masked in blood. 'Our three friends. What became of our three friends?'

'Dead.'

'Dead?' Schaffer groaned and shook his head. 'Tell me about it sometime. But not now.'

'He doesn't know what he's missing,' Smith said unsympathetically. 'The drama of it all escapes him, which is perhaps just as well. Is the door up above there still standing or are the hinges or padlocks going? Is someone rushing towards the winch controls – Is there—'

'Stop it!' Mary's voice was sharp, high-pitched and carried overtones of hysteria. 'Stop talking like that!'

'Sorry,' Smith said contritely. He reached out and touched her shoulder. 'Just whistling in the dark, that's all. Here comes the last pylon. Another minute or so and we're home and dry.'

'Home and dry,' Schaffer said bitterly. 'Wait till I have that Savoy Grill menu in my hand. *Then* I'll be home and dry.'

'Some people are always thinking of their stomachs,' Smith observed. At that moment he was thinking of his own and it didn't feel any too good. No stomach does when it feels as if it has a solid lead ball, a chilled lead ball lodged in it with an icy hand squeezing from the outside. His heart was thumping slowly, heavily, painfully in his chest and he was having difficulty in speaking for all the saliva seemed to have evaporated from his mouth. He became suddenly aware that he was unconsciously leaning backward, bracing himself for the moment when the cable-car jerked to a stand-still then started climbing back up to the Schloss Adler again. I'll count to ten, he said to himself, then if we get that far without being checked, I'll count to nine, and then – And then he caught sight of Mary's face, a dead-white, scared and almost haggard face that made her look fifteen years older than she was, and felt suddenly ashamed of himself. He sat on the bench, and squeezed her shoulder. 'We'll be all right,' he said confidently. All of a sudden he found it easy to speak again. 'Uncle John has just said so, hasn't he? You wait and see.'

She looked up at him, trying to smile. 'Is Uncle John always right?'

'Always,' Smith said firmly.

Twenty seconds passed. Smith rose to his feet, walked to the front of the cable-car and peered down. Though the moon was obscured he could just dimly discern the shape of the lower section. He turned to look at the others. They were all looking at him.

'Not much more than a hundred feet to go,' Smith said. 'I'm going to open that door in a minute. Well, a few seconds. By that time we won't be much more than fifteen feet above the ground. Twenty, at the most. If the car stops, we jump. There's two or three feet of snow down there. Should cushion our fall enough to give an even chance of not breaking anything.'

Schaffer parted his lips to make some suitable remark, thought better of it and returned head to hands in weary silence. Smith opened the leading door, did his best to ignore the icy blast of wind that gusted in through the opening, and looked vertically downwards, realizing that he had been over-optimistic in his assessment of the distance between cable-car and ground. The distance was at least fifty feet, a distance sufficient to arouse in even the most optimistic mind dismaying thoughts of fractured femurs and tibias. And then he dismissed the thought, for an even more dismaying factor had now to be taken into consideration: in the far distance could be heard the sound of sirens, in the far distance could be seen the wavering beams of approaching headlamps. Schaffer lifted his head. The muzziness had now left him, even if his sore head had not.

'Enter, left, reinforcements,' he announced. 'This wasn't on the schedule, boss. Radio gone, telephone gone, helicopter gone—'

'Just old-fashioned.' Smith pointed towards the rear window. 'They're using smoke signals.'

'Jeez!' Schaffer stared out the rear windows, his voice awe-struck. 'For stone, it sure burns good!'

Schaffer was in no way exaggerating. For stone, it burnt magnificently. The Schloss Adler was well and truly alight, a conflagration in which smoke had suddenly become an inconsiderable and, indeed, a very minor element. It was wreathed in flames, almost lost to sight in flames, towering flames that now reached up almost to the top of the great round tower to the north-east. Perched on its volcanic plug half-way up the mountain-side against the dimly seen back-drop of the unseen heights of the Weissspitze, the blazing castle, its effulgence now beginning to light up the entire valley and quite drowning out the pale light of a moon again showing through, was an incredibly fantastic sight from some equally incredible and fantastic fairy tale.

'One trusts that they are well insured,' Schaffer said. He was on his feet now, peering down towards the lower station. 'How far, boss? And how far down?'

'Thirty feet. Maybe twenty-five. And fifteen feet down.' The lights of the leading cars were passing the still smouldering embers of the station. 'We have it made, Lieutenant Schaffer.'

'We have it made.' Schaffer cursed and staggered as the car jerked to a violent and abrupt stop. 'Almost, that is.'

'All out!' Smith shouted. 'All out!'

'There speaks the eternal shop steward,' Schaffer said. 'Stand back, I've got two good hands.' He brushed by Smith, clutched the door jamb with his left hand, pulled Mary towards him, transferred his grip from waist to wrist and dropped her out through the leading door, lowering her as far as the stretch of his left arm would permit. When he let her go, she had less than three feet to fall. Within three seconds he had done the same with Carnaby-Jones. The cable-car jerked and started to move back up the valley. Schaffer practically bundled Smith out of the car, wincing in pain as he momentarily took all of Smith's two hundred pound weight, then slid out of the doorway himself, hung momentarily from the doorway at the full stretch of his arms, then dropped six feet into the soft yielding snow. He staggered, but maintained balance.

Smith was beside him. He had fished out a plastic explosive from the bag on his back and torn off the friction fuse. He handed the package to Schaffer and said: 'You have a good right arm.'

'I have a good right arm. Horses, no. Baseball, yes.' Schaffer took aim and lobbed the explosive neatly through the doorway of the disappearing cable-car. 'Like that?'

'Like that. Come on.' Smith turned and, catching Mary by the arm while Schaffer hustled Carnaby-Jones along, ran down the side of the lower station and into the shelter of the nearest house bare seconds before a command car, followed by several trucks crammed with soldiers, slid to a skidding halt below the lower station. Soldiers piled out of the trucks, following an officer, clearly identifiable as Colonel Weissner, up the steps into the lower station.

The castle burned more fiercely than ever, a fire obviously totally out of control. Suddenly, there was the sharp crack of an explosion and the ascending cable-car burst into flames. The car, half-way up to the first pylon, swung in great arcs across the valley, its flames fanned by the wind, and climbed steadily upwards into the sky until its flame was lost in the greater flame of the Schloss Adler.

Crouched in the shelter of the house, Schaffer touched Smith's arm. 'Sure you wouldn't like to go and burn down the station as well?'

'Come on,' Smith said. 'The garage.'

Chapter Eleven

Colonel Wyatt-Turner leaned over in the co-pilot's seat, pressed his face against the side-screen and stared down unhappily at the ground. The Mosquito bomber, all engines and plywood, was, he was well aware, the fastest warplane in the world: even so, he hadn't been prepared for anything quite so fast as this.

Normal flying, of course, imparts no sensation of speed, but then, Wing Commander Carpenter wasn't engaged in normal flying; he was engaged in what Wyatt-Turner regarded as highly abnormal flying and flying, moreover, that was liable to bring them to disaster at any second. Carpenter was giving a ground-level performance of some spectacular note, skimming across fields, brushing tree-tops, skirting small hills that stood in his way, and Wyatt-Turner didn't like any of it one little bit. What he liked even less was the appalling speed of their own moon-shadow flitting over the ground beneath them; and what he liked least of all was the increasing number of occasions on which plane and shadow came within almost touching distance of each other. In an effort to keep his mind off what must inevitably happen when and if the gap were finally closed he withdrew his almost mesmerised stare and glanced at his watch.

'Twenty-five minutes.' He looked at the relaxed figure in the pilot's seat, at the world-weary face that contrasted so oddly with the magnificent panache of the red handlebar moustache. 'Can you make it in time?'

'I can make it,' Carpenter said comfortably. 'Point is, will they?'

'God only knows. I don't see how they can. Both the Admiral and I are convinced that they're trapped in the Schloss Adler. Besides, the whole countryside must be up in arms by this time. What chance *can* they have?'

'And that is why you came?'

'I sent them,' Wyatt-Turner said emptily. He glanced through the side-screen and recoiled as plane and shadow seemed to touch as they skimmed over the top of a pine forest. He said plaintively: 'Must you fly so close to the damned ground?'

'Enemy radar, old chap,' Carpenter said soothingly. 'We're safer down here among the bushes.'

Smith, with Mary and Jones behind him and Schaffer bringing up the rear, skirted the backs of the houses on the east side of the village street and cautiously made their way through the automobile junkyard to the rear double doors of Sulz's garage. Smith had his skeleton keys in his hand and was just reaching for the padlock when one of the doors opened quietly inwards. Heidi stood there. She stared at them as if they were creatures from another world, then up at the burning castle, then wordlessly, questioningly, at Smith.

'All here in black and white.' Smith patted his tunic. 'Into the bus.'

Smith waited till they had filed through the door, closed it, crossed to a small barred window at the front of the garage and peered out cautiously.

The street was packed with a milling crowd of people, most of them soldiers, nearly all unarmed men who had come hurrying out from the various *Weinstuben* to watch the burning Schloss Adler. But there were plenty of armed soldiers nearby – two truck-loads not thirty yards from the garage, not to mention three more truck-loads even farther up the street at the foot of the lower station. Farther down the street a motor-cycle patrol was parked outside 'Zum Wilden Hirsch'. The one real physical obstacle in the way of their escape was a small command car, manned, parked directly outside the doors of Sulz's garage. Smith looked at the car thoughtfully, decided that this was an obstacle that could be overcome. He withdrew from the window and crossed over to the doors to check that the four bolts were still withdrawn.

Mary and Carnaby-Jones had already made their way into the bus. As Heidi went to follow, Schaffer caught her by the shoulders, kissed her briefly and smiled at her. She looked at him in surprise.

'Well, aren't you glad to see me?' Schaffer demanded. 'I've had a *terrible* time up there. Good God, girl, I might have been killed.'

'Not as handsome as you were two hours ago.' She smiled, gently touched his face where Carraciola's handiwork with the Schmeisser had left its bloody mark, and added over her shoulder as she climbed into the bus: 'And that's as long as you've known me.'

'Two hours! I've aged twenty years tonight. And that, lady, is one helluva long courtship. Oh, God!' He watched in wearily resigned despair as Smith climbed into the driver's seat and switched on the ignition. 'Here we go for another twenty. On the floor, everyone.'

'How about you?' Heidi asked.

'Me?' Schaffer's surprise seemed genuine. He smashed the front window with the butt of the Schmeisser, reversed the gun, released the trigger and knelt on the floor. 'I'm the conductor. It's against regulations.'

The middle finger of Smith's blood-stained, bandaged hand reached for the starter button and the big diesel caught at once. Smith started to back towards the rear of the garage. Two perfectly good cars, a Mercedes and an Opel, lay in his way and by the time that Smith – whose expression betrayed no awareness of their presence – reached the back of the garage neither were fit for anything other than the scrap-heap that lay beyond the rear doors. Smith stopped, engaged first gear, revved up the engine and let in the clutch with a bang. The bus jerked forward, gathering speed as it went.

Smith aimed the angled point of the massive snow-plough at the junction of the double doors and for all the resistance the doors offered they might have been made of brown paper. With a splintering crash that sent shattered door-planks flying through the air like so much confetti, the bus roared out into the street, Smith spinning the wheel violently to the right as they careened into the crowded thoroughfare.

Crowded the thoroughfare might have been, but the pedestrians, the rubber-neckers gazing at the funeral pyre of the Schloss Adler, had had at least sufficient warning given them by the accelerating clamour of the post-bus's diesel to fling themselves clear as the bus came crashing through the doors. But the command car had no such opportunity for escape. Before either of the two occupants of the front seat – a sergeant with his hands resting lightly on the wheel, a major with a radio telephone in one hand, a thin cigar with a long ash in the other – were properly aware of what was happening, their car was swept up and carried away on the post-bus's snow-plough. For fifteen, perhaps even twenty yards, the command car was carried along, precariously balanced, on the broad blade of the snow-plough, before dropping off to one side. Miraculously enough, it landed on even keel, all four wheels still on the ground. The dazed major still had the telephone in one hand, the cigar in the other: he hadn't even lost the ash from his cigar.

Farther down the street, outside 'Zum Wilden Hirsch', a group of Alpenkorps motor-cyclists standing just outside the door stared incredulously up the street. Their first reaction, their immediate conclusion was either that Zep Salzmann, the highly popular driver of the post-bus, had gone mad or that the accelerator had jammed on the floor-boards. Disillusionment was rapid. They heard the unmistakable sound of an engine changing up quickly through the gears and caught a brief glimpse of Smith hunched over the steering wheel and of Schaffer crouched behind, the Schmeisser sticking out through the right-hand shattered windscreen: then the post-bus's headlamps switched on and they could see no more. But they had seen enough. One quick command from their sergeant and the motor-cycle patrol leapt for their machines, began to kick them into life.

But Smith also had seen enough. He blew a warning blast on his town horn, twisted the wheel and slewed the bus into the side of the street. His intentions were unmistakable and the motor-cycle patrol's decision to elect for discretion in lieu of suicidal valour was as immediate as it was automatic. They frantically abandoned their machines and flung themselves for their lives up the steps of 'Zum Wilden Hirsch'.

There was a thunderous series of metallic bangs interspersed with the eldritch screeches of torn and tortured metal as the snow-plough smashed into the motor-cycles and swept them along in its giant maw. As Smith straightened out into the middle of the road again several of them slid off the angled blade and crashed with a great splintering of wood and buckling of metal into the boarded sidewalk: the machines were no longer recognisable as motor-cycles. Two of them, however, still remained perched on the blade.

The post-bus was still accelerating with Smith's accelerator foot flat on the floor-boards. The headlamps were flashing rapidly, alternately main beam and dipped, and the streets ahead were clearing with corresponding rapidity: but the moment when the last few straggling pedestrians were galvanized into jumping for safety came when Smith switched on the Alpine horn.

In the mountains, the Alpine post-bus has absolute priority over every other vehicle in the road and its penetrating and stentorian three-toned post-horn is the symbol of its total authority, of its unquestioned right to complete priority at all times. The sound of that horn – whether the post-bus is in sight or not – is the signal for all vehicles or pedestrians to stop or move well into the side of the road, a signal that is immediately and automatically obeyed, for the absolute entitlement to the right of way of the official post-bus is deeply ingrained into the minds of all Alpine dwellers, and has been from earliest childhood. A magic wand might have made a better job of clearing that village street, but not all that much better; vehicles and pedestrians alike pressed into the sides of the street as if some powerful magnetic affinity had just been developed between them and the walls of the houses. The expression on faces ranged from astonishment to blank incomprehension. Hostility there was none: there had been no time for any to develop for events were moving far too swiftly and comprehension hadn't even begun to overtake the events. The bus had now reached the end of the village street and still not one shot had been fired.

At the sharp left-hand corner at the foot of the street the two remaining motor-cycles slid off the snow-plough and smashed into a low stone wall: two more absolute certainties, Smith thought inconsequentially, for the automobile cemetery behind Sulz's garage. Ahead of him now he could see the road stretch almost arrow-straight alongside the dark waters of the Blau See. He switched off the Alpine horn button, changed his mind and switched it on again: that horn was worth a pair of machine-guns any day.

'Don't you know any other tunes?' Schaffer asked irritably. He shivered in the icy blast from the smashed front window, and sat on the floor to get what little shelter he could. 'Give me a call when you require my services. A mile from now, I'd say.'

'What do you mean, a mile from now?'

'The barrack gates. That guy in the command car had a radio phone.'

'He had, had he?' Smith spared him a brief glance. 'Why didn't you shoot him?'

'I'm a changed man, boss.' Schaffer sighed. 'Something splendid has just come into my life.'

'Besides, you didn't have a chance.'

'Besides, as you say, I didn't have a chance.' Schaffer twisted round and looked through the rear windows of the bus for signs of pursuit, but the road behind them was empty. For all that, Schaffer reflected, the rearward view was one not lacking in interest: the Schloss Adler, now completely enveloped in flames, a reddish-white inferno by this time lighting up for half a mile around the startling incongruity of its snow and ice covered setting, was clearly beyond saving: arsonist's dream or fireman's nightmare, the castle was finished: before dawn it would be an empty and desolate shell, a gaunt and blackened ruin to haunt and desecrate for generations to come the loveliest fairy-tale valley he had ever seen.

Schaffer shortened his gaze and tried to locate the three others, but all were on the floor, under seats and completely concealed. He cursed as the shaking and shuddering bus lurched violently, throwing him against the right-hand front door, then straightened and peered at the illuminated dashboard.

'God save us all,' he said piously. 'Ninety!'

'Kilometres,' Smith said patiently.

'Ah!' Schaffer said as he watched Smith's foot move quickly from accelerator to brake, hoisted a wary eye over the lower edge of the shattered windscreen and whistled softly. The barrack gates were barely two hundred yards away: both the area around the guard-house and the parade ground beyond were brilliantly illuminated by overhead flood-lamps: scores of armed soldiers seemed to be running around in purposeless confusion, a totally erroneous impression as Schaffer almost immediately realized. They were running towards and scrambling aboard trucks and command cars and they weren't wasting any time about it either.

'A hive of activity and no mistake,' Schaffer observed. 'I wonder—' He broke off, his eyes widening. A giant tank came rumbling into view past the guard-house, turned right on to the road, stopped, swivelled 180° on its tracks, completely blocking the road: the gun turret moved fractionally until it was lined up on the headlights of the approaching bus. 'Oh, my gosh!' Schaffer's shocked whisper was just audible over the fading sound of the post-bus's diesel. 'A Tiger tank. And that's an 88-millimetre cannon, boss.'

'It's not a pop-gun, and that's a fact,' Smith agreed. 'Flat on the floor.' He reached forward, pulled a switch, and the eighteen-inch long semaphore indicator began to wave gently up and down. Smith first dipped his main headlights, then switched them off altogether, covering the last thirty yards on side-lamps alone and praying that all those signs of peaceful normality might help to keep nervous fingers away from the firing button of the most lethal tank cannon ever devised.

The fingers, for whatever reason, left the button alone. Smith slowed to a walking pace, turned right through the guard-house gates and stopped. Taking care to keep his injured right hand well out of sight, he wound down his window and leaned out, left elbow over the sill as three guards, led by a sergeant and all with machine-pistols at the ready, closed in on the driver's cab.

'Quickly!' Smith shouted. 'Telephone. Surgeon to the sick-bay.' He jerked his thumb over his shoulder. 'Colonel Weissner. They got him twice. Through the lungs. For God's sake, don't just *stand* there!'

'But – but the post-bus!' the sergeant protested. 'We had a call from—'

'Drunk, by God!' Smith swore savagely. 'He'll be court-martialled in the morning.' His voice dropped menacingly. 'And you, if the Colonel dies. Move!'

Smith engaged gear and drove off, still at walking pace. The sergeant, reassured by the sight of a major's uniform, the fact that the bus was moving into the barracks, the slow speed with which it was moving and, above all, by the authoritative clamour of the Alpine horn which Smith still had not switched off, ran for the nearest phone.

Still crawling along in first gear, Smith carefully edged the post-bus through the press of men and machines, past a column of booted and gauntleted soldiers mounted on motor-cycles, past armoured vehicles and trucks, all with engines already running, some already moving towards the gates – but not moving as quickly towards the gates as Smith would have wished. Ahead of the post-bus was a group of officers, most of them obviously senior, talking animatedly. Smith slowed down the bus even more and leaned from the window.

'They're trapped!' he called excitedly. 'Upstairs in "Zum Wilden Hirsch". They've got Colonel Weissner as hostage. Hurry, for God's sake!'

He broke off as he suddenly recognised one of the officers as the Alpenkorps captain to whom in his temporary capacity of Major Bernd Himmler, he'd spoken in 'Zum Wilden Hirsch' earlier that evening. A second later the recognition was mutual, the captain's mouth fell open in total incredulity and before he had time to close it Smith's foot was flat on the accelerator and the bus heading for the southern gates, soldiers flinging themselves to both sides to avoid the scything sweep of the giant snow-plough. Such was the element of surprise that fully thirty yards had been covered before most of the back windows of the bus were holed and broken, the shattering of glass mingling with the sound of the ragged fusillade of shots from behind. And then Smith, wrenching desperately on the wheel, came careering through the southern gates back on to the main road, giving them at least temporary protection from the sharp-shooters on the parade ground.

But they had, it seemed, only changed from the frying pan to the fire. Temporary protection they might have obtained from one enemy – but from another and far deadlier enemy they had no protection at all. Smith all but lost control of the bus as something struck a glancing blow low down on his cab door, ricocheted off into the night with a viciously screaming whine and exploded in a white flash of snow-flurried light less than fifty yards ahead.

'The Tiger tank,' Schaffer shouted. 'That goddamned 88-millimetre—'

'Get down!' Smith jack-knifed down and to one side of the wheel until his eyes were only an inch above the foot of the windscreen. 'That one was low. The next one—'

The next one came through the top of the back door, traversed the length of the bus and exited through the front of the roof, just above the windscreen. This time there was no explosion.

'A dud?' Schaffer said hopefully. 'Or maybe a dummy practice—'

'Dummy nothing!' Upright again, Smith was swinging the bus madly, dangerously, from side to side of the road in an attempt to confuse the tank gunner's aim. 'Armour-piercing shells, laddie, designed to go through two inches of steel plate in a tank before they explode.' He winced and ducked low as a third shell took out most of the left-hand windows of the bus, showering himself and Schaffer with a flying cloud of shattered glass fragments. 'Just let one of those shells strike a chassis member, instead of thin sheet metal, or the engine block, or the snow-plough—'

'Don't!' Schaffer begged. 'Just let it creep up on me all unbeknownst, like.' He paused, then continued: 'Taking his time, isn't he? Lining up for the Sunday one.'

'No,' Smith glanced in the rear-view mirror and steadied the wildly swaying bus up on a steadier course. 'Never thought I'd be glad to see a few car-loads or truck loads of Alpenkorps coming after me.' He changed into top gear and pushed the accelerator to the floor. 'I'm happy to make an exception this time.'

Schaffer turned and looked through the shattered rear windows. He could count at least three pairs of headlights on the road behind them, with two others swinging out through the southern gates: between them, they effectively blotted the post-bus from the view of the tank gunner.

'Happy isn't the word for it. Me, I'm ecstatic. Tiger tanks are one thing but little itsy-bitsy trucks are another.' Schaffer strode rapidly down the central aisle, passing by Mary, Heidi and Carnaby-Jones, all of whom were struggling rather shakily to their feet, and looked at the crates stacked in the rear seats.

'Six crates!' he said to Heidi. 'And we asked for only two. Honey, you're going to make me the happiest man alive.' He opened the rear door and began to empty the contents of the crate on to the road. A few of the bottles just bounced harmlessly on ridges of hard-packed snow, but the speed of the bus was now such that most of them shattered on impact.

The first of the two leading pursuit cars was within three hundred yards of the bus when it ran into the area of broken glass. From Schaffer's point of view it was impossible to tell what exactly happened, but such indications as could be gathered by long-range sight and sound were satisfying enough.

The headlights of the leading car suddenly began to slew violently from side to side, the screeching of brakes was clearly audible above the sound of the post-bus's diesel, but not nearly as loud as the rending crash of metal as the second car smashed into the rear of the first. For a few seconds both cars seemed locked together, then they skidded wildly out of control, coming to rest with the nose of the first car in the right hand ditch, the tail of the second in the left hand ditch. The headlamps of both cars had failed just after the moment of impact but there was more than sufficient illumination from the lamps of the first of the trucks coming up behind them to show that the road was completely blocked.

'Neat,' Schaffer said admiringly. 'Very neat, Schaffer.' He called to Smith: 'That'll hold them, boss.'

'Sure, it'll hold them,' Smith said grimly. 'It'll hold them for all of a minute. You can't burst heavy truck tyres that way and it won't take them long to bull-doze those cars out of the way. Heidi?'

Heidi walked forward, shivering in the icy gale blowing through both the shattered front and side windows. 'Yes, Major?'

'How far to the turn off?'

'A mile.'

'And to the wooden bridge – what do you call it, Zur Alten Brücke?'

'Another mile.'

'Three minutes. At the most, that.' He raised his voice. 'Three minutes, Lieutenant. Can you do it?'

'I can do it.' Schaffer was already lashing together packages of plastic explosives. He used transparent adhesive tape, leaving long streamers dangling from the bound packages. He had just secured the last package in position when he lurched heavily as the post-bus, now clear of the Blau See and running through a pine forest, swung abruptly to the left on to a side road.

'Sorry,' Smith called. 'Almost missed that one. Less than a mile, Lieutenant.'

'No panic,' Schaffer said cheerfully. He fished out a knife to start cutting the fuses to their shortest possible length, then went very still indeed as he glanced through where the rear windows had once been. In the middle distance were the vertically wavering beams of powerful headlights, closing rapidly. The cheerfulness left Schaffer's voice. 'Well, maybe there is a little bit panic, at that. I've got bad news, boss.'

'And I have a rear mirror. How far, Heidi?'

'Next corner.'

While Schaffer worked quickly on the fuses, Smith concentrated on getting the post-bus round the next corner as quickly as possible without leaving the road. And then they were on and round the corner and the bridge was no more than a hundred yards away.

It was not, Smith thought, a bridge he would have chosen to have crossed with a bicycle, much less a six ton bus. Had it been a bridge crossing some gently meandering stream, then, yes, possibly: but not a bridge such as this one was, a fifty-foot bridge surfaced with untied railway sleepers, spanning a ravine two hundred feet in depth and supported by trestles, very ancient wooden trestles which, from what little he could see of them from his acute angle of approach, he wouldn't have trusted to support the tables at the vicar's garden party.

Smith hit this elderly and decrepit edifice at forty miles per hour. A more cautious and understandable approach might have been to crawl over it at less than walking pace but Smith's conviction that the less time he spent on each ancient sleeper the better was as instantaneous as it was complete. The heavy snow chains on each tyre bit into and dislodged each successive sleeper with a terrifying rumble, the post-bus bounced up and down as if on a giant cake-walk while the entire structure of the bridge swayed from side to side like the bridge of a destroyer at speed in a heavy cross-sea. It had been Smith's original intention to stop in the middle of the bridge but once embarked upon the crossing he would no more have done so than dallied to pick up an edelweiss in the path of an Alpine avalanche. Ten feet from the edge of the bridge he stamped on the brakes and skidded to a sliding halt, on solid ground again, in less than twenty yards.

Schaffer had already the back door open and the two packages of plastic explosives in his hands before the bus stopped. Five seconds after hitting the road he was back on the bridge again, skipping nimbly over a dozen dislodged sleepers until he had arrived at the main supports of the central trestle. It took him less than twenty seconds to tape one package to the right hand support, cross the bridge and tape the second package to the left hand support. He heard the deepening roar of a rapidly approaching engine, glanced up, saw the swathe of unseen headlamp beams shining round the corner they had just passed, tore off the ignition fuse, crossed the bridge, tore off the other and raced for the bus. Smith had already the bus in gear and was moving away when Schaffer flung himself through the back doorway and was hauled inside by helping hands.

Schaffer twisted round till he was sitting on the passage-way, his legs dangling through the open doorway, just in time to see the headlamps of the pursuing car sweep into sight round the corner. It was now less than a hundred yards from the bridge, and accelerating. For a brief, almost panic-stricken, moment, Schaffer wondered wildly if he had cut the fuses short enough, he hadn't realized the following car had been quite as close as it was: and from the tense and strained expressions on the faces of the two girls and the man beside him, expressions sensed rather than seen, he knew that exactly the same thought was in their minds.

The two loud, flat detonations, each fractionally preceded by the brilliant white flash characteristic of the plastic explosive, came within one second of each other. Baulks of timber and railway sleepers were hurled forty feet into the air, spinning lazily around in a curious kind of slow motion, many of them falling back again on to the now tottering support structure with an impact sufficient to carry away the central trestle. One moment, a bridge: the next, an empty ravine with, on the far side of it, the wildly swinging headlamp beams as the driver flung his car from side to side in a nothing-to-be-lost attempt to prevent the car from sliding over the edge of the ravine. It seemed certain that he must fail until the moment when the car, sliding broadside on along the road, struck a large rock, rolled over twice and came to a halt less than six feet from the edge of the ravine.

Schaffer shook his head in wonder, rose, closed the rear door, sat in the back seat, lit a cigarette, tossed the spent match through the smashed rear window and observed: 'You're a lucky lot to have me around.'

'All this and modesty too,' Heidi said admiringly.

'A rare combination,' Schaffer acknowledged. 'You'll find lots of other pleasant surprises in store for you as we grow old together. How far to this airfield now?'

'Five miles. Perhaps eight minutes. But this is the only road in. With the bridge gone, there's no hurry now.'

'That's as maybe. Schaffer is anxious to be gone. Tell me, honey, were *all* those beer bottles empty?'

'The ones we threw away were.'

'I just simply don't deserve you,' Schaffer said reverently.

'We're thinking along the same lines at last,' Heidi said acidly.

Schaffer grinned, took two beer bottles and went forward to relieve Smith, who moved out only too willingly with the bus still in motion. Smith's right hand, Schaffer saw, hadn't a scrap of bandage left that wasn't wholly saturated in blood and the face was very pale. But he made no comment.

Three minutes later they were out of the forest, running along through open farm-land, and five minutes after that, acting on Heidi's directions, Schaffer swung the bus through a narrow gateway on the left hand side of the road. The headlamps successively illuminated two small hangars, a narrow, cleared runway stretching into the distance and, finally, a bullet-riddled Mosquito bomber with a crumpled under-carriage.

'Ain't that a beautiful sight, now?' Schaffer nodded at the damaged plane. 'Carnaby-Jones's transport?'

Smith nodded. 'It began with a Mosquito and it will end – we hope – in a Mosquito. This is Oberhausen airfield HQ of the Bavarian Mountain Rescue pilots.'

'Three cheers for the Bavarian Mountain Rescue pilots.' Schaffer stopped the bus facing up the length of the runway, switched off the lights and turned off the engine. They sat silently in the darkness, waiting.

Colonel Wyatt-Turner glanced through the side-screen and breathed with relief as, for the first time that night, the ground fell away sharply beneath the Mosquito. He said sarcastically: 'Losing your nerve, Wing Commander?'

'I lost that September 3rd, 1939,' Carpenter said cheerfully. 'Got to climb. Can't expect to see any recognition signals down among the bushes there.'

'You're sure we're on the right course?'

'No question. That's the Weissspitze there. Three minutes' flying time.' Carpenter paused and went on thoughtfully. 'Looks uncommon like Guy Fawkes night up there, don't you think.'

The Wing Commander was hardly exaggerating. In the far distance the silhouette of the Weissspitze was but dimly seen, but there was no mistaking the intensity of the great fire blazing half-way up the mountain-side. Occasionally, great gouts of red flame and what looked like gigantic fireworks could be seen soaring high above the main body of the fire.

'Explosives or boxes of ammunition going up, I'd say,' Carpenter said pensively. 'That's the Schloss Adler, of course. Were any of your boys carrying matches?'

'They must have been.' Wyatt-Turner stared impassively at the distant blaze. 'It's quite a sight.'

'It's all of that,' Carpenter agreed. He touched Wyatt-Turner's arm and pointed forwards and down. 'But there's a sight that's far finer, the most beautiful sight I've ever seen.'

Wyatt-Turner followed the pointing finger. Less than two miles away, about five hundred feet below, a pair of headlamps were flashing regularly on and off, once every two seconds. With a conscious effort of will he looked away and glanced briefly at Carpenter, but almost at once was back on the flashing headlamps. He stared at them hypnotically and shook his head in slow and total disbelief.

Schaffer had the headlights switched on main beam, illuminating the runway, and the post-bus engine running as the black squat shape of the Mosquito, air-brakes fully extended, lined up for its approach to the runway, and had the bus itself moving, accelerating quickly through the gears, as the Mosquito sank down over the top of the bus and settled down beautifully without the slightest suspicion of a bounce.

Within a minute Schaffer brought the bus to a skidding halt only yards from the now stationary plane. Half a minute later, with all five of them safely inside the plane, Carpenter had the Mosquito turned through 180° and was standing hard on the brakes as he brought the engines up to maximum revolutions. And then they were on their way, gathering speed so rapidly that they were air-borne two hundred yards before the end of the runway. For the first mile of their climb Carpenter kept the plane heading almost directly towards the blazing castle that now redly illuminated the entire valley, then the funeral pyre of the Schloss Adler vanished for the last time as the Mosquito banked and headed for the north-west and home.

Chapter Twelve

Wing Commander Carpenter took the Mosquito up to five thousand feet and kept it there. The time for dodging around among the bushes was past for, on the outward journey, Carpenter had been concerned only that no German station pick him up long enough to form even a rough guess as to where he was going. But now he didn't care if every radar station in the country knew where he was going: he was going home to England, mission accomplished, and there wasn't a warplane in Europe that could catch him. Wing Commander Carpenter pulled luxuriously at his evil-smelling briar. He was well content.

His five newly-acquired passengers were, perhaps, a fraction less content. They lacked Carpenter's well-upholstered pilot's seat. The interior of the Mosquito made no concessions whatsoever to passenger comfort. It was bleak, icy, cramped – it didn't require much space to carry a 4000 lb. bomb load, the Mosquito's maximum – and totally devoid of seating in any form. The three men and the two girls squatted uncomfortably on thin palliasses, the expressions on their faces pretty accurately reflecting their acute discomfort. Colonel Wyatt-Turner, still holding across his knees the Sten gun he'd had at the ready in case any trouble had developed on the ground or the flashing lights of the truck had been a German ruse, was sitting sideways in the co-pilot's seat so that he could see and talk to the pilot and the passengers at the same time. He had accepted without question or apparent interest Smith's brief explanation of the two girls' presence as being necessary to escape Gestapo vengeance. Colonel Wyatt-Turner had other and weightier matters on his mind.

Smith looked up from the bleeding mangled hand that Mary was rebandaging with the plane's first aid kit and said to the Colonel: 'It was good of you to come in person to meet us, sir.'

'It wasn't good of me at all,' Wyatt-Turner said frankly. 'I'd have gone mad if I'd stayed another minute in London – I *had* to know. It was I who sent you all out here.' He sat without speaking for some time, then went on heavily: 'Torrance-Smythe gone, Sergeant Harrod, and now, you say, Carraciola, Christiansen and Thomas. All dead. A heavy price, Smith, a terrible price. My best men.'

'All of them, sir?' Smith asked softly.

'I'm getting old.' Wyatt-Turner shook his head wearily and drew a hand across his eyes. 'Did you find out who—'

'Carraciola.'

'Carraciola! Ted Carraciola? Never! I can't believe it.'

'*And* Christiansen.' Smith's voice was still quiet, still even. '*And* Thomas.'

'And Christiansen? And Thomas?' He looked consideringly at Smith. 'You've been through a lot, Major Smith. You're not well.'

'I'm not as well as I was,' Smith admitted. 'But I was well enough when I killed them?'

'You – *you* killed them?'

'I've killed a traitor before now. You know that.'

'But – but traitors! All three of them. Impossible. I can't believe it! I *won't* believe it!'

'Then maybe you'll believe this, sir.' Smith produced one of the notebooks from his tunic and handed it to Wyatt-Turner. 'The names and addresses or contacts of every German agent in southern England *and* the names of all British agents in north-west Europe who have been supplanted by German agents. You will recognise Carraciola's writing. He wrote this under duress.'

Slowly, like a man in a dream, Wyatt-Turner reached out and took the note-book. For three minutes he examined the contents, leafing slowly, almost reluctantly through the pages, then finally laid the book down with a sigh.

'This is the most important document in Europe, the most important document I have even seen.' Wyatt-Turner sighed. 'The nation is deeply in your debt, Major Smith.'

'Thank you, sir.'

'Or would have been. It's a great pity it will never have the chance to express its gratitude.' He lifted the Sten from his knees and pointed it at Smith's heart. 'You will do nothing foolish, will you, Major Smith?'

'What in God's name—' Carpenter twisted in his seat and stared at Wyatt-Turner in startled and total disbelief.

'Concentrate on your flying, my dear Wing Commander.' Wyatt-Turner waved the Sten gently in Carpenter's direction. 'Your course will do for the present. We'll be landing at Lille airport within the hour.'

'The guy's gone nuts!' Schaffer's voice was a shocked whisper.

'If he has,' Smith said drily, 'he went nuts some years ago. Ladies and gentlemen, I give you the most dangerous spy in Europe, the most successful double agent of all time.' He paused for reaction, but the silence remained unbroken: the enormity of the revelation of Wyatt-Turner's duplicity was too great for immediate comprehension. Smith continued: 'Colonel Wyatt-Turner, you will be court-martialled this afternoon, sentenced, removed to the Tower then taken out, blind-folded and shot at eight o'clock tomorrow morning.'

'You knew?' Wyatt-Turner's affable self-confidence had completely deserted him and his voice, low and strained, was barely distinguishable above the clamour of the engines. 'You knew about me?'

'I knew about you,' Smith nodded. 'But we all knew about you, didn't we, Colonel? Three years, you claimed, behind the German lines, served with the Wehrmacht and finally penetrated the Berlin High Command. Sure you did. With the help of the Wehrmacht and the High Command. But when the tide of war turned and you could no longer feed the Allies with false and misleading reports about proposed German advances, then you were allowed to escape back to England to feed the Germans true and accurate reports about Allied planes – *and* give them all the information they required to round up British agents in north-west Europe. How many million francs do you have in your numbered account in Zurich, Colonel?'

Wing Commander Carpenter stared straight ahead through the windscreen, and said very slowly: 'Frankly, old chap, this is preposterous.'

'Try batting an eyelid and see just how preposterous that Sten gun is,' Smith suggested. He looked at Wyatt-Turner again. 'You underestimated Admiral Rolland, I'm afraid. He's had his suspicions about you and the four section leaders of Department C for months. But he was wrong about Torrance-Smythe.'

'Guess away.' Wyatt-Turner had recovered his composure and most of his self-confidence. 'It'll pass the time till we get to Lille.'

'Unfortunately for you, there is no guess-work. Admiral Rolland recalled me – and Mary – from Italy: he could no longer be sure of anyone in London. You know how corruption spreads? Played it very clever, did the Admiral. He told you he had his suspicions about one of his section leaders, but didn't know which. So, when General Carnaby crashed, he put up to you the idea of sending the section officers to the rescue – and made damn sure that you never once had the opportunity of talking to any of them in private before they took off.'

'That – that was why I was called in?' Schaffer looked as if he had been sand-bagged. 'Because you couldn't trust—'

'For all we knew, MI6 was riddled ... Well, Colonel, you weren't too happy until Rolland asked *you* to pick the leader. So you picked me. Rolland knew you would. You'd only just met me for the first time, but you knew from Kesselring's military intelligence chief, through your pal Admiral Canaris, that I was their top double agent. Or thought you did. Rolland was the only man on either side who knew I wasn't. For you, I was the ideal choice. Rolland made certain that you didn't have the chance of talking to *me* either, but you weren't worried. You knew that I would know what to do.' Smith smiled bleakly. 'I'm happy to say I did. It must have been quite a shock to your system this afternoon when he told you what I really was.'

'You knew that? You knew all that?' Wyatt-Turner's newfound composure had vanished, his voice was quiet and vicious. He lifted the Sten slightly. 'What goes on, Smith?'

'All pre-arranged to force your hand. We had everything – except proof – about you. I got that proof this evening. Colonel Kramer *knew* that we were coming, *knew* we were after General Carnaby.' He nodded towards Jones. 'Incidentally meet Cartwright Jones, an American actor.'

'What?' Wyatt-Turner forced out the word as if a pair of powerful hands were squeezing on his wind-pipe.

'General Carnaby is spending a quiet weekend at the Admiral's country house in Wiltshire. As a stand-in, Mr Jones was quite admirable. He had them all as deceived as that faked plane crash – you will have realized by now that it was a deliberate crash-landing.' Wyatt-Turner tried to speak, but the words failed to come: his mouth was working and the colour had drained from his ruddy face. 'And why did Kramer know? He knew because you had informed Berlin as soon as Rolland had put the plan to you. *Nobody else had the chance to. And* he knew that we would be in "Zum Wilden Hirsch" this evening. He knew because I told you on the radio broadcast this morning and you lost no time in passing the good word on.'

'Are you sure?' Heidi asked. 'Couldn't the informant have been whichever of the men – Carraciola or Christiansen or Thomas – who killed Torrance-Smythe. There's a phone box just outside the inn.'

'I know. No, he didn't have time. I left the inn for exactly seven minutes. Three minutes after I'd left, Torrance-Smythe did the same – to follow one of the three others he'd just seen leaving. Smithy was clever and he knew something was far wrong. He—'

'*How* did he know?' Schaffer demanded.

'We'll never be sure. I think we'll find that he was a highly-skilled lip-reader. Anyway, he caught the man he'd seen leaving in the phone booth outside the Post Office – before he'd had time to get through to either Weissner or Kramer. There was a fight to the death. By the time the killer had dragged Smithy around to the back and returned to the booth, someone else was occupying it. I saw him. So the killer had to go back into the inn. Kramer it was who told Weissner – and the Colonel here who told Kramer.'

'Very interesting.' There was a sneer in Wyatt-Turner's voice, but a sneer belied by the deep unease in his face. 'Fascinating, in fact. Quite finished, Major Smith?'

'Finished.' Smith sighed. 'You just had to come to meet us, hadn't you, Colonel? This was the last door to life left open to you. In my final broadcast I told the Admiral "I have it all". He told you what that meant – all the names, all the addresses. We could never have got at you through Carraciola, Christiansen or Thomas – they were too close to you in MI6, you were too cagey and they never knew who they were working for. You used intermediaries – and all their names are in that book. You *knew* they'd put the finger on you – when it's a choice between taking a walk to the gallows and talking – well, it's not much of a choice, is it?'

Wyatt-Turner didn't answer. He turned to Carpenter and said: 'Lay off a course for Lille airport.'

'Don't bother,' Smith said.

Wyatt-Turner lined his Sten on Smith. 'Give me one good reason why I shouldn't shoot you now.'

'I can do that,' Smith nodded. 'Why do you think that Admiral Rolland accompanied you to the airport. He never has before.'

'Go on.' Wyatt's voice was hard, abrupt, but his eyes were sick, sick with the sudden certainty of defeat and death.

'To make quite certain that you took that Sten and only that Sten with you. Tell me, can you see two parallel scores where the stock meets the barrel?'

Wyatt-Turner stared at him for a long moment than glanced down quickly at the Sten. There were two unmistakable parallel scratches exactly where Smith had said they would be. Wyatt-Turner looked up again, his face contorted, desperation replacing the sickness in his eyes.

'That's right,' Smith said. 'I personally filed off the firing pin exactly thirty-six hours ago.' With his left hand Smith reached awkwardly under his tunic flap and brought out his silenced Luger. Wyatt-Turner, with his Sten lined up on Smith's head and the muzzle less than three feet from Smith's face, squeezed the trigger time and again, and each convulsive contraction of his forefinger was rewarded by a dry and empty click. With a stunned almost uncomprehending expression on his face, Wyatt-Turner slowly lowered the Sten to the floor, then quickly whirled in his seat, jerked open the door and threw the note-book out into the night. He turned and smiled bleakly at Smith.

'The most important document in Europe, I believe I called it.'

'So you did.' Smith handed his gun to Schaffer, reached under his tunic and brought out two more books. 'Duplicates.'

'Duplicates!' The smile slowly faded from the heavily-jowled face, leaving it frozen in defeat. 'Duplicates,' he whispered. He looked slowly around them all and then finally back at Smith, who had retrieved his gun from Schaffer. He said: 'Are you going to shoot me?'

'No.'

Wyatt-Turner nodded, slid back the door to its widest extent and said: 'Can you really see me in the Tower?' He stepped forward into the doorway.

'No.' Smith shook his head. 'No, I can't see that.'

'Mind the step,' said Schaffer. His voice was cold and empty, his face was carved from stone.

'Well, now, time to make a call.' Smith slid shut the door, scrambled painfully into the co-pilot's seat and looked at Mary. 'The Admiral must be getting worried by this time.'

'Time to make a call,' Mary repeated mechanically. She stared at him as if seeing a ghost. 'How can you sit there – just after – how can you be so *calm*?'

'Because it's no shock to me, silly. I *knew* he was going to die.'

'You knew – of course, of course,' she murmured.

'Now then,' Smith went on, deliberately brisk-voiced as he took her hand. 'You realize what this means, don't you?'

'Do I realize what what means?' She was still ashen-faced.

'You and I are all washed up,' Smith explained patiently. 'Finished. In Italy, in north-west Europe. I won't even be allowed to fight as a soldier because if I were captured I'd still be shot as a spy.'

'So?'

'So, for us, the war is over. For the first time we can think of ourselves.

OK?' He squeezed her hand and she smiled shakily in reply. 'OK. Wing Commander, may I use your radio?'

'So that's the way he went.' Admiral Rolland, telephone in hand and standing by the big transceiver in his London Operations HQ, looked old and very very tired. 'Maybe it's all for the best, Smith. And you have all the information you want?'

Smith's voice crackled over the earphone. 'Everything, sir.'

'Magnificent, magnificent! I have all the police forces in the country alerted. As soon as we get that book . . . There's a car waiting for you at the airport. See you in an hour.'

'Yes, sir. There's one thing, sir, a small thing. I want to get married this morning.'

'You what?' Grey bushy eyebrows lifted towards the mane of white hair.

'I want to get married,' Smith explained slowly and patiently. 'To Miss Mary Ellison.'

'But you can't,' Rolland protested. 'This morning! Impossible! There are such things as banns, permits, the registrar's office will be shut today—'

'After all I've done for you,' Smith interrupted reproachfully.

'Blackmail, sir! You play on an old man's gratitude. Downright blackmail!' Rolland banged down the phone, smiled tiredly and picked up another phone. 'Operator? Put me through to the Forgery Section.'

Wing Commander Carpenter, his pipe well alight and by his elbow a cup of coffee newly poured from a vacuum flask, was his old imperturbable self again. Smith talked quietly to Mary while Jones had his eyes closed and appeared to be asleep.

Farther aft in the fuselage, Schaffer had his arm around Heidi, who was making no attempt to fight him off.

'Right,' Schaffer said. 'So we go to this pub tonight, see—'

'You said the Savoy Grill,' Heidi reminded him.

'A rose by any other name . . . So we go to this pub, and we'll have paté, smoked trout, sirloin of Aberdeen-Angus—'

'Aberdeen-Angus!' Heidi looked at him in amusement. 'Forgotten the war, haven't you? Forgotten rationing? More like a sirloin of horse meat.'

'Honey.' Schaffer took her hands and spoke severely and earnestly. 'Honey, don't ever again mention that word to me. I'm allergic to horses.'

'You eat them?' Heidi gazed at him in astonishment. 'In Montana?'

'I fall off them,' Schaffer said moodily. 'Everywhere.'

Alistair MacLean

Ice Station Zebra

Ice Station Zebra
To Lachlan, Michael and Alistair

U.S.S. DOLPHIN

1. Rudder
2. Stern Room
3. Nucleonics Room
4. Manoeuvring Room
5. Engine Room
6. Machinery space
7. Passage over reactor
8. Reactor Room
9. Sail
10. Bridge
11. Radio Room (port)
12. Control Room
13. Captain's Cabin (port)
    Sickbay (starboard)
14. Wardroom
15. Inertial Navigation Room
16. Electronics Room
17. Crew's Quarters
18. Galley
19. Medical Store
20. Disposal chute
21. Periscope (retracted)
22. Torpedo Storage Room
23. Collision Space
24. Torpedo Room
25. Torpedo Tubes
26. Bow Caps

ICE STATION ZEBRA

| COOK-HOUSE | GENERATOR ROOM | MAIN BUNKHOUSE | LABORATORY |

| RADIO ROOM | MAJOR HALLIWELL'S HUT | FUEL STORE | METEOR-OLOGICAL HUT | TRACTOR |

N

Chapter One

Commander James D. Swanson of the United States Navy was short, plump and crowding forty. He had jet black hair topping a pink cherubic face, and with the deep permanent creases of laughter lines radiating from his eyes and curving round his mouth he was a dead ringer for the cheerful, happy-go-lucky extrovert who is the life and soul of the party where the guests park their brains along with their hats and coats. That, anyway, was how he struck me at first glance but on the reasonable assumption that I might very likely find some other qualities in the man picked to command the latest and most powerful nuclear submarine afloat I took a second and closer look at him and this time I saw what I should have seen the first time if the dank grey fog and winter dusk settling down over the Firth of Clyde hadn't made seeing so difficult. His eyes. Whatever his eyes were they weren't those of the gladhanding wisecracking *bon vivant*. They were the coolest, clearest grey eyes I'd ever seen, eyes that he used as a dentist might his probe, a surgeon his lancet or a scientist his electronic microscope. Measuring eyes. They measured first me and then the paper he held in his hand but gave no clue at all as to the conclusions arrived at on the basis of measurements made.

'I'm sorry, Dr Carpenter.' The south-of-the-Mason–Dixon-line voice was quiet and courteous, but without any genuine regret that I could detect, as he folded the telegram back into its envelope and handed it to me. 'I can accept neither this telegram as sufficient authorization nor yourself as a passenger. Nothing personal, you know that; but I have my orders.'

'Not sufficient authorization?' I pulled the telegram from its cover and pointed to the signature. 'Who do you think this is – the resident window-cleaner at the Admiralty?'

It wasn't funny, and as I looked at him in the failing light I thought maybe I'd overestimated the depth of the laughter lines in the face. He said precisely: 'Admiral Hewson is commander of the Nato Eastern Division. On Nato exercises I come under his command. At all other times I am responsible only to Washington. This is one of those other times. I'm sorry. And I must point out, Dr Carpenter, that you could have arranged for anyone in London to send this telegram. It's not even on a naval message form.'

He didn't miss much, that was a fact, but he was being suspicious about nothing. I said: 'You could call him up by radio-telephone, Commander.'

'So I could,' he agreed. 'And it would make no difference. Only accredited American nationals are allowed aboard this vessel – and the authority must come from Washington.'

'From the Director of Underseas Warfare or Commander Atlantic submarines?' He nodded, slowly, speculatively, and I went on: 'Please radio them and ask them to contact Admiral Hewson. Time is very short, Commander.' I might have added that it was beginning to snow and that I was getting colder by the minute, but I refrained.

He thought for a moment, nodded, turned and walked a few feet to a portable dockside telephone that was connected by a looping wire to the long dark shape lying at our feet. He spoke briefly, keeping his voice low, and hung up. He barely had time to rejoin me when three duffel-coated figures came hurrying up an adjacent gangway, turned in our direction and stopped when they reached us. The tallest of the three tall men, a lean rangy character with wheat-coloured hair and the definite look of a man who ought to have had a horse between his legs, stood slightly in advance of the other two. Commander Swanson gestured towards him.

'Lieutenant Hansen, my executive officer. He'll look after you till I get back.' The commander certainly knew how to choose his words.

'I don't need looking after,' I said mildly. 'I'm all grown up now and I hardly ever feel lonely.'

'I shall be as quick as I can, Dr Carpenter,' Swanson said. He hurried off down the gangway and I gazed thoughtfully after him. I put out of my mind any idea I might have had about the Commander US Atlantic Submarines picking his captains from the benches in Central Park. I had tried to effect an entrance aboard Swanson's ship and if such an entrance was unauthorized he didn't want me taking off till he'd found out why. Hansen and his two men, I guessed, would be the three biggest sailors on the ship.

The ship. I stared down at the great black shape lying almost at my feet. This was my first sight of a nuclear-engined submarine, and the *Dolphin* was like no submarine that I had ever seen. She was about the same length as a World War II long-range ocean-going submarine but there all resemblance ceased. Her diameter was at least twice that of any conventional submarine. Instead of having the vaguely boat-shaped lines of her predecessors, the *Dolphin* was almost perfectly cylindrical in design: instead of the usual V-shaped bows, her fore end was completely semi-spherical. There was no deck, as such: the rounded sheer of sides and bows rose smoothly to the top of the hull then fell as smoothly away again, leaving only a very narrow fore-and-aft working space so dangerously treacherous in its slippery convexity that it was permanently railed off in harbour. About a hundred feet back from the bows the slender yet massive conning-tower reared over twenty feet above the deck, for all the world like the great dorsal fin of some monstrous shark: half-way up the sides of the conning-tower and thrust out stubbily at right angles were the sweptback auxiliary diving planes of the submarine. I tried to see what lay farther aft but the fog and the thickening snow swirling down from the north of Loch Long defeated me. Anyway, I was losing interest. I'd only a thin raincoat over my clothes and I could feel my skin start to gooseflesh under the chill fingers of that winter wind.

'Nobody said anything about us having to freeze to death,' I said to Hansen. 'That naval canteen there. Would your principles prevent you from accepting a cup of coffee from Dr Carpenter, that well-known espionage agent?'

He grinned and said: 'In the matter of coffee, friend, I have no principles. Especially to-night. Someone should have warned us about those Scottish winters.' He not only looked like a cowboy, he talked like one: I was an expert on cowboys as I was sometimes too tired to rise to switch off the TV set. 'Rawlings, go tell the captain that we are sheltering from the elements.'

While Rawlings went to the dockside phone Hansen led the way to the nearby neon-lit canteen. He let me precede him through the door then made for the counter while the other sailor, a red-complexioned character about the size and shape of a polar bear, nudged me gently into an angled bench seat in one corner of the room. They weren't taking too many chances with me. Hansen came and sat on the other side of me, and when Rawlings returned he sat squarely in front of me across the table.

'As neat a job of corralling as I've seen for a long time,' I said approvingly. 'You've got nasty suspicious minds, haven't you?'

'You wrong us,' Hansen said sadly. 'We're just three friendly sociable guys carrying out our orders. It's Commander Swanson who has the nasty suspicious mind, isn't that so, Rawlings?'

'Yes, indeed, Lieutenant,' Rawlings said gravely. 'Very security-minded, the captain is.'

I tried again. 'Isn't this very inconvenient for you?' I asked. 'I mean, I should have thought that every man would have been urgently required aboard if you're due to sail in less than two hours' time.'

'You just keep on talking, Doc,' Hansen said encouragingly. There was nothing encouraging about his cold blue Arctic eyes. 'I'm a right good listener.'

'Looking forward to your trip up to the ice-pack?' I inquired pleasantly.

They operated on the same wavelength, all right. They didn't even look at one another. In perfect unison they all hitched themselves a couple of inches closer to me, and there was nothing imperceptible about the way they did it either. Hansen waited, smiling in a pleasantly relaxed fashion until the waitress had deposited four steaming mugs of coffee on the table, then said in the same encouraging tone: 'Come again, friend. Nothing we like to hear better than top classified information being bandied about in canteens. How the hell do *you* know where we're going?'

I reached up my hand beneath my coat lapel and it stayed there, my right wrist locked in Hansen's right hand.

'We're not suspicious or anything,' he said apologetically. 'It's just that we submariners are very nervous on account of the dangerous life we lead. Also, we've a very fine library of films aboard the *Dolphin* and every time a character in one of those films reaches up under his coat it's always for the same reason and that's not just because he's checking to see if his wallet's still there.'

I took his wrist with my free hand, pulled his arm away and pushed it down on the table. I'm not saying it was easy, the US Navy clearly fed its submariners on a high protein diet, but I managed it without bursting a blood-vessel. I pulled a folded newspaper out from under my coat and laid it down. 'You wanted to know how the hell I knew where you were going,' I said. 'I can read, that's why. That's a Glasgow evening paper I picked up in Renfrew Airport half an hour ago.'

Hansen rubbed his wrist thoughtfully, then grinned. 'What did you get your doctorate in, Doc? Weight-lifting? About that paper – how could you have got it in Renfrew half an hour ago?'

'I flew down here. Helicopter.'

'A whirlybird, eh? I heard one arriving a few minutes ago. But that was one of ours.'

'It had US Navy written all over it in four-foot letters,' I conceded, 'and the pilot spent all his time chewing gum and praying out loud for a quick return to California.'

'Did you tell the skipper this?' Hansen demanded.

'He didn't give me the chance to tell him anything.'

'He's got a lot on his mind and far too much to see to,' Hansen said. He unfolded the paper and looked at the front page. He didn't have far to look to find what he wanted: the two-inch banner headlines were spread over seven columns.

'Well, would you look at this.' Lieutenant Hansen made no attempt to conceal his irritation and chagrin. 'Here we are, pussy-footing around in this God-forsaken dump, sticking-plaster all over our mouths, sworn to eternal secrecy about mission and destination and then what? I pick up this blasted Limey newspaper and here are all the top-secret details plastered right across the front page.'

'You are kidding, Lieutenant,' said the man with the red face and the general aspect of a polar bear. His voice seemed to come from his boots.

'I am not kidding, Zabrinski,' Hansen said coldly, 'as you would appreciate if you had ever learned to read. "Nuclear submarine to the rescue," it says. "Dramatic dash to the North Pole." God help us, the North Pole. And a picture of the *Dolphin*. And of the skipper. Good lord, there's even a picture of me.'

Rawlings reached out a hairy paw and twisted the paper to have a better look at the blurred and smudged representation of the man before him. 'So there is. Not very flattering, is it, Lieutenant? But a speaking likeness, mind you, a speaking likeness. The photographer has caught the essentials perfectly.'

'You are utterly ignorant of the first principles of photography,' Hansen said witheringly. 'Listen to this lot. "The following joint statement was issued simultaneously a few minutes before noon (GMT) to-day in both London and Washington: 'In view of the critical condition of the survivors of Drift Ice Station Zebra and the failure either to rescue or contact them by conventional means, the United States Navy has willingly agreed that the United States nuclear submarine *Dolphin* be dispatched with all speed to try to effect contact with the survivors.

' "The *Dolphin* returned to its base in the Holy Loch, Scotland, at dawn this morning after carrying out extensive exercises with the Nato naval forces in the Eastern Atlantic. It is hoped that the *Dolphin* (Commander James D. Swanson, USN, commanding) will sail at approximately 7 p.m. (GMT) this evening.

' "The laconic understatement of this communique heralds the beginning of a desperate and dangerous rescue attempt which must be without parallel in the history of the sea or the Arctic. It is now sixty hours—" '

' "Desperate," you said, Lieutenant?' Rawlings frowned heavily. ' "Dangerous," you said? The captain will be asking for volunteers?'

'No need. I told the captain that I'd already checked with all eighty-eight enlisted men and that they'd volunteered to a man.'

'You never checked with me.'

'I must have missed you out. Now kindly clam up, your executive officer is talking. "It is now sixty hours since the world was electrified to learn of the disaster which had struck Drift Ice Station Zebra, the only British meteorological station in the Arctic, when an English-speaking ham radio operator in Bodo, Norway picked up the faint SOS from the top of the world.

' "A further message, picked up less than twenty-four hours ago by the British trawler *Morning Star* in the Barents Sea makes it clear that the position of the survivors of the fuel oil fire that destroyed most of Drift Ice Station Zebra in the early hours of Tuesday morning is desperate in the extreme. With their oil fuel reserves completely destroyed and their food stores all but wiped out, it is feared that those still living cannot long be expected to survive in the twenty-below temperatures – fifty degrees of frost – at present being experienced in that area.

' "It is not known whether all the prefabricated huts, in which the expedition members lived, have been destroyed.

' "Drift Ice Station Zebra, which was established only in the late summer of this year, is at present in an estimated position of 85° 40′ N 21° 30′ E, which is only about three hundred miles from the North Pole. Its position cannot be known with certainty because of the clockwise drift of the polar ice-pack.

' "For the past thirty hours long-range supersonic bombers of the American, British and Russian air forces have been scouring the polar ice-pack searching for Station Zebra. Because of the uncertainty about the Drift Station's actual position, the complete absence of daylight in the Arctic at this time of year and the extremely bad weather conditions they were unable to locate the station and forced to return." '

'They didn't have to locate it,' Rawlings objected. 'Not visually. With the instruments those bombers have nowadays they could home in on a hummingbird a hundred miles away. The radio operator at the Drift Station had only to keep on sending and they could have used that as a beacon.'

'Maybe the radio operator is dead,' Hansen said heavily. 'Maybe his radio has packed up on him. Maybe the fuel that was destroyed was essential for running the radio. All depends what source of power he used.'

'Diesel-electric generator,' I said. 'He had a standby battery of Nife cells. Maybe he's conserving the batteries, using them only for emergencies. There's also a hand-cranked generator, but its range is pretty limited.'

'How do you know that?' Hansen asked quietly. 'About the type of power used?'

'I must have read it somewhere.'

'You must have read it somewhere.' He looked at me without expression, then turned back to his paper. ' "A report from Moscow," ' he read on, ' "states that the atomic-engined *Dvina*, the world's most powerful ice-breaker, sailed from Murmansk some twenty hours ago and is proceeding at high speed towards the Arctic pack. Experts are not hopeful about the outcome for at this late period of the year the ice-pack had already thickened and compacted into a solid mass which will almost certainly defy the efforts of any vessel, even those of the *Dvina*, to smash its way through.

' "The use of the submarine *Dolphin* appears to offer the only slender hope of life for the apparently doomed survivors of Station Zebra. The odds against success must be regarded as heavy in the extreme. Not only will the *Dolphin* have to travel several hundred miles continuously submerged under the polar ice-cap, but the possibilities of its being able to break through the ice-cap at any given place or to locate the survivors are very remote. But undoubtedly if any ship in the world can do it it is the *Dolphin*, the pride of the United States Navy's nuclear submarine fleet." '

Hansen broke off and read on silently for a minute. Then he said: 'That's about all. A story giving all the known details of the *Dolphin*. That, and a lot of ridiculous rubbish about the enlisted men in the *Dolphin*'s crew being the *èlite* of the cream of the US Navy.'

Rawlings looked wounded. Zabrinski, the polar bear with the red face, grinned, fished out a pack of cigarettes and passed them around. Then he became serious again and said: 'What are those crazy guys doing up there at the top of the world anyway?'

'Meteorological, lunkhead,' Rawlings informed him. 'Didn't you hear the lieutenant say so? A big word, mind you,' he conceded generously, 'but he made a pretty fair stab at it. Weather station to you, Zabrinski.'

'I still say they're crazy guys,' Zabrinski rumbled. 'Why do they do it, Lieutenant?'

'I suggest you ask Dr Carpenter about it,' Hansen said dryly. He stared through the plate-glass windows at the snow whirling greyly through the gathering darkness, his eyes bleak and remote, as if he were already visualizing the doomed men drifting to their death in the frozen immensity of the polar ice-cap. 'I think he knows a great deal more about it than I do.'

'I know a little,' I admitted. 'There's nothing mysterious or sinister about what I know. Meteorologists now regard the Arctic and the Antarctic as the two great weather factories of the world, the areas primarily responsible for the weather that affects the rest of the hemisphere. We already know a fair amount about Antarctic conditions, but practically nothing about the Arctic. So we pick a suitable ice-floe, fill it with huts crammed with technicians and all sorts of instruments and let them drift around the top of the world for six months or so. Your own people have already set up two or three of those stations. The Russians have set up at least ten, to the best of my knowledge, most of them in the East Siberian Sea.'

'How do they establish those camps, Doc?' Rawlings asked.

'Different ways. Your people prefer to establish them in winter-time, when the pack freezes up enough for plane landings to be made. Someone flies out from, usually, Point Barrow in Alaska and searches around the polar pack till they find a suitable ice-floe – even when the ice is compacted and frozen together into one solid mass an expert can tell which pieces are going to remain as good-sized floes when the thaw comes and the break-in begins. Then they fly out all huts, equipment, stores and men by ski-plane and gradually build the place up.

'The Russians prefer to use a ship in summer-time. They generally use the *Lenin*, a nuclear-engined ice-breaker. It just batters its way into the summer pack, dumps everything and everybody on the ice and takes off before the big freeze-up starts. We used the same technique for Drift Ice Station Zebra – our one and only ice station. The Russians lent us the *Lenin* – all countries are only too willing to co-operate on meteorological research as everyone benefits by it – and took us pretty deep into the ice-pack north of Franz Josef Land. Zebra has already moved a good bit from its original position – the polar ice-cap, just sitting on top of the Arctic Ocean, can't quite manage to keep up with the west-east spin of the earth so that it has a slow westward movement in relation to the earth's crust. At the present moment it's about four hundred miles due north of Spitzbergen.'

'They're still crazy,' Zabrinski said. He was silent for a moment then looked speculatively at me. 'You in the Limey navy, Doc?'

'You must forgive Zabrinski's manners, Dr Carpenter,' Rawlings said coldly. 'But he's denied the advantages that the rest of us take for granted. I understand he was born in the Bronx.'

'No offence,' Zabrinski said equably. 'Royal Navy, I meant. Are you, Doc?'

'Attached to it, you might say.'

'Loosely, no doubt,' Rawlings nodded. 'Why so keen on an Arctic holiday, Doc? Mighty cool up there, I can tell you.'

'Because the men on Drift Station Zebra are going to be badly in need of medical aid. If there are any survivors, that is.'

'We got our own medico on board and he's no slouch with a stethoscope, or so I've heard from several who have survived his treatment. A well-spoken-of quack.'

'Doctor, you ill-mannered lout,' Zabrinski said severely.

'That's what I meant,' Rawlings apologized. 'It's not often that I get the chance to talk to an educated man like myself, and it just kinda slipped out. The point is, the *Dolphin*'s already all buttoned up on the medical side.'

'I'm sure it is.' I smiled. 'But any survivors we might find are going to be suffering from advanced exposure, frostbite and probably gangrene. The treatment of those is rather a speciality of mine.'

'Is it now?' Rawlings surveyed the depths of his coffee cup. 'I wonder how a man gets to be a specialist in those things?'

Hansen stirred and withdrew his gaze from the darkly-white world beyond the canteen windows.

'Dr Carpenter is not on trial for his life,' he said mildly. 'The counsel for the prosecution will kindly pack it in.'

They packed it in. This air of easy familiarity between officer and men, the easy camaraderie, the mutually tolerant disparagement with the deceptively misleading overtones of knock-about comedy, was something very rare in my experience but not unique. I'd seen it before, in first-line RAF bomber crews, a relationship found only among a close-knit, close-living group of superbly trained experts each of whom is keenly aware of their complete interdependence. The casually informal and familiar attitude was a token not of the lack of discipline but of the complete reverse: it was the token of a very high degree of self-discipline, of the regard one man held for another not only as a highly-skilled technician in his own field but also as a human being. It was clear, too, that a list of unwritten rules governed their conduct. Off-hand and frequently completely lacking in outward respect though Rawlings and Zabrinski were in their attitude towards Lieutenant Hansen, there was an invisible line of propriety over which it was inconceivable that they would ever step: for Hansen's part, he scrupulously avoided any use of his authority when making disparaging remarks at the expense of the two enlisted men. It was also clear, as now, who was boss.

Rawlings and Zabrinski stopped questioning me and had just embarked upon an enthusiastic discussion of the demerits of the Holy Loch in particular and Scotland in general as a submarine base when a jeep swept past the canteen windows, the snow whirling whitely, thickly, through the swathe of the headlights. Rawlings jumped to his feet in mid-sentence, then subsided slowly and thoughtfully into his chair.

'The plot,' he announced, 'thickens.'

'You saw who it was?' Hansen asked.

'I did indeed. Andy Bandy, no less.'

'I didn't hear that, Rawlings,' Hansen said coldly.

'Vice-Admiral John Garvie, United States Navy, sir.'

'Andy Bandy, eh?' Hansen said pensively. He grinned at me. 'Admiral Garvie, Officer Commanding US Naval Forces in Nato. Now this is very interesting, I submit. I wonder what he's doing here.'

'World War III has just broken out,' Rawlings announced. 'It's just about time for the Admiral's first martini of the day and no lesser crisis—'

'He didn't by any chance fly down with you in that chopper from Renfrew this afternoon?' Hansen interrupted shrewdly.

'No.'

'Know him, by any chance?'

'Never even heard of him until now.'

'Curiouser and curiouser,' Hansen murmured.

A few minutes passed in desultory talk – the minds of Hansen and his two men were obviously very much on the reason for the arrival of Admiral Garvie – and then a snow-filled gust of chilled air swept into the canteen as the door opened and a blue-coated sailor came in and crossed to our table.

'The captain's compliments, Lieutenant. Would you bring Dr Carpenter to his cabin, please?'

Hansen nodded, rose to his feet and led the way outside. The snow was beginning to lie now, the darkness was coming down fast and the wind from the north was bitingly chill. Hansen made for the nearest gangway, halted at its head as he saw seamen and dockyard workers, insubstantial and spectral figures in the swirling flood-lit snow, carefully easing a slung torpedo down the for'ard hatch, turned and headed towards the after gangway. We clambered down and at the foot Hansen said: 'Watch your step, Doc. It's a mite slippery hereabouts.'

It was all that, but with the thought of the ice-cold waters of the Holy Loch waiting for me if I put a foot wrong I made no mistake. We passed through the hooped canvas shelter covering the after hatch and dropped down a steep metal ladder into a warm, scrupulously clean and gleaming engine-room packed with a baffling complexity of grey-painted machinery and instrument panels, its every corner brightly illuminated with shadowless fluorescent lighting.

'Not going to blindfold me, Lieutenant?' I asked.

'No need.' He grinned. 'If you're on the up and up, it's not necessary. If you're not on the up and up it's still not necessary, for you can't talk about what you've seen – not to anyone that matters – if you're going to spend the next few years staring out from behind a set of prison bars.'

I saw his point. I followed him for'ard, our feet soundless on the black rubber decking past the tops of a couple of huge machines readily identifiable as turbo-generator sets for producing electricity. More heavy banks of instruments, a door, then a thirty-foot-long very narrow passageway. As we passed along its length I was conscious of a heavy vibrating hum from beneath my feet. The *Dolphin*'s nuclear reactor had to be somewhere. This would be it, here. Directly beneath us. There were circular hatches on the passageway deck and those could only be covers for the heavily-leaded glass windows, inspection ports which would provide the nearest and only approach to the nuclear furnace far below.

The end of the passage, another heavily-clipped door, and then we were into what was obviously the control centre of the *Dolphin*. To the left was a partitioned-off radio room, to the right a battery of machines and dialled panels of incomprehensible purpose, straight ahead a big chart table. Beyond that again, in the centre were massive mast housings and, still farther on, the periscope stand with its twin periscopes. The whole control room was twice the size of any I'd ever seen in a conventional submarine but, even so, every square inch of bulkhead space seemed to be taken up by one type or another of highly-complicated looking machines or instrument banks: even the deckhead was almost invisible, lost to sight above thickly twisted festoons of wires, cables and pipes of a score of different kinds.

The for'ard port side of the control room was for all the world like a replica of the flight-deck of a modern multi-engined jet airliner. There were two separate yoke aircraft-type control columns, facing on to banks of hooded calibrated dials. Behind the yokes were two padded leather chairs, each chair, I could see, fitted with safety-belts to hold the helmsman in place. I wondered vaguely what type of violent manoeuvres the *Dolphin* might be capable of when such safety-belts were obviously considered essential to strap the helmsman down.

Opposite the control platform, on the other side of the passageway leading forward from the control room, was a second partitioned-off room. There was no indication what this might be and I wasn't given time to wonder. Hansen hurried down the passage, stopped at the first door on his left, and knocked. The door opened and Commander Swanson appeared.

'Ah, there you are. Sorry you've been kept waiting, Dr Carpenter. We're sailing at six-thirty, John' – this to Hansen. 'You can have everything buttoned up by then?'

'Depends how quickly the loading of the torpedoes goes, Captain.'

'We're taking only six aboard.'

Hansen lifted an eyebrow, made no comment. He said: 'Loading them into the tubes?'

'In the racks. They have to be worked on.'

'No spares?'

'No spares.'

Hansen nodded and left. Swanson led me into his cabin and closed the door behind him.

Commander Swanson's cabin was bigger than a telephone booth, I'll say that for it, but not all that much bigger to shout about. A built-in bunk, a folding washbasin, a small writing-bureau and chair, a folding camp-stool, a locker, some calibrated repeater instrument dials above the bunk and that was it. If you'd tried to perform the twist in there you'd have fractured yourself in a dozen places without ever moving your feet from the centre of the floor.

'Dr Carpenter,' Swanson said, 'I'd like you to meet Admiral Garvie, Commander US Nato Naval Forces.'

Admiral Garvie put down the glass he was holding in his hand, rose from the only chair and stretched out his hand. As he stood with his feet together, the far from negligible clearance between his knees made it easy to understand the latter part of his 'Andy Bandy' nickname: like Hansen, he'd have been at home on the range. He was a tall florid-faced man with white hair, white eyebrows and a twinkle in the blue eyes below: he had that certain indefinable something about him common to all senior naval officers the world over, irrespective of race or nationality.

'Glad to meet you, Dr Carpenter. Sorry for the – um – lukewarm reception you received, but Commander Swanson was perfectly within his rights in acting as he did. His men have looked after you?'

'They permitted me to buy them a cup of coffee in the canteen.'

He smiled. 'Opportunists all, those nuclear men. I feel that the good name of American hospitality is in danger. Whisky, Dr Carpenter?'

'I thought American naval ships were dry, sir.'

'So they are, my boy, so they are. Except for a little medicinal alcohol, of course. My personal supply.' He produced a hip-flask about the size of a canteen, reached for a convenient tooth-glass. 'Before venturing into the remoter fastnesses of the Highlands of Scotland the prudent man takes the necessary precautions. I have to make an apology to you, Dr Carpenter. I saw your Admiral Hewson in London last night and had intended to be here this morning to persuade Commander Swanson here to take you aboard. But I was delayed.'

'Persuade, sir?'

'Persuade.' He sighed. 'Our nuclear submarine captains, Dr Carpenter, are a touchy and difficult bunch. From the proprietary attitude they adopt towards their submarines you'd think that each one of them was a majority shareholder in the Electric Boat Company of Groton, where most of those boats are built.' He raised his glass. 'Success to the commander and yourself. I hope you manage to find those poor devils. But I don't give you one chance in a thousand.'

'I think we'll find them, sir. Or Commander Swanson will.'

'What makes you so sure?' He added slowly, 'Hunch?'

'You could call it that.'

He laid down his glass and his eyes were no longer twinkling. 'Admiral Hewson was most evasive about you, I must say. Who are you, Carpenter? *What* are you?'

'Surely he told you, Admiral? Just a doctor attached to the navy to carry out—'

'A naval doctor?'

'Well, not exactly. I—'

'A civilian, is it?'

I nodded, and the admiral and Swanson exchanged looks which they were at no pains at all to conceal from me. If they were happy at the prospect of having aboard America's latest and most secret submarine a man who was not only a foreigner but a civilian to boot, they were hiding it well. Admiral Garvie said: 'Well, go on.'

'That's all. I carry out environmental health studies for the services. How men react to extremes of environmental conditions, such as in the Arctic or the tropics, how they react to conditions of weightlessness in simulated space flights or to extremes of pressure when having to escape from submarines. Mainly—'

'Submarines.' Admiral Garvie pounced on the word. 'You have been to sea in submarines, Dr Carpenter. Really sailed in them, I mean?'

'I had to. We found that simulated tank escapes were no substitute for the real thing.'

The admiral and Swanson looked unhappier than ever. A foreigner – bad. A foreign civilian – worse. But a foreign civilian with at least a working knowledge of submarines – terrible. I didn't have to be beaten over the head to see their point of view. I would have felt just as unhappy in their shoes.

'What's your interest in Drift Ice Station Zebra, Dr Carpenter?' Admiral Garvie asked bluntly.

'The Admiralty asked me to go there, sir.'

'So I gather, so I gather,' Garvie said wearily. 'Admiral Hewson made that quite plain to me already. Why *you*, Carpenter?'

'I have some knowledge of the Arctic, sir. I'm supposed to be an expert on the medical treatment of men subjected to prolonged exposure, frostbite and gangrene. I might be able to save lives or limbs that your own doctor aboard might not.'

'I could have half a dozen such experts here in a few hours,' Garvie said evenly. 'Regular serving officers of the United States Navy, at that. That's not enough, Carpenter.'

This was becoming difficult. I tried again. I said: 'I know Drift Station Zebra. I helped select the site. I helped establish the camp. The commandant, a Major Halliwell, has been my closest friend for many years.' The last was only half the truth but I felt that this was neither the time nor the place for over-elaboration.

'Well, well,' Garvie said thoughtfully. 'And you still claim you're just an ordinary doctor?'

'My duties are flexible, sir.'

'I'll say they are. Well, then, Carpenter, if you're just a common-or-garden sawbones, how do you explain this?' He picked a signal form from the table and handed it to me. 'This has just arrived in reply to Commander Swanson's radioed query to Washington about you.'

I looked at the signal. It read: 'Dr Neil Carpenter's bonafides beyond question. He may be taken into your fullest, repeat fullest confidence. He is to be extended every facility and all aid short of actually endangering the safety of your submarine and the lives of your crew.' It was signed by the Director of Naval Operations.

'Very civil of the Director of Naval Operations, I must say.' I handed back the signal. 'With a character reference like this, what are you worrying about. That ought to satisfy anyone.'

'It doesn't satisfy me,' Garvie said heavily. 'The ultimate responsibility for the safety of the *Dolphin* is mine. This signal more or less gives you *carte blanche* to behave as you like, to ask Commander Swanson to act in ways that might be contrary to his better judgment. I can't have that.'

'Does it matter what you can or can't have? You have your orders. Why don't you obey them?'

He didn't hit me. He didn't even bat an eyelid. He wasn't activated by pique about the fact that he wasn't privy to the reason for the seeming mystery of my presence there, he was genuinely concerned about the safety of the submarine. He said: 'If I think it more important that the *Dolphin* should remain on an active war footing rather than to go haring off on a wild-goose chase to the Arctic, or if I think you constitute a danger to the submarine, I can countermand the DNO's orders. I'm the C-in-C on the spot. And I'm not satisfied.'

This was damnably awkward. He meant every word he said and he didn't look the type who would give a hoot for the consequences if he believed himself to be in the right. I looked at both men, looked at them slowly and speculatively, the unmistakable gaze, I hoped, of a man who was weighing others in the balance: what I was really doing was thinking up a suitable story that would satisfy both. After I had given enough time to my weighing-up – and my thinking – I dropped my voice a few decibels and said: 'Is that door soundproof?'

'More or less,' Swanson said. He'd lowered his own voice to match mine.

'I won't insult either of you by swearing you to secrecy or any such rubbish,' I said quietly. 'I want to put on record the fact that what I am about to tell you I am telling you under duress, under Admiral Garvie's threat to refuse me transport if I don't comply with his wishes.'

'There will be no repercussions,' Garvie said.

'How do you know? Not that it matters now. Well, gentlemen, the facts are these. Drift Ice Station Zebra is officially classed as an Air Ministry meteorological station. Well, it belongs to the Air Ministry all right, but there's not more than a couple of qualified meteorologists among its entire personnel.'

Admiral Garvie refilled the toothglass and passed it to me without a word, without a flicker of change in his expression. The old boy certainly knew how to play it cool.

'What you will find there,' I went on, 'are some of the most highly skilled men in the world in the fields of radar, radio, infra-red and electronic computers, operating the most advanced instruments ever used in those fields. We know now, never mind how, the count-down succession of signals the Russians use in the last minute before launching a missile. There's a huge dish aerial in Zebra that can pick up and amplify any such signals within seconds of it beginning. Then long-range radar and infra-red home in on that bearing and within three minutes of the rocket's lift-off they have its height, speed and course pin-pointed to an infinitesimal degree of error. The computers do this, of course. One minute later the information is in the hands of all the anti-missile stations between Alaska and Greenland. One minute more and solid fuel infra-red homing anti-missile rockets are on their way; then the enemy missiles will be intercepted and harmlessly destroyed while still high over the Arctic regions. If you look at a map you will see that in its present position Drift Ice Station Zebra is sitting practically on Russia's missile doorstep. It's hundreds of miles in advance of the present DEW line – the distant early warning system. Anyway, it renders the DEW line obsolete.'

'I'm only the office boy around those parts,' Garvie said quietly. 'I've never heard of any of this before.'

I wasn't surprised. I'd never heard any of it myself either, not until I'd just thought it up a moment ago. Commander Swanson's reactions, if and when we ever got to Drift Station Zebra, were going to be very interesting. But I'd cross that bridge when I came to it. At present, my only concern was to get there.

'Outside the Drift Station itself,' I said, 'I doubt if a dozen people in the world know what goes on there. But now you know. And you can appreciate how vitally important it is to the free world that this base be maintained in being. If anything has happened to it we want to find out just as quick as possible *what* has happened so that we can get it operating again.'

'I still maintain that you're not an ordinary doctor,' Garvie smiled. 'Commander Swanson, how soon can you get under way?'

'Finish loading the torpedoes, move alongside the *Hunley*, load some final food stores, pick up extra Arctic clothing and that's it, sir.'

'Just like that? You said you wanted to make a slow-time dive out in the loch to check the planes and adjust the underwater trim – those missing torpedoes up front are going to make a difference you know.'

'That's before I heard Dr Carpenter. Now I want to get up there just as fast as he does, sir. I'll see if immediate trim checks are necessary: if not, we can carry them out at sea.'

'It's your boat,' Garvie acknowledged. 'Where are you going to accommodate Dr Carpenter, by the way?'

'There's space for a cot in the Exec's and Engineer's cabin.' He smiled at me. 'I've already had your suitcase put in there.'

'Did you have much trouble with the lock?' I inquired.

He had the grace to colour slightly. 'It's the first time I've ever seen a combination lock on a suitcase,' he admitted. 'It was that, more than anything else – and the fact that we couldn't open it – that made the admiral and myself so suspicious. I've still one or two things to discuss with the admiral, so I'll take you to your quarters now. Dinner will be at eight to-night.'

'I'd rather skip dinner, thanks.'

'No one ever gets seasick on the *Dolphin*, I can assure you,' Swanson smiled.

'I'd appreciate the chance to sleep instead. I've had no sleep for almost three days and I've been travelling non-stop for the past fifty hours. I'm just tired, that's all.'

'That's a fair amount of travelling.' Swanson smiled. He seemed almost always to be smiling, and I supposed vaguely that there would be some people foolish enough to take that smile always at its face value. 'Where were you fifty hours ago, Doctor?'

'In the Antarctic.'

Admiral Garvie gave me a very old-fashioned look indeed, but he let it go at that.

Chapter Two

When I awoke I was still heavy with sleep, the heaviness of a man who has slept for a long time. My watch said nine-thirty, and I knew it must be the next morning, not the same evening: I had been asleep for fifteen hours.

The cabin was quite dark. I rose, fumbled for the light switch, found it and looked around. Neither Hansen nor the engineer officer was there: they must have come in after I had gone to sleep and left before I woke. I looked around some more, and then I listened. I was suddenly conscious of the almost complete quiet, the stillness, the entire lack of any perceptible motion. I might have been in the bedroom of my own house. What had gone wrong? What hold-up had occurred? Why in God's name weren't we under way? I'd have sworn the previous night that Commander Swanson had been just as conscious of the urgency as I had been.

I had a quick wash in the folding Pullman-type basin, passed up the need for a shave, pulled on shirt, trousers and shoes and went outside. A few feet away a door opened off starboard off the passage. I went along and walked in. The officers' wardroom, without a doubt, with one of them still at breakfast, slowly munching his way through a huge plateful of steak, eggs and French fries, glancing at a magazine in a leisurely fashion and giving every impression of a man enjoying life to the luxurious full. He was about my own age, big, inclined to fat – a common condition, I was to find, among the entire crew who ate so well and exercised so little – with close-cropped black hair already greying at the temples and a cheerful intelligent face. He caught sight of me, rose and stretched out a hand.

'Dr Carpenter, it must be. Welcome to the wardroom. I'm Benson. Take a seat, take a seat.'

I said something, appropriate but quick, then asked: 'What's wrong? What's been the hold-up? Why aren't we under way?'

'That's the trouble with the world to-day,' Benson said mournfully. 'Rush, rush, rush. And where does all the hurry get them? I'll tell you—'

'Excuse me. I must see the captain.' I turned to leave but he laid a hand on my arm.

'Relax, Dr Carpenter. We *are* at sea. Take a seat.'

'At sea? On the level? I don't feel a thing.'

'You never do when you're three hundred feet down. Maybe four hundred. I don't,' he said expansively, 'concern myself with those trifles. I leave them to the mechanics.'

'Mechanics?'

'The captain, engineer officer, people like those.' He waved a hand in a generously vague gesture to indicate the largeness of the concept he understood by the term 'mechanics'. 'Hungry?'

'We've cleared the Clyde?'

'Unless the Clyde extends to well beyond the north of Scotland, the answer to that is, yes, we have.'

'Come again?'

He grinned. 'At the last check we were well into the Norwegian Sea, about the latitude of Bergen.'

'This is still only Tuesday morning?' I don't know if I looked stupid: I certainly felt it.

'It's still only Tuesday morning.' He laughed. 'And if you can work out from that what kind of speed we have been making in the last fifteen hours we'd all be obliged if you'd keep it to yourself.' He leaned back in his seat and lifted his voice. 'Henry!'

A steward, white-jacketed, appeared from what I took to be the pantry. He was a tall thin character with a dark complexion and the long lugubrious face of a dyspeptic spaniel. He looked at Benson and said in a meaningful voice: '*Another* plate of French fries, Doc?'

'You know very well that I never have more than one helping of that carbohydrated rubbish,' Benson said with dignity. 'Not, at least, for breakfast. Henry, this is Dr Carpenter.'

'Howdy,' Henry said agreeably.

'Breakfast, Henry,' Benson said. 'And, remember, Dr Carpenter is a Britisher. We don't want him leaving with a low opinion of the chow served up in the United States Navy.'

'If anyone aboard this ship has a low opinion of the food,' Henry said darkly, 'they hide it pretty well. Breakfast. The works. Right away.'

'Not the works, for heaven's sake,' I said. 'There are some things we decadent Britishers can't face up to first thing in the morning. One of them is French fries.'

He nodded approvingly and left. I said: 'Dr Benson, I gather.'

'Resident medical officer aboard the *Dolphin*, no less,' he admitted. 'The one who's had his professional competence called into question by having a competing practitioner called in.'

'I'm along for the ride. I assure you I'm not competing with anyone.'

'I know you're not,' he said quickly. Too quickly. Quickly enough so that I could see Swanson's hand in this, could see him telling his officers to lay of quizzing Carpenter too much. I wondered again what Swanson was going to say when and if we ever arrived at the Drift Station and he found out just how fluent a liar I was. Benson went on, smiling, 'There's no call for even one medico aboard this boat, far less two.'

'You're not overworked?' From the leisurely way he was going about his breakfast it seemed unlikely.

'Overworked! I've sickbay call once a day and no one ever turns up – except the morning after we arrive in port with a long cruise behind us and then there are liable to be a few sore heads around. My main job, and what is supposed to be my speciality, is checking on radiation and atmosphere pollution of one kind or another – in the olden submarine days the atmosphere used to get pretty foul after only a few hours submerged but we have to stay down for months, if necessary.' He grinned. 'Neither job is very exacting. We issue each member of the crew with a dosimeter and periodically check a film badge for radiation dosage – which is invariably less than you'd get sitting on the beach on a moderately warm day.

'The atmospheric problem is even easier. Carbon dioxide and carbon monoxide are the only things we have to worry about. We have a scrubbing machine that absorbs the breathed-out carbon dioxide from the atmosphere and pumps it out into the sea. Carbon monoxide – which we could more or less eliminate if we forbade cigarette smoking, only we don't want a mutiny on our hands when we're three hundred feet down – is burned to dioxide by a special heater and then scrubbed as usual. And even that hardly worries me, I've a very competent engineman who keeps those machines in tip-top condition.' He sighed. 'I've a surgery here that will delight your heart, Dr Carpenter. Operating table, dentist's chair, the lot, and the biggest crisis I've had yet is a cigarette burn between the fingers sustained by a cook who fell asleep during one of the lectures.'

'Lectures?'

'I've got to do something if I'm not to go round the bend. I spend a couple of hours a day keeping up with all the latest medical literature but what good is that if you don't get a chance to practise it? So I lecture. I read up about places we're going to visit and everyone listens to those talks. I give lectures on general health and hygiene and some of them listen to those. I give lectures on the perils of overeating and under-exercise and no one listens to those. I don't listen to them myself. It was during one of those that the cook got burned. That's why our friend Henry, the steward, adopts his superior and critical attitude towards the eating habits of those who should obviously be watching their habits. He eats as much as any two men aboard but owing to some metabolic defect he remains as thin as a rake. Claims it's all due to dieting.'

'It all sounds a bit less rigorous than the life of the average G.P.'

'It is, it is.' He brightened. 'But I've got one job – a hobby to me – that the average G.P. can't have. The ice-machine. I've made myself an expert on that.'

'What does Henry think about it?'

'What? Henry?' He laughed. 'Not that kind of ice-machine. I'll show you later.'

Henry brought food and I'd have liked the *maîtres d'hôtel* of some allegedly five-star hotels in London to be there to see what a breakfast should be like. When I'd finished and told Benson that I didn't see that his lectures on the dangers of overweight were going to get him very far, he said: 'Commander Swanson said you might like to see over the ship. I'm at your complete disposal.'

'Very kind of you both. But first I'd like to shave, dress and have a word with the captain.'

'Shave if you like. No one insists on it. As for dress, shirt and pants are the rig of the day here. And the captain told me to tell you that he'd let you know immediately anything came through that could possibly be of any interest to you.'

So I shaved and then had Benson take me on a conducted tour of this city under the sea: the *Dolphin*, I had to admit made any British submarine I'd ever seen look like a relic from the Ice Age.

To begin with, the sheer size of the vessel was staggering. So big had the hull to be to accommodate the huge nuclear reactor that it had internal accommodation equivalent to that of a 3,000-ton surface ship, with three decks instead of the usual one and lower hold found in the conventional submarine. The size, combined with the clever use of pastel paints for all accommodation spaces, working spaces and passageways, gave an over-whelming impression of lightness, airiness and above all, spaciousness.

He took me first, inevitably, to his sickbay. It was at once the smallest and most comprehensively equipped surgery I'd ever seen, whether a man wanted a major operation or just a tooth filled, he could have himself accommodated there. Neither clinical nor utilitarian, however, was the motif Benson had adopted for the decoration of the one bulkhead in his surgery completely free from surgical or medical equipment of any kind – a series of film stills in colour featuring every cartoon character I'd ever seen, from Popeye to Pinnochio, with, as a two-foot square centrepiece, an immaculately cravatted Yogi Bear industriously sawing off from the top of a wooden signpost the first word of a legend which read 'Don't feed the bears.' From deck to deckhead, the bulkhead was covered with them.

'Makes a change from the usual pin-ups,' I observed.

'I get inundated with those, too,' Benson said regretfully. 'Film librarian, you know. Can't use them, supposed to be bad for discipline. However. Lightens the morgue-like atmosphere, what? Cheers up the sick and suffering, I like to think – and distracts their attention while I turn up page 217 in the old textbook to find out what's the matter with them.'

From the surgery we passed through the wardroom and officers' quarters and dropped down a deck to the crew's living quarters. Benson took me through the gleaming tiled washrooms, the immaculate bunk-room, then into the crew's mess hall.

'The heart of the ship,' he announced. 'Not the nuclear reactor, as the uninformed maintain, but here. Just look at it. Hifi, juke box, record player, coffee machine, ice-cream machine, movie theatre, library and the home of all the card-sharps on the ship. What chance has a nuclear reactor against this lot? The old-time submariners would turn in their graves if they could see this: compared to the prehistoric conditions they lived in we must seem completely spoiled and ruined. Maybe we are, then again maybe we're not: the old boys never had to stay submerged for months at a time. This is also where I send them to sleep with my lectures on the evils of overeating.' He raised his voice for the benefit of seven or eight men who were sitting about the tables, drinking coffee, smoking and reading. 'You can observe for yourself, Dr Carpenter, the effects of my lectures in dieting and keeping fit. Did you ever see a bunch of more out-of-condition fat-bellied slobs in your life?'

The men grinned cheerfully. They were obviously well used to this sort of thing: Benson was exaggerating and they knew it. Each of them looked as if he knew what to do with a knife and fork when he got them in his hands, but that was about as far as it went. All had a curious similarity, big men and small men, the same characteristic as I'd seen in Zabrinski and Rawlings – an air of calmly relaxed competence, a cheerful imperturbability, that marked them out as being the men apart that they undoubtedly were.

Benson conscientiously introduced me to everyone, telling me exactly what their function aboard ship was and in turn informing them that I was a Royal Navy doctor along for an acclimatization trip. Swanson would have told him to say this, it was near enough the truth and would stop speculation on the reason for my presence there.

Benson turned into a small compartment leading off the mess hall. 'The air purification room. This is Engineman Harrison. How's our box of tricks, Harrison?'

'Just fine, Doc, just fine. CO reading steady on thirty parts a million.' He entered some figures up in a log book, Benson signed it with a flourish, exchanged a few more remarks and left.

'Half my day's toil done with one stroke of the pen,' he observed. 'I take it you're not interested in inspecting sacks of wheat, sides of beef, bags of potatoes and about a hundred different varieties of canned goods.'

'Not particularly. Why?'

'The entire for'ard half of the deck beneath our feet – a storage hold, really – is given up mainly to that. Seems an awful lot, I know, but then a hundred men can get through an awful lot of food in three months, which is the minimum time we must be prepared to stay at sea if the need arises. We'll pass up the inspection of the stores, the sight of all that food just makes me feel I'm fighting a losing battle all the time, and have a look where the food's cooked.'

He led the way for'ard into the galley, a small square room all tiles and glittering stainless steel. A tall, burly, white-coated cook turned at our entrance and grinned at Benson. 'Come to sample to-day's lunch, Doc?'

'I have not,' Benson said coldly. 'Dr Carpenter, the chief cook and my arch-enemy, Sam MacGuire. What form does the excess of calories take that you are proposing to thrust down the throats of the crew to-day?'

'No thrusting required,' said MacGuire happily. 'Cream soup, sirloin of beef, no less, roast potatoes and as much apple pie as a man can cope with. All good nourishing food.'

Benson shuddered. He made to leave the galley, stopped and pointed at a heavy bronze ten-inch tube that stood about four feet above the deck of the galley. It had a heavy hinged lid and screwed clamps to keep the lid in position. 'This might interest you, Dr Carpenter. Guess what?'

'A pressure cooker?'

'Looks like it, doesn't it? This is our garbage disposal unit. In the old days when a submarine had to surface every few hours garbage disposal was no problem, you just tipped the stuff over the side. But when you spend weeks on end cruising at three hundred feet you can't just walk up to the upper deck and tip the waste over the side: garbage disposal becomes quite a problem. This tube goes right down to the bottom of the *Dolphin*. There's a heavy watertight door at the lower end corresponding to this one, with interlocking controls which made it impossible for both doors to be open at the same time – it would be curtains for the *Dolphin* if they were. Sam here, or one of his henchmen, sticks the garbage into nylon mesh or polythene bags, weighs them with bricks— '

'Bricks, you said?'

'Bricks. Sam, how many bricks aboard this ship?'

'Just over a thousand at the latest count, Doc.'

'Regular builder's yard, aren't we?' Benson grinned. 'Those bricks are to ensure that the garbage bags sink to the bottom of the sea and not float to the surface – even in peacetime we don't want to give our position away to anyone. In go three or four bags, the top door is clamped shut and the bags pumped out under pressure. Then the outer door is closed again. Simple.'

'Yes.' For some reason or other this odd contraption had a curious fascination for me. Days later I was to remember my inexplicable interest in it and wonder whether, after all, I wasn't becoming psychic with advancing years.

'It's not worth all that attention,' Benson said good-humouredly. 'Just an up-to-date version of the old rubbish chute. Come on, a long way to go yet.'

He led the way from the galley to a heavy steel door set in a transverse bulkhead. Eight massive clips to release, then replace after we had passed through the doorway.

'The for'ard torpedo storage room.' Benson's voice was lowered, for at least half of the sixteen or so bunks that lined the bulkheads or were jammed up close to the torpedoes and racks were occupied and every man occupying them was sound asleep. 'Only six torpedoes as you can see. Normally there's stowage for twelve plus another six constantly kept loaded in the torpedo tubes. But those six are all we have just now. We had a malfunction in two of our torpedoes of the newest and more or less untested radio-controlled type – during the Nato exercises just ended – and Admiral Garvie ordered the lot removed for inspection when we got back to the Holy Loch. The *Hunley*, that's our depot ship, carries experts for working on those things. However, they were no sooner taken off yesterday morning than this Drift Station operation came our way and Commander Swanson insisted on having at least six of them put back on straight away.' Benson grinned. 'If there's one thing a submarine skipper hates it's putting to sea without his torpedoes. He feels he might just as well stay at home.'

'Those torpedoes are still not operational?'

'I don't know whether they are or not. Our sleeping warriors here will do their best to find out when they come to.'

'Why aren't they working on them now?'

'Because before our return to the Clyde they were working on them for nearly sixty hours non-stop trying to find out the cause of the malfunction – and if it existed in the other torpedoes. I told the skipper that if he wanted to blow up the *Dolphin* as good a way as any was to let those torpedo-men keep on working – they were starting to stagger around like zombies and a zombie is the last person you want to have working on the highly-complicated innards of a torpedo. So he pulled them off.'

He walked the length of the gleaming torpedoes and halted before another steel door in a cross bulkhead. He opened this, and beyond, four feet away, was another such heavy door set in another such bulkhead. The sills were about eighteen inches above deck level.

'You don't take many chances in building these boats, do you?' I asked. 'It's like breaking into the Bank of England.'

'Being a nuclear sub doesn't mean that we're not as vulnerable to underwater hazards as the older ships,' Benson said. 'We are. Ships have been lost before because the collision bulkhead gave way. The hull of the *Dolphin* can withstand terrific pressures, but a relatively minor tap from a sharp-edged object can rip us wide like an electric can-opener. The biggest danger is surface collision which nearly always happens at the bows. So, to make doubly sure in the event of a bows collision, we have those double collision bulkheads – the first submarine ever to have them. Makes fore and aft movement here a bit difficult but you've no idea how much more soundly we all sleep at night.'

He closed the after door behind him and opened the for'ard one: we found ourselves in the for'ard torpedo room, a narrow cramped compartment barely long enough to permit torpedoes to be loaded or withdrawn from their tubes. Those tubes,with their heavy-hinged rear doors, were arranged close together in two vertical banks of three. Overhead were the loading rails with heavy chain tackles attached. And that was all. No bunks in here and I didn't wonder: I wouldn't have liked to be the one to sleep for'ard of those collision bulkheads.

We began to work our way aft and had reached the mess hall when a sailor came up and said that the captain wanted to see me. I followed him up the wide central stairway into the control room, Dr Benson a few paces behind to show that he wasn't being too inquisitive. Commmander Swanson was waiting for me by the door of the radio room.

'Morning Doctor. Slept well?'

'Fifteen hours. What do you think? And breakfasted even better. What's up, Commander.' Something was up, that was for sure: for once, Commander Swanson wasn't smiling.

'Message coming through about Drift Station Zebra. Has to be decoded first but that should take minutes only.' Decoding or not, it seemed to me that Swanson already had a fair idea of the content of that message.

'When did we surface?' I asked. A submarine loses radio contact as soon as it submerges.

'Not since we left the Clyde. We are close on three hundred feet down right now.'

'This is a *radio* message that's coming through?'

'What else? Times have changed. We still have to surface to transmit but we can receive down to our maximum depth. Somewhere in Connecticut is the world's largest radio transmitter using an extremely low frequency which can contact us at this depth far more easily than any other radio station can contact a surface ship. While we're waiting, come and meet the drivers.'

He introduced me to some of his control centre crew – as with Benson it seemed to be a matter of complete indifference to him whether it was officer or enlisted man – finally stopped by an officer sitting just aft of the periscope stand, a youngster who looked as if he should still be in high school. 'Will Raeburn,' Swanson said. 'Normally we pay no attention to him but after we move under the ice he becomes the most important man on the ship. Our navigation officer. Are we lost, Will?'

'We're just there, Captain.' He pointed to a tiny pin-point of light on the Norwegian Sea chart spread out below the glass on the plotting-table. 'Gyro and sins are checking to a hair.'

'Sins?' I said.

'You may well look surprised, Dr Carpenter,' Swanson said. 'Lieutenant Raeburn here is far too young to have any sins. He is referring to S.I.N.S. – Ship's Inertial Navigational System – a device once used for guiding intercontinental missiles and now adapted for submarine use, specifically nuclear submarines. No point in my elaborating, Will's ready to talk your head off about it if he manages to corner you.' He glanced at the chart position. 'Are we getting along quickly enough to suit you, Doctor?'

'I still don't believe it,' I said.

'We cleared the Holy Loch a bit earlier than I expected, before seven,' Swanson admitted. 'I had intended to carry out some slow-time dives to adjust trim – but it wasn't necessary. Even the lack of twelve torpedoes up in the nose didn't make her as stern-heavy as I'd expected. She's so damned big that a few tons more or less here or there doesn't seem to make any difference to her. So we just came haring on up—'

He broke off to accept a signal sheet from a sailor, and read through it slowly, taking his time about it. Then he jerked his head, walked to a quiet corner of the control centre and faced me as I came up to him. He still wasn't smiling.

'I'm sorry,' he said. 'Major Halliwell, the commandant of the Drift Station – you said last night he was a very close friend of yours?'

I felt my mouth begin to go dry. I nodded, took the message from him. It read: 'A further radio message, very broken and difficult to decipher, was received 0945 Greenwich Mean Time from Drift Ice Station Zebra by the British trawler *Morning Star*, the vessel that picked up the previous broadcast. Message stated that Major Halliwell, Officer Commanding, and three others unnamed critically injured or dead, no indication who or how many of the four are dead. Others, number again unknown, suffering severely from burns and exposure. Some message about food and fuel, atmospheric conditions and weakness in transmission made it quite indecipherable. Understood from very garbled signal that survivors in one hut, unable to move because of weather. Word 'icestorm' clearly picked up. Apparently details of wind speed and temperature but unable to make out.

'*Morning Star* several times attempted contact Drift Station Zebra immediately afterwards. No acknowledgment.

'*Morning Star*, at request of British Admiralty, has abandoned fishing grounds and is moving closer in to Barrier to act as listening post. Message ends.'

I folded the paper and handed it back to Swanson. He said again: 'Sorry about this, Carpenter.'

'Critically injured or dead,' I said. 'In a burnt-out station on the ice-cap in winter, what's the difference?' My voice fell upon my ears as the voice of another man, a voice flat and lifeless, a voice empty of all emotion. 'Johnny Halliwell and three of his men. Johnny Halliwell. Not the kind of man you would meet often, Commander. A remarkable man. Left school at fifteen when his parents died to devote himself to the support of a brother eight years younger than himself. He slaved, he scraped, he sacrificed, he devoted many of the best years of his life to doing everything for his young brother, including putting him through a six-year University course. Not till then did he think of himself, not till then did he get married. He leaves a lovely wife and three marvellous kids. Two nieces and a nephew not yet six months old.'

'Two nieces—' He broke off and stared at me. 'Good God, your brother? *Your* brother?' He didn't, for the moment seem to find anything peculiar in the difference of surname.

I nodded silently. Young Lieutenant Raeburn approached us, an odd expression of anxiety on his face, but Swanson abruptly waved him away without seeming even to glance in his direction. He shook his head slowly and was still shaking it when I said abruptly: 'He's tough. He may be one of the survivors. He may live. We must get Drift Station Zebra's position. We *must* get it.'

'Maybe they haven't got it themselves,' Swanson said. You could see he was grateful for something to talk about. 'It *is* a drifting station, remember. The weather being what it is, it may have been days since they got their last fixes – and for all we know their sextants, chronometers and radio direction finders have been lost in the fire.'

'They must know what their latest fix was, even although it was a week ago. They must have a fairly accurate idea of the speed and direction of their drift. They'll be able to provide approximate data. The *Morning Star* must be told to keep transmitting non-stop with a continuous request for their position. If you surface now, can you contact the *Morning Star*?'

'I doubt it. The trawler must be the best part of a thousand miles north of us. His receiver wouldn't be big enough to pull us in – which is another way of saying that our transmitter is too small.'

'The BBC have plenty of transmitters that are big enough. So have the Admiralty. Please ask one or other to contact the *Morning Star* and ask it to make a continuous send for Zebra's position.'

'They could do that themselves direct.'

'Sure they could. But they couldn't hear the reply. The *Morning Star* can – if there's any reply. And she's getting closer to them all the time.'

'We'll surface now,' Swanson nodded. He turned away from the chart table we'd been standing beside and headed for the diving stand. As he passed the plotting table he said to the navigator: 'What was it you wanted, Will?'

Lieutenant Raeburn turned his back on me and lowered his voice, but my hearing has always been a little abnormal. He whispered: 'Did you see his face, Captain? I thought he was going to haul off and clobber you one.'

'I thought the same thing myself,' Swanson murmured. 'For a moment. But I think I just happened to be in his line of vision, that's all.'

I went forward to my cabin and lay down in the cot.

Chapter Three

'There it is, then,' said Swanson. 'That's the Barrier.'

The *Dolphin*, heading due north, her great cylindrical bulk at one moment completely submerged, the next showing clear as she rolled heavily through the steep quartering seas, was making less than three knots through the water, the great nuclear-powered engines providing just enough thrust to the big twin eight-foot propellers to provide steerage way and no more: thirty feet below where we stood on the bridge the finest sonar equipment in the world was ceaselessly probing the waters all around us but even so Swanson was taking no chances on the effects of collision with a drifting ice-block. The noonday Arctic sky was so overcast that the light was no better than that of late dusk. The bridge thermometer showed the sea temperature as 28° F, the air temperature as −16° F. The gale-force wind from the north-east was snatching the tops off the rolling steel-grey waves and subjecting the steep-walled sides of the great conning-tower – sail, the crew called it – to the ceaseless battering of a bullet-driven spray that turned to solid ice even as it struck. The cold was intense.

Shivering uncontrollably, wrapped in heavy duffel-coat and oilskins and huddled against the illusory shelter of the canvas wind-dodger, I followed the line of Swanson's pointing arm: even above the high thin shrill whine of the wind and the drum-fire of the flying spray against the sail, I could hear the violent chattering of his teeth. Less than two miles away a long, thin, greyish-white line, at that distance apparently smooth and regular, seemed to stretch the entire width of the northern horizon. I'd seen it before and it wasn't much to look at but it was a sight a man never got used to, not because of itself but because of what it represented, the beginning of the polar ice-cap that covered the top of the world, at this time of year a solid compacted mass of ice that stretched clear from where we lay right across to Alaska on the other side of the world. And we had to go under that mass. We had to go under it to find men hundreds of miles away, men who might be already dying, men who might be already dead. Who probably were dead. Men, dying or dead, whom we had to seek out by guess and by God in that great wasteland of ice stretching out endlessly before us, for we did not know where they were.

The relayed radio message we had received just forty-nine hours previously had been the last. Since then, there had been only silence. The trawler *Morning Star* had been sending almost continuously in the intervening two days, trying to raise Drift Station Zebra, but out of that bleak desert of ice to the north had come nothing but silence. No word, no signal, no faintest whisper of sound had come out of that desolation.

Eighteen hours previously the Russian atomic-engined *Dvina* had reached the Barrier and had started on an all-out and desperate attempt to smash its way into the heart of the ice-cap. In this early stage of winter the ice was neither so thick nor so compacted as it would be at the time of its maximum density, in March, and the very heavily armoured and powerfully engined *Dvina* was reputed to be able to break through ice up to a thickness of eighteen feet: given fair conditions, the *Dvina* was widely believed to be capable of battering its way to the North Pole. But the conditions of the rafted ice had proved abnormal to a degree and the attempt a hopeless one. The *Dvina* had managed to crash its way over forty miles into the ice-cap before being permanently stopped by a thick wall of rafter ice over twenty feet in height and probably more than a hundred deep. The *Dvina*, according to reports, had sustained heavy damage to its bows and was still in the process of extricating itself, with the greatest difficulty, from the pack. A very gallant effort that had achieved nothing except an improvement in East-West relations to an extent undreamed of for many years.

Nor had the Russian efforts stopped there. Both they and the Americans had made several flights over the area with front-line long-range bombers. Through the deep overcast and driving ice- and snow-filled winds those planes had criss-crossed the suspected area a hundred times, searching with their fantastically accurate radar. But not one single radar sighting had been reported. Various reasons had been put forward to explain the failure, especially the failure of the Strategic Air Command's B52 bomber whose radar was known to be easily capable of picking out a hut against contrasting background from ten thousand feet and in pitch darkness. It had been suggested that the huts were no longer there: that the radar's eye was unable to distinguish between an ice-sheathed hut and the thousands of ice-hummocks which dot the polar cap in winter; and that they had been searching in the wrong area in the first place. The most probable explanation was that the radar waves had been blurred and deflated by the dense clouds of ice-spicules blowing over the area. Whatever the reason, Drift Ice Station Zebra remained as silent as if no life had ever been there, as lost as if it had never existed.

'There's no percentage in staying up here and getting frozen to death.' Commander Swanson's voice was a half-shout, it had to be to make him heard. 'If we're going under that ice, we might as well go now.' He turned his back to the wind and stared out to the west where a big broad-beamed trawler was rolling heavily and sluggishly in the seas less than a quarter of a mile away. The *Morning Star*, which had closed right up to the edge of the ice-pack over the last two days, listening, waiting, and all in vain, was about to return to Hull: her fuel reserves were running low.

'Make a signal,' Swanson said to the seaman by his side. ' "We are about to dive and proceed under the ice. We do not expect to emerge for minimum four days, are prepared to remain maximum fourteen." ' He turned to me and said: 'If we can't find them in that time . . .' and left the sentence unfinished.

I nodded, and he went on: ' "Many thanks for your splendid co-operation. Good luck and a safe trip home." ' As the signalman's lamp started chattering out its message, he said wonderingly: 'Do those fishermen trawl up in the Arctic the entire winter?'

'They do.'

'The whole winter. Fifteen minutes and I'm about dead. Just a bunch of decadent Limeys, that's what they are.' A lamp aboard the *Morning Star* flickered for some seconds and Swanson said: 'What reply?'

' "Mind your heads under that ice. Good luck and goodbye." '

'Everybody below,' Swanson said. As the signalman began to strip the canvas dodger I dropped down a ladder into a small compartment beneath, wriggled through a hatch and down a second ladder to the pressure hull of the submarine, another hatch, a third ladder and then I was on the control deck of the *Dolphin*. Swanson and the signalman followed, then last of all Hansen, who had to close the two heavy watertight doors above.

Commander Swanson's diving technique would have proved a vast disappointment to those brought up on a diet of movie submarines. No frenzied activity, no tense steely-eyed men hovering over controls, no Tannoy calls of "Dive, dive, dive," no blaring of klaxons. Swanson reached down a steel-spring microphone, said quietly: 'This is the captain. We are about to move under the ice. Diving now,' hung up and said: 'Three hundred feet.'

The chief electronics technician leisurely checked the rows of lights indicating all hatches, surface openings and valves closed to the sea. The disc lights were out: the slot lights burned brightly. Just as leisurely he re-checked them, glanced at Swanson and said: 'Straight line shut, sir.' Swanson nodded. Air hissed loudly out of the ballast tanks, and that was it. We were on our way. It was about as wildly exciting as watching a man push a wheelbarrow. And there was something oddly reassuring about it all.

Ten minutes later Swanson came up to me. In the past two days I'd come to know Commander Swanson fairly well, like him a lot and respect him tremendously. The crew had complete and implicit faith in him. I was beginning to have the same thing. He was a kindly genial man with a vast knowledge of every aspect of submarining, a remarkable eye for detail, an even more remarkably acute mind and an imperturbability that remained absolute under all conditions. Hansen, his executive officer and clearly no respecter of persons, had said flatly that Swanson was the best submarine officer in the Navy. I hoped he was right, that was the kind of man I wanted around in conditions like those.

'We're about to move under the ice now, Dr Carpenter,' he said. 'How do you feel about it?'

'I'd feel better if I could see where we were going.'

'We can see,' he said. 'We've the best eyes in the world aboard the *Dolphin*. We've got eyes that look down, around, ahead and straight up. Our downward eye is the fathometer or echo-sounder that tells us just how deep the water below our keel is – and as we have about five thousand feet of water below our keel at this particular spot we're hardly likely to bump into underwater projections and its use right now is purely a formality. But no responsible navigation officer would ever think of switching it off. We have two sonar eyes for looking around and ahead, one sweeping the ship, another searching out a fifteen-degree path on either side of the bow. Sees everything, hears everything. You drop a spanner on a warship twenty miles away and we know all about it. Fact. Again it seems purely a formality. The sonar is searching for underwater ice stalactites forced down by the pressure of rafted ice above, but in five trips under the ice and two to the Pole I've never seen underwater stalactites or ridges deeper than 200 feet, and we're at 300 feet now. But we still keep them on.'

'You might bump into a whale?' I suggested.

'We might bump into another submarine.' He wasn't smiling. 'And that would be the end of both of us. What with the Russian and our own nuclear submarines busy criss-crossing to and fro across the top of the world the underside of the polar ice-cap is getting more like Times Square every day.'

'But surely the chances—'

'What are the chances of mid-air collision to the only two aircraft occupying ten thousand square miles of sky? On paper, they don't exist. There have been three such collisions this year already. So we keep the sonar pinging. But the really important eye, when you're under the ice, is the one that looks up. Come and have a squint at it.'

He led the way to the after starboard end of the control room where Dr Benson and another man were busy studying a glassed-in eye-level machine which outwardly consisted of a seven-inch-wide moving ribbon of paper and an inked stylus that was tracing a narrow straight black line along it. Benson was engrossed in adjusting some of the calibrated controls.

'The surface fathometer,' Swanson said. 'Better known as the ice-machine. It's not really Dr Benson's machine at all, we have two trained operators aboard, but as we see no way of separating him from it without actually court-martialling him, we take the easy way out and let him be.' Benson grinned, but his eye didn't leave the line traced by the stylus. 'Same principle as the echo-sounding machine, it just bounces an echo back from the ice – when there is any. That thin black line you see means open water above. When we move under the ice the stylus has an added vertical motion which not only indicates the presence of ice but also gives us its thickness.'

'Ingenious,' I said.

'It's more than that. Under the ice it can be life or death for the *Dolphin*. It certainly means life or death for Drift Station Zebra. If we ever get its position we can't get at it until we break through the ice and this is the only machine that can tell us where the ice is thinnest.'

'No open water at this time of year? No leads?'

'Polynyas, we call them. None. Mind you, the ice-pack is never static, not even in winter, and surface pressure changes can very occasionally tear the ice apart and expose open water. With air temperatures such as you get in winter you can guess how long the open water stays in a liquid condition. There's a skin of ice on it in five minutes, an inch in an hour and a foot inside two days. If we get to one of those frozen over polynyas inside, say, three days, we've a fair chance of breaking through.'

'With the conning-tower?'

'That's it. The sail. All new nuclear subs have specially strengthened sails designed for one purpose only – breaking through Arctic ice. Even so we have to go pretty gently as the shock, of course, is transmitted to the pressure hull.'

I thought about this a bit then said: 'What happens to the pressure hull if you come up too fast – as I understand may happen with a sudden change in salinity and sea temperature – and you find out at the last minute that you've drifted away from the indicated area of thin ice and have ten solid feet of the stuff above you?'

'That's it,' he said. 'Like you say, it's the last minute. Don't even think about such things, far less talk about them: I can't afford to have nightmares on this job.' I looked at him closely, but he wasn't smiling any more. He lowered his voice. 'I don't honestly think that there is one member of the crew of the *Dolphin* who doesn't get a little bit scared when we move in under the ice. I know I do. I think this is the finest ship in the world, Dr Carpenter, but there are still a hundred things that can go wrong with it and if anything happens to the reactor or the steam turbines or the electrical generators – then we're already in our coffin and the lid screwed down. The ice-pack above is the coffin lid. In the open sea most of those things don't matter a damn – we just surface or go to snorkel depth and proceed on our diesels. But for diesels you need air – and there's no air under the ice-pack. So if anything happens we either find a polynya to surface in, one chance in ten thousand at this time of year, before our standby battery packs up or – well, that's it.'

'This is all very encouraging,' I said.

'Isn't it?' He smiled, none too soon for me. 'It'll never happen. What's the worthy Benson making all the racket about?'

'Here it is,' Benson called. 'The first drift-block. And another. And another! Come and have a look, Doctor.'

I had a look. The stylus, making a faint soft hissing sound, was no longer tracing out a continuously horizontal line but was moving rapidly up and down across the paper, tracing out the outline of the block of ice passing astern above us. Another thin straight line, more agitated vertical movements of the stylus, and again another block of ice had gone. Even as I watched the number of thin horizontal lines became fewer and fewer and shorter and shorter until eventually they disappeared altogether.

'That's it, then,' Swanson nodded. 'We'll take her deep now, real deep, and open up all the stops.'

When Commander Swanson had said he was going to hurry, he'd meant every word of it. In the early hours of the following morning I was awakened from a deep sleep by a heavy hand on my shoulder. I opened my eyes, blinked against the glare of the overhead light then saw Lieutenant Hansen.

'Sorry about the beauty sleep, Doc,' he said cheerfully. 'But this is it.'

'This is what?' I said irritably.

'85° 35′ north, 21° 20′ east – the last estimated position of Drift Station Zebra. At least, the last estimated position with estimated correction for polar drift.'

'Already?' I glanced at my watch, not believing it. 'We're there already?'

'We have not,' Hansen said modestly, 'been idling. The skipper suggests you come along and watch us at work.'

'I'll be right with you.' When and if the *Dolphin* managed to break through the ice and began to try her one in a million chance of contacting Drift Station Zebra, I wanted to be there.

We left Hansen's cabin and had almost reached the control room when I lurched, staggered and would have fallen but for a quick grab at a handrail that ran along one side of the passageway. I hung on grimly as the *Dolphin* banked violently sideways and round like a fighter plane in a tight turn. No submarine in my experience had ever been able to begin to behave even remotely in that fashion. I understood now the reasons for the safety belts on the diving control seats.

'What the hell's up?' I said to Hansen. 'Avoiding some underwater obstruction ahead?'

'Must be a possible polynya. Some place where the ice is thin, anyway. As soon as we spot a possible like that we come around like a chicken chasing its own tail just so we don't miss it. It makes us very popular with the crew, especially when they're drinking coffee or soup.'

We passed into the control room. Commander Swanson, flanked by the navigator and another man, was bent over the plotting table, examining something intently. Farther aft a man at the surface fathometer was reading out ice thickness figures in a quiet unemotional voice. Commander Swanson looked up from the chart.

'Morning, Doctor. John, I think we may have something here.'

Hansen crossed to the plot and peered at it. There didn't seem to be much to peer at – a tiny pin-point of light shining through the glass top of the plot and a squared sheet of chart paper marked by a most unseamanlike series of wavering black lines traced out by a man with a pencil following the track of the tiny moving light. There were three red crosses superimposed on the paper, two very close together, and just as Hansen was examining the paper the crewman manning the ice-machine – Dr Benson's enthusiasm for his toy did not, it appeared, extend to the middle of the night – called out 'Mark!' Immediately the black pencil was exchanged for a red and a fourth cross made.

' "Think" and "may" are just about right, Captain,' Hansen said. 'It looks awfully narrow to me.'

'It looks the same way to me, too,' Swanson admitted. 'But it's the first break in the heavy ice that we've had in an hour, almost. And the farther north we go, the poorer our chances. Let's give it a go. Speed?'

'One knot,' Raeburn said.

'All back one-third,' Swanson said. No sharp imperatives, not ever, in the way Swanson gave his orders, more a quiet and conversational suggestion, but there was no mistaking the speed with which one of the crewmen strapped into the diving-stand bucket seat leaned forward to telegraph the order to the engine-room. 'Left full rudder.'

Swanson bent over to check the plot, closely watching the tiny pin-point of light and tracing pencil move back towards the approximate centre of the elongated quadrangle formed by the four red crosses. 'All stop,' he went on. 'Rudder amidships.' A pause then: 'All ahead one-third. So. All stop.'

'Speed zero,' Raeburn said.

'120 feet,' Swanson said to the diving officer. 'But gently, gently.'

A strong steady hum echoed in the control centre. I asked Hansen: 'Blowing ballast?'

He shook his head. 'Just pumping the stuff out. Gives a far more precise control of rising speed and makes it easier to keep the sub on an even keel. Bringing a stopped sub up on a dead even keel is no trick for beginners. Conventional subs never try this sort of thing.'

The pumps stopped. There came the sound of water flooding back into the tanks as the diving officer slowed up the rate of ascent. The sound faded. 'Secure flooding,' the diving officer said. 'Steady on 120 feet.'

'Up periscope,' Swanson said to the crewman by his side. An overhead lever was engaged and we could hear the hiss of high-pressure oil as the hydraulic piston began to lift the starboard periscope off its seating. The gleaming cylinder rose slowly against the pressure of the water outside until finally the foot of the periscope cleared its well. Swanson opened the hinged handgrips and peered through the eyepiece.

'What does he expect to see in the middle of the night at this depth?' I asked Hansen.

'Never can tell. It's rarely completely dark, as you know. Maybe a moon, maybe only stars – but even starlight will show as a faint glow through the ice – if the ice is thin enough.'

'What's the thickness of the ice above, in this rectangle?'

'The sixty-four thousand dollar question,' Hansen admitted, 'and the answer is that we don't know. To keep that ice-machine to a reasonable size the graph scale has to be very small. Anything between four and forty inches. Four inches we go through like the icing on a wedding cake: forty inches and we get a very sore head indeed.' He nodded across to Swanson. 'Doesn't look so good. That grip he's twisting is to tilt the periscope lens upwards and that button is for focusing. Means he's having trouble in finding anything.'

Swanson straightened. 'Black as the earl of hell's waistcoat,' he said conversationally. 'Switch on hull and sail floodlights.'

He stooped and looked again. For a few seconds only. 'Pea-soup. Thick and yellow and strong. Can't see a thing. Let's have the camera, shall we?'

I looked at Hansen, who nodded to a white screen that had just been unshuttered on the opposite bulkhead. 'All mod cons, Doc. Closed circuit TV. Camera is deck mounted under toughened glass and can be remotely controlled to look up or round.'

'You could do with a new camera, couldn't you?' The TV screen was grey, fuzzy, featureless.

'Best that money can buy,' Hansen said. 'It's the water. Under certain conditions of temperature and salinity it becomes almost completely opaque when floodlit. Like driving into a heavy fog with your headlights full on.'

'Floodlights off,' Swanson said. The screen became quite blank. 'Floodlights on.' The same drifting misty grey as before. Swanson sighed and turned to Hansen. 'Well, John?'

'If I were paid for imagining things,' Hansen said carefully, 'I could imagine I see the top of the sail in that left corner. Pretty murky out there, Captain. Heigh-ho for the old blind man's buff, is that it?'

'Russian roulette, I prefer to call it.' Swanson had the clear unworried face of a man contemplating a Sunday afternoon in a deck-chair. 'Are we holding position?'

'I don't know.' Raeburn looked up from the plot. 'It's difficult to be sure.'

'Sanders?' This to the man at the ice-machine.

'Thin ice, sir. Still thin ice.'

'Keep calling. Down periscope.' He folded the handles up and turned to the diving officer. 'Take her up like we were carrying a crate of eggs atop the sail and didn't want to crack even one of them.'

The pumps started again. I looked around the control room. Swanson excepted, everyone was quiet and still and keyed-up. Raeburn's face was beaded with sweat and Sanders's voice was too calm and impersonal by half as he kept repeating: 'Thin ice, thin ice,' in a low monotone. You could reach out and touch the tension in the air. I said quietly to Hansen: 'Nobody seems very happy. There's still a hundred feet to go.'

'There's forty feet,' Hansen said shortly. 'Readings are taken from keel level and there's sixty feet between the keel and the top of the sail. Forty feet minus the thickness of the ice – and maybe a razor-sharp or needle-pointed stalactite sticking down ready to skewer the *Dolphin* through the middle. You know what that means?'

'That it's time I started getting worried too?'

Hansen smiled, but he wasn't feeling like smiling. Neither was I, not any more.

'Ninety feet,' the diving officer said.

'Thin ice, thin ice,' Sanders intoned.

'Switch off the deck flood, leave the sail flood on,' Swanson said. 'And keep that camera moving. Sonar?'

'All clear,' the sonar operator reported. 'All clear all round.' A pause, then: 'No, hold it, hold it! Contact dead astern!'

'How close?' Swanson asked quickly.

'Too close to say. Very close.'

'She's jumping!' the diving officer called out sharply. '80, 75.' The *Dolphin* had hit a layer of colder water or extra salinity.

'Heavy ice, heavy ice!' Sanders called out urgently.

'Flood emergency!' Swanson ordered – and this time it was an order.

I felt the sudden build-up of air pressure as the diving officer vented the negative tank and tons of sea-water poured into the emergency diving tank, but it was too late. With a shuddering jarring smash that sent us staggering the *Dolphin* crashed violently into the ice above, glass tinkled, lights went out and the submarine started falling like a stone.

'Blow negative to the mark!' the diving officer called. High pressure air came boiling into the negative tank – at our rate of falling we would have been flattened by the sea-pressure before the pumps could even have begun to cope with the huge extra ballast load we had taken aboard in seconds. Two hundred feet, two hundred and fifty and we were still falling. Nobody spoke, everybody just stood or sat in a frozen position staring at the diving stand. It required no gift for telepathy to know the thought in every mind. It was obvious that the *Dolphin* had been struck aft by some underwater pressure ridge at the same instant as the sail had hit the heavy ice above: if the *Dolphin* had been holed aft this descent wasn't going to stop until the pressure of a million tons of water had crushed and flattened the hull and in a flicker of time snuffed out the life of every man inside it.

'Three hundred feet,' the diving officer called out. 'Three fifty – and she's slowing! She's slowing.'

The *Dolphin* was still falling, sluggishly passing the four-hundred-foot mark, when Rawlings appeared in the control room, tool-kit in one hand, a crate of assorted lamps in the other.

'It's unnatural,' he said. He appeared to be addressing the shattered lamp above the plot which he had immediately begun to repair. 'Contrary to the laws of nature, I've always maintained. Mankind was never meant to probe beneath the depths of the ocean. Mark my words, those new-fangled inventions will come to a bad end.'

'So will you, if you don't keep quiet,' Commander Swanson said acidly. But there was no reprimand in his face, he appreciated as well as any of us the therapeutic breath of fresh air that Rawlings had brought into that tension-laden atmosphere. 'Holding?' he went on to the diving officer.

The diving officer raised a finger and grinned. Swanson nodded, swung the coiled-spring microphone in front of him. 'Captain here,' he said calmly. 'Sorry about that bump. Report damage at once.'

A green light flashed in the panel of a box beside him. Swanson touched a switch and a loudspeaker in the deckhead crackled.

'Manoeuvring room here.' The manoeuvring room was in the after end of the upper level engine-room, towards the stern. 'Hit was directly above us here. We could do with a box of candles and some of the dials and gauges are out of kilter. But we still got a roof over our heads.'

'Thank you, Lieutenant. You can cope?'

'Sure we can.'

Swanson pressed another switch. 'Stern room?'

'We still attached to the ship?' a cautious voice inquired.

'You're still attached to the ship,' Swanson assured him. 'Anything to report?'

'Only that there's going to be an awful lot of dirty laundry by the time we get back to Scotland. The washing-machine's had a kind of fit.'

Swanson smiled and switched off. His face was untroubled, he must have had a special sweat-absorbing mechanism on his face, I felt I could have done with a bath towel. He said to Hansen: 'That was bad luck. A combination of a current where a current had no right to be, a temperature inversion where a temperature inversion had no right to be, and a pressure ridge where we least expected it. Not to mention the damned opacity of the water. What's required is a few circuits until we know this polynya like the backs of our hands, a small offset to allow for drift and a little precautionary flooding as we approach the ninety-foot mark.'

'Yes, sir. That's what's required. Point is, what are we going to do?'

'Just that. Take her up and try again.'

I had my pride so I refrained from mopping my brow. They took her up and tried again. At 200 feet and for fifteen minutes Swanson juggled propellers and rudder till he had the outline of the frozen polynya above as accurately limned on the plot as he could ever expect to have it. Then he positioned the *Dolphin* just outside one of the boundary lines and gave an order for a slow ascent.

'One twenty-feet,' the diving officer said. 'One hundred ten.'

'Heavy ice,' Sanders intoned. 'Still heavy ice.'

Sluggishly the *Dolphin* continued to rise. Next time in the control room, I promised myself, I wouldn't forget that bath towel. Swanson said: 'If we've overestimated the speed of the drift, there's going to be another bump I'm afraid.' He turned to Rawlings who was still busily repairing lights. 'If I were you, I'd suspend operations for the present. You may have to start all over again in a moment and we don't carry all that number of spares aboard.'

'One hundred feet,' the diving officer said. He didn't sound as unhappy as his face looked.

'The water's clearing,' Hansen said suddenly. 'Look.'

The water had cleared, not dramatically so, but enough. We could see the top corner of the sail clearly outlined on the TV screen. And then suddenly, we could see something else again, heavy ugly ridged ice not a dozen feet above the sail.

Water flooding into the tanks. The diving officer didn't have to be told what to do, we'd gone up like an express lift the first time we'd hit a different water layer and once like that was enough in the life of any submarine.

'Ninety feet,' he reported. 'Still rising.' More water flooded in, then the sound died away. 'She's holding. Just under ninety feet.'

'Keep her there.' Swanson stared at the TV screen. 'We're drifting clear and into the polynya – I hope.'

'Me too,' Hansen said. 'There can't be more than a couple of feet between the top of the sail and that damned ugly stuff.'

'There isn't much room,' Swanson acknowledged. 'Sanders?'

'Just a moment, sir. The graph looks kinda funny – no we're clear.' He couldn't keep the excitement out of his voice. 'Thin ice!'

I looked at the screen. He was right. I could see the vertical edge of a wall of ice move slowly across the screen, exposing clear water above.

'Gently, now, gently,' Swanson said. 'And keep the camera on the ice wall at the side, then straight up, turn about.'

The pumps began to throb again. The ice wall, less than ten yards away, began to drift slowly down past us.

'Eighty-five feet,' the diving officer reported. 'Eighty.'

'No hurry,' Swanson said. 'We're sheltered from that drift by now.'

'Seventy-five feet.' The pumps stopped, and water began to flood into the tanks. 'Seventy.' The *Dolphin* was almost stopped now, drifting upwards as gently as thistledown. The camera switched upwards, and we could see the top corner of the sail clearly outlined with a smooth ceiling of ice floating down to meet it. More water gurgled into the tanks, the top of the sail met the ice with a barely perceptible bump and the *Dolphin* came to rest.

'Beautifully done,' Swanson said warmly to the diving officer. 'Let's give that ice a nudge. Are we slewing?'

'Bearing constant.'

Swanson nodded. The pumps hummed, pouring out water, lightening ship, steadily increasing positive buoyancy. The ice stayed where it was. More time passed, more water pumped out, and still nothing happened. I said softly to Hansen: 'Why doesn't he blow the main ballast? You'd get a few hundred tons of positive buoyancy in next to no time and even if that ice is forty inches thick it couldn't survive all that pressure at a concentrated point.'

'Neither could the *Dolphin*,' Hansen said grimly. 'With a suddenly induced big positive buoyancy like that, once she broke through she'd go up like a cork from a champagne bottle. The pressure hull might take it, I don't know, but sure as little apples the rudder would be squashed flat as a piece of tin. Do you want to spend what little's left of your life travelling in steadily decreasing circles under the polar ice-cap?'

I didn't want to spend what little was left of my life in travelling in steadily decreasing circles under the ice-cap so I kept quiet. I watched Swanson as he walked across to the diving stand and studied the banked dials in silence for some seconds. I was beginning to become a little apprehensive about what Swanson would do next: I was beginning to realize, and not slowly either, that he was a lad who didn't give up very easily.

'That's enough of that lot,' he said to the diving officer. 'If we go through now with all this pressure behind us we'll be airborne. This ice is even thicker than we thought. We've tried the long steady shove and it hasn't worked. A sharp tap is obviously what is needed. Flood her down, but gently, to eighty feet or so, a good sharp whiff of air into the ballast tanks and we'll give our well-known imitation of a bull at a gate.'

Whoever had installed the 240-ton air-conditioning unit in the *Dolphin* should have been prosecuted, it just wasn't working any more. The air was very hot and stuffy – what little there was of it, that was. I looked around cautiously and saw that everyone else appeared to be suffering from this same shortage of air, all except Swanson, who seemed to carry his own built-in oxygen cylinder around with him. I hoped Swanson was keeping in mind the fact that the *Dolphin* had cost 120 million dollars to build. Hansen's narrowed eyes held a definite core of worry and even the usually imperturbable Rawlings was rubbing a bristly blue chin with a hand the size and shape of a shovel. In the deep silence after Swanson had finished speaking the scraping noise sounded unusually loud, then was lost in the noise of water flooding into the tanks.

We stared at the screen. Water continued to pour into the tanks until we could see a gap appear between the top of the sail and the ice. The pumps started up, slowly, to control the speed of descent. On the screen, the cone of light thrown on to the underside of the ice by the flood-lamp grew fainter and larger as we dropped, then remained stationary, neither moving nor growing in size. We had stopped.

'Now,' said Swanson. 'Before that current gets us again.'

There came the hissing roar of compressed air under high pressure entering the ballast tanks. The *Dolphin* started to move sluggishly upwards while we watched the cone of light on the ice slowly narrow and brighten.

'More air,' Swanson said.

We were rising faster now, closing the gap to the ice all too quickly for my liking. Fifteen feet, twelve feet, ten feet.

'More air,' Swanson said.

I braced myself, one hand on the plot, the other on an overhead grab bar. On the screen, the ice was rushing down to meet us. Suddenly the picture quivered and danced, the *Dolphin* shuddered, jarred and echoed hollowly along its length, more lights went out, the picture came back on the screen, the sail was still lodged below the ice, then the *Dolphin* trembled and lurched and the deck pressed against our feet like an ascending elevator. The sail on the TV vanished, nothing but opaque white taking its place. The diving officer, his voice high with strain that had not yet found relief, called out. 'Forty feet, forty feet.' We had broken through.

'There you are now,' Swanson said mildly. 'All it needed was a little perseverance.' I looked at the short plump figure, the round good-humoured face, and wondered for the hundredth time why the nerveless iron men of this world so very seldom look the part.

I let my pride have a holiday. I took my handkerchief from my pocket, wiped my face and said to Swanson: 'Does this sort of thing go on all the time?'

'Fortunately, perhaps, no.' He smiled. He turned to the diving officer. 'We've got our foothold on this rock. Let's make sure we have a good belay.'

For a few second more compressed air was bled into the tanks, then the diving officer said: 'No chance of her dropping down now, Captain.'

'Up periscope.'

Again the long gleaming silver tube hissed up from its well. Swanson didn't even bother folding down the hinged handles. He peered briefly into the eyepiece, then straightened.

'Down periscope.'

'Pretty cold up top?' Hansen asked.

Swanson nodded. 'Water on the lens must have frozen solid as soon as it hit that air. Can't see a thing.' He turned to the diving officer. 'Steady at forty?'

'Guaranteed. And all the buoyancy we'll ever want.'

'Fair enough.' Swanson looked at the quartermaster who was shrugging his way into a heavy sheepskin coat. 'A little fresh air, Ellis, don't you think?'

'Right away, sir.' Ellis buttoned his coat and added: 'Might take some time.'

'I don't think so,' Swanson said. 'You may find the bridge and hatchways jammed with broken ice but I doubt it. My guess is that that ice is so thick that it will have fractured into very large sections and fallen outside clear of the bridge.'

I felt my ears pop with the sudden pressure change as the hatch swung up and open and snapped back against its standing latch. Another more distant sound as the second hatch-cover locked open and then we heard Ellis on the voice-tube.

'All clear up top.'

'Raise the antennae,' Swanson said. 'John, have them start transmitting and keep transmitting until their fingers fall off. Here we are and here we stay – until we raise Drift Ice Station Zebra.'

'If there's anyone left alive there,' I said.

'There's that, of course,' Swanson said. He couldn't look at me. 'There's always that.'

Chapter Four

This, I thought, death's dreadful conception of a dreadful world, must have been what had chilled the hearts and souls of our far-off Nordic ancestors when life's last tide slowly ebbed and they had tortured their failing minds with fearful imaginings of a bleak and bitter hell of eternal cold. But it had been all right for the old boys, all they had to do was to imagine it, we had to experience the reality of it and I had no doubt at all in my mind as to which was the easier. The latter-day Eastern conception of hell was more comfortable altogether, at least a man could keep reasonably warm there.

One thing sure, nobody could keep reasonably warm where Rawlings and I were, standing a half-hour watch on the bridge of the *Dolphin* and slowly freezing solid. It had been my own fault entirely that our teeth were chattering like frenzied castanets. Half an hour after the radio room had started transmitting on Drift Ice Station Zebra's wavelength and all without the slightest whisper by way of reply or acknowledgment, I had suggested to Commander Swanson that Zebra might possibly be able to hear us without having sufficient power to send a reply but that they might just conceivably let us have an acknowledgment some other way. I'd pointed out that Drift Stations habitually carried rockets – the only way to guide home any lost members of the party if radio communication broke down – and radio-sondes and rockoons. The sondes were radio-carrying balloons which could rise to a height of twenty miles to gather weather information: the rockoons, radio rockets fired from balloons, could rise even higher. On a moonlit night such as this, those balloons, if released, would be visible at least twenty miles away: if flares were attached to them, at twice that distance. Swanson had seen my point, called for volunteers for the first watch and in the circumstances I hadn't had much option. Rawlings had offered to accompany me.

It was a landscape – if such a bleak, barren and featureless desolation could be called a landscape – from another and ancient world, weird and strange and oddly frightening. There were no clouds in the sky, but there were no stars either: this I could not understand. Low on the southern horizon a milky misty moon shed its mysterious light over the dark lifelessness of the polar ice-cap. Dark, not white. One would have expected moonlit ice to shine and sparkle and glitter with the light of a million crystal chandeliers – but it was dark. The moon was so low in the sky that the dominating colour on the ice-cap came from the blackness of the long shadows cast by the fantastically ridged and hummocked ice: and where the moon did strike directly the ice had been so scoured and abraded by the assaults of a thousand ice-storms that it had lost almost all its ability to reflect light of any kind.

This ridged and hummocked ice-cap had a strange quality of elusiveness, of impermanence, of evanescence: one moment there, definitively hard and harsh and repellent in its coldly contrasting blacks and whites, the next, ghost-like blurring coalescing and finally vanishing like a shimmering mirage fading and dying in some ice-bound desert. But this was no trick of the eye or imagination, it was the result of a ground-level ice-storm that rose and swirled and subsided at the dictates of an icy wind that was never less than strong and sometimes gusted up to gale force, a wind that drove before it a swirling rushing fog of billions of needle-pointed ice-spicules. For the most part, standing as we were on the bridge twenty feet above the level of the ice – the rest of the *Dolphin* might never have existed as far as the eye could tell – we were above this billowing ground-swell of ice particles; but occasionally the wind gusted strongly, the spicules lifted, drummed demoniacally against the already ice-sheathed starboard side of the sail, drove against the few exposed inches of our skin with all the painfully stinging impact of a sand-blaster held at arm's length; but unlike a sand-blaster, the pain-filled shock of those spear-tipped spicules was only momentary, each wasp-like sting carried with it its own ice-cold anaesthetic and all surface sensation was quickly lost. Then the wind would drop, the furious rattling on the sail would fade and in the momentary contrast of near-silence we could hear the stealthy rustling as of a million rats advancing as the ice-spicules brushed their blind way across the iron-hard surface of the polar cap. The bridge thermometer stood at −21° F. −53° of frost. If I were a promoter interested in developing a summer holiday resort, I thought, I wouldn't pay very much attention to this place.

Rawlings and I stamped our feet, flailed our arms across our chests, shivered non-stop, took what little shelter we could from the canvas wind-break, rubbed our goggles constantly to keep them clear, and never once, except when the ice-spicules drove into our faces, stopped examining every quarter of the horizon. Somewhere out there on those frozen wastes was a lost and dying group of men whose lives might depend upon so little a thing as the momentary misting up of one of our goggles. We stared out over those shifting ice-sands until our eyes ached. But that was all we had for it, just aching eyes. We saw nothing, nothing at all. The ice-cap remained empty of all signs of life. Dead.

When our relief came Rawlings and I got below with all the speed our frozen and stiffened limbs would allow. I found Commander Swanson sitting on a canvas stool outside the radio room. I stripped off outer clothes, face coverings and goggles, took a steaming mug of coffee that had appeared from nowhere and tried not to hop around too much as the blood came pounding back into arms and legs.

'How did you cut yourself like that?' Swanson asked, concern in his voice. 'You've a half-inch streak of blood right across your forehead.'

'Flying ice, it just looks bad.' I felt tired and pretty low. 'We're wasting our time transmitting. If the men on Drift Station Zebra were without any shelter it's no wonder all signals ceased long ago. Without food and shelter no one could last more than a few hours in that lot. Neither Rawlings nor I is a wilting hothouse flower but after half an hour up there we've both just about had it.'

'I don't know,' Swanson said thoughtfully. 'Look at Amundsen. Look at Scott, at Peary. They *walked* all the way to the Poles.'

'A different breed of men, Captain. Either that or the sun shone for them. All I know is that half an hour is too long to be up there. Fifteen minutes is enough for anyone.'

'Fifteen minutes it shall be.' He looked at me, face carefully empty of all expression. 'You haven't much hope?'

'If they're without shelter. I've none.'

'You told me they had an emergency power pack of Nife cells for powering their transmitter,' he murmured. 'You also said those batteries will retain their charge indefinitely, years if necessary, irrespective of the weather conditions under which they are stored. They must have been using that battery a few days ago when they sent out their first SOS. It wouldn't be finished already.'

His point was so obvious that I didn't answer. The battery wasn't finished: the men were.

'I agree with you,' he went on quietly. 'We're wasting our time. Maybe we should just pack up and go home. If we can't raise them, we'll never find them.'

'Maybe not. But you're forgetting your directive from Washington, Commander.'

'How do you mean?'

'Remember? I'm to be extended every facility and all aid short of actually endangering the safety of the submarine and the lives of the crew. At the present moment we're doing neither. If we fail to raise them I'm prepared for a twenty-mile sweep on foot round this spot in the hope of locating them. If that fails we could move to another polynya and repeat the search. The search area isn't all that big, there's a fair chance, but a chance, that we might locate the station eventually. I'm prepared to stay up here all winter till we do find them.'

'You don't call that endangering the lives of my men? Making extended searches of the ice-cap, on foot, in mid-winter?'

'Nobody said anything about endangering the lives of your men.'

'You mean – you mean you'd go it alone.' Swanson stared down at the deck and shook his head. 'I don't know what to think. I don't know whether to say you're crazy or whether to say I'm beginning to understand why they – whoever "they" may be – picked you for the job, Dr Carpenter.' He sighed, then regarded me thoughtfully. 'One moment you say there's no hope, the next that you're prepared to spend the winter here, searching. If you don't mind my saying so, Doctor, it just doesn't make sense.'

'Stiff-necked pride,' I said. 'I don't like throwing my hand in on a job before I've even started it. I don't know what the attitude of the United States Navy is on that sort of thing.'

He gave me another speculative glance, I could see he believed me the way a fly believes the spider on the web who has just offered him safe accommodation for the night. He smiled. He said: 'The United States Navy doesn't take offence all that easily, Dr Carpenter. I suggest you catch a couple of hours' sleep while you can. You'll need it all if you're going to start walking towards the North Pole.'

'How about yourself? You haven't been to bed at all to-night.'

'I think I'll wait a bit.' He nodded towards the door of the radio room. 'Just in case anything comes through.'

'What are they sending? Just the call sign?'

'Plus request for position and a rocket, if they have either. I'll let you know immediately anything comes through. Good night, Dr Carpenter. Or rather, good morning.'

I rose heavily and made my way to Hansen's cabin.

The atmosphere round the 8 a.m. breakfast table in the wardroom was less than festive. Apart from the officer on deck and the engineer lieutenant on watch, all the *Dolphin*'s officers were there, some just risen from their bunks, some just heading for them, none of them talking in anything more than monosyllables. Even the ebullient Dr Benson was remote and withdrawn. It seemed pointless to ask whether any contact had been established with Drift Station Zebra, it was painfully obvious that it hadn't. And that after almost five hours' continuous sending. The sense of despondency and defeat, the unspoken knowledge that time had run out for the survivors of Drift Station Zebra hung heavy over the wardroom.

No one hurried over his meal – there was nothing to hurry for – but by and by they rose one by one and drifted off, Dr Benson to his sick-bay call, the young torpedo officer, Lieutenant Mills, to supervise the efforts of his men who had been working twelve hours a day for the past two days to iron out the faults in the suspect torpedoes, a third to relieve Hansen, who had the watch, and three others to their bunks. That left only Swanson, Raeburn and myself. Swanson, I knew, hadn't been to bed at all the previous night, but for all that he had the rested clear-eyed look of a man with eight solid hours behind him.

The steward, Henry, had just brought in a fresh pot of coffee when we heard the sound of running footsteps in the passageway outside and the quartermaster burst into the wardroom. He didn't quite manage to take the door off its hinges, but that was only because the Electric Boat Company put good solid hinges on the doors of their submarines.

'We got it made!' he shouted, and then perhaps recollecting that enlisted men were expected to conduct themselves with rather more decorum in the wardroom, went on: 'We've raised them, Captain, we've raised them!'

'What!' Swanson could move twice as fast as his comfortable figure suggested and he was already half-out of his chair.

'We are in radio contact with Drift Ice Station Zebra, sir,' Ellis said formally.

Commander Swanson got to the radio room first, but only because he had a head start on Raeburn and myself. Two operators were on watch, both leaning forward towards their transmitters, one with his head bent low, the other with his cocked to one side, as if those attitudes of concentrated listening helped them to isolate and amplify the slightest sounds coming through the earphones clamped to their heads. One of them was scribbling away mechanically on a signal pad. DSY, he was writing down, DSY repeated over and over again. DSY. The answering call-sign of Drift Station Zebra. He stopped writing as he caught sight of Swanson out of the corner of one eye.

'We've got 'em, Captain, no question. Signal very weak and intermittent but—'

'Never mind the signal!' It was Raeburn who made this interruption without any by-your-leave from Swanson. He tried, and failed, to keep the rising note of excitement out of his voice and he looked more than ever like a youngster playing hookey from high school. 'The bearing? Have you got their bearing? That's all that matters.'

The other operator swivelled in his seat and I recognized my erstwhile guard, Zabrinski. He fixed Raeburn with a sad and reproachful eye.

'Course we got their bearing, Lieutenant. First thing we did. O-forty-five, give or take a whisker. North-east, that is.'

'Thank you, Zabrinski,' Swanson said dryly. 'O-forty-five is north-east. The navigating officer and I wouldn't have known. Position?'

Zabrinski shrugged and turned to his watchmate, a man with a red face, leather neck and a shining polished dome where his hair ought to have been. 'What's the word, Curly?'

'Nothing. Just nothing.' Curly looked at Swanson. 'Twenty times I've asked for his position. No good. All he does is send out his call-sign. I don't think he's hearing us at all, he doesn't even know we're listening, he just keeps sending his call-sign over and over again. Maybe he hasn't switched his aerial in to "receive".'

'It isn't possible,' Swanson said.

'It is with this guy,' Zabrinski said. 'At first Curly and I thought that it was the signal that was weak, then we thought it was the operator who was weak or sick, but we were wrong, he's just a ham-handed amateur.'

'You can tell?' Swanson asked.

'You can always tell. You can—' He broke off, stiffened and touched his watchmate's arm.

Curly nodded. 'I got it,' he said matter-of-factly. 'Position unknown, the man says.'

Nobody said anything, not just then. It didn't seem important that he couldn't give us his position, all that mattered was that we were in direct contact. Raeburn turned and ran forward across the control room. I could hear him speak rapidly on the bridge telephone. Swanson turned to me.

'Those balloons you spoke of earlier. The ones on Zebra. Are they free or captive?'

'Both.'

'How do the captive ones work?'

'A free-running winch, nylon cord marked off in hundreds and thousands of feet.'

'We'll ask them to send a captive balloon up to 5,000 feet,' Swanson decided. 'With flares. If they're within thirty or forty miles we ought to see it, and if we get its elevation and make an allowance for the effect of wind on it, we should get a fair estimate of distance . . . What is it, Brown?' This to the man Zabrinski called 'Curly.'

'They're sending again,' Curly said. 'Very broken, fades a lot. "God's sake, hurry." Just like that, twice over. "God's sake hurry." '

'Send this,' Swanson said. He dictated a brief message about the balloons. 'And send it real slow.'

Curly nodded and began to transmit. Raeburn came running back into the radio room.

'The moon's not down yet,' he said quickly to Swanson. 'Still a degree or two above the horizon. I'm taking a sextant up top and taking a moon-sight. Ask them to do the same. That'll give us the latitude difference and if we know they're o-forty-five of us we can pin them down to a mile.'

'It's worth trying,' Swanson said. He dictated another message to Brown. Brown transmitted the second message immediately after the first. We waited for the answer. For all of ten minutes we waited. I looked at the men in the radio room, they all had the same remote withdrawn look of men who are there only physically, men whose minds are many miles away. They were all at the same place and I was too, wherever Drift Ice Station Zebra was.

Brown started writing again, not for long. His voice this time was still matter-of-fact, but with overtones of emptiness. He said: ' "All balloons burnt. No moon." '

'No moon.' Raeburn couldn't hide the bitterness, the sharpness of his disappointment. 'Damn! Must be pretty heavy overcast up there. Or a bad storm.'

'No,' I said. 'You don't get local weather variations like that on the ice-cap. The conditions will be the same over 50,000 square miles. The moon is down. For them, the moon is down. Their latest estimated position must have been pure guesswork, and bad guesswork at that. They must be at least a hundred miles farther north and east than we had thought.'

'Ask them if they have any rockets,' Swanson said to Brown.

'You can try,' I said. 'It'll be a waste of time. If they are as far off as I think, their rockets would never get above our horizon. Even if they did, we wouldn't see them.'

'It's always a chance, isn't it?' Swanson asked.

'Beginning to lose contact, sir,' Brown reported. 'Something there about food but it faded right out.'

'Tell them if they have any rockets to fire them at once,' Swanson said. 'Quickly now, before you lose contact.'

Four times in all Brown sent the message before he managed to pick up a reply. Then he said: 'Message reads: "Two minutes." Either this guy is pretty far through or his transmitter batteries are. That's all. "Two minutes," he said.'

Swanson nodded wordlessly and left the room. I followed. We picked up coats and binoculars and clambered up to the bridge. After the warmth and comfort of the control room, the cold seemed glacial, the flying ice-spicules more lancet-like than ever. Swanson uncapped the gyro-repeater compass, gave us the line of o-forty-five, told the two men who had been keeping watch what to look for and where.

A minute passed, two minutes, five. My eyes began to ache from staring into the ice-filled dark, the exposed part of my face had gone completely numb and I knew that when I removed those binoculars I was going to take a fair bit of skin with them.

A phone bell rang. Swanson lowered his glasses, leaving two peeled and bloody rings round his eyes – he seemed unaware of it, the pain wouldn't come until later – and picked up the receiver. He listened briefly, hung up.

'Radio room,' he said. 'Let's get below. All of us. The rockets were fired three minutes ago.'

We went below. Swanson caught sight of his face reflected in a glass gauge and shook his head. 'They must have shelter,' he said quietly. 'They must. Some hut left. Or they would have been gone long ago.' He went into the radio room. 'Still in contact?'

'Yeah.' Zabrinski spoke. 'Off and on. It's a funny thing. When a dicey contact like this starts to fade it usually gets lost and stays lost. But this guy keeps coming back. Funny.'

'Maybe he hasn't even got batteries left,' I said. 'Maybe all they have is a hand-cranked generator. Maybe there's no one left with the strength to crank it for more than a few moments at a time.'

'Maybe,' Zabrinski agreed. 'Tell the captain that last message, Curly.'

' "Can't late many tours," ' Brown said. 'That's how the message came through. "Can't late many tours." I think it should have read "Can't last many hours." Don't see what else it can have been.'

Swanson looked at me briefly, glanced away again. I hadn't told anyone else that the commandant of the base was my brother and I knew he hadn't told anyone either. He said to Brown: 'Give them a time-check. Ask them to send their call-signs five minutes every hour on the hour. Tell them we'll contact them again within six hours at most, maybe only four. Zabrinski, how accurate was that bearing?'

'Dead accurate, Captain. I've had plenty of re-checks. O-forty-five exactly.'

Swanson moved out into the control centre. 'Drift Station Zebra can't see the moon. If we take Dr Carpenter's word for it that weather conditions are pretty much the same all over, that's because the moon is below their horizon. With the elevation we have of the moon, and knowing their bearing, what's Zebra's minimum distance from us?'

'A hundred miles, as Dr Carpenter said,' Raeburn confirmed after a short calculation. 'At least that.'

'So. We leave here and take a course o-forty. Not enough to take us very far from their general direction but it will give us enough offset to take a good cross-bearing eventually. We will go exactly a hundred miles and try for another polynya. Call the executive officer, secure for diving.' He smiled at me. 'With two cross-bearings and an accurately measured base-line, we can pin them down to a hundred yards.'

'How do you intend to measure a hundred miles under the ice? Accurately, I mean?'

'Our inertia navigation computer does it for me. It's very accurate, you wouldn't believe just how accurate. I can dive the *Dolphin* off the eastern coast of the United States and surface again in the Eastern Mediterranean within five hundred yards of where I expect to be. Over a hundred miles I don't expect to be twenty yards out.'

Radio aerials were lowered, hatches screwed down and within five minutes the *Dolphin* had dropped down from her hole in the ice and was on her way. The two helmsmen at the diving stand sat idly smoking, doing nothing: the steering controls were in automatic interlock with the inertial navigation system which steered the ship with a degree of accuracy and sensitivity impossible to human hands. For the first time I could feel a heavy jarring vibration rumbling throughout the length of the ship: 'can't last many hours' the message had said: the *Dolphin* was under full power.

I didn't leave the control room that morning. I spent most of the time peering over the shoulder of Dr Benson who had passed his usual five minutes in the sick-bay waiting for the patients who never turned up and then had hurried to his seat by the ice-machine. The readings on that machine meant living or dying to the Zebra survivors. We had to find another polynya to surface in to get a cross-bearing: no cross-bearing, no hope. I wondered for the hundredth time how many of the survivors of the fire were still alive. From the quiet desperation of the few garbled messages that Brown and Zabrinski had managed to pick up I couldn't see that there would be many.

The pattern traced out by the hissing stylus on the chart was hardly an encouraging sight. Most of the time it showed the ice overhead to be of a thickness of ten feet or more. Several times the stylus dipped to show thicknesses of thirty to forty feet, and once it dipped down almost clear of the paper, showing a tremendous inverted ridge of at least 150 feet in depth. I tried to imagine what kind of fantastic pressures created by piled-up log-jams of rafted ice on the surface must have been necessary to force ice down to such a depth: but I just didn't have the imagination to cope with that sort of thing.

Only twice in the first eighty miles did the stylus trace out the thin black line that meant thin ice overhead. The first of those polynyas might have accommodated a small rowing boat, but it would certainly never have looked at the *Dolphin*: the other had hardly been any bigger.

Shortly before noon the hull vibration died away as Swanson gave the order for a cutback to a slow cruising speed. He said to Benson: 'How does it look?'

'Terrible. Heavy ice all the way.'

'Well, we can't expect a polynya to fall into our laps straight away,' Swanson said reasonably, 'We're almost there. We'll make a grid search. Five miles east, five miles west, a quarter-mile farther to the north each time.'

The search began. An hour passed, two, then three. Raeburn and his assistant hardly ever raised their heads from the plotting table where they were meticulously tracing every movement the *Dolphin* was making in its criss-cross search under the sea. Four o'clock in the afternoon. The normal background buzz of conversation, the occasional small talk from various groups in the control centre, died away completely. Benson's occasional 'Heavy ice, still heavy ice,' growing steadily quieter and more dispirited, served only to emphasize and deepen the heavy brooding silence that had fallen. Only a case-hardened undertaker could have felt perfectly at home in that atmosphere. At the moment, undertakers were the last people I wanted to think about.

Five o'clock in the afternoon. People weren't looking at each other any more, far less talking. Heavy ice, still heavy ice. Defeat, despair, hung heavy in the air. Heavy ice, still heavy ice. Even Swanson had stopped smiling, I wondered if he had in his mind's eye what I now constantly had in mine, the picture of a haggard, emaciated, bearded man with his face all but destroyed with frostbite, a frozen, starving, dying man draining away the last few ounces of his exhausted strength as he cranked the handle of his generator and tapped out his call-sign with lifeless fingers, his head bowed as he strained to listen above the howl of the ice-storm for the promise of aid that never came. Or maybe there was no one tapping out a call-sign any more. They were no ordinary men who had been sent to man Drift Ice Station Zebra but there comes a time when even the toughest, the bravest, the most enduring will abandon all hope and lie down to die. Perhaps he had already lain down to die. Heavy ice, still heavy ice.

At half past five Commander Swanson walked across to the ice-machine and peered over Benson's shoulder. He said: 'What's the average thickness of that stuff above?'

'Twelve to fifteen feet,' Benson said. His voice was low and tired. 'Nearer fifteen, I would say.'

Swanson picked up a phone. 'Lieutenant Mills? Captain here. What is the state of readiness of those torpedoes you're working on? . . . Four? . . . Ready to go? . . . Good. Stand by to load. I'm giving this search another thirty minutes, then it's up to you. Yes that is correct. We shall attempt to blow a hole through the ice.' He replaced the phone.

Hansen said thoughtfully: 'Fifteen feet of ice is a helluva lot of ice. And that ice will have a tamping effect and will direct 90 per cent of the explosive force down the way. You think we *can* blow a hole through fifteen feet of ice, Captain?'

'I've no idea,' Swanson admitted. 'How can anyone know until we try it?'

'Nobody ever tried to do this before?' I asked.

'No. Not in the US Navy, anyway. The Russians may have tried it, I wouldn't know. They don't,' he added dryly, 'keep us very well informed on those matters.'

'Aren't the underwater shock waves liable to damage the *Dolphin*?' I asked. I didn't care for the idea at all, and that was a fact.

'If they do, the Electric Boat Company can expect a pretty strong letter of complaint. We shall explode the warhead electronically about 1,000 yards after it leaves the ship – it has to travel eight hundred yards anyway before a safety device unlocks and permits the warhead to be armed. We shall be bows-on to the detonation and with a hull designed to withstand the pressures this one is, the shock effects should be negligible.'

'Very heavy ice,' Benson intoned. 'Thirty feet, forty feet, fifty feet. Very, very heavy ice.'

'Just too bad if your torpedo ended up under a pile like the stuff above us just now,' I said. 'I doubt if it would even chip off the bottom layer.'

'We'll take care that doesn't happen. We'll just find a suitably large layer of ice of normal thickness, kind of back off a thousand yards and then let go.'

'Thin ice!' Benson's voice wasn't a shout, it was a bellow. 'Thin ice. No, by God, clear water! Clear water! Lovely clear, clear water!'

My immediate reaction was that either the ice-machine or Benson's brain had blown a fuse. But the officer at the diving panel had no such doubts for I had to grab and hang on hard as the *Dolphin* heeled over violently to port and came curving round, engines slowing, in a tight circle to bring her back to the spot where Benson had called out. Swanson watched the plot, spoke quietly and the big bronze propellers reversed and bit into the water to bring the *Dolphin* to a stop.

'How's it looking now, Doc?' Swanson called out.

'Clear, clear water,' Benson said reverently. 'I got a good picture of it. It's pretty narrow, but wide enough to hold us. It's long, with a sharp left-hand dog-leg, for it followed us round through the first forty-five degrees of our curve.'

'One fifty feet,' Swanson said.

The pumps hummed. The *Dolphin* drifted gently upwards like an airship rising from the ground. Briefly, water flooded back into the tanks. The *Dolphin* hung motionless.

'Up periscope,' Swanson said.

The periscope hissed up slowly into the raised position. Swanson glanced briefly through the eyepiece, then beckoned me. 'Take a look,' he beamed. 'As lovely a sight as you'll ever see.'

I took a look. If you'd made a picture of what could be seen above and framed it you couldn't have sold the result even if you added Picasso's name to it: but I could see what he meant. Solid black masses on either side with a scarcely lighter strip of dark jungle green running between them on a line with the fore-and-aft direction of the ship. An open lead in the polar pack.

Three minutes later we were lying on the surface of the Arctic Ocean, just under two hundred and fifty miles from the Pole.

The rafted, twisted ice-pack reared up into contorted ridges almost fifty feet in height, towering twenty feet above the top of the sail, so close you could almost reach out and touch the nearest ridge. Three or four of those broken and fantastically hummocked icehills we could see stretching off to the west and then the light of the floodlamp failed and we could see no more. Beyond that there was only blackness.

To the east we could see nothing at all. To have stared out to the east with opened eyes would have been to be blinded for life in a very few seconds: even goggles became clouded and scarred after the briefest exposure. Close in to the *Dolphin*'s side you could, with bent head and hooded eyes, catch, for a fleeting part of a second, a glimpse of black water, already freezing over: but it was more imagined than seen.

The wind, shrieking and wailing across the bridge and through raised antennae, showed at consistently over 60 m.p.h. on the bridge anemometer. The ice-storm was no longer the gusting, swirling fog of that morning but a driving wall of stiletto-tipped spears, near-lethal in its ferocity, high speed ice-spicule lances that would have skewered their way through the thickest cardboard or shattered in a second a glass held in your hand. Over and above the ululating threnody of the wind we could hear an almost constant grinding, crashing and deep-throated booming as millions of tons of racked and tortured ice, under the influence of the gale and some mighty pressure centre, heaven knew how many hundreds of miles away, reared and twisted and tore and cracked, one moment forming another rafted ridge as a layer of ice, perhaps ten feet thick, screeched and roared and clambered on to the shoulders of another and then another, the next rending apart in indescribably violent cacophony to open up a new lead, black wind-torn water that started to skim over with ice almost as soon as it was formed.

'Are we both mad? Let's get below.' Swanson cupped his hands to my ear and had to shout, but even so I could hardly hear him above that hellish bedlam of sound.

We clambered down into the comparatively sudden stillness of the control room. Swanson untied his parka hood and pulled off scarf and goggles that had completely masked his face. He looked at me and shook his head wonderingly.

'And some people talk about the white silence of the Arctic. My God, a boilermaker's shop is like a library reading-room compared to that lot.' He shook his head again. 'We stuck our noses out a few times above the ice-pack last year, but we never saw anything like this. Or heard it. Winter-time, too. Cold, sure, damned cold, and windy, but never so bad that we couldn't take a brief stroll on the ice, and I used to wonder about those stories of explorers being stuck in their tents for days on end, unable to move. But I know now why Captain Scott died.'

'It is pretty nasty,' I admitted. 'How safe are we here, Commander?'

'That's anybody's guess,' Swanson shrugged. 'The wind's got us jammed hard against the west wall of this polynya and there's maybe fifty yards of open water to starboard. For the moment we're safe. But you can hear and see that pack is on the move, and not slowly either. The lead we're in was torn open less than an hour ago. How long? Depends on the configuration of the ice, but those polynyas can close up damned quickly at times, and while the hull of the *Dolphin* can take a fair old pressure, it can't take a million tons of ice leaning against it. Maybe we can stay here for hours, maybe only for minutes. Whichever it is, as soon as that east wall comes within ten feet of the starboard side we're dropping down out of it. You know what happens when a ship gets caught in the ice.'

'I know. They get squeezed flat, are carried round the top of the world for a few years then one day are released and drop to the bottom, two miles straight down. The United States Government wouldn't like it, Commander.'

'The prospects of further promotion for Commander Swanson would be poor,' Swanson admitted. 'I think—'

'Hey!' The shout came from the radio room. 'Hey, c'm here.'

'I rather think Zabrinski must be wanting me,' Swanson murmured. He moved off with his usual deceptive speed and I followed him into the radio room. Zabrinski was sitting half-turned in his chair, an ear-to-ear beam on his face, the earphones extended in his left hand. Swanson took them, listened briefly, then nodded.

'DSY,' he said softly. 'DSY, Dr Carpenter. We have them. Got the bearing? Good.' He turned to the doorway, saw the quartermaster. 'Ellis, ask the navigating officer to come along as soon as possible.'

'We'll pick 'em all up yet, Captain,' Zabrinski said jovially. The smile on the big man's face, I could see now, didn't extend as far as his eyes. 'They must be a pretty tough bunch of boys out there.'

'Very tough, Zabrinski,' Swanson said absently. His eyes were remote and I knew he was listening to the metallic cannonading of the ice-spicules, a billion tiny pneumatic chisels drumming away continuously against the outer hull of the submarine, a sound loud enough to make low speech impossible. 'Very tough. Are you in two-way contact?'

Zabrinski shook his head and turned away. He'd stopped smiling. Raeburn came in, was handed a sheet of paper and left for his plotting table. We went with him. After a minute or two he looked up, and said: 'If anyone fancies a Sunday afternoon's walk, this is it.'

'So close?' Swanson asked.

'So very close. Five miles due east, give or take half a mile. Pretty fair old bloodhounds, aren't we?'

'We're just lucky,' Swanson said shortly. He walked back to the radio room. 'Talking to them yet?'

'We've lost them altogether.'

'Completely?'

'We only had 'em a minute, Captain. Just that. Then they faded. Got weaker and weaker. I think Doc Carpenter here is right, they're using a hand-cranked generator.' He paused, then said idly: 'I've a six-year-old-daughter who could crank one of those machines for five minutes without turning a hair.'

Swanson looked at me, then turned away without a word. I followed him to the unoccupied diving stand. From the bridge access hatch we could hear the howl of the storm, the grinding ice with its boom and scream that spanned the entire register of hearing. Swanson said: 'Zabrinski put it very well . . . I wonder how long this damnable storm is going to last?'

'Too long. I have a medical kit in my cabin, a fifty-ounce flask of medicinal alcohol and cold-weather clothes. Could you supply me with a thirty-pound pack of emergency rations, high protein high-calorie concentrates, Benson will know what I mean.'

'Do you mean what I think you mean?' Swanson said slowly. 'Or am I just going round the bend?'

'What's this about going round the bend?' Hansen had just come through the doorway leading to the for'ard passageway, and the grin on his face was clear enough indication that though he'd caught Swanson's last words he'd caught neither the intonation nor the expression on Swanson's face. 'Very serious state of affairs, going round the bend. I'll have to assume command

and put you in irons, Captain. Something about it in regulations, I dare say.'

'Dr Carpenter is proposing to sling a bag of provisions on his back and proceed to Drift Station Zebra on foot.'

'You've picked them up again?' Just for the moment Hansen had forgotten me. 'You really got them? And a cross-bearing?'

'Just this minute. We've hit it almost on the nose. Five miles, young Raeburn says.'

'My God! Five miles. Only five miles!' Then the elation vanished from voice and face as if an internal switch had been touched. 'In weather like this it might as well be five hundred. Even old Amundsen couldn't have moved ten yards through this stuff.'

'Dr Carpenter evidently thinks he can improve on Amundsen's standard's,' Swanson said dryly. 'He's talking about walking there.'

Hansen looked at me for a long and considering moment, then turned back to Swanson. 'I think maybe it's Doc Carpenter we should be clapping in the old irons.'

'I think maybe it is,' Swanson said.

'Look,' I said. 'There are men out there on Drift Station Zebra. Maybe not many, not now, but there are some. One, anyway. Men a long way past being sick. Dying men. To a dying man it takes only the very smallest thing to spell out the difference between life and death. I'm a doctor, I know. The smallest thing. An ounce of alcohol, a few ounces of food, a hot drink, some medicine. Then they'll live. Without those little things they will surely die. They're entitled to what smallest aid they can get, and I'm entitled to take whatever risks I care to see they get it. I'm not asking anyone else to go, all I'm asking is that you implement the terms of your orders from Washington to give me all possible assistance without endangering the *Dolphin* or its crew. Threatening to stop me is not my idea of giving assistance. And I'm not asking you to endanger your submarine or the lives of your men.'

Swanson gazed at the floor. I wondered what he was thinking of: the best way to stop me, his orders from Washington, or the fact that he was the only man who knew that the commandant on Zebra was my brother. He said nothing.

'You must stop him, Captain,' Hansen said urgently. 'Any other man you saw putting a pistol to his head or a razor to his throat, you'd stop that man. This is the same. He's out of his mind, he's wanting to commit suicide.' He tapped the bulkhead beside him. 'Good God, Doc, why do you think we have the sonar operators in here on duty even when we're stopped. So that they can tell us when the ice wall on the far side of the polynya starts to close in on us, that's why. And *that's* because it's impossible for any man to last thirty seconds on the bridge or see an inch against the ice-storm up there. Just take a quick twenty-second trip up there, up on the bridge, and you'll change your mind fast enough, I guarantee.'

'We've just come down from the bridge,' Swanson said matter-of-factly.

'And he still wants to go? It's like I say, he's crazy.'

'We could drop down now,' Swanson said. 'We have the position. Perhaps we can find a polynya within a mile, half a mile of Zebra. That would be a different proposition altogether.'

'Perhaps you could find a needle in a haystack,' I said. 'It took you six hours to find this one, and even at that we were lucky. And don't talk about torpedoes, the ice in this area is rafted anything up to a hundred feet in depth. Pretty much all over. You'd be as well trying to blast your way through with a .22. Might be twelve hours, might be days before we could break through again. I can get there in two-three hours.'

'*If* you don't freeze to death in the first hundred yards,' Hansen said. '*If* you don't fall down a ridge and break your leg. *If* you don't get blinded in a few minutes. *If* you don't fall into a newly-opened polynya that you can't see, where you'll either drown or, if you manage to get out, freeze solid in thirty seconds. And even if you do survive all those things, I'd be grateful if you'd explain to me exactly how you propose to find your way blind to a place five miles away. You can't carry a damn' great gyro weighing about half a ton on your back, and a magnetic compass is useless in those latitudes. The magnetic north pole is a good bit *south* of where we are now and a long way to the west. Even if you *did* get some sort of bearing from it, in the darkness and the ice-storm you could still miss the camp – or what's left of it – by only a hundred yards and never know it. And even if by one chance in a million you do manage to find your way there, how on earth do you ever expect to find your way back again. Leave a paper-trail? A five-mile ball of twine. Crazy is hardly the word for it.'

'I may break a leg, drown or freeze,' I conceded. 'I'll take my chance on that. Finding my way there and back is no great trick. You have a radio bearing on Zebra and know exactly where it lies. You can take a radio bearing on any transmitter. All I have to do is to tote a receiver-transmitter radio along with me, keep in touch with you and you can keep me on the same bearing as Zebra. It's easy.'

'It would be,' Hansen said, 'except for one little thing. We don't have any such radio.'

'I have a twenty-mile walkie-talkie in my case,' I said.

'Coincidence, coincidence,' Hansen murmured. 'Just happened to bring it along, no doubt. I'll bet you have all sorts of funny things in that case of yours, haven't you, Doc?'

'What Dr Carpenter has in his case is really no business of ours,' Swanson said in mild reproof. He hadn't thought so earlier. 'What does concern us is his intention to do away with himself. You really can't expect us to consent to this ridiculous proposal, Dr Carpenter.'

'No one's asking you to consent to anything,' I said. 'Your consent is not required. All I'm asking you to do is to stand to one side. And to arrange for that food provision pack for me. If you won't, I'll have to manage without.'

I left and went to my cabin. Hansen's cabin, rather. But even although it wasn't my cabin that didn't stop me from turning the key in the lock as soon as I had passed through the door.

Working on the likely supposition that if Hansen did come along soon he wasn't going to be very pleased to find the door of his own cabin locked against him, I wasted no time. I spun the combination lock on the case and opened the lid. At least three-quarters of the available space was taken up by Arctic survival clothing, the very best that money could buy. It hadn't been my money that had bought it.

I stripped off the outer clothes I was wearing, pulled on long open-mesh underwear, woollen shirt and cord breeches, then a triple-knit wool parka lined with pure silk. The parka wasn't quite standard, it had a curiously shaped suède-lined pocket below and slightly to the front of the left armpit, and a differently shaped suède-lined pocket on the right-hand side. I dug swiftly to the bottom of my case and brought up three separate items. The first of these, a nine-millimetre Mannlicher-Schoenauer automatic, fitted into the left-hand pocket as securely and snugly as if the pocket had been specially designed for it, which indeed it had: the other items, spare magazine clips, fitted as neatly into the right-hand pocket.

The rest of the dressing didn't take long. Two pairs of heavy-knit woollen socks, felt undershoes and then the furs – caribou for the outer parka and trousers, wolverine for the hood, sealskin for the boots and reindeer for the gloves, which were pulled on over other layers of silk gloves and woollen mittens. Maybe a polar bear would have had a slight edge over me when it came to being equipped to survive an Arctic blizzard, but there wouldn't have been much in it.

I hung snow-mask and goggles round my neck, stuck a rubberized waterproofed torch into the inside pocket of the fur parka, unearthed my walkie-talkie and closed the case. I set the combination again. There was no need to set the combination any more, not now that I had the Mannlicher-Schoenauer under my arm, but it would give Swanson something to do while I was away. I shoved my medicine case and a steel flask of alcohol in a rucksack and unlocked the door.

Swanson was exactly where I'd left him in the control room. So was Hansen. So were two others who had not been there when I had left, Rawlings and Zabrinski. Hansen, Rawlings, and Zabrinski, the three biggest men in the ship. The last time I'd seen them together was when Swanson had whistled them up from the *Dolphin* in the Holy Loch to see to it that I didn't do anything he didn't want me to do. Maybe Commander Swanson had a one-track mind. Hansen, Rawlings, and Zabrinski. They looked bigger than ever.

I said to Swanson: 'Do I get those iron rations or not?'

'One last formal statement,' Swanson said. His first thoughts, as I came waddling into the control centre, must have been that a grizzly bear was loose inside his submarine, but he hadn't batted an eyelid. 'For the record. Your intentions are suicidal, your chances are non-existent. I cannot give my consent.'

'All right, your statement is on record, witnesses and all. The iron rations.'

'I cannot give my consent because of a fresh and dangerous development One of our electronic technicians was carrying out a routine calibration test on the ice-machine just now and an overload coil didn't function. Electric motor burnt out. No spares, it will have to be rewired. You realize what that means. If we're forced to drop down I can't find my way to the top again. Then it's curtains for everybody – everybody left above the ice, that is.'

I didn't blame him for trying, but I was vaguely disappointed in him: he'd had time to think up a better one than that. I said: 'The iron rations, Commander. Do I get them?'

'You mean to go through with this? After what I've said?'

'Oh, for God's sake. I'll do without the food.'

'My executive officer, Torpedoman Rawlings and Radioman Zabrinski,' Swanson said formally, 'don't like this.'

'I can't help what they like or don't like.'

'They feel they can't let you go through with it,' he persisted.

They were more than big. They were huge. I could get past them the way a lamb gets past a starving lion. I had a gun all right but with that one-piece parka I was wearing I'd practically have to undress myself to get at it and Hansen, in that Holy Loch canteen, had shown just how quickly he could react when he saw anyone making a suspicious move. And even if I did get my gun out, what then? Men like Hansen, like Rawlings and Zabrinski, didn't scare. I couldn't bluff them with a gun. And I couldn't use the gun. Not against men who were just doing their duty.

'They *won't* let you go through with it,' Swanson went on, 'unless, that is, you will permit them to accompany you, which they have volunteered to do.'

'Volunteered,' Rawlings sniffed. 'You, you, and you.'

'I don't want them,' I said.

'Gracious, ain't he?' Rawlings asked of no one in particular. 'You might at least have said thanks, Doc.'

'You are putting the lives of your men in danger, Commander Swanson. You know what your orders said.'

'Yes. I also know that in Arctic travels, as in mountaineering and exploring, a party has always double the chances of the individual. I also know that if it became known that we had permitted a civilian doctor to set off on his own for Drift Station Zebra while we were all too scared to stir from our nice warm sub, the name of the United States Navy would become pretty muddy.'

'What do your men think of your making them risk their lives to save the good name of the submarine service?'

'You heard the captain,' Rawlings said. 'We're volunteers. Look at Zabrinski there, anyone can see that he is a man cast in a heroic mould.'

'Have you thought of what happens' I said, 'if the ice closes in when we're away and the captain has to take the ship down?'

'Don't even talk of it,' Zabrinski urged. 'I'm not all that heroic.'

I gave up. I'd no option but to give up. Besides, like Zabrinski, I wasn't all that heroic and I suddenly realized that I would be very glad indeed to have those three men along with me.

Chapter Five

Lieutenant Hansen was the first man to give up. Or perhaps 'give up' is wrong, the meaning of the words was quite unknown and the thought totally alien to Hansen, it would be more accurate to say that he was the first of us to show any glimmerings of common sense. He caught my arm, brought his head close to mine, pulled down his snow mask and shouted: 'No farther, Doc. We must stop.'

'The next ridge,' I yelled back. I didn't know whether he'd heard me or not, as soon as he'd spoken he'd pulled his mask back up into position again to protect the momentarily exposed skin against the horizontally driving ice-storm, but he seemed to understand for he eased his grip on the rope round my waist and let me move ahead again. For the past two and a half hours Hansen, Rawlings and I had each taken his turn at being the lead man on the end of the rope, while the other three held on to it some ten yards behind, the idea being not that the lead man should guide the others but that the others should save the life of the lead man, should the need arise. And the need already had arisen, just once, Hansen, slipped and scrambling on all-fours across a fractured and upward sloping raft of ice, had reached gropingly forward with his arms into the blindness of the night and the storm and found nothing there. He had fallen eight vertical feet before the rope had brought him up with a vicious jerk that had been almost as painful for Rawlings and myself, who had taken the brunt of the shock, as it had been for Hansen. For nearly two minutes he'd dangled above the wind-torn black water of a freshly opened lead before we'd managed to drag him back to safety. It had been a close thing, far too close a thing, for in far sub-zero temperatures with a gale-force wind blowing, even a few seconds' submersion in water makes the certainty of death absolute, the process of dissolution as swift as it is irreversible. In those conditions the clothes of a man pulled from the water become a frozen and impenetrable suit of armour inside seconds, an armour that can neither be removed nor chipped away. Petrified inside this ice-shroud, a man just simply and quickly freezes to death – in the unlikely event, that is, of his heart having withstood the thermal shock of the body surface being exposed to an almost instantaneous hundred degree drop in temperature.

So now I stepped forward very cautiously, very warily indeed, feeling the ice ahead of me with a probe we'd devised after Hansen's near accident – a chopped-off five foot length of rope which we'd dipped into the water of the lead then exposed to the air until it had become as rigid as a bar of steel. At times I walked, at times I stumbled, at times, when a brief lull in the gale-force wind, as sudden as it was unexpected, would catch me off balance I'd just fall forward and continue on hands and knees, for it was quite as easy that way. It was during one of those periods when I was shuffling blindly forward on all-fours that I realized that the wind had, for the time being, lost nearly all of its violence and that I was no longer being bombarded by that horizontally driving hail of flying ice-spicules. Moments later my probe made contact with some solid obstacle in my path: the vertical wall of a rafted ice ridge. I crawled thankfully into its shelter, raised my goggles and pulled out and switched on my torch as the others came blindly up to where I lay.

Blindly. With arms outstretched they pawed at the air before them like sightless men, which for the past two and a half hours was exactly what they had been. For all the service our goggles had given us we might as well have stuck our heads in gunny sacks before leaving the *Dolphin*. I looked at Hansen, the first of the three to come up. Goggles, snow-mask, hood, clothing – the entire front part of his body from top to toe was deeply and solidly encrusted in a thick and glittering layer of compacted ice, except for some narrow cracks caused by joint movements of legs and arms. As he drew close to me I could hear him splintering and crackling a good five feet away.

Long ice-feathers streamed back from his head, shoulders and elbows; as an extra-terrestrial monster from one of the chillier planets, such as Pluto, he'd have been a sensation in any horror movie. I suppose I looked much the same.

We huddled close together in the shelter of the wall. Only four feet above our heads the ice-storm swept by in a glittering grey-white river. Rawlings, sitting on my left, pushed up his goggles, looked down at his ice-sheathed furs and started to beat himself with his fist across the chest to break up the covering. I reached out a hand and caught his arm.

'Leave it alone,' I said.

'Leave it alone?' Rawling's voice was muffled by his snow-mask, but not so muffled that I couldn't hear the chattering of his teeth. 'This damn' suit of armour weighs a ton. I'm out of training for this kind of weight-lifting, Doc.'

'Leave it alone. If it weren't for that ice, you'd have frozen to death by this time: it's insulating you from that wind and the ice-storm. Let's see the rest of your face. And your hands.'

I checked him and the two others for frost-bite, while Hansen checked me. We were still lucky. Blue and mottled and shaking with cold, but no frost-bite. The furs of the other three might not have been quite as fancy as mine, but they were very adequate indeed. Nuclear subs always got the best of everything, and Arctic clothing was no exception. But although they weren't freezing to death I could see from their faces and hear from their breathing that they were pretty far gone in exhaustion. Thrusting into the power of that ice-storm was like wading upstream against the current of a river of molasses: that was energy-sapping enough, but the fact that we had to spend most of our time clambering over, slipping on, sliding and falling across fractured ice or making detours round impassable ridges while being weighed down with forty pound packs on our back and heaven only knew how many additional pounds of ice coating our furs in front had turned our trudge across that contorted treacherous ice into a dark and frozen nightmare.

'The point of no return, I think,' Hansen said. His breathing, like Rawlings's, was very quick, very shallow, almost gasping. 'We can't take much more of this, Doc.'

'You ought to listen to Dr Benson's lectures a bit more.' I said reprovingly. 'All this ice-cream and apple pie and lolling around in your bunks is no training for this sort of thing.'

'Yeah?' He peered at me. 'How do *you* feel?'

'A mite tired,' I admitted. 'Nothing much to speak of.' Nothing much to speak of, my legs felt as if they were falling off, that was all, but the goad of pride was always a useful one to have to hand. I slipped off my rucksack and brought out the medicinal alcohol. 'I suggest fifteen minutes' break. Any more and we'll just start stiffening up completely. Meantime, a little drop of what we fancy will help keep the old blood corpuscles trudging around.'

'I thought medical opinion was against alcohol in low temperatures,' Hansen said doubtfully. 'Something about opening the pores.'

'Name me any form of human activity,' I said, 'and I'll find you a group of doctors against it. Spoilsports. Besides, this isn't alcohol, it's very fine Scotch whisky.'

'You should have said so in the first place. Pass it over. Not too much for Rawlings and Zabrinski, they're not used to the stuff. Any word, Zabrinski?'

Zabrinski, with the walkie-talkie's aerial up and one earphone tucked in below the hood of his parka, was talking into the microphone through cupped hands. As the radio expert, Zabrinski had been the obvious man to handle the walkie-talkie and I'd given it to him before leaving the submarine. This was also the reason why Zabrinski wasn't at any time given the position of lead man in our trudge across the pack ice. A heavy fall or immersion in water would have finished the radio he was carrying slung on his back: and if the radio were finished then so would we be, for without the radio not only had we no hope of finding Drift Station Zebra, we wouldn't have a chance in a thousand of ever finding our way back to the *Dolphin* again. Zabrinski was built on the size and scale of a medium-sized gorilla and was about as durable; but we couldn't have treated him more tenderly had he been made of Dresden china.

'It's difficult,' Zabrinski said. 'Radio's O.K., but this ice-storm causes such damn' distortion and squeaking – no, wait a minute, though, wait a minute.'

He bent his head over the microphone, shielding it from the sound of the storm, and spoke again through cupped hands. 'Zabrinski here . . . Zabrinski. Yeah, we're all kinda tuckered out, but Doc here seems to think we'll make it. . . . Hang on, I'll ask him.'

He turned to me. 'How far do you reckon we've come, they want to know.'

'Four miles.' I shrugged. 'Three and a half, four and a half. You guess it.'

Zabrinski spoke again, looked interrogatively at Hansen and myself, saw our headshakes and signed off. He said: 'Navigating officer says we're four-five degrees north of where we should be and that we'll have to cut south if we don't want to miss Zebra by a few hundred yards.'

It could have been worse. Over an hour had passed since we'd received the last bearing position from the *Dolphin* and, between radio calls, our only means of navigating had been by judging the strength and direction of the wind in our faces. When a man's face is completely covered and largely numb it's not a very sensitive instrument for gauging wind direction – and for all we knew the wind might be either backing or veering. It could have been a lot worse and I said so to Hansen.

'It could be worse,' he agreed heavily. 'We could be travelling in circles or we could be dead. Barring that, I don't see how it could be worse.' He gulped down the whisky, coughed, handed the flask top back to me. 'Things look brighter now. You honestly think we can make it?'

'A little luck, that's all. You think maybe our packs are too heavy? That we should abandon some of it here?' The last thing I wanted to do was to abandon any of the supplies we had along with us: eighty pounds of food, a stove, thirty pounds of compressed fuel tablets, 100 ounces of alcohol, a tent, and a very comprehensive medical kit; but if it was to be abandoned I wanted the suggestion to be left to them, and I was sure they wouldn't make it.

'We're abandoning nothing,' Hansen said. Either the rest or the whisky had done him good, his voice was stronger, his teeth hardly chattering at all.

'Let the thought die stillborn,' Zabrinski said. When first I'd seen him in Scotland he had reminded me of a polar bear and now out here on the ice-cap, huge and crouched in his ice-whitened furs, the resemblance was redoubled. He had the physique of a bear, too, and seemed completely tireless; he was in far better shape than any of us. 'This weight on my bowed shoulders is like a bad leg: an old friend that gives me pain, but I wouldn't be without it.'

'You?' I asked Rawlings.

'I am conserving my energy,' Rawlings announced. 'I expect to have to carry Zabrinski later on.'

We pulled the starred, abraded and now thoroughly useless snow-goggles over our eyes again, hoisted ourselves stiffly to our feet and moved off to the south to find the end of and round the high ridge that here blocked our path. It was by far the longest and most continuous ridge we'd encountered yet, but we didn't mind, we required to make a good offing to get us back on course and not only were we doing just that but we were doing it in comparative shelter and saving our strength by so doing. After perhaps four hundred yards the ice wall ended so abruptly, leading to so sudden and unexpected an exposure to the whistling fury of the ice-storm that I was bowled completely off my feet. An express train couldn't have done it any better. I hung on to the rope with one hand, clawed and scrambled my way back on to my feet with the help of the other, shouted a warning to the others, and then we were fairly into the wind again, holding it directly in our faces and leaning far forward to keep our balance.

We covered the next mile in less than half an hour. The going was easier now, much easier than it had been, although we still had to make small detours round rafted, compacted and broken ice: on the debit side, we were all of us, Zabrinski excepted, pretty far gone in exhaustion, stumbling and falling far more often than was warranted by the terrain and the strength of the ice-gale: for myself, my leaden dragging legs felt as if they were on fire, each step now sent a shooting pain stabbing from ankle clear to the top of the thigh. For all that, I think I could have kept going longer than any of them, even Zabrinski, for I had the motivation, the driving force that would have kept me going hours after my legs would have told me that it was impossible to carry on a step farther. Major John Halliwell. My elder, my only brother. Alive or dead. Was he alive or was he dead, this one man in the world to whom I owed everything I had or had become? Was he dying, at that very moment when I was thinking of him, was he dying? His wife, Mary, and his three children who spoilt and ruined their bachelor uncle as I spoilt and ruined them: whatever way it lay they would have to know and only I could tell them. Alive or dead? My legs weren't mine, the stabbing fire that tortured them belonged to some other man, not to me. I had to know, I had to know, and if I had to find out by covering whatever miles lay between me and Drift Ice Station Zebra on my hands and knees, then I would do just that. I would find out. And over and above the tearing anxiety as to what had happened to my brother there was yet another powerful motivation, a motivation that the world would regard as of infinitely more importance than the life or death of the commandant of the station. As infinitely more important than the living or dying of the score of men who manned that desolate polar outpost. Or so the world would say.

The demented drumming of the spicules on my mask and ice-sheathed furs suddenly eased, the gale wind fell away and I found myself standing in the grateful shelter of an ice-ridge even higher than the last one we'd used for shelter. I waited for the others to come up, asked Zabrinski to make a position check with the *Dolphin* and doled out some more of the medicinal alcohol. More of it than on the last occasion. We were in more need of it.

Both Hansen and Rawlings were in a very distressed condition, their breath whistling in and out of their lungs in the rapid, rasping, shallow panting of a long-distance runner in the last tortured moments of his final exhaustion. I became gradually aware that the speed of my own breathing matched theirs almost exactly, it required a concentrated effort of will-power to hold my breath even for the few seconds necessary to gulp down my drink. I wondered vaguely if perhaps Hansen hadn't had the right of it, maybe the alcohol wasn't good for us. But it certainly tasted as if it were.

Zabrinski was already talking through cupped hands into the microphone. After a minute or so he pulled the earphones out from under his parka and buttoned up the walkie-talkie set. He said: 'We're either good or lucky or both. The *Dolphin* says we're exactly on the course we ought to be on.' He drained the glass I handed him and sighed in satisfaction. 'Well, that's the good part of the news. Here comes the bad part. The sides of the polynya the *Dolphin* is lying in are beginning to close together. They're closing pretty fast. The captain estimates he'll have to get out of it in two hours. Two at the most.' He paused, then finished slowly: 'And the ice-machine is still on the blink.'

'The ice-machine,' I said stupidly. Well, anyway, I felt stupid, I don't know how I sounded. 'Is the ice—?'

'It sure is, brother,' Zabrinski said. He sounded tired. 'But you didn't believe the skipper, did you, Dr Carpenter? You were too clever for that.'

'Well, that's a help,' Hansen said heavily. 'That makes everything just perfectly splendid. The *Dolphin* drops down, the ice closes up, and there we are, the *Dolphin* below, us on top and the whole of the polar ice-cap between us. They'll almost certainly never manage to find us again, even if they do fix the ice-machine. Shall we just lie down and die now or shall we first stagger around in circles for a couple of hours and then lie down and die?'

'It's tragic,' Rawlings said gloomily. 'Not the personal aspect of it, I mean the loss to the United States Navy. I think I may fairly say, Lieutenant, that we are – or were – three promising young men. Well, you and me, anyway. I think Zabrinski there had reached the limit of his potentialities. He reached them a long time ago.'

Rawlings got all this out between chattering teeth and still painful gasps of air. Rawlings, I reflected, was very much the sort of person I would like to have by my side when things began to get awkward, and it looked as if things were going to become very awkward indeed. He and Zabrinski had, as I'd found out, established themselves as the home-spun if slightly heavy-handed humorists on the *Dolphin*; for reasons known only to themselves both men habitually concealed intelligence of a high order and advanced education under a cloak of genial buffoonery.

'Two hours yet,' I said. 'With this wind at our back we can be back in the sub in well under an hour. We'd be practically blown back there.'

'And the men on Drift Station Zebra?' Zabrinski asked.

'We'd have done our best. Just one of those things.'

'We are profoundly shocked, Dr Carpenter,' Rawlings said. The tone of genial buffoonery was less noticeable than usual.

'Deeply dismayed,' Zabrinski added, 'by the very idea.' The words were light, but the lack of warmth in the voice had nothing to do with the bitter wind.

'The only dismaying thing around here is the level of intelligence of certain simple-minded sailors,' Hansen said with some asperity. He went on, and I wondered at the conviction in his voice: 'Sure, Dr Carpenter thinks we should go back. That doesn't include him. Dr Carpenter wouldn't turn back now for all the gold in Fort Knox.' He pushed himself wearily to his feet. 'Can't be much more than half a mile to go now. Let's get it over with.'

In the backwash of light from my torch I saw Rawlings and Zabrinski glance at each other, saw them shrug their shoulders at the same moment. Then they, too, were on their feet and we were on our way again.

Three minutes later Zabrinski broke his ankle.

It happened in an absurdly simple fashion, but for all its simplicity it was a wonder that nothing of the same sort had happened to any of us in the previous three hours. After starting off again, instead of losing our bearing by working to the south and north until we had rounded the end of the ice ridge blocking our path, we elected to go over it. The ridge was all of ten feet high but by boosting and pulling each other we reached the top without much difficulty. I felt my way forward cautiously, using the ice-probe – the torch was useless in that ice-storm and my goggles completely opaque. After twenty feet crawling across the gently downward sloping surface I reached the far side of the ridge and stretched down with the probe.

'Five feet,' I called to the others as they came up. 'It's only five feet.' I swung over the edge, dropped down and waited for the others to follow. Hansen came first, then Rawlings, both sliding down easily beside me. What happened to Zabrinski was impossible to see, he either misjudged his distance from the edge or a sudden easing of the wind made him lose his footing. Whatever the cause, I heard him call out, the words whipped away and lost by the wind, as he jumped down beside us. He seemed to land squarely and lightly enough on his feet, then cried out sharply and fell heavily to the ground.

I turned my back to the ice-storm, raised the useless snow-goggles and pulled out my torch. Zabrinski was half-sitting, half-lying on the ice, propped up on his right elbow and cursing steadily and fluently and, as far as I could tell because of the muffling effect of his snow-mask, without once repeating himself. His right heel was jammed in a four-inch crack in the ice, one of the thousands of such fractures and fissures that criss-crossed the pressure areas of the pack: his right leg was bent over at an angle to the outside, an angle normally impossible for any leg to assume. I didn't need to have a medical diploma hung around my neck to tell that the ankle was gone: either that or the lowermost part of the tibia, for the ankle was so heavily encased in a stout boot with lace binding that most of the strain must have fallen on the shin bone. I hoped it wasn't a compound fracture, but it was an unreasonable hope: at that acute angle the snapped bone could hardly have failed to pierce the skin. Compound or not, it made no immediate difference, I'd no intention of examining it: a few minutes' exposure of the lower part of his leg in those temperatures was as good a way as any of ensuring that Zabrinski went through the rest of his life with one foot missing.

We lifted his massive bulk, eased the useless foot out of the crack in the ice and lowered him gently to a sitting position. I unslung the medical kit from my back, knelt beside him and asked: 'Does it hurt badly?'

'No, it's numb, I hardly feel a thing.' He swore disgustedly. 'What a crazy thing to do. A little crack like that. How stupid can a man get?'

'You wouldn't believe me if I told you,' Rawlings said acidly. He shook

his head. 'I prophesied this, I prophesied this. I said it would end up with
me carrying this gorilla here.'

I had splints to the injured leg and taped them as tightly as possible over
the boot and the furs, trying not to think of the depth of trouble we were in
now. Two major blows in one. Not only had we lost the indispensable
services of the strongest man in our party, we now had an extra 220 lbs. –
at least – of weight, of dead-weight, to carry along with us. Not to mention
his 40-lb. pack. Zabrinski might almost have read my thoughts.

'You'll have to leave me here, Lieutenant,' he said to Hansen. His teeth
were rattling, with shock and cold. 'We must be almost there now. You can
pick me up on the way back.'

'Don't talk rubbish,' Hansen said shortly. 'You know damn' well we'd
never find you again.'

'Exactly,' Rawlings said. His teeth were like Zabrinski's, stuttering away
irregularly like an asthmatic machine-gun. He knelt on the ice to support
the injured man's bulk. 'No medals for morons. It says so in the ship's
articles.'

'But you'll never get to Zebra,' Zabrinski protested. 'If you have to carry
me—'

'You heard what I said,' Hansen interrupted. 'We're not leaving you.'

'The lieutenant is perfectly correct,' Rawlings agreed. 'You aren't the hero
type, Zabrinski. You haven't the face for it, for one thing. Now clam up
while I get some of this gear off your back.'

I finished tightening the splints and pulled mittens and fur gloves back
on my silk-clad but already frozen hands. We shared out Zabrinski's load
among the three of us, pulled goggles and snow-masks back into position,
hoisted Zabrinski to his one sound leg, turned into the wind and went on
our way again. It would be truer to say that we staggered on our way again.

But now, at last and when we most needed it, luck was with us. The ice-
cap stretched away beneath our feet level and smooth as the surface of a
frozen river. No ridges, no hummocks, no crevasses, not even the tiny cracks
one of which had crippled Zabrinski. Just billiard flat unbroken ice and not
even slippery, for its surface had been scoured and abraded by the flying ice-
storm.

Each of us took turns at being lead man, the other two supporting a
Zabrinski who hopped along in uncomplaining silence on one foot. After
maybe three hundred yards of this smooth ice, Hansen, who was in the lead
at the moment, stopped so suddenly and unexpectedly that we bumped into
him.

'We're there!' he yelled above the wind. 'We've made it. We're there!
Can't you smell it?'

'Smell what?'

'Burnt fuel oil. Burnt rubber. Don't you get it?'

I pulled down my snow-mask, cupped my hands to my face and sniffed
cautiously. One sniff was enough. I hitched up my mask again, pulled
Zabrinski's arm more tightly across my shoulder and followed on after
Hansen.

The smooth ice ended in another few feet. The ice sloped up sharply to
a level plateau and it took the three of us all of what pitifully little strength
remained to drag Zabrinski up after us. The acrid smell of burning seemed
to grow more powerful with every step we took. I moved forward, away

from the others, my back to the storm, goggles down and sweeping the ice with semicircular movements of my torch. The smell was strong enough now to make my nostrils wrinkle under the mask. It seemed to be coming from directly ahead. I turned round into the wind, protectively cupped hand over my eyes, and as I did my torch struck something hard and solid and metallic. I lifted my torch and vaguely through the driving ice I could just make out the ghostly hooped steel skeleton, ice-coated on the windward side, fire-charred on the leeward side, of what had once been a nissen-shaped hut.

We had found Drift Ice Station Zebra.

I waited for the others to come up, guided them past the gaunt and burnt-out structure, then told them to turn backs to wind and lift their goggles. For maybe ten seconds we surveyed the ruin in the light of my torch. No one said anything. Then we turned round into the wind again.

Drift Station Zebra had consisted of eight separate huts, four in each of two parallel rows, thirty feet between the two rows, twenty feet between each two huts in the rows – this to minimize the hazard of fire spreading from hut to hut. But the hazard hadn't been minimized enough. No one could be blamed for that. No one, except in the wildest flights of nightmarish imagination, could have envisaged what must indeed have happened – exploding tanks and thousands of gallons of blazing oil being driven through the night by a gale-force wind. And, by a double inescapable irony, fire, without which human life on the polar ice-cap cannot survive, is there the most dreaded enemy of all: for although the entire ice-cap consists of water, frozen water, there is nothing that can melt that water and so put out the fire. Except fire itself. I wondered vaguely what had happened to the giant chemical fire-extinguishers housed in every hut.

Eight huts, four in each row. The first two on either side were completely gutted. No trace remained of the walls, which had been of two layers of weather-proofed bonded ply that had enclosed the insulation of shredded glass-fibre and kapok: on all of them even the aluminium-sheeted roofs had disappeared. In one of the huts we could see charred and blackened generator machinery, ice-coated on the windward side, bent and twisted and melted almost out of recognition: one could only wonder at the furnace ferocity of the heat responsible.

The fifth hut – the third on the right-hand side – was a gutted replica of the other four, the framing even more savagely twisted by the heat. We were just turning away from this, supporting Zabrinski and too sick at heart even to speak to each other, when Rawlings called out something unintelligible. I leaned closer to him and pulled back my parka hood.

'A light!' he shouted. 'A light. Look, Doc – across there!'

And a light there was, a long narrow strangely white vertical strip of light from the hut opposite the charred wreck by which we stood. Leaning sideways into the storm we dragged Zabrinski across the intervening gap. For the first time my torch showed something that was more than a bare framework of steel. This was a hut. A blackened, scorched and twisted hut with a roughly nailed-on sheet of plywood where its solitary window had been, but nevertheless a hut. The light was coming from a door standing just ajar at the sheltered end. I laid my hand on the door, the one unscorched thing I'd seen so far in Drift Station Zebra. The hinges creaked like a rusty gate in a cemetery at midnight and the door gave beneath my hand. We passed inside.

Suspended from a hook in the centre of the ceiling a hissing Coleman lamp threw its garish light, amplified by the glittering aluminium ceiling, over every corner and detail of that eighteen by ten hut. A thick but transparent layer of ice sheathed the aluminium roof except for a three-foot circle directly above the lamp, and the ice spread from the ceiling down the plywood walls all the way to the door. The wooden floor, too, was covered with ice, except where the bodies of the men lay. There may have been ice under them as well. I couldn't tell.

My first thought, conviction rather, and one that struck at me with a heart-sapping sense of defeat, with a chill that even the polar storm outside had been unable to achieve, was that we had arrived too late. I had seen many dead men in my life, I knew what dead men looked like, and now I was looking at just that many more. Shapeless, huddled, lifeless forms lying under a shapeless mass of blankets, mackinaws, duffels and furs, I wouldn't have bet a cent on my chances of finding one heart-beat among the lot of them. Lying packed closely together in a rough semicircle at the end of the room remote from the door, they were utterly still, as unmoving as men would be if they had been lying that way for a frozen eternity. Apart from the hissing of the pressure-lamp there was no sound inside the hut other than the metallic drumfire of the ice-spicules against the ice-sheathed eastern wall of the hut.

Zabrinski was eased down into a sitting position against a wall. Rawlings unslung the heavy load he was carrying on his back, unwrapped the stove, pulled off his mittens and started fumbling around for the fuel tablets. Hansen pulled the door to behind him, slipped the buckles of his rucksack and wearily let his load of tinned food drop to the floor of the shack.

For some reason, the voice of the storm outside and the hissing of the Coleman inside served only to heighten the deathly stillness in the hut, and the unexpected metallic clatter of the falling cans made me jump. It made one of the dead men jump, too. The man nearest to me by the left-hand wall suddenly moved, rolled over and sat up, bloodshot faded eyes staring out unbelievingly from a frostbitten, haggard and cruelly burnt face, the burns patchily covered by a long dark stubble of beard. For long seconds he looked at us unblinkingly, then, some obscure feeling of pride making him ignore the offer of my outstretched arm, he pushed himself shakily and with obvious pain to his feet. Then the cracked and peeling lips broke into a grin.

'You've been a bleedin' long time getting here.' The voice was hoarse and weak and cockney as the Bow Bells themselves. 'My name's Kinnaird. Radio operator.'

'Whisky?' I asked.

He grinned again, tried to lick his cracked lips, and nodded. The stiff tot of whisky went down his throat like a man in a barrel going over the Niagara Falls, one moment there, the next gone for ever. He bent over, coughing harshly until the tears came to his eyes, but when he straightened life was coming back into those same lack-lustre eyes and colour touching the pale emaciated cheeks.

'If you go through life saying "Hallo" in this fashion, mate,' he observed, 'then you'll never lack for friends.' He bent and shook the shoulder of the man beside whom he had been lying. 'C'mon, Jolly, old boy, where's your bleedin' manners. We got company.'

It took quite a few shakes to get Jolly, old boy, awake, but when he did come to he was completely conscious and on his feet with remarkable speed in the one case and with remarkable nimbleness in the other. He was a short, chubby character with china-blue eyes, and although he was as much in need of a shave as Kinnaird, there was still colour in his face and the round good-humoured face was far from emaciated: but frost-bite had made a bad mess of both mouth and nose. The china-blue eyes, flecked with red and momentarily wide in surprise, crinkled into a grin of welcome. Jolly, old boy, I guess, would always adjust fast to circumstances.

'Visitors, eh?' His deep voice held a rich Irish brogue. 'And damned glad we are to see you, too. Do the honours, Jeff.'

'We haven't introduced ourselves,' I said. 'I'm Dr Carpenter and this—'

'Regular meeting of the BMA, old boy,' Jolly said. I was to find out later that he used the phrase 'old boy' in every second or third sentence, a mannerism which went strangely with his Irish accent.

'Dr Jolly?'

'The same. Resident medical officer, old boy.'

'I see. This is Lieutenant Hansen of the United States Navy submarine *Dolphin*—'

'Submarine?' Jolly and Kinnaird stared at each other, then at us. 'You said "submarine," old top?'

'Explanations can wait. Torpedoman Rawlings. Radioman Zabrinski.' I glanced down at the huddled men on the floor, some of them already stirring at the sound of voices, one or two propping themselves up on their elbows. 'How are they?'

'Two or three pretty bad burn cases,' Jolly said. 'Two or three far gone with cold and exhaustion, but not so far gone that food and warmth wouldn't have them right as rain in a few days. I made them all huddle together like this for mutual warmth.'

I counted them. Including Jolly and Kinnaird, there were twelve all told. I said: 'Where are the others?'

'The others?' Kinnaird looked at me in momentary surprise, then his face went bleak and cold. He pointed a thumb over his shoulder. 'In the next hut, mate.'

'Why?'

'Why?' He rubbed a weary forearm across bloodshot eyes. 'Because we don't fancy sleeping with a roomful of corpses, that's why.'

'Because you don't—' I broke off and stared down at the men at my feet. Seven of them were awake now, three of them propped on elbows, four still lying down, all seven registering various degrees of dazed bewilderment: the three who were still asleep – or unconscious – had their faces covered by blankets. I said slowly. 'There were nineteen of you.'

'Nineteen of us,' Kinnaird echoed emptily. 'The others – well, they never had a chance.'

I said nothing. I looked carefully at the faces of the conscious men, hoping to find among them the one face I wanted to see, hoping perhaps that I had not immediately recognized it because frost-bite or hunger or burns had made it temporarily unrecognizable. I looked very carefully indeed and I knew that I had never seen any of those faces before.

I moved over to the first of the three still sleeping figures and lifted the blanket covering the face. The face of a stranger. I let the blanket drop. Jolly said in puzzlement: 'What's wrong? What do you want?'

I didn't answer him. I picked my way round recumbent men, all staring uncomprehendingly at me, and lifted the blanket from the face of the second sleeping man. Again I let the blanket drop and I could feel my mouth go dry, the slow heavy pounding of my heart. I crossed to the third man, then stood there hesitating, knowing I must find out, dreading what I must find. Then I stooped quickly and lifted the blanket. A man with a heavily bandaged face. A man with a broken nose and a thick blond beard. A man I had never seen in my life before. Gently I spread the blanket over his face and straightened up. Rawlings, I saw, already had the solid-fuel stove going.

'That should bring the temperature up to close to freezing,' I said to Dr Jolly. 'We've plenty of fuel. We've also brought food, alcohol, a complete medical kit. If you and Kinnaird want to start in on those things now I'll give you a hand in a minute. Lieutenant, that was a polynya, that smooth stretch we crossed just before we got here? A frozen lead?'

'Couldn't be anything else.' Hansen was looking at me peculiarly, a wondering expression on his face. 'These people are obviously in no fit state to travel a couple of hundred yards, far less four or five miles. Besides, the skipper said he was going to be squeezed down pretty soon. So we whistle up the Dolphin and have them surface at the back door?'

'Can he find that polynya – without the ice-machine, I mean?'

'Nothing simpler. I'll take Zabrinski's radio, move a measured two hundred yards to the north, send a bearing signal, move two hundred yards to the south and do the same. They'll have our range to a yard. Take a couple of hundred yards off that and the *Dolphin* will find itself smack in the middle of the polynya.'

'But still under it. I wonder how thick that ice is. You had an open lead to the west of the camp some time ago, Dr Jolly. How long ago?'

'A month. Maybe five weeks. I can't be sure.'

'How thick?' I asked Hansen.

'Five feet, maybe six. Couldn't possibly break through it. But the captain's always had a hankering to have a go with his torpedoes.' He turned to Zabrinski. 'Still fit to operate that radio of yours?'

I left them to it. I'd hardly been aware of what I'd been saying, anyway. I felt sick and old and empty and sad, and deathly tired. I had my answer now. I'd come 12,000 miles to find it, I'd have gone a million to avoid it. But the inescapable fact was there and now nothing could ever change it. Mary, my sister-in-law and her three wonderful children – she would never see her husband again, they would never see their father again. My brother was dead and no one was ever going to see him again. Except me. I was going to see him now.

I went out, closing the door behind me, moved round the corner of the hut and lowered my head against the storm. Ten seconds later I reached the door of the last hut in the line. I used the torch to locate the handle, twisted it, pushed and passed inside.

Once it had been a laboratory: Now it was a charnel house, a house of the dead. The laboratory equipment had all been pushed roughly to one side and the cleared floor space covered with the bodies of dead men. I knew they were dead men, but only because Kinnaird had told me so: hideously charred and blackened and grotesquely misshapen as they were, those carbonized and contorted lumps of matter could have been any form of life or indeed no form of life at all. The stench of incinerated flesh and burnt diesel fuel was dreadful. I wondered which of the men in the other hut had had the courage, the iron resolution, to bring those grisly burdens, the shockingly disfigured remains of their former comrades into this hut. They must have had strong stomachs.

Death must have been swift, swift for all of them. Theirs had not been the death of men trapped by fire, it had been the death of men who had themselves been on fire. Caught, drenched, saturated by a gale-borne sea of burning oil, they must have spent the last few seconds of life as incandescently blazing human torches before dying in insane screaming agony. They must have died as terribly as men can ever die.

Something about one of the bodies close to me caught my attention. I stooped and focused the torch beam on what had once been a right hand, now no more than a blackened claw with the bone showing through. So powerful had been the heat that it had warped, but not melted, the curiously shaped gold ring on the third finger. I recognized that ring, I had been with my sister-in-law when she had bought it.

I was conscious of no grief, no pain, no revulsion. Perhaps, I thought dully, those would come later when the initial shock had worn off. But I didn't think so. This wasn't the man I remembered so well, the brother to whom I owed everything, a debt that could never now be repaid. This charred mass of matter before me was a stranger, so utterly different from the man who lived on in my memory, so changed beyond all possibility of recognition that my numbed mind in my exhausted body just could not begin to bridge the gap.

As I stood there, staring down, something ever so slightly off-beat about the way the body lay caught my professional attention. I stooped low, very low, and remained bent over for what seemed a long time. I straightened, slowly, and as I did I heard the door behind me open. I whirled round and saw that it was Lieutenant Hansen. He pulled down his snow-mask, lifted up his goggles, looked at me and then at the man at my feet. I could see shock draining expression and colour from his face. Then he looked up at me.

'So you lost out, Doc?' I could hardly hear the husky whisper above the voice of the storm. 'God, I'm sorry.'

'What do you mean?'

'Your brother?' He nodded at the man at my feet.

'Commander Swanson told you?'

'Yeah. Just before we left. That's why we came.' His gaze moved in horrified fascination over the floor of the hut, and his face was grey, like old parchment. 'A minute, Doc, just a minute.' He turned and hurried through the doorway.

When he came back he looked better, but not much. He said: 'Commander Swanson said that that was why he had to let you go.'

'Who else knows?'

'Skipper and myself. No one else.'

'Keep it that way, will you? As a favour to me.'

'If you say so, Doc.' There was curiosity in his face now, and puzzlement, but horror was still the dominant expression. 'My God, have you ever seen anything like it?'

'Let's get back to the others,' I said. 'We're doing nobody any good by staying here.'

He nodded without speaking. Together we made our way back to the other hut. Apart from Dr Jolly and Kinnaird, three other men were on their feet now, Captain Folsom, an extraordinarily tall thin man with savagely burnt face and hands who was second in command of the base, Hewson, a dark-eyed taciturn character, a tractor driver and engineer who had been responsible for the diesel generators, and a cheerful Yorkshireman, Naseby, the camp cook. Jolly, who had opened my medical kit and was applying fresh bandages to the arms of the men still lying down, introduced them, then turned back to his job. He didn't seem to need my help, not for the moment anyway. I heard Hansen say to Zabrinski: 'In contact with the *Dolphin?*'

'Well, no.' Zabrinski stopped sending his call-sign and shifted slightly to ease his broken ankle. 'I don't quite know how to put this, Lieutenant, but the fact is that this little ol' set here seems to have blown a fuse.'

'Well, now,' Hansen said heavily. 'That *is* clever of you, Zabrinski. You mean you can't raise them?'

'I can hear them, they can't hear me.' He shrugged, apologetically. 'Me and my clumsy feet, I guess. It wasn't just only my ankle that went when I took that tumble out there.'

'Well, can't you repair the damn' thing?'

'I don't think so, Lieutenant.'

'Damn it, you're supposed to be a radioman.'

'That's so,' Zabrinski acknowledged reasonably. 'But I'm not a magician. And with a couple of numbed and frozen hands, no tools, an old-type set without a printed circuit and the code signs in Japanese – well, even Marconi would have called it a day.'

'*Can* it be repaired?' Hansen insisted.

'It's a transistor set. No valves to smash. I expect it could be repaired. But it might take hours, Lieutenant – I'd even have to fake up a set of tools first.'

'Well, fake them. Anything you like. Only get that thing working.'

Zabrinski said nothing. He held out the headphones to Hansen. Hansen looked at Zabrinski, then at the phones, took them without a word and listened briefly. Then he shrugged, handed back the phones and said: 'Well, I guess there *is* no hurry to repair that radio.'

'Yeah,' Zabrinski said. 'Awkward, you might say, Lieutenant.'

'What's awkward,' I asked.

'Looks as if *we're* going to be next on the list for a rescue party,' Hansen said heavily. 'They're sending a more or less continuous signal: "Ice closing rapidly, return at once." '

'I was against this madness from the very beginning,' Rawlings intoned from the floor. He stared down at the already melting lumps of frozen tinned soup and stirred it moodily with a fork. 'A gallant attempt, men, but foredoomed to failure.'

'Keep your filthy fingers out of that soup and kindly clam up,' Hansen said coldly. He turned suddenly to Kinnaird. 'How about *your* radio set. Of course, that's it. We have fit men here to crank your generator and—'

'I'm sorry.' Kinnaird smiled the way a ghost might smile. 'It's not a hand-powered generator, that was destroyed, it's a battery set. The batteries are finished. Completely finished.'

'A battery set, you said?' Zabrinski looked at him in mild surprise. 'Then what caused all the power fluctuations when you were transmitting?'

'We kept changing over the nickel cadmium cells to try to make the most of what little power was left in them: we'd only fifteen left altogether, most of them were lost in the fire. That caused the power fluctuations. But even Nife cells don't last for ever. They're finished, mate. The combined power left in those cells would light a pencil torch.'

Zabrinski didn't say anything. No one said anything. The ice-spicules drummed incessantly against the east wall, the Coleman hissed, the solid-fuel stove purred softly: but the sole effect of those three sounds was to make the silence inside seem that little bit more absolute. No one looked at his neighbours, everyone stared down at the floor with the fixed and steadfast gaze of an entomologist hunting for traces of woodworm. Any newspaper printing a picture taken at that instant wouldn't have found it any too easy to convince its readers that the men on Drift Ice Station Zebra had been rescued just ten minutes previously, and rescued from certain death at that. The readers would have pointed out that one might have expected a little more jubilation in the atmosphere, a touch, perhaps, of lighthearted relief, and they wouldn't have been far wrong at that, there wasn't very much gaiety around.

After the silence had gone on just that little too long I said to Hansen: 'Well, that's it, then. We don't have to hire any electronic computer to work this one out. Someone's got to get back to the *Dolphin* and get back there now. I'm nominating myself.'

'No!' Hansen said violently, then more quietly: 'Sorry, friend, but the skipper's orders didn't include giving permission to anyone to commit suicide. You're staying here.'

'So I stay here,' I nodded. This wasn't the time to tell him I didn't need his permission for anything, far less was it the time to start flourishing the Mannlicher-Schoenauer. 'So we all stay here. And then we all die here. Quietly, without any fighting, without any fuss, we just lie down and die here. I suppose you reckon that comes under the heading of inspiring leadership. Amundsen would have loved that.' It wasn't fair, but then I wasn't feeling fairminded at the moment.

'Nobody's going any place,' Hansen said. 'I'm not my brother's keeper, Doc, but for all that I'll be damned if I let you kill yourself. You're not fit, none of us is fit to make the return trip to the *Dolphin* – not after what we've just been through. That's one thing. The next thing is that without a transmitter from which the *Dolphin* can pick up our directional bearings, we could never hope to find the *Dolphin* again. The third thing is that the closing ice will probably have forced the *Dolphin* to drop down before anyone could get half-way there. And the last thing is that if we failed to find the *Dolphin* either because we missed her or because she was gone, we could never make our way back to Zebra again: we wouldn't have the strength and we would have nothing to guide us back anyway.'

'The odds offered aren't all that attractive,' I admitted.

'What odds are you offering on the ice-machine being repaired?'

Hansen shook his head, said nothing. Rawlings started stirring his soup again, carefully not looking up, he didn't want to meet the anxious eyes, the desperate eyes, in that circle of haggard and frost-bitten faces any more than I did. But he looked up as Captain Folsom pushed himself away from the support of a wall and took a couple of unsteady steps towards us. It didn't require any stethoscope to see that Folsom was in a pretty bad way.

'I am afraid that we don't understand,' he said. His voice was slurred and indistinct, the puffed and twisted lips had been immobilized by the savage charring of his face: I wondered bleakly how many months of pain would elapse, how many visits to the surgeon's table, before Folsom could show that face to the world again. In the very remote event, that was, of our ever getting him to hospital. 'Would you please explain? What is the difficulty?'

'Simply this,' I said. 'The *Dolphin* has an ice fathometer, a device for measuring the thickness of the overhead ice. Normally, even if Commander Swanson – the captain of the *Dolphin* – didn't hear from us, we could expect him on our doorstep in a matter of hours. He has the position of this Drift Station pinned down pretty closely. All he would have to do is to drop down, come under us here, start a grid search with his ice fathometer and it would be only minutes before he would locate the relatively thin ice out in that lead there. But things aren't normal. The ice-machine has broken down and if it stays that way he'll never find that lead. That's why I want to go back there. Now. Before Swanson's forced to dive by the closing ice.'

'Don't see it, old boy,' Jolly said. 'How's that going to help? Can *you* fix this ice what-you-may-call-it.'

'I don't have to. Commander Swanson knows his distance from this camp give or take a hundred yards. All I have to do is to tell him to cover the distance less quarter of a mile and loose off a torpedo. That ought—'

'Torpedo?' Jolly asked. 'Torpedo? To break through the ice from beneath?'

'That's it. It's never been tried before. I suppose there's no reason why it shouldn't work if the ice is thin enough and it won't be all that thick in the lead out there. I don't really know.'

'They'll be sending planes, you know, Doc,' Zabrinski said quietly. 'We started transmitting the news as soon as we broke through and everybody will know by now that Zebra has been found – at least, they'll know exactly where it is. They'll have the big bombers up here in a few hours.'

'Doing what?' I asked. 'Sculling around uselessly in the darkness up above? Even if they do have the exact position, they still won't be able to see what's left of this station because of the darkness and the ice-storm. Perhaps they can with radar, it's unlikely, but even if they do, what then? Drop supplies? Maybe. But they won't dare drop supplies directly on us for fear of killing us. They'd have to drop them some distance off – and even a quarter-mile would be too far away for any chance we'd ever have of finding stuff in those conditions. As for landing – even if weather conditions were perfect, no plane big enough to have the range to fly here could ever hope to land on the ice-cap. You know that.'

'What's your middle name, Doc?' Rawlings asked dolefully. 'Jeremiah?'

'The greatest good of the greatest number,' I said. 'The old yardstick, but there's never been a better one. If we just hole up here without making any attempt to help ourselves and the ice-machine remains useless, then we're all dead. All sixteen of us. If I make it there safely, then we're all alive. Even if I don't, the ice-machine may be fixed and there would only be one lost then.' I started pulling on my mittens. 'One is less than sixteen.'

'We might as well make it two,' Hansen sighed and began to pull on his own gloves. I was hardly surprised, when he'd last spoken he'd talked at first of 'you' having no chance and finished by saying that 'we' had none and it hadn't required any psychiatrist to follow his quick shift in mental orientation: whatever men like Hansen were hand-picked for, it wasn't for any predilection for shifting the load to others' shoulders when the going became sticky.

I didn't waste time arguing with him.

Rawlings got to his feet.

'One skilled volunteer for the soup-stirring,' he requested. 'Those two wouldn't get as far as the door there without my holding their hands. I shall probably get a medal for this. What's the highest decoration awarded in peace-time, Lieutenant?'

'There are no medals given for soup-stirring, Rawlings,' Hansen said, 'which is what you are going to keep on doing. You're staying right here.'

'Uh-uh.' Rawlings shook his head. 'Prepare yourself to deal with your first mutiny, Lieutenant. I'm coming with you. I can't lose. If we get to the *Dolphin* you'll be too damned glad and happy to have made it to dream of reporting me, apart from being a fair-minded man who will have to admit that our safe arrival back at the ship will be entirely due to Torpedoman Rawlings.' He grinned. 'And if we don't make it – well, you can't very well report it, can you, Lieutenant?'

Hansen walked across to him. He said quietly: 'You know that there's more than an even chance that we won't reach the *Dolphin*. That would leave twelve pretty sick men here, not to mention Zabrinski with a broken ankle, and with no one to look after them. They must have one fit man to look after them. You couldn't be that selfish, now, could you, Rawlings? Look after them, will you? As a favour to me?'

Rawlings looked at him for long seconds, then squatted down and started stirring the soup again.

'As a favour to me, you mean,' he said bitterly. 'OK, I'll stay. As a favour to me. Also to prevent Zabrinski tripping over his legs again and breaking another ankle.' He stirred the soup viciously. Well, what are you waiting for? The skipper may be making up his mind to dive any minute.'

He had a point. We brushed off protests and attempts to stop us made by Captain Folsom and Dr Jolly and were ready to leave in thirty seconds. Hansen was through the door first. I turned and looked at the sick and emaciated and injured survivors of Drift Station Zebra. Folsom, Jolly, Kinnaird, Hewson, Naseby and seven others. Twelve men altogether. They couldn't all be in cahoots together, so it had to be a single man, maybe two, acting in concert. I wondered who those men might be, those men I would have to kill, that person or persons who had murdered my brother and six other men on Drift Ice Station Zebra.

I pulled the door to behind me and followed Hansen out into the dreadful night.

Chapter Six

We had been tired, more than tired, even before we had set out. We had been leaden-legged, bone-weary, no more than a short hand-span from total exhaustion. But for all that we flitted through the howling darkness of that night like two great white ghosts across the dimly seen whiteness of a nightmare lunar landscape. We were no longer bowed under the weight of heavy packs. Our backs were to that gale-force wind so that for every laborious plodding step we had made on our way to Zebra, we now covered five, with so little a fraction of our earlier toil that at first it seemed all but effortless. We had no trouble in seeing where we were going, no fear of falling into an open lead or of crippling ourselves against some unexpected obstacle, for with our useless goggles removed and powerful torch beams dancing erratically ahead of us as we jog-trotted along, visibility was seldom less than five yards, more often near to ten. Those were the physical aids that helped us on our way but even more sharply powerful as spur to our aching legs was that keen and ever-growing fear that dominated our minds to the exclusion of all else, the fear that Commander Swanson had already been compelled to drop down and that we would be left to die in that shrieking wasteland: with our lacking both shelter and food, the old man with the scythe would not be keeping us waiting too long.

We ran, but we did not run too fast, for to have done that would have been to have the old man tapping us on the shoulder in very short order indeed. In far sub-zero temperatures, there is one thing that the Eskimo avoids as he would the plague – over-exertion, in those latitudes more deadly, even than the plague itself. Too much physical effort while wearing heavy furs inevitably results in sweat, and when the effort ceases, as eventually cease it must, the sweat freezes on the skin: the only way to destroy that film of ice is by further exertion, producing even more sweat, the beginnings of a vicious and steadily narrowing circle that can have only one end. So though we ran it was only at a gentle jog-trot, hardly more than a fast walk: we took every possible precaution against overheating.

After half an hour, perhaps a little more, I called for a brief halt in the shelter of a steep ice-wall. Twice in the past two minutes Hansen had stumbled and fallen where there hadn't appeared to be any reason to stumble and fall: and I had noticed that my own legs were more unsteady than the terrain warranted.

'How are you making out?' I asked.

'Pretty bushed, Doc.' He sounded it, too, his breathing quick and rasping and shallow. 'But don't write me off yet. How far do you reckon we've come?'

'Three miles, near enough.' I patted the ice-wall behind us. 'When we've had a couple of minutes I think we should try climbing this. Looks like a pretty tallish hummock to me.'

'To try to get into the clear above the ice-storm?' I nodded my head and he shook his. 'Won't do you any good, Doc. This ice-storm must be at least twenty feet thick, and even if you do get above it the *Dolphin* will still be below it. She's only got the top of her sail clear above the ice.'

'I've been thinking,' I said. 'We've been so lost in our own woes and sorrows that we have forgotten about Commander Swanson. I think we have been guilty of underestimating him pretty badly.'

'It's likely enough. Right now I'm having a full-time job worrying about Lieutenant Hansen. What's on your mind?'

'Just this. The chances are better than fifty-fifty that Swanson believes we are on the way back to the *Dolphin*. After all, he's been ordering us to return for quite some time; and if he thinks we didn't get the order because something has happened to us or to the radio, he'll still figure that we will be returning.'

'Not necessarily. Radio or not, we might still be pushing on for Drift Station Zebra.'

'No. Definitely not. He'll be expecting us to be smart enough to figure it the way he would; and smart enough to see that that is the way he *would* figure it. He would know that if our radio broke down before we got to Zebra that it would be suicidal for us to try to find it without radio bearing – but that it *wouldn't* be suicidal for us to try to make it back to the *Dolphin*, for he would be hoping that we would have sufficient savvy to guess that he would put a lamp in the window to guide the lost sheep home.'

'My God, Doc, I believe you've got it! Of course he would, of course he would. Lordy, lordy, what am I using for brains?' He straightened and turned to face the ice-wall.

Pushing and pulling, we made it together to the top. The summit of the rafted ice hummock was less than twenty feet above the level of the ice-pack and not quite high enough. We were still below the surface of that gale-driven river of ice-spicules. Occasionally, for a brief moment of time, the wind force would ease fractionally and let us have a brief glimpse of the clear sky above but only occasionally and for a fraction of a second. And if there was anything to be seen in that time, we couldn't see it.

'There'll be other hummocks,' I shouted in Hansen's ear. 'Higher hummocks.' He nodded without answering. I couldn't see the expression on his face but I didn't have to see it. The same thought was in both our minds: we could see nothing because there was nothing to see. Commander Swanson hadn't put a lamp in the window, for the window was gone, the *Dolphin* forced to dive to avoid being crushed by the ice.

Five times in the next twenty mintues we climbed hummocks, and five times we climbed down, each time more dejected, more defeated. By now I was pretty far gone, moving in a pain-filled nightmare: Hansen was in even worse case, lurching and staggering around like a drunken man. As a doctor, I knew well of the hidden and unsuspected resources that an exhausted man can call on in times of desperate emergency; but I knew too, that those resources are not limitless and that we were pretty close to the end. And when that end came we would just lie down in the lee of an ice-wall and wait for the old man to come along: he wouldn't keep us waiting long.

Our sixth hummock all but defeated us. It wasn't that it was hard to climb, it was well ridged with foot and hand holds in plenty, but the sheer physical effort of climbing came very close to defeating us. And then I dimly began to realize that part of the effort was due to the fact that this was by far the highest hummock we had found yet. Some colossal pressures had concentrated on this one spot, rafting and log-jamming the ice-pack until it had risen a clear thirty feet above the general level: the giant underwater ridge beneath must have stretched down close on two hundred feet towards the black floor of the Arctic.

Eight feet below the summit our heads were in the clear: on the summit itself, holding on to each other for mutual support against the gale, we could look down on the ice-storm whirling by just beneath our feet: a fantastic sight, a great grey-white sea of undulating turbulence, a giant rushing river that stretched from horizon to horizon. Like so much else in the high Arctic the scene had an eerie and terrifying strangeness about it, a mindless desolation that belonged not to earth but to some alien and long-dead planet.

We scanned the horizon to the west until our eyes ached. Nothing. Nothing at all. Just that endless desolation. From due north to due south, through 180°, we searched the surface of that great river; and still we saw nothing. Three minutes passed. Still nothing. I began to feel the ice running in my blood.

On the remote off-chance that we might already have by-passed the *Dolphin* to the north or south, I turned and peered towards the east. It wasn't easy, for that far sub-zero gale of wind brought tears to the eyes in an instant of time; but at least it wasn't impossible, we no longer had to contend with the needle-pointed lances of the ice-spicules. I made another slow 180° sweep of the eastern horizon, and again, and again. Then I caught Hansen's arm.

'Look there,' I said. 'To the north-east. Maybe quarter of a mile away, maybe half a mile. Can you see anything?'

For several seconds Hansen squinted along the direction of my outstretched hand, then shook his head. 'I see nothing. What do you think you see?'

'I don't know. I'm not sure. I can imagine I see a very faint touch of luminescence on the surface of the ice-storm there, maybe just a fraction of a shade whiter than the rest.'

For a full half-minute Hansen stared out through cupped hands. Finally he said: 'It's no good. I don't see it. But then my eyes have been acting up on me for the past half-hour. But I can't even *imagine* I see anything.'

I turned away to give my streaming eyes a rest from that icy wind and then looked again. 'Damn it,' I said, 'I can't be sure that there is anything there; but I can't be sure that there isn't, either.'

'What do you fancy it would be?' Hansen's voice was dispirited, with overtones of hopelessness. 'A light?'

'A searchlight shining vertically upwards. A searchlight that's not able to penetrate that ice-storm.'

'You're kidding yourself, Doc,' Hansen said wearily. 'The wish father to the thought. Besides, that would mean that we had already passed the *Dolphin*. It's not possible.'

'It's not impossible. Ever since we started climbing those damned ice-hummocks I've lost track of time and space. It *could* be.'

'Do you still see it?' The voice was empty, uninterested, he didn't believe me and he was just making words.

'Maybe my eyes are acting up, too,' I admitted. 'But, damn it, I'm still not sure that I'm not right.'

'Come on, Doc, let's go.'

'Go where?'

'I don't know.' His teeth chattered so uncontrollably in that intense cold that I could scarcely follow his words. 'I guess it doesn't matter very much where—'

With breath-taking abruptness, almost in the centre of my imagined patch of luminescence and not more than four hundred yards away, a swiftly climbing rocket burst through the rushing river of ice-spicules and climbed high into the clear sky trailing behind it a fiery tale of glowing red sparks. Five hundred feet it climbed, perhaps six hundred, then burst into a brilliantly incandescent shower of crimson stars, stars that fell lazily back to earth again, streaming away to the west on the wings of the gale and dying as they went, till the sky was colder and emptier than ever before.

'You still say it doesn't matter very much where we go?' I asked Hansen. 'Or maybe you didn't see that little lot?'

'What I just saw,' he said reverently, 'was the prettiest ol' sight that Ma Hansen's little boy ever did see – or ever will see.' He thumped me on the back, so hard that I had to grab him to keep my balance. 'We got it made, Doc!' he shouted. 'We got it made. Suddenly I have the strength of ten. Home sweet home, here we come.'

Ten minutes later we were home.

'God this is wonderful,' Hansen sighed. He stared in happy bemusement from the captain to me to the glass in his hand to the water dripping from the melting ice on his furs on to the corticene decking of the captain's tiny cabin. 'The warmth, the light, the comfort and home sweet home. I never thought I'd see any of it again. When that rocket went up, Skipper, I was just looking around to pick a place to lay me down and die. And don't think I'm joking, for I'm not.'

'And Dr Carpenter?' Swanson smiled.

'Defective mental equipment somewhere,' Hansen said. 'He doesn't seem to know how to set about giving up. I think he's just mule-headed. You get them like that.'

Hansen's slightly off-beat, slightly irrational talk had nothing to do with the overwhelming relief and relaxation that comes after moments of great stress and tension. Hansen was too tough for that. I knew that and I knew that Swanson knew it also. We'd been back for almost twenty minutes now, we'd told our story, the pressure was off, a happy ending for all seemed in sight and normalcy was again almost the order of the day. But when the strain is off and conditions are back to normal a man has time to start thinking about things again. I knew only too well what was in Hansen's mind's eye, that charred and huddled shapelessness that had once been my brother. He didn't want me to talk about him, and for that I didn't blame him; he didn't want me even to think about him, although he must have known that that was impossible. The kindest men nearly always are like that, hard and tough and cynical on the outside, men who have been too kind and showed it.

'However it was,' Swanson smiled, 'you can consider yourselves two of the luckiest men alive. That rocket you saw was the third last we had, it's been a regular fourth of July for the past hour or so. And you reckon Rawlings, Zabrinski and the survivors on Zebra are safe for the present?'

'Nothing to worry about for the next couple of days,' Hansen nodded. 'They'll be OK. Cold, mind you, and a good half of them desperately in need of hospital treatment, but they'll survive.'

'Fine. Well, this is how it is. This lead here stopped closing in about half an hour ago, but it doesn't matter now, we can drop down any time and still hold our position. What does matter is that we have located the fault in the ice-machine. It's a damnably tricky and complicated job and I expect it will take several hours to fix. But I think we'll wait until it is fixed before we try anything. I'm not too keen on this idea of making a dead reckoning approach to this lead near Zebra then loosing off a shot in the dark. Since there's no desperate hurry, I'd rather wait till we got the ice fathometer operating again, make an accurate survey of this lead then fire a torpedo up through the middle. If the ice is only four or five feet thick there, we shouldn't have much trouble blowing a hole through.'

'That would be best,' Hansen agreed. He finished off his medicinal alcohol – an excellent bourbon – rose stiffly to his feet and stretched. 'Well, back to the old treadmill again. How many torpedoes in working order?'

'Four, at the last count.'

'I may as well go help young Mills load them up now. If that's OK by you, Skipper.'

'It is not OK by me,' Swanson said mildly, 'and if you'll take a quick gander at that mirror there you'll understand why. You're not fit to load a slug into an airgun far less a torpedo into its tube. You haven't just been on a Sunday afternoon stroll, you know. A few hours' sleep, John, then we'll see.'

Hansen didn't argue. I couldn't imagine anyone arguing with Commander Swanson. He made for the door. 'Coming, Doc?'

'In a moment. Sleep well.'

'Yeah. Thanks.' He touched me lightly on the shoulder and smiled through bloodshot and exhausted eyes. 'Thanks for everything. Good-night, all.'

When he was gone Swanson said: 'It was pretty wicked out there to-night?'

'I wouldn't recommend it for an old ladies' home Sunday afternoon outing.'

'Lieutenant Hansen seems to imagine he's under some kind of debt to you,' he went on inconsequentially.

'Imagination, as you say. They don't come any better than Hansen. You're damned lucky to have him as an exec.'

'I know that.' He hesitated, then said quietly: 'I promise you, I won't mention this again – but, well, I'm most damnably sorry, Doctor.'

I looked at him and nodded slowly. I knew he meant it, I knew he had to say it, but there's not much you can say in turn to anything like that. I said: 'Six others died with him, Commander.'

He hesitated again. 'Do we – do we take the dead back to Britain with us?'

'Could I have another drop of that excellent bourbon, Commander. Been a very heavy run on your medicinal alcohol in the past few hours, I'm afraid.' I waited till he had filled my glass then went on: 'We don't take them back with us. They're not dead men, they're just unrecognizable and unidentifiable lumps of charred matter. Let them stay here.'

His relief was unmistakable and he was aware of it for he went on hurriedly, for something to say: 'All this equipment for locating and tracking the Russian missiles. Destroyed?'

'I didn't check.' He'd find out for himself soon enough that there had been no such equipment. How he'd react to that discovery in light of the cock-and-bull story I'd spun to himself and Admiral Garvie in the Holy Loch I couldn't even begin to guess. At the moment I didn't even care. It didn't seem important, nothing seemed important, not any more. All at once I felt tired, not sleepy, just deathly tired, so I pushed myself stiffly to my feet, said good-night and left.

Hansen was in his bunk when I got back to his cabin, his furs lying where he had dropped them. I checked that he was no longer awake, slipped off my own furs, hung them up and replaced the Mannlicher-Schoenauer in my case. I lay down in my cot to sleep, but sleep wouldn't come. Exhausted though I was, I had never felt less like sleep in my life.

I was too restless and unsettled for sleep, too many problems coming all at once were causing a first-class log-jam in my mind. I got up, pulled on shirt and denim pants, and made my way to the control room. I spent the better part of what remained of the night there, pacing up and down, watching two technicians repairing the vastly complicated innards of the ice-machine, reading the messages of congratulation which were still coming in, talking desultorily to the officer on deck and drinking endless cups of coffee. It passed the night for me and although I hadn't closed an eye I felt fresh and almost relaxed by the time morning came.

At the wardroom breakfast table that morning everyone seemed quietly cheerful. They knew they had done a good job, the whole world was telling them they had done a magnificent job, and you could see that they all regarded that job as being as good as over. No one appeared to doubt Swanson's ability to blow a hole through the ice. If it hadn't been for the presence of the ghost at the feast, myself, they would have been positively jovial.

'We'll pass up the extra cups of coffee this morning, gentlemen,' Swanson said. 'Drift Station Zebra is still waiting for us and even although I'm assured everyone there will survive, they must be feeling damned cold and miserable for all that. The ice-machine has been in operation for almost an hour now, at least we hope it has. We'll drop down right away and test it and after we've loaded the torpedoes – two should do it, I fancy – we'll blow our way up into this lead at Zebra.'

Twenty minutes later the *Dolphin* was back where she belonged, 150 feet below the surface of the sea – or the ice-cap. After ten minutes' manoeuvring, with a close check being kept on the plotting table to maintain our position relative to Drift Station Zebra, it was clear that the ice-machine was behaving perfectly normally again, tracing out the inverted ridges and valleys in the ice with its usual magical accuracy. Commander Swanson nodded his satisfaction.

'That's it, then.' He nodded to Hansen and Mills, the torpedo officer. 'You can go ahead now. Maybe you'd like to accompany them, Dr Carpenter. Or is loading torpedoes old hat to you?'

'Never seen it,' I said truthfully. 'Thanks, I'd like to go along.' Swanson was as considerate towards men as he was towards his beloved *Dolphin* which was why every man in the ship swore by him. He knew, or suspected that, apart from the shock I felt at my brother's death, I was worried stiff about other things: he would have heard, although he hadn't mentioned it to me and hadn't even asked me how I had slept, that I'd spent the night prowling aimlessly and restlessly above the control room: he knew I would be grateful for any distraction, for anything that would relieve my mind, however temporarily, of whatever it was that was troubling it. I wondered just how much that extraordinarily keen brain knew or guessed. But that was an unprofitable line of thought so I put it out of my mind and went along with Hansen and Mills. Mills was another like Raeburn, the navigation officer, he looked to me more like a college undergraduate than the highly competent officer he was, but I supposed it was just another sign that I was growing old.

Hansen crossed to a panel by the diving console and studied a group of lights. The night's sleep had done Hansen a great deal of good and, apart from the abraded skin on his forehead and round the cheekbones where the ice-spicules of last night had done their work, ihe was again his normal cheerfully-cynical relaxed self, fresh and rested and fit. He waved his hand at the panel.

'The torpedo safety light, Dr Carpenter. Each green light represents a closed torpedo tube door. Six doors that open to the sea – bow caps, we call them – six rear doors for loading the torpedoes. Only twelve lights but we study them very, very carefully – just to make sure that all the lights are green. For if any of them were red – any of the top six, that is, which represent the sea doors – well, that wouldn't be so good, would it?' He looked at Mills. 'All green?'

'All green,' Mills echoed.

We moved for'ard along the wardroom passage, and dropped down the wide companionway into the crew's mess. From there we moved into the for'ard torpedo storage room. Last time I'd been there, on the morning after our departure from the Clyde, nine or ten men had been sleeping in their bunks; now all the bunks were empty. Five men were waiting for us: four ratings and a Petty Officer Bowen whom Hansen, no stickler for protocol, addressed as Charlie.

'You will see now,' Hansen observed to me, 'why officers are more highly paid than enlisted men, and deservedly so. While Charlie and his gallant men skulk here behind two sets of collision bulkheads, we must go and test the safety of the tubes. Regulations. Still, a cool head, and an iron nerve: we do it gladly for our men.'

Bowen grinned and unclipped the first collision bulkhead door. We stepped over the eighteen-inch sill, leaving the five men behind, and waited until the door had been clipped up again before opening the for'ard collision bulkhead door and stepping over the second sill into the cramped torpedo room. This time the door was swung wide open and hooked back on a heavy standing catch.

'All laid down in the book of rules,' Hansen said. 'the only time the two doors can be opened at the same time is when we're actually loading the torpedoes.' He checked the position of metal handles at the rear of the tubes, reached up, swung down a steel-spring microphone and flicked a switch. 'Ready to test tubes. All manual levers shut. All lights showing green?'

'All lights still green.' The answering voice from the overhead squawk box was hollow, metallic, queerly impersonal.

'You already checked,' I said mildly.

'So we check again. Same old book of rules.' He grinned. 'Besides, my grandpa died at ninety-seven and I aim to beat his record. Take no chances and you run no risk. What are they to be, George?'

'Three and four.' I could see the brass plaques on the circular rear doors of the tubes, 2, 4 and 6 on the port side, 1, 3 and 5 on the starboard. Lieutenant Mills was proposing to use the central tubes on each side.

Mills unhooked a rubber torch from the bulkhead and approached number 3 first. Hansen said: 'Still no chances. First of all George opens the test cock in the rear door which will show if there is any water at all in the tubes. Shouldn't be, but sometimes a little gets past the bow caps. If the test cock shows nothing, then he opens the door and shines his torch up to examine the bow cap and see that there is no obstruction in the tube. How's it, George?'

'OK, number three.' Three times Mills lifted the test cock handle and no trace of water appeared. 'Opening the door now.'

He hauled on the big lever at the rear, pulled it clear and swung back the heavy circular door. He shone his torch up the gleaming inside length of the tube, then straightened. 'Clean as a whistle and dry as a bone.'

'That's not the way he was taught to report it,' Hansen said sorrowfully. 'I don't know what the young officers are coming to these days. Right, George, number four.'

Mills grinned, secured the rear door on number 3 and crossed to number 4. He lifted the test cock handle and said: 'Oh-oh.'

'What is it?' Hansen asked.

'Water,' Mills said tersely.

'Is there much? Let's see?'

'Just a trickle.'

'Is that bad?' I asked.

'It happens,' Hansen said briefly. He joggled the handle up and down and another spoonful of water appeared. 'You can get a slightly imperfect bow-cap and if you go deep enough to build up sufficient outside pressure you can get a trickle of water coming in. Probably what has happened in this case. If the bow-cap was open, friend, at this depth the water would come out of that spout like a bullet. But no chances, no chances.' He reached for the microphone again. 'Number four bow-cap still green? We have a little water here.'

'Still green.'

Hansen looked down at Mills. 'How's it coming?'

'Not so much now.'

'Control centre,' Hansen said into the microphone. 'Check the trim chit, just to make sure.'

There was a pause, then the box crackled again.

'Captain here. All tubes showing "Empty." Signed by Lieutenant Hansen and the foreman engineer.'

'Thank you, sir.' Hansen switched off and grinned. 'Lieutenant Hansen's word is good enough for me any day. How's it now?'

'Stopped.'

'Open her up.'

Mills tugged the heavy lever. It moved an inch or two, then stuck. 'Uncommon stiff,' he commented.

'You torpedomen never heard of anything called lubricating oil?' Hansen demanded. 'Weight, George, weight.'

Mills applied more weight. The lever moved another couple of inches. Mills scowled, shifted his feet to get maximum purchase and heaved just as Hansen shouted: 'No! Stop! For God's sake, stop!'

He was too late. He was a lifetime too late. The lever snapped clear, the heavy circular rear door smashed open as violently as if it had been struck by some gigantic battering ram and a roaring torrent of water burst into the for'ard torpedo room. The sheer size, the enormous column of water was staggering. It was like a giant hosepipe, like one of the outlet pipes of the Boulder Dam. It caught up Lieutenant Mills, already badly injured by the flailing sweep of that heavy door and swept him back across the torpedo room to smash heavily against the after bulkhead; for a moment he half-stood there, pinned by the power of that huge jet, then slid down limply to the deck.

'Blow all main ballast!' Hansen shouted into the microphone. He was hanging on to a rear torpedo door to keep from being carried away and even above the thunderous roar of the waters his voice carried clearly. 'Emergency. Blow all main ballast. Number four tube open to the sea. Blow all main ballast!' He released his grip, staggered across the deck trying to keep his balance in the madly swirling already foot-deep waters. 'Get out of here, for God's sake.'

He should have saved his energy and breath. I was already on my way out of there. I had Mills under the arms and was trying to drag him over the high sill of the for'ard collision bulkhead and I was making just no headway at all. The proper trim of a submarine is a delicate thing at the best of times and even after these few seconds the nose of the *Dolphin*, heavy with the tons of water that had already poured in, was beginning to cant sharply downwards: trying to drag Mills and at the same time keep my balance on that sloping deck with knee-high water boiling around me was more than I could do; but suddenly Hansen had Mills by the feet and I stumbled off-balance, tripped over the high sill and fell backwards into the confined space between the two collision bulkheads, dragging Mills after me.

Hansen was still on the other side of the bulkhead. I could hear him cursing steadily, monotonously and as if he meant it as he struggled to unhook the heavy door from its standing catch. Because of the steep downward pitch of the *Dolphin*'s deck he had to lean all his weight against the massive steel door to free the catch, and with his insecure footing among the swirling waters on that sloping slippery deck he was obviously having the devil's own time trying to release it. I let Mills lie, jumped over the sill, flung my shoulder against the door and with the suddenly added pressure the latch clicked free. The heavy door at once swung half-shut, carrying us along with it and knocking us both off our feet into the battering-ram path of that torrent still gushing from number 4 tube. Coughing and spluttering we scrambled upright again, crossed the sill and, hanging on to a clip handle apiece, tried to drag the door shut.

Twice we tried and twice we failed. The water boiled in through the tube and its level was now almost lipping the top of the sill. With every second that passed the downward angle of the *Dolphin* increased and with every extra degree of steepness the task of pulling that door uphill against the steadily increasing gravity became more and more difficult.

The water began to spill over the sill on to our feet.

Hansen grinned at me. At least, I thought for a moment he was grinning, but the white teeth were clamped tightly together and there was no amusement at all in his eyes. He shouted above the roar of the water: 'It's now or never.'

A well-taken point. It was indeed now or never. At a signal from Hansen we flung our combined weights on to those clip-handles each with one hand to a clip while the other braced against the bulkhead to give maximum purchase. We got the door to within four inches. It swung open. We tried again. Still four inches and I knew that all our strength had gone into that one.

'Can you hold it for a moment?' I shouted.

He nodded. I shifted both hands to the lower corner clip, dropped to the deck, braced my feet against the sill and straightened both legs in one convulsive jerk. The door crashed shut, Hansen jammed his clip home, I did the same with mine and we were safe. For the moment we were safe.

I left Hansen to secure the remaining clips and started knocking the clips off the after collision bulkhead door. I'd only got as far as the first one when the others started falling off by themselves. Petty Officer Bowen and his men, on the other side of that door, needed no telling that we wanted out of there just as fast as possible. The door was pulled open and my ear drums popped with the abrupt fall in air pressure. I could hear the steady echoing roar of air blasting into the ballast tanks under high pressure. I hoisted Mills by the shoulders, strong competent hands lifted him out and over the sill and a couple of seconds later Hansen and I were beside him.

'In God's name!' Petty Officer Bowen said to Hansen. 'What's gone wrong?'

'Number four tube open to the sea.'

'Jesus!'

'Clip up that door,' Hansen ordered. 'But good.' He left at a dead run, clawing his way up the sharply sloping deck of the torpedo storage room. I took a look at Lieutenant Mills – one short look was all I needed – and followed after Hansen. Only I didn't run. Running wasn't going to help anybody now.

The roar of compressed air filled the ship, the ballast tanks were rapidly emptying, but still the *Dolphin* continued on its deadly dive, arrowing down for the dark depths of the Arctic: not even the massive compressed-air banks of the submarine could hope to cope so soon with the effects of the scores of tons of sea-water that had already flooded into the for'ard torpedo room: I wondered bleakly if they would ever be able to cope at all. As I walked along the wardroom passage, using the hand-rail to haul myself up that crazily canted deck, I could feel the entire submarine shudder beneath my feet. No doubt about what that was, Swanson had the great turbines turning over at maximum revolutions, the big bronze propellers threshing madly in reverse, trying to bite deep into the water to slow up the diving submarine.

You can smell fear. You can smell it and you can see it and I could do both as I hauled my way into the control centre of the *Dolphin* that morning. Not one man as much as flickered an eye in my direction as I passed by the sonar room. They had no eyes for me. They had no eyes for anybody: tense, strained, immobile, with hunted faces, they had eyes for one thing only – the plummetting needle on the depth gauge.

The needle was passing the six-hundred-feet mark. Six hundred feet. No conventional submarine I'd ever been on could have operated at this depth. Could have survived at this depth. Six hundred and fifty. I thought of the fantastic outside pressure that represented and I felt far from happy. Someone else was feeling far from happy also, the young seaman manning the inboard diving seat. His fists were clenched till the knuckles showed, a muscle was jumping in his cheek, a nerve twitching in his neck and he had the look on his face of a man who sees the bony finger of death beckoning.

Seven hundred feet. Seven hundred and fifty. Eight hundred. I'd never heard of a submarine that had reached that depth and lived. Neither, apparently, had Commander Swanson.

'We have just set up a new mark, men,' he said. His voice was calm and relaxed and although he was far too intelligent a man not to be afraid, no trace of it showed in tone or manner. 'Lowest recorded dive ever, as far as I am aware. Speed of descent?'

'No change.'

'It will change soon. The torpedo room must be about full now – apart from the pocket of air compressed under high pressure.' He gazed at the dial and tapped his teeth thoughtfully with a thumb-nail – this, for Swanson, was probably the equivalent of going into hysterics. 'Blow the diesel tanks: blow the fresh-water tanks.' Imperturbable though he sounded, Swanson was close to desperation for this was the counsel of despair: thousands of miles from home and supplies, yet jettisoning all the diesel and drinking water, the lack of either of which could make all the difference between life and death. But, at that moment, it didn't matter: all that mattered was lightening ship.

'Main ballast tanks empty,' the diving officer reported. His voice was hoarse and strained.

Swanson nodded, said nothing. The volume of the sound of the compressed air had dropped at least seventy-five per cent and the suddenly comparative silence was sinister, terrifying, as if it meant that the *Dolphin* was giving up the fight. Now we had only the slender reserves of the fresh water and diesel to save us: at the rate at which the *Dolphin* was still diving I didn't see how it could.

Hansen was standing beside me. I noticed blood dripping from his left hand to the deck and when I looked more closely I could see that two of his fingers were broken. It must have happened in the torpedo room. At the moment, it didn't seem important. It certainly didn't seem important to Hansen. He was entirely oblivious of it.

The pressure gauge fell farther and still farther. I knew now that nothing could save the *Dolphin*. A bell rang. Swanson swung down a microphone and pressed a button.

'Engine-room here,' a metallic voice came through. 'We must slow down. Main bearings beginning to smoke, she'll seize up any moment.'

'Maintain revolutions.' Swanson swung back the microphone. The young-ster at the diving console, the one with the jumping cheek muscles and the nervous twitch, started to mumble, 'Oh, dear God, oh, dear God,' over and over again, softly at first, then the voice climbing up the scale to hysteria. Swanson moved two paces, touched him on the shoulder. 'Do you mind, laddie? I can hardly hear myself think.' The mumblings stopped and the boy sat quite still, his face carved from grey granite, the nerve in his neck going like a trip-hammer.

'How much more of this will she take?' I asked casually. At least, I meant it to sound casual but it came out like the croak of an asthmatic bullfrog.

'I'm afraid we're moving into the realms of the unknown,' Swanson admitted calmly. 'One thousand feet plus. If that dial is right, we passed the theoretical implosion point – where the hull should have collapsed – fifty feet ago. At the present moment she's being subjected to well over a million tons of pressure.' Swanson's repose, his glacial calm, was staggering, they must have scoured the whole of America to find a man like that. If ever there was the right man in the right place at the right time it was Commander Swanson in the control room of a runaway submarine diving to depths hundreds of feet below what any submarine had ever experienced before.

'She's slowing,' Hansen whispered.

'She's slowing,' Swanson nodded.

She wasn't slowing half fast enough for me. It was impossible that the pressure hull could hold out any longer. I wondered vaguely what the end would be like, then put the thought from my mind, I would never know anything about it, anyway. At that depth the pressure must have been about twenty tons to the square foot, we'd have been squashed as flat as flounders before our senses could even begin to record what was happening to us.

The engine-room call-up bell rang again. The voice this time was imploring, desperate. 'We must ease up, Captain. Switch gear is turning red hot. We can see it glowing.'

'Wait till it's white hot, then you can complain about it,' Swanson said curtly. If the engines were going to break down they were going to break down; but until they did he'd tear the life out of them in an attempt to save the *Dolphin*. Another bell rang.

'Control room?' The voice was harsh, high-pitched. 'Crew's mess deck here. Water is beginning to come in.' For the first time, every eye in the control room turned away from the depth gauge and fixed itself on that loudspeaker. The hull was giving at last under the fantastic pressure, the crushing weight. One little hole, one tiny threadlike crack as a starting point and the pressure hull would rip and tear and flatten like a toy under a steam-hammer. A quick glance at the strained, shocked faces showed this same thought in every mind.

'Where?' Swanson demanded.

'Starboard bulkhead.'

'How much?'

'A pint or two, just trickling down the bulkhead. And it's getting worse. It's getting worse all the time. For God's sake, Captain, what are we going to do?'

'What are you going to do?' Swanson echoed. 'Mop the damn' stuff up, of course. You don't want to live in a dirty ship, do you?' He hung up.

'She's stopped. She's stopped.' Four words and a prayer. I'd been wrong about every eye being on the loudspeaker, one pair of eyes had never left the depth gauge, the pair belonging to the youngster at the console.

'She's stopped,' the diving officer confirmed. His voice had a shake in it.

No one spoke. The blood continued to drip unheeded from Hansen's crushed fingers. I thought that I detected, for the first time, a faint sheen of sweat on Swanson's brow, but I couldn't be sure. The deck still shuddered beneath our feet as the giant engines strove to lift the *Dolphin* out of those deadly depths, the compressed air still hissed into the diesel and fresh-water tanks. I could no longer see the depth gauge, the diving officer had drawn himself up so close to it that he obscured most of it from me.

Ninety seconds passed, ninety seconds that didn't seem any longer than a leap year, ninety interminable seconds while we waited for the sea to burst into our hull and take us for its own, then the diving officer said: 'Ten feet. *Up*'

'Are you sure?' Swanson asked.

'A year's pay.'

'We're not out of the wood yet,' Swanson said mildly. 'The hull can still go – it should have gone a damn' long time ago. Another hundred feet – that means a couple of tons less pressure to the square foot – and I think we'll have a chance. At least a fifty-fifty chance. And after that the chances will improve with every foot we ascend; and as we ascend the highly compressed air in the torpedo room will expand, driving out water and so lightening ship.'

'Still rising,' the diving officer said. 'Still rising. Speed of ascent changed.'

Swanson walked across to the diving stand and studied the slow movement of the depth gauge dial. 'How much fresh water left?'

'Thirty per cent.'

'Secure blowing fresh-water ballast. Engines all back two-thirds.'

The roar of compressed air fell away and the deck vibration eased almost to nothing as the engine revolutions fell from emergency power to two-third full speed.

'Speed of ascent unchanged,' the diving officer reported. 'One hundred feet up.'

'Secure blowing diesel.' The roar of compressed air stopped completely. 'All back one-third.'

'Still rising. Still rising.'

Swanson took a silk handkerchief from his pocket and wiped his face and neck. 'I was a little worried there,' he said to no one in particular, 'and I don't much care who knows it.' He reached for a microphone and I could hear his voice booming faintly throughout the ship.

'Captain here. All right, you can all start breathing again. Everything is under control, we're on our way up. As a point of interest we're still over three hundred feet deeper than the lowest previous submarine dive ever recorded.'

I felt as if I had just been through the rollers of a giant mangle. We all looked as if we'd just been through the rollers of a giant mangle. A voice said: 'I've never smoked in my life, but I'm starting now. Someone give me a cigarette.' Hansen said: 'When we get back to the States do you know what I'm going to do?'

'Yes,' Swanson said. 'You're going to scrape together your last cent, go up to Groton and throw the biggest, the most expensive party ever for the men who built this boat. You're too late, Lieutenant, I thought of it first.' He checked abruptly and said sharply: 'What's happened to your hand?'

Hansen lifted his left hand and stared at it in surprise. 'I never even knew I'd been scratched. Must have happened with that damn' door in the torpedo room. There's a medical supply box there, Doc. Would you fix this.'

'You did a damn' fine job there, John,' Swanson said warmly. 'Getting that door closed, I mean. Couldn't have been easy.'

'It wasn't. All pats on the back to our friend here,' Hansen said. 'He got it closed, not me. And if we hadn't got it closed—'

'Or if I'd let you load the torpedoes when you came back last night,' Swanson said grimly. 'When we were sitting on the surface and the hatches wide open. We'd have been eight thousand feet down now and very, very dead.'

Hansen suddenly snatched his hand away. 'My God!' he said remorsefully. 'I'd forgotten. Never mind this damned hand of mine. George Mills, the torpedo officer. He caught a pretty bad smack. You'd better see him first. Or Doc Benson.'

I took his hand back. 'No hurry for either of us. Your fingers first. Mills isn't feeling a thing.'

'Good lord!' Astonishment showed in Hansen's face, maybe shock at my callousness. 'When he recovers consciousness—'

'He'll never recover consciousness again,' I said. 'Lieutenant Mills is dead.'

'What!' Swanson's fingers bit deeply, painfully into my arm. ' "Dead," did you say?'

'That column of water from number four tube came in like an express train,' I said tiredly. 'Flung him right back against the after bulkhead and smashed in the occiput – the back of his head – like an eggshell. Death must have been instantaneous.'

'Young George Mills,' Swanson whispered. His face had gone very pale. 'Poor young beggar. His first trip on the *Dolphin*. And now – just like that. Killed.'

'Murdered,' I said.

'What!' If Commander Swanson didn't watch out with his fingers he'd have my upper arm all black and blue. 'What was that you said?'

' "Murdered," I said. "Murdered," I meant.'

Swanson stared at me for a long moment, his face empty of expression, but the eyes strained and tired and suddenly somehow old. He wheeled, walked across to the diving officer, spoke a few words to him and returned. 'Come on,' he said abruptly. 'You can fix up the lieutenant's hand in my cabin.'

Chapter Seven

'You realize the seriousness of what you are saying?' Swanson asked. 'You are making a grave accusation—'

'Come off it,' I said rudely. 'This is not a court of law and I'm not accusing anyone. All I say is that murder has been done. Whoever left that bow-cap door open is directly responsible for the death of Lieutenant Mills.'

'What do you mean "left the door open"? Who says anyone left the door open? It could have been due to natural causes. And even if – I can't see it – that door had been left open, you can't accuse a man of murder because of carelessness or forgetfulness or because—'

'Commander Swanson,' I said. 'I'll go on record as saying that you are probably the best naval officer I have ever met. But being best at that doesn't mean that you're best at everything. There are noticeable gaps in your education, Commander, especially in the appreciation of the finer points of skulduggery. You require an especially low and devious type of mind for that and I'm afraid that you just haven't got it. Doors left open by natural causes, you say. What natural causes?'

'We've hit the ice a few hefty smacks,' Swanson said slowly. 'That could have jarred it open. Or when we poked through the ice last night a piece of ice, a stalactite, say, could have—'

'Your tubes are recessed, aren't they. Mighty oddly-shaped stalactite that would go down then bend in at a right angle to reach the door – and even then it would only shut it more tightly.'

'The doors are tested every time we're in harbour,' Commander Swanson persisted quietly. 'They're also opened when we open tubes to carry out surface trimming tests in dock. Any dockyard has pieces of waste, rope and other rubbish floating around that could easily have jammed a door open.'

'The safety lights showed the doors shut.'

'They could have been opened just a crack, not enough to disengage the safety contact.'

'Open a crack! Why do you think Mills is dead? If you've ever seen the jet of water that hits the turbine blades in a hydro-electric plant, then you'll know how that water came in. A crack? My God! How are those doors operated?'

'Two ways. Remote control, hydraulic, just press a button: then there are manually-operated levers in the torpedo room itself.'

I turned to Hansen. He was sitting on the bunk beside me, his face pale as I splinted his broken fingers. I said: 'Those hand-operated levers. Were they in the shut position?'

'You heard me say so in there. Of course they were. First thing we always check.'

'Somebody doesn't like you,' I said to Swanson. 'Or somebody doesn't like the *Dolphin*. Or somebody knew that the *Dolphin* was going searching for the Zebra survivors and they didn't like that either. So they sabotaged the ship. You will remember you were rather surprised you didn't have to correct the *Dolphin*'s trim? It had been your intention to carry out a slow-time dive to check the underwater trim because you thought that would have been affected by the fact that you had no torpedoes in the for'ard tubes. But surprise, surprise. She didn't need any correction.'

'I'm listening,' Swanson said quietly. He was with me now. He was with me all the way. He cocked an eyebrow as we heard water flooding back into the tanks. The repeater gauge showed 200 feet, Swanson must have ordered his diving officer to level off at that depth. The *Dolphin* was still canted nose downwards at an angle of about 25°.

'She didn't need any correcting because some of her tubes were already full of water. For all I know maybe number three tube, the one we tested and found OK is the only one that is *not* full of water. Our clever little pal left the doors open, disconnected the hand-operated levers so that they appeared to be in the shut position when they were actually open and crossed over a few wires in a junction box so that the open position showed green while the closed showed red. A man who knew what he was about could have done it in a few minutes. Two men who knew what they were about could have done it in no time at all. I'll lay anything you like that when you're eventually in a position to check you'll find the levers disconnected, the wires crossed and the inlets of the test-cocks blocked with sealing-wax, quick-drying paint or even chewing-gum so that when the test-cocks were opened nothing would show and you would assume the tubes to be empty.'

'There was a trickle from the test-cock in number four tube,' Hansen objected.

'Low-grade chewing-gum.'

'The murderous swine,' Swanson said calmly. His restraint was far more effective than the most thunderous denunciations could ever have been. 'He could have murdered us all. But for the grace of God and the Groton boatyard shipwrights he would have murdered us all.'

'He didn't mean to,' I said. 'He didn't mean to kill anyone. You had intended to carry out a slow-time dive to check trim in the Holy Loch before you left that evening. You told me so yourself. Did you announce it to the crew, post it up in daily orders or something like that?'

'Both.'

'So. Our pal knew. He also knew that you carried out those checks when the boat is still awash or just under the surface. When you checked the tubes to see if they were OK, water would come in, too much water to permit the rear doors to be shut again, but not under such high pressure that you wouldn't have time and to spare to close the for'ard collision bulkhead door and make a leisurely retreat in good order. What would have happened? Not much. At the worst you would have settled down slowly to the bottom and stayed there. Not deep enough to worry the *Dolphin*. In a submarine of even ten years ago it might have been fatal for all, because of the limited air supply. Not to-day when your air purifying machines can let you stay down for months at a time. You just float up your emergency indicator buoy and telephone, tell your story, sit around and drink coffee till a naval diver comes down and replaces the bow cap, pump out the torpedo room and surface again. Our unknown pal – or pals – didn't mean to kill anyone. But they did mean to delay you. And they would have delayed you. We know now that you could have got to the surface under your own steam, but even so your top brass would have insisted that you go into dock for a day or two to check that everything was OK.'

'Why should anyone want to delay us?' Swanson asked. I though he had an unnecessarily speculative look in his eyes, but it was hard to be sure, Commander Swanson's face showed exactly what Commander Swanson wanted it to show and no more.

'My God, do you think I know the answer to that one?' I said irritably.

'No. No, I don't think so.' He could have been more emphatic about it. 'Tell me, Dr Carpenter, do you suspect some member of the *Dolphin*'s crew to be responsible?'

'Do you really need an answer to that one?'

'I supppose not,' he sighed. 'Going to the bottom of the Arctic Ocean is not a very attractive way of committing suicide, and if any member of the crew had jinxed things he'd damn' soon have unjinxed them as soon as he realized that we weren't going to carry out trim checks in shallow water. Which leaves only the civilian dockyard workers in Scotland – and every one of them has been checked and rechecked and given a top-grade security clearance.'

'Which means nothing. There are plushy Moscow hotels and British and American prisons full of people who had top-grade security clearances . . . What are you going to do now, Commander. About the *Dolphin*, I mean?'

'I've been thinking about it. In the normal course of events the thing to do would be to close the bow-cap of number four and pump out the torpedo room, then go in and close the rear door of number four. But the bow-cap door won't close. Within a second of John's telling us that number four was open to the sea the diving officer hit the hydraulic button – the one that closes it by remote control. You saw for yourself that nothing happened. It must be jammed.'

'You bet your life it's jammed,' I said grimly. 'A sledgehammer might do some good but pressing buttons won't.'

'I could go back to that lead we've just left, surface again and send a diver under the ice to investigate and see what he can do, but I'm not going to ask any man to risk his life doing that. I could retreat to the open sea, surface and fix it there, but not only would it be a damned slow and uncomfortable trip with the *Dolphin* canted at this angle, it might take us days before we got back here again. And some of the Drift Station Zebra men are pretty far through. It might be too late.'

'Well, then,' I said. 'You have the man to hand, Commander. I told you when I first met you that environmental health studies were my speciality, especially in the field of pressure extremes when escaping from submarines. I've done an awful lot of simulated sub escapes, Commander. I do know a fair amount about pressures, how to cope with them and how I react to them myself.'

'How do you react to them, Dr Carpenter?'

'A high tolerance. They don't worry me much.'

'What do you have in mind?'

'You know damn' well what I have in mind,' I said impatiently. 'Drill a hole in the door of the after collision bulkhead, screw in a high-pressure hose, open the door, shove someone in the narrow space between the two

collision bulkheads and turn up the hose until the pressure between the
collision bulkheads equals that in the torpedo room. You have the clips eased
off the for'ard collision door. When the pressures are equalized it opens at
a touch, you walk inside, close number four rear door and walk away again.
That's what you had in mind wasn't it?'

'More or less,' he admitted. 'Except that *you* are no part of it. Every man
on this ship has made simulated escapes. They all know the effects of
pressure. And most of them are a great deal younger than you.'

'Suit yourself,' I said. 'But age has little to do with the ability to stand
stresses. You didn't pick a teen-ager as the first American to orbit the earth,
did you? As for simulated escapes, making a free ascent up a hundred-foot
tank is a different matter altogether from going inside an iron box, waiting
for the slow build-up of pressure, working under that pressure, then waiting
for the slow process of decompression. I've seen young men, big, tough, very,
very fit young men break up completely under those circumstances and
almost go crazy trying to get out. The combination of physiological and
psychological factors involved is pretty fierce.'

'I think,' Swanson said slowly, 'that I'd sooner have you – what do the
English say, batting on a sticky wicket – than almost any man I know. But
there's a point you've overlooked. What would the Admiral Commanding
Atlantic Submarines say to me if he knew I'd let a civilian go instead of one
of my own men?'

'If you *don't* let me go, I know what he'll say. He'll say: "We must reduce
Commander Swanson to lieutenant, j-g., because he had on board the
Dolphin an acknowledged expert in this speciality and refused, out of stiff-
necked pride, to use him, thereby endangering the lives of his crew and the
safety of his ship."'

Swanson smiled a pretty bleak smile, but with the desperately narrow
escape we had just had, the predicament we were still in and the fact that
his torpedo officer was lying dead not so many feet away, I hardly expected
him to break into gales of laughter. He looked at Hansen: 'What do you say,
John?'

'I've seen more incompetent characters than Dr Carpenter,' Hansen said.
'Also, he gets about as nervous and panic-stricken as a bag of Portland
cement.'

'He has qualifications you do not look to find in the average medical man,'
Swanson agreed. 'I shall be glad to accept your offer. One of my men will
go with you. That way the dictates of common sense and honour are both
satisfied.'

It wasn't all that pleasant, not by quite a way, but it wasn't all that terribly
bad either. It went off exactly as it could have been predicted it would go
off. Swanson cautiously eased the *Dolphin* up until her stern was just a few
feet beneath the ice: this reduced the pressure in the torpedo room to a
minimum, but even at that the bows were still about a hundred feet down.

A hole was drilled in the after collision bulkhead door and an armoured
high-pressure hose screwed into position. Dressed in porous rubber suits
and equipped with an aqualung apiece, a young torpedoman by the name
of Murphy and I went inside and stood in the gap between the two collision
bulkheads. High-powered air hissed into the confined space. Slowly the
pressure rose: twenty, thirty, forty, fifty pounds to the square inch. I could

feel the pressure on lungs and ears, the pain behind the eyes, the slight wooziness that comes from the poisonous effect of breathing pure oxygen under such pressure. But I was used to it, I knew it wasn't going to kill me: I wondered if young Murphy knew that. This was the stage where the combined physical and mental effects became too much for most people, but if Murphy was scared or panicky or suffering from bodily distress he hid it well. Swanson would have picked his best man and to be the best man in a company like that Murphy had to be something very special.

We eased off the clips on the for'ard bulkhead door, knocked them off cautiously as the pressures equalized. The water in the torpedo room was about two feet above the level of the sill and as the door came ajar the water boiled whitely through into the collision space while compressed air hissed out from behind us to equalize the lowering pressure of the air in the torpedo room. For about ten seconds we had to hang on grimly to hold the door and maintain our balance while water and air fought and jostled in a seething maelstrom to find their own natural levels. The door opened wide. The water level now extended from about thirty inches up on the collision bulkhead to the for'ard deckhead of the torpedo room. We crossed the sill, switched on our waterproof torches and ducked under.

The temperature of that water was about 28° F. – four below freezing. Those porous rubber suits were specially designed to cope with icy waters but even so I gasped with the shock of it – as well as one can gasp when breathing pure oxygen under heavy pressure. But we didn't linger, for the longer we remained there the longer we would have to spend decompressing afterwards. We half-walked, half-swum towards the fore end of the compartment, located the rear door on number 4 tube and closed it, but not before I had a quick look at the inside of the pressure cock. The door itself seemed undamaged: the body of the unfortunate Lieutenant Mills had absorbed its swinging impact and prevented it from being wrenched off its hinges. It didn't seem distorted in any way, and fitted snugly into place. We forced its retaining lever back into place and left.

Back in the collision compartment we gave the prearranged taps on the door. Almost at once we heard the subdued hum of a motor as the high-speed extraction pumps in the torpedo room got to work, forcing the water out through the hull. Slowly the water level dropped and as it dropped the air pressure as slowly decreased. Degree by degree the *Dolphin* began to come back on even keel. When the water was finally below the level of the for'ard sill we gave another signal and the remaining over-pressure air was slowly bled out through the hose.

A few minutes later, as I was stripping off the rubber suit, Swanson asked: 'Any trouble?'

'None. You picked a good man in Murphy.'

'The best. Many thanks, Doctor.' He lowered his voice. 'You wouldn't by any chance—'

'You know damned well I would,' I said. 'I did. Not sealing-wax, not chewing-gum, not paint. Glue, Commander Swanson. That's how they blocked the test-cock inlet. The old-fashioned animal hide stuff that comes out of a tube. Ideal for the job.'

'I see,' he said, and walked away.

The *Dolphin* shuddered along its entire length as the torpedo hissed out of its tube – number 3 tube, the only one in the submarine Swanson could safely rely upon.

'Count it down,' Swanson said to Hansen. 'Tell me when we should hit, tell me when we should hear it hit.'

Hansen looked at the stop-watch in his bandaged hand and nodded. The seconds passed slowly. I could see Hansen's lips move silently. Then he said: 'We should be hitting – now,' and two or three seconds later: 'We should be hearing – now.'

Whoever had been responsible for the settings and time calculations on that torpedo had known what he was about. Just on Hansen's second 'now' we felt as much as heard the clanging vibration along the *Dolphin*'s hull as the shock-waves from the exploding war-head reached us. The deck shook briefly beneath our feet but the impact was nowhere nearly as powerful as I had expected. I was relieved. I didn't have to be a clairvoyant to know that everyone was relieved. No submarine had ever before been in the vicinity of a torpedo detonating under the ice-pack: no one had known to what extent the tamping effect of overhead ice might have increased the pressure and destructive effect of the lateral shock-waves.

'Nicely,' Swanson murmured. 'Very nicely done indeed. Both ahead one-third. I hope that bang had considerably more effect on the ice than it had on our ship.' He said to Benson at the ice-machine: 'Let us know as soon as we reach the lead, will you?'

He moved to the plotting table. Raeburn looked up and said: 'Five hundred yards gone, five hundred to go.'

'All stop,' Swanson said. The slight vibration of the engine died away. 'We'll just mosey along very carefully indeed. That explosion may have sent blocks of ice weighing a few tons apiece pretty far down into the sea. I don't want to be doing any speed at all if we meet any of them on the way up.'

'Three hundred yards to go,' Raeburn said.

'All clear. All clear all round,' the sonar room reported.

'Still thick ice,' Benson intoned. 'Ah! That's it. We're under the lead. Thin ice. Well, five or six feet.'

'Two hundred yards,' Raeburn said. 'It checks.'

We drifted slowly onwards. At Swanson's orders the propellers kicked over once or twice then stopped again.

'Fifty yards,' Raeburn said. 'Near enough.'

'Ice reading?'

'No change? Five feet, about.'

'Speed?'

'One knot.'

'Position?'

'One thousand yards exactly. Passing directly under target area.'

'And nothing on the ice-machine. Nothing at all?'

'Not a thing.' Benson shrugged and looked at Swanson. The captain walked across and watched the inked stylus draw its swiftly etched vertical lines on the paper.

'Peculiar, to say the least of it,' Swanson murmured. 'Seven hundred pounds of very high-grade amatol in that lot. Must be uncommonly tough ice in those parts. Again to say the least of it. We'll go up to ninety feet and make a few passes under the area. Floodlights on, TV on.'

So we went up to ninety feet and made a few passes and nothing came of it. The water was completely opaque, the floods and camera useless. The ice-machine stubbornly registered four to six feet – it was impossible to be more accurate – all the time.

'Well, that seems to be it,' Hansen said. 'We back off and have another go?'

'Well, I don't know,' Swanson said pensively. 'What say we just try to shoulder our way up?'

'Shoulder our way up?' Hansen wasn't with him: neither was I. 'What kind of shoulder is going to heave five feet of ice to one side?'

'I'm not sure. The thing is, we've been working from unproved assumptions and that's always a dangerous basis. We've been assuming that if the torpedo didn't blow the ice to smithereens it would at least blow a hole in it. Maybe it doesn't happen that way at all. Maybe there's just a big upward pressure of water distributed over a fair area that heaves the ice up and breaks it into pretty big chunks that just settle back into the water again in their original position in the pattern of a dried-up mud hole with tiny cracks all round the isolated sections. But with cracks all round. Narrow cracks, but there. Cracks so narrow that the ice-machine couldn't begin to register them even at the slow speed we were doing.' He turned to Raeburn. 'What's our position?'

'Still in the centre of the target area, sir.'

'Take her up till we touch the ice,' Swanson said.

He didn't have to add any cautions about gentleness. The diving officer took her up like floating thistledown until we felt a gentle bump.

'Hold her there,' Swanson said. He peered at the TV screen but the water was so opaque that all definition vanished half-way up the sail. He nodded to the diving officer. 'Kick her up – hard.'

Compressed air roared into the ballast tanks. Seconds passed without anything happening then all at once the *Dolphin* shuddered as something very heavy and very solid seemed to strike the hull. A moment's pause, another solid shock then we could see the edge of a giant segment of ice sliding down the face of the TV screen.

'Well, now, I believe I might have had a point there,' Swanson remarked. 'We seem to have hit a crack between two chunks of ice almost exactly in the middle. Depth?'

'Forty-five.'

'Fifteen feet showing. And I don't think we can expect to lift the hundreds of tons of ice lying over the rest of the hull. Plenty of positive buoyancy?'

'All we'll ever want.'

'Then we'll call it a day at that. Right, Quartermaster, away you go up top and tell us what the weather is like.'

I didn't wait to hear what the weather was like. I was interested enough it in, but I was even more interested in ensuring that Hansen didn't come along to his cabin in time to find me putting on the Mannlicher-Schoenauer along with my furs. But this time I stuck it not in its special holster but in the outside pocket of my caribou trousers. I thought it might come in handier there.

It was exactly noon when I clambered over the edge of the bridge and used a dangling rope to slide down a great rafted chunk of ice that slanted up almost to the top of the sail. The sky had about as much light in it as a late twilight in winter when the sky is heavy with grey cloud. The air was as bitter as ever, but the weather had improved for all that. The wind was down now, backed round to the north-east, seldom gusting at more than twenty m.p.h., the ice-spicules rising no more than two or three feet above the ice-cap. Nothing to tear your eyes out. To be able to see where you were going on that damned ice-cap made a very pleasant change.

There were eleven of us altogether – Commander Swanson himself, Dr Benson, eight enlisted men and myself. Four of the men were carrying stretchers with them.

Even seven hundred pounds of the highest grade conventional explosive on the market hadn't managed to do very much damage to the ice in that lead. Over an area of seventy yards square or thereabouts the ice had fractured into large fragments curiously uniform in size and roughly hex-agonal in shape but fallen back so neatly into position that you couldn't have put a hand down most of the cracks between the adjacent fragments of ice: many of the cracks, indeed, were already beginning to bind together. A poor enough performance for a torpedo war-head – until you remembered that though most of its disruptive power must have been directed downwards it had still managed to lift and fracture a chunk of ice-cap weighing maybe 5,000 tons. Looked at in that way, it didn't seem such a puny effort after all. Maybe we'd been pretty lucky to achieve what we had.

We walked across to the eastern edge of the lead, scrambled up on to the ice-pack proper and turned round to get our bearings, to line up on the unwaver-ing white finger of the searchlight that reached straight up into the gloom of the sky. No chance of getting lost this time. While the wind stayed quiet and the spicules stayed down you could see that lamp in the window ten miles away.

We didn't even need to take any bearings. A few steps away and up from the edge of the lead and we could see it at once. Drift Station Zebra. Three huts, one of them badly charred, five blackened skeletons of what had once been huts. Desolation.

'So that's it,' Swanson said in my ear. 'Or what's left of it. I've come a long way to see this.'

'You nearly went a damned sight longer and never saw it,' I said. 'To the floor of the Arctic, I mean. Pretty, isn't it?'

Swanson shook his head slowly, moved on. There were only a hundred yards to go. I led the way to the nearest intact hut, opened the door and passed inside.

The hut was about thirty degrees warmer than the last time I had been there, but still bitterly cold. Only Zabrinski and Rawlings were awake. The hut smelt of burnt fuel, disinfectant, iodine, morphine and a peculiar aroma arising from a particularly repulsive looking hash that Rawlings was indus-triously churning around in a dixie over the low stove.

'Ah, there you are,' Rawlings said conversationally. He might have been hailing a neighbour who'd phoned a minute previously to see if he could come across to borrow the lawnmower rather than greeting men he'd been fairly certain he'd never see again. 'The time is perfect – just about to ring the dinner bell, Captain. Care for some Maryland chicken – I think.'

'Not just at the moment, thank you,' Swanson said politely. 'Sorry about the ankle, Zabrinski. How is it?'

'Just fine, Captain, just fine. In a plaster cast.' He thrust out a foot, stiffly.

'The Doc here – Dr Jolly – fixed me up real nice. Had much trouble last night?' This was for me.

'Dr Carpenter had a great deal of trouble last night,' Swanson said. 'And we've had a considerable amount since. But later. Bring that stretcher in here. You first, Zabrinski. As for you, Rawlings, you can stop making like Escoffier. The *Dolphin*'s less than a couple of hundred yards from here. We'll have you all aboard in half an hour.'

I heard a shuffling noise behind me. Dr Jolly was on his feet, helping Captain Folsom to his. Folsom looked even weaker than he had done yesterday: his face, bandaged though it was, certainly looked worse.

'Captain Folsom,' I introduced him. 'Dr Jolly. This is Commander Swanson, captain of the *Dolphin*. Dr Benson.'

'*Doctor* Benson, you said, old boy?' Jolly lifted an eyebrow. 'My word, the pill-rolling competition's getting a little fierce in these parts. And Commander. By jove, but we're glad to see you fellows.' The combination of the rich Irish brogue and the English slang of the twenties fell more oddly than ever on my ear, he reminded me of educated Singhalese I'd met with their precise, lilting, standard southern English interlarded with the catch-phrases of forty years ago. Topping, old bean, simply too ripping for words.

'I can understand that,' Swanson smiled. He looked around the huddled unmoving men on the floor, men who might have been living or dead but for the immediate and smoky condensation from their shallow breathing, and his smile faded. He said to Captain Folsom: 'I cannot tell you how sorry I am. This has been a dreadful thing.'

Folsom stirred and said something but we couldn't make out what it was. Although his shockingly burnt face had been bandaged since I'd seen him last it didn't seem to have done him any good: he was talking inside his mouth all right but the ravaged cheek and mouth had become so paralysed that his speech didn't emerge as any recognizable language. The good side of his face, the left, was twisted and furrowed and the eye above almost completely shut. This had nothing to do with any sympathetic neuro-muscular reaction caused by the wickedly charred right cheek. The man was in agony. I said to Jolly: 'No morphine left?' I'd left him, I'd thought, with more than enough of it.

'Nothing left,' he said tiredly. 'I used the lot. The lot.'

'Dr Jolly worked all through the night,' Zabrinski said quietly. 'Eight hours. Rawlings and himself and Kinnaird. They never stopped once.'

Benson had his medical kit open. Jolly saw it and smiled, a smile of relief, a smile of exhaustion. He was in far worse case than he'd been the previous evening. He hadn't had all that much in him when he'd started. But he'd worked. He'd worked a solid eight hours. He'd even fixed up Zabrinski's ankle. A good doctor. Conscientious, Hippocratic, anyway. He was entitled to relax. Now that there were other doctors here, he'd relax. But not before.

He began to ease Folsom into a sitting position and I helped him. He slid down himself, his back to the wall. 'Sorry, and all that, you know,' he said. His bearded frost-bitten face twisted into the semblance of a grin. 'A poor host.'

'You can leave everything to us now, Dr Jolly,' Swanson said quietly. 'You've got all the help that's going. One thing. All those men fit to be moved?'

'I don't know.' Jolly rubbed an arm across bloodshot, smudged eyes. 'I don't know. One or two of them slipped pretty far back last night. It's the cold. Those two. Pneumonia, I think. Something an injured man could fight off in a few days back home can be fatal here. It's the cold,' he repeated. 'Uses up ninety per cent of his energy not in fighting illness and infection but just generating enough heat to stay alive.'

'Take it easy,' Swanson said. 'Maybe we'd better change our minds about that half-hour to get you all aboard. Who's first for the ambulance, Dr Benson?' Not Dr Carpenter. Dr Benson. Well, Benson was his own ship's doctor. But pointed, all the same. A regrettable coolness, as sudden in its onset as it was marked in degree, had appeared in his attitude towards me, and I didn't have to be beaten over the head with a heavy club to guess at the reason for the abrupt change.

'Zabrinski, Dr Jolly, Captain Folsom and this man here,' Benson said promptly.

'Kinnaird, radio operator,' Kinnaird identified himself. 'We never thought you'd make it, mate.' This to me. He dragged himself somehow to his feet and stood there swaying. 'I can walk.'

'Don't argue,' Swanson said curtly. 'Rawlings stop stirring that filthy mush and get to your feet. Go with them. How long would it take you to run a cable from the boat, fix up a couple of big electric heaters in here, some lights?'

'Alone?'

'All the help you want, man.'

'Fifteen minutes. I could rig a phone, sir.'

'That would be useful. When the stretcher bearers come back bring blankets, sheets, hot water. Wrap the water containers in the blankets. Anything else, Dr Benson?'

'Not now, sir.'

'That's it then. Away you go.'

Rawlings lifted the spoon from the pot, tasted it, smacked his lips in appreciation and shook his head sadly. 'It's a crying shame,' he said mournfully. 'It really is.' He went out in the wake of the stretcher bearers.

Of the eight men left lying on the floor, four were conscious. Hewson the tractor-driver, Naseby the cook, and two others who introduced themselves as Harrington. Twins. They'd even been burnt and frost-bitten in the same places. The other four were either sleeping or in coma. Benson and I started looking them over, Benson much more carefully than myself, very busy with thermometer and stethoscope. Looking for signs of pneumonia. I didn't think he'd have to look very far. Commander Swanson looked speculatively around the cabin, occasionally throwing a very odd look in my direction, occasionally flailing his arms across his chest to keep the circulation going. He had to. He didn't have the fancy furs I had and in spite of the solid-fuel stove the place was like an ice-box.

The first man I looked at was lying on his side in the far right-hand corner of the room. He had half-open eyes, just showing the lower arcs of his pupils, sunken temples, marble-white forehead and the only part of his face that wasn't bandaged was as cold as the marble in a winter graveyard. I said: 'Who is this?'

'Grant. John Grant.' Hewson, the dark quiet tractor-driver answered me. 'Radio operator. Kinnaird's side-kick. How's it with him?'

'He's dead. He's been dead quite some time.'

'Dead?' Swanson said sharply. 'You sure?' I gave him my aloof professional look and said nothing. He went on to Benson: 'Anybody too ill to be moved?'

'Those two here, I think,' Benson said. He wasn't noticing the series of peculiar looks Swanson was letting me have, so he handed me his stethoscope. After a minute I straightened and nodded.

'Third-degree burns,' Benson said to Swanson. 'What we can see of them, that is. Both high temperatures, both very fast, very weak and erratic pulses, both with lung fluids.'

'They'd have a better chance inside the *Dolphin*,' Swanson said.

'You'll kill them getting there,' I said. 'Even if you could wrap them up warmly enough to take them back to the ship, hauling them up to the top of the sail and then lowering them vertically through those hatchways would finish them off.'

'We can't stay out in that lead indefinitely,' Swanson said. 'I'll take the responsibility for moving them.'

'Sorry, Captain.' Benson shook his head gravely. 'I agree with Dr Carpenter.'

Swanson shrugged and said nothing. Moments later the stretcher bearers were back, followed soon after by Rawlings and three other enlisted men carrying cables, heaters, lamps and a telephone. It took only a few minutes to button the heaters and lamps on to the cable. Rawlings cranked the call-up generator of his field-phone and spoke briefly into the mouthpiece. Bright lights came on and the heaters started to crackle and after a few seconds glow.

Hewson, Naseby and the Harrington twins left by stretcher. When they'd gone I unhooked the Coleman lamp. 'You won't be needing this now,' I said. 'I won't be long.'

'Where are you going?' Swanson's voice was quiet.

'I won't be long,' I repeated. 'Just looking around.'

He hesitated, then stood to one side. I went out, moved round a corner of the hut and stopped. I heard the whirr of the call-up bell, a voice on the telephone. It was only a murmur to me, I couldn't make out what was being said. But I'd expected this.

The Coleman storm lantern flickered and faded in the wind, but didn't go out. Stray ice-spicules struck against the glass, but it didn't crack or break, it must have been one of those specially toughened glasses immune to a couple of hundred degrees' temperature range between the inside and the outside.

I made my way diagonally across to the only hut left on the south side. No trace of burning, charring or even smoke-blackening on the outside walls. The fuel store must have been the one next to it, on the same side and to the west, straight downwind: that almost certainly must have been its position to account for the destruction of all the other huts, and the grotesquely buckled shape of its remaining girders made this strong probability a certainty. Here had been the heart of the fire.

Hard against the side of the undamaged hut was a lean-to shed, solidly built. Six feet high, six wide, eight long. The door opened easily. Wooden floor, gleaming aluminium for the sides and ceiling, big black heaters bolted to the inside and outside walls. Wires led from those and it was no job for an Einstein to guess that they led – or had led – to the now destroyed generator house. This lean-to shed would have been warm night and day. The squat low-slung tractor that took up nearly all the floor space inside would have started any time at the touch of a switch. It wouldn't start at the turn of a switch now, it would take three or four blow-torches and the same number of strong men even to turn the engine over once. I closed the door and went into the main hut.

It was packed with metal tables, benches, machinery and every modern device for the automatic recording and interpretation of every conceivable observed detail of the Arctic weather. I didn't know what the functions of most of the instruments were and I didn't care. This was the meteorological office and that was enough for me. I examined the hut carefully but quickly and there didn't seem to be anything odd or out of place that I could see. In one corner, perched on an empty wooden packing-case. was a portable radio transmitter with listening phones – transceivers, they called them nowadays. Near it, in a box of heavy oiled wood, were fifteen Nife cells connected up in series. Hanging from a hook on the wall was a two-volt test lamp. I touched its bare leads to the outside terminals of the battery formed by the cells. Had those cells left in them even a fraction of their original power that test lamp should have burnt out in a white flash. It didn't even begin to glow. I tore a piece of flex from a nearby lamp and touched its ends to the terminals. Not even the minutest spark. Kinnaird hadn't been lying when he had said that his battery had been completely dead. But, then, I hadn't for a moment thought he'd been lying.

I made my way to the last hut – the hut that held the charred remnants of the seven men who had died in the fire. The stench of charred flesh and burnt diesel seemed stronger, more nauseating than ever. I stood in the doorway and the last thing I wanted to do was to approach even an inch closer. I peeled off fur and woollen mittens, set the lamp on a table, pulled out my torch and knelt by the first dead man.

Ten minutes passed and all I wanted was out of there. There are some things that doctors, even hardened pathologists, will go a long way to avoid. Bodies that have been too long in the sea is one; bodies that have been in the immediate vicinity of under-water explosion is another; and men who have literally been burned alive is another. I was beginning to feel more than slightly sick; but I wasn't going to leave there until I was finished.

The door creaked open. I turned and watched Commander Swanson come in. He'd been a long time, I'd expected him before then. Lieutenant Hansen, his damaged left hand wrapped in some thick woollen material, came in after him. That was what the phone call had been about, the Commander calling up reinforcements. Swanson switched off his torch, pushed up his snow-goggles and pulled down his mask. His eyes narrowed at the scene before him, his nostrils wrinkled in involuntary disgust, and the colour drained swiftly from his ruddy cheeks. Both Hansen and I had told him what to expect, but he hadn't been prepared for this: not often can the imagination encompass the reality. For a moment I thought he was going to be sick, but then I saw a slight tinge of colour touch the cheekbones and I knew he wasn't.

'Dr Carpenter,' he said in a voice in which the unsteady huskiness seemed only to emphasize the stilted formality, 'I wish you to return at once to the ship where you will remain confined to your quarters. I would prefer you went voluntarily, accompanied by Lieutenant Hansen here. I wish no trouble. I trust you don't either. If you do, we can accommodate you. Rawlings and Murphy are waiting outside that door.'

'Those are fighting words, Commander,' I said, 'and very unfriendly. Rawlings and Murphy are going to get uncommon cold out there.' I put my right hand in my caribou pants pocket – the one with the gun in it – and surveyed him unhurriedly. 'Have you had a brainstorm?'

Swanson looked at Hansen and nodded in the direction of the door. Hansen half-turned, then stopped as I said: 'Very high-handed, aren't we? I'm not worth an explanation, is that it?'

Hansen looked uncomfortable. He didn't like any part of this. I suspected Swanson didn't either, but he was going to do what he had to do and let his feelings look elsewhere.

'Unless you're a great deal less intelligent than I believe – and I credit you with a high intelligence – you know exactly what the explanation is. When you came aboard the *Dolphin* in the Holy Loch both Admiral Garvie and myself were highly suspicious of you. You spun us a story about being an expert in Arctic conditions and of having helped set up this station here. When we wouldn't accept that as sufficient authority or reason to take you along with us you told a highly convincing tale about this being an advanced missile-warning outpost and even although it was peculiar that Admiral Garvie had never heard of it, we accepted it. The huge dish aerial you spoke of, the radar masts, the electronic computers – what's happened to them, Dr Carpenter? A bit insubstantial, weren't they? Like all figments of the imagination.'

I looked at him, considering, and let him go on.

'There never were any of those things, were there? You're up to the neck in something very murky indeed, my friend. What it is I don't know nor, for the moment, do I care. All I care for is the safety of the ship, the welfare of the crew and bringing the Zebra survivors safely back home and I'm taking no chances at all.'

'The wishes of the British Admiralty, the orders from your own Director of Underseas Warfare – those mean nothing to you?'

'I'm beginning to have very strong reservations about the way those orders were obtained,' Swanson said grimly. 'You're altogether too mysterious for my liking, Dr Carpenter – as well as being a fluent liar.'

'Those are harsh, harsh words, Commander.'

'The truth not infrequently sounds that way. Will you please come?'

'Sorry. I'm not through here yet.'

'I see. John, will you—'

'I can give you an explanation. I see I have to. Won't you listen?'

'A third fairy-story?' A headshake. 'No.'

'And I'm not ready to leave. Impasse.'

Swanson looked at Hansen, who turned to go. I said: 'Well, if you're too stiff-necked to listen to me, call up the bloodhounds. Isn't it just luck, now, that we have three fully-qualified doctors here?'

'What do you mean?'

'I mean this.' Guns have different characteristics in appearance. Some look relatively harmless, some ugly, some business-like, some wicked-looking. The Mannlicher-Schoenauer in my hand just looked plain downright wicked. Very wicked indeed. The white light from the Coleman glittered off the blued metal, menacing and sinister. It was a great gun to terrify people with.

'You wouldn't use it,' Swanson said flatly.

'I'm through talking. I'm through asking for a hearing. Bring on the bailiffs, friend.'

'You're bluffing, mister,' Hansen said savagely. 'You don't dare.'

'There's too much at stake for me not to dare. Find out now. Don't be a coward. Don't hide behind your enlisted men's backs. Don't order them to get themselves shot.' I snapped off the safety-catch. 'Come and take it from me yourself.'

'Stay right where you are, John,' Swanson said sharply. 'He means it. I suppose you have a whole armoury in that combination-lock suitcase of yours,' he said bitterly.

'That's it. Automatic carbines, six-inch naval guns, the lot. But for a small-size situation a small-size gun. Do I get my hearing?'

'You get your hearing.'

'Send Rawlings and Murphy away. I don't want anyone else to know anything about this. Anyway, they're probably freezing to death.'

Swanson nodded. Hansen went to the door, opened it, spoke briefly and returned. I laid the gun on the table, picked up my torch and moved some paces away. I said: 'Come and have a look at this.'

They came. Both of them passed by the table with the gun lying there and didn't even look at it. I stopped before one of the grotesquely misshapen charred lumps lying on the floor. Swanson came close and stared down. His face had lost whatever little colour it had regained. He made a queer noise in his throat.

'That ring, that gold ring—' he began, then stopped short.

'I wasn't lying about that.'

'No. No you weren't. I – I don't know what to say. I'm most damnably—'

'It doesn't matter,' I said roughly. 'Look here. At the back. I'm afraid I had to remove some of the carbon.'

'The neck,' Swanson whispered. 'It's broken.'

'Is that what you think?'

'Something heavy, I don't know, a beam from one of the huts, must have fallen—'

'You've just seen one of those huts. They have no beams. There's an inch and half of the vertebrae missing. If anything sufficiently heavy to smash off an inch and a half of the backbone had struck him, the broken piece would be imbedded in his neck. It's not. It was blown out. He was shot from the front, through the base of the throat. The bullet went out the back of the neck. A soft-nosed bullet – you can tell by the size of the exit hole – from a powerful gun, something like a .38 Colt or Luger or Mauser.'

'Good God above!' For the first time, Swanson was badly shaken. He stared at the thing on the floor, then at me. 'Murdered. You mean he was murdered.'

'Who would have done this?' Hansen said hoarsely. 'Who, man, who? And in God's name, why?'

'I don't know who did it.'

Swanson looked at me, his eyes strange. 'You just found this out?'

'I found out last night.'

'You found out last night.' The words were slow, far-spaced, a distinct hiatus between each two. 'And all the time since, aboard the ship, you never said – you never showed – my God, Carpenter, you're inhuman.'

'Sure,' I said. 'See that gun there. It makes a loud bang and when I use it to kill the man who did this I won't even blink. I'm inhuman, all right.'

'I was speaking out of turn. Sorry.' Swanson was making a visible effort to bring himself under normal control. He looked at the Mannlicher-Schoenauer, then at me, then back at the gun. 'Private revenge is out, Carpenter. No one is going to take the law into his own hands.'

'Don't make me laugh out loud. A morgue isn't a fit place for it. Besides, I'm not through showing you things yet. There's more. Something that I've just found out now. Not last night.' I pointed to another huddled black shape on the ground. 'Care to have a look at this man here?'

'I'd rather not,' Swanson said steadily. 'Suppose you tell us?'

'You can see from where you are. The head. I've cleaned it up. Small hole in the front, in the middle of the face and slightly to the right; larger exit hole at the back of the top of the head. Same gun. Same man behind the gun.'

Neither man said anything. They were too sick, too shocked to say anything.

'Queer path the bullet took,' I went on. 'Ranged sharply upwards. As if the man who fired the shot had been lying or sitting down while his victim stood above him.'

'Yes.' Swanson didn't seem to have heard me. 'Murder. Two murders. This is a job for the authorities, for the police.'

'Sure,' I said. 'For the police. Let's just ring the sergeant at the local station and ask him if he would mind stepping this way for a few minutes.'

'It's not a job for us,' Swanson persisted. 'As captain of an American naval vessel with a duty to discharge I am primarily interested in bringing my ship and the Zebra survivors back to Scotland again.'

'Without endangering the ship?' I asked. 'With a murderer aboard the possibility of endangering the ship does not arise?'

'We don't know he is – or will be – aboard.'

'You don't even begin to believe that yourself. You know he will be. You know as well as I do why this fire broke out and you know damn' well that it was no accident. If there was any accidental element about it it was just the size and extent of the fire. The killer may have miscalculated that. But both time and weather conditions were against him: I don't think he had very much option. The only possible way in which he could obliterate all traces of his crime was to have a fire of sufficient proportions to obliterate those traces. He would have got off with it too, if I hadn't been here, if I hadn't been convinced before we left port that something was very far wrong indeed. But he would take very good care that he wouldn't obliterate himself in the process. Like it or not, Commander, you're going to have a killer aboard your ship.'

'But all of those men have been burned, some very severely—'

'What the hell did you expect? That the unknown X would go about without a mark on him, without as much as a cigarette burn, proclaiming to the world that he had been the one who had been throwing matches about and had then thoughtfully stood to one side? Local colour. He *had* to get himself burnt.'

'It doesn't follow,' Hansen said. 'He wasn't to know that anyone was going to get suspicious and start investigating.'

'You'll be well advised to join your captain in keeping out of the detecting racket,' I said shortly. 'The men behind this are top-flight experts with far-reaching contacts – part of a criminal octopus with tentacles so long that it can even reach out and sabotage your ship in the Holy Loch. Why they did that, I don't know. What matters is that top-flight operators like those *never* take chances. They always operate on the assumption that they *may* be found out. They take every possible precaution against every possible eventuality. Besides, when the fire was at its height – we don't know the story of that, yet – the killer would have had to pitch in and rescue those trapped. It would have seemed damned odd if he hadn't. And so he got burnt.'

'My God.' Swanson's teeth were beginning to chatter with the cold but he didn't seem to notice it. 'What a hellish set-up.'

'Isn't it? I dare say there's nothing in your navy regulations to cover this lot.'

'But what – what are we going to do?'

'We call the cops. That's me.'

'What do you mean?'

'What I say. I have more authority, more official backing, more scope, more power and more freedom of action than any cop you ever saw. You must believe me. What I say is true.'

'I'm beginning to believe it *is* true,' Swanson said in slow thoughtfulness. 'I've been wondering more and more about you in the past twenty-four hours. I've kept telling myself I was wrong, even ten minutes before I kept telling myself. You're a policeman? Or detective?'

'Naval officer. Intelligence. I have credentials in my suitcase which I am empowered to show in an emergency.' It didn't seem the time to tell him just how wide a selection of credentials I did have. 'This is the emergency.'

'But – but you are a doctor.'

'Sure I am. A navy doctor – on the side. My speciality is investigating sabotage in the UK armed forces. The cover-up of research doctor is the ideal one. My duties are deliberately vague and I have the power to poke and pry into all sorts of corners and situations and talk to all sorts of people on the grounds of being an investigating psychologist that would be impossible for the average serving officer.'

There was a long silence, then Swanson said bitterly: 'You might have told us before this.'

'I might have broadcast it all over your Tannoy system. Why the hell should I? I don't want to trip over blundering amateurs every step I take. Ask any cop. The biggest menace of his life is the self-appointed Sherlock. Besides, I couldn't trust you, and before you start getting all hot and bothered about that I might add that I don't mean you'd deliberately give me away or anything like that but that you may inadvertently give me away. Now I've no option but to tell you what I can and chance the consequences. Why couldn't you just have accepted that directive from your Director of Naval Operations and acted accordingly?'

'Directive?' Hansen looked at Swanson. 'What directive?'

'Orders from Washington to give Dr Carpenter here *carte blanche* for practically everything. Be reasonable, Carpenter. I don't like operating in the dark and I'm naturally suspicious. You came aboard in highly questionable circumstances. You knew too damn' much about submarines. You were as evasive as hell. You had this sabotage theory all cut and dried. Damn it, man, of course I had reservations. Wouldn't you have had, in my place?'

'I suppose so. I don't know. Me, I obey orders.'

'Uh-huh. And your orders in this case?'

'Meaning what exactly is all this about,' I sighed. 'It would have to come to this. You must be told now – and you'll understand why your Director of Naval Operations was so anxious that you give me every help possible.'

'We can believe this one?' Swanson asked.

'You can believe this one. The story I spun back in the Holy Loch wasn't all malarkey – I just dressed it up a bit to make sure you'd take me along. They did indeed have a very special item of equipment here – an electronic marvel that was used for monitoring the count-down of Soviet missiles and pin-pointing their locations. This machine was kept in one of the huts now destroyed – the second from the west in the south now. Night and day a giant captive radio-sonde balloon reached thirty thousand feet up into the sky – but it had no radio attached. It was just a huge aerial. Incidentally, I should think that is the reason why the oil fuel appears to have been flung over so large an area – an explosion caused by the bursting of the hydrogen cylinders used to inflate the balloons. They were stored in the fuel hut.'

'Did everybody in Zebra know about this monitoring machine?'

'No. Most of them thought it a device for investigating cosmic rays. Only four people knew what it really was – my brother and the three others who all slept in the hut that housed this machine. Now the hut is destroyed. The free world's most advanced listening-post. You wonder why your DNO was so anxious?'

'Four men?' Swanson looked at me, a faint speculation still in his eye. 'Which four men, Dr Carpenter?'

'Do you have to ask? Four of the seven men you see lying here, Commander.'

He stared down at the floor then looked quickly away. He said: 'You mentioned that you were convinced even before we left port that something was far wrong. Why?'

'My brother had a top-secret code. We had messages sent by himself – he was an expert radio operator. One said that there had been two separate attempts to wreck the monitor. He didn't go into details. Another said that he had been attacked and left unconscious when making a midnight check and found someone bleeding off the gas from the hydrogen cylinders – without the radio-sonde aerial the monitor would have been useless. He was lucky, he was out only for a few minutes, as long again and he would have frozen to death. In the circumstances did you expect me to believe that the fire was unconnected with the attempts to sabotage the monitor?'

'But how would anyone *know* what it was?' Hansen objected. 'Apart from your brother and the other three men, that is?' Like Swanson, he glanced at the floor and, like Swanson looked as hurriedly away. 'For my money this is the work of a psycho. A madman. A coldly calculating criminal would – well, he wouldn't go in for wholesale murder like this. But a psycho would.'

'Three hours ago,' I said, 'before you loaded the torpedo into number three tube you checked the manually controlled levers and the warning lights for the tube bow-caps. In the one case you found that the levers had been disconnected in the open position: in the other you found that the wires had been crossed in a junction-box. Do you think that was the work of a psycho? Another psycho?'

He said nothing. Swanson said: 'What can I do to help, Dr Carpenter?'

'What are you willing to do, Commander?'

'I will not hand over command of the *Dolphin*.' He smiled, but he wasn't feeling like smiling. 'Short of that, I – and the crew of the *Dolphin* – are at your complete disposal. You name, it, Doctor, that's all.'

'This time you believe my story?'

'This time I believe your story.'

I was pleased about that, I almost believed it myself.

Chapter Eight

The hut where we'd found all the Zebra survivors huddled together was almost deserted when we got back to it – only Dr Benson and the two very sick men remained. The hut seemed bigger now, somehow, bigger and colder, and very shabby and untidy like the remnants of a church rummage sale where the housewives have trained for a couple of months before moving up to battle stations. Pieces of clothing, bedding, frayed and shredded blankets, gloves, plates, cutlery and dozens of odds and ends of personal possessions lay scattered all over the floor. The sick men had been too sick – and too glad to be on their way – to worry overmuch about taking too many of their various knick-knacks out of there. All they had wanted out of there was themselves. I didn't blame them.

The two unconscious men had their scarred and frost-bitten faces towards us. They were either sleeping or in a coma. But I took no chances. I beckoned Benson and he came and stood with us in the shelter of the west wall.

I told Benson what I'd told the commander and Hansen. He had to know. As the man who would be in the most constant and closest contact with the sick men, he had to know. I suppose he must have been pretty astonished and shaken, but he didn't show it. Doctors' faces behave as doctors tell them to, when they come across a patient in a pretty critical state of health they don't beat their breasts and break into loud lamentations, as this tends to discourage the patient. This now made three men from the *Dolphin*'s crew who knew what the score was – well, half the score, anyway. Three was enough. I only hoped it wasn't too much.

Thereafter Swanson did the talking: Benson would take it better from him than he would from me. Swanson said: 'Where were you thinking of putting the sick men we've sent back aboard?'

'In the most comfortable places I can find. Officers' quarters, crew's quarters, scattered all over so that no one is upset too much. Spread the load, so to speak.' He paused. 'I didn't know of the latest – um – development at the time. Things are rather different now.'

'They are. Half of them in the wardroom, the other half in the crew's mess – no, the crew's quarters. No reason why they shouldn't be fixed up comfortably. If they wonder at this, you can say it's for ease of medical treatment and that they can all be under constant medical watch, like heart patients in a ward. Get Dr Jolly behind you in this, he seems a co-operative type. And I've no doubt he'll support you in your next move – that all patients are to be stripped, bathed and provided with clean pyjamas. If they're too ill to move, bed-bath. Dr Carpenter here tells me that prevention of infection is of paramount importance in cases of severe burn injuries.'

'And their clothes?'

'You catch on more quickly than I did,' Swanson grunted. 'All their clothes to be taken away and labelled. All contents to be removed and labelled. The clothes, for anyone's information, are to be disinfected and laundered.'

'It might help if I am permitted to know just what we are looking for,' Benson suggested.

Swanson looked at me.

'God knows,' I said. 'Anything and everything. One thing certain – you won't find a gun. Be especially careful in labelling gloves – when we get back to Britain we'll have the experts test them for nitrates from the gun used.'

'If anyone has brought aboard anything bigger than a postage stamp I'll find it,' Benson promised.

'Are you sure?' I asked. 'Even if you brought it aboard yourself?'

'Eh? Me? What the devil are you suggesting?'

'I'm suggesting that something may have been shoved inside your medical kit, even your pockets, when you weren't looking.'

'Good lord.' He dug feverishly into his pockets. 'The idea never occurred to me.'

'You haven't the right type of nasty suspicious mind,' Swanson said dryly. 'Off you go. You too, John.'

They left, and Swanson and I went inside. Once I'd checked that the two men really were unconscious, we went to work. It must have been many years since Swanson had policed a deck or parade-ground, far less doubled as scavenger, but he took to it in the manner born. He was assiduous, painstaking, and missed nothing. Neither did I. We cleared a corner of the hut and brought across there every single article that was either lying on the floor or attached to the still ice-covered walls. Nothing was missed. It was either shaken, turned over, opened or emptied according to what it was. Fifteen minutes and we were all through. If there was anything bigger than a matchstick to be found in that room then we would have found it. But we found nothing. Then we scattered everything back over the floor again until the hut looked more or less as it had been before our search. If either of the two unconscious men came to I didn't want him knowing that we had been looking for anything.

'We're no great shakes in the detecting business,' Swanson said. He looked slightly discouraged.

'We can't find what isn't there to be found. And it doesn't help that we don't know what we're looking for. Let's try for the gun now. May be anywhere, he may even have thrown it away on the ice-cap, though I think that unlikely. A killer never likes to lose his means of killing – and he couldn't have been sure that he wouldn't require it again. There aren't so very many places to search. He wouldn't have left it here, for this is the main bunkhouse and in constant use. That leaves only the met. office and the lab. where the dead are lying.'

'He could have hidden it among the ruins of one of the burnt-out huts,' Swanson objected.

'Not a chance. Our friend has been here for some months now, and he must know exactly the effect those ice-storms have. The spicules silt up against any object that lies in their path. The metal frameworks at the bases of the destroyed buildings are still in position, and the floors of the huts – or where the wooden floors used to be – are covered with solid ice to a depth of from four to six inches. He would have been as well to bury his gun in quick-setting concrete.'

We started on the meteorological hut. We looked in every shelf, every box, every cupboard and had just started ripping the backs off the metal cabinets that housed the meteorological equipment when Swanson said abruptly: 'I have an idea. Back in a couple of minutes.'

He was better than his word. He was back in a minute flat, carrying in his hands four objects that glittered wetly in the lamplight and smelled strongly of petrol. A gun – a Luger automatic – the haft and broken-off blade of a knife and two rubber-wrapped packages which turned out to be spare magazines for the Luger. He said: 'I guess this was what you were looking for.'

'Where did you find them?'

'The tractor. In the petrol tank.'

'What made you think of looking there?'

'Just luck. I got to thinking about your remark that the guy who had used this gun might want to use it again. But if he was to hide it anywhere where it was exposed to the weather it might have become jammed up with ice. Even if it didn't, he might have figured that the metal would contract so that the shells wouldn't fit or that the firing mechanism and lubricating oil would freeze solid. Only two things don't freeze solid in these sub-zero temperatures – alcohol and petrol. You can't hide a gun in a bottle of gin.'

'It wouldn't have worked,' I said. 'Metal would still contract – the petrol is as cold as the surrounding air.'

'Maybe he didn't know that. Or if he did, maybe he just thought it was a good place to hide it, quick and handy.' He looked consideringly at me as I broke the butt and looked at the empty magazine, then said sharply: 'You're smearing that gun a little, aren't you?'

'Fingerprints? Not after being in petrol. He was probably wearing gloves anyway.'

'So why did you want it?'

'Serial number. May be able to trace it. It's even possible that the killer had a police permit for it. It's happened before, believe it or not. And you must remember that the killer believed there would be no suspicion of foul play, far less that a search would be carried out for the gun.

'Anyway, this knife explains the gun. Firing guns is a noisy business and I'm surprised – I was surprised – that the killer risked it. He might have waked the whole camp. But he had to take the risk because he'd gone and snapped off the business end of this little sticker here. This is a very slender blade, the kind of blade it's very easy to snap unless you know exactly what you're doing, especially when extreme cold makes the metal brittle. He probably struck a rib or broke the blade trying to haul it out – a knife slides in easily enough but it can jam against cartilage or bone when you try to remove it.'

'You mean – you mean the killer murdered a *third* man?' Swanson asked carefully. 'With this knife?'

'The third man but the first victim,' I nodded. 'The missing half of the blade will be stuck inside someone's chest. But I'm not going to look for it – it would be pointless and take far too long.'

'I'm not sure that I don't agree with Hansen,' Swanson said slowly. 'I know it's impossible to explain away the sabotage on the boat – but, my God, this looks like the work of a maniac. All this – all this senseless killing.'

'All this killing,' I agreed. 'But not senseless – not from the point of view of the killer. No, don't ask me, I don't know what his point of view was – or is. I know – you know – why he started the fire: what we don't know is why he killed those men in the first place.'

Swanson shook his head, then said: 'Let's get back to the other hut. I'll phone for someone to keep a watch over those sick men. I don't know about you, but I'm frozen stiff. And you had no sleep last night.'

'I'll watch them meantime,' I said. 'For an hour or so. And I've some thinking to do, some very hard thinking.'

'You haven't much to go on, have you?'

'That's what makes it so hard.'

I'd said to Swanson that I didn't have much to go on, a less than accurate statement, for I didn't have anything to go on at all. So I didn't waste any time thinking. Instead I took a lantern and went once again to the lab. where the dead men lay. I was cold and tired and alone, and the darkness was falling and I didn't very much fancy going there. Nobody would have fancied going there, a place of dreadful death which any sane person would have avoided like the plague. And that was why I was going there, not because I wasn't sane, but because it was a place that no man would ever voluntarily visit – unless he had an extremely powerful motivation, such as the intention of picking up some essential thing he had hidden there in the near certainty that no one else would ever go near the place. It sounded complicated, even to me. I was very tired. I made a fuzzy mental note to ask around, when I got back to the *Dolphin*, to find out who had suggested shifting the dead men in there.

The walls of the lab. were lined with shelves and cupboards containing jars and bottles and retorts and test-tubes and such-like chemical junk, but I didn't give them more than a glance. I went to the corner of the hut where the dead men lay most closely together, shone my torch along the side of the room and found what I was looking for in a matter of seconds – a floorboard standing slightly proud of its neighbours. Two of the blackened contorted lumps that had once been men lay across that board. I moved them just far enough, not liking the job at all, then lifted one end of the loose floorboard.

It looked as if someone had had it in mind to start up a supermarket. In the six-inch space between the floor and the base of the hut were stacked dozens of neatly arranged cans – soup, beef, fruit, vegetables, a fine varied diet with all the proteins and vitamins a man could want. Someone had had no intention of going hungry. There was even a small pressure-stove and a couple of gallons of kerosene to thaw out the cans. And to one side, lying flat, two rows of gleaming Nife cells – there must have been about forty in all.

I replaced the board, left the lab. and went across to the meteorological hut again. I spent over an hour there, unbuttoning the backs of metal cabinets and peering into their innards, but I found nothing. Not what I had hoped to find, that was. But I did come across one very peculiar item, a small green metal box six inches by four by two, with a circular control that was both switch and tuner, and two glassed-in dials with neither figures nor marking on them. At the side of the box was a brass-rimmed hole.

I turned the switch and one of the dials glowed green, a magic-eye tuning device with the fans spread well apart. The other dial stayed dead. I twiddled the tuner control but nothing happened. Both the magic eye and the second dial required something to activate them – something like a pre-set radio signal. The hole in the side would accommodate the plug of any standard telephone receiver. Not many people would have known what this was, but I'd seen one before – a transistorized homing device for locating the direction of a radio signal, such as emitted by the 'Sarah' device on American space capsules which enables searchers to locate it once it has landed in the sea.

What legitimate purpose could be served by such a device in Drift Ice Station Zebra? When I'd told Swanson and Hansen of the existence of a console for monitoring rocket-firing signals from Siberia, that much of my story, anyway, had been true. But that had called for a giant aerial stretching far up into the sky: this comparative toy couldn't have ranged a twentieth of the distance to Siberia.

I had another look at the portable radio transmitter and the now exhausted Nife batteries that served them. The dialling counter was still tuned into the waveband which the *Dolphin* had picked up the distress signals. There was nothing for me there. I looked more closely at the nickel-cadmium cells and saw that they were joined to one another and to the radio set by wire-cored rubber leads with very powerfully spring-loaded saw-tooth clips on the terminals: those last ensured perfect electrical contact as well as being very convenient to use. I undid two of the clips, brought a torch-beam to bear and peered closely at the terminals. The indentations made by the sharpened steel saw-teeth were faint but unmistakable.

I made my way back to the laboratory hut, lifted the loose floorboard again and shone the torch on the Nife cells lying there. At least half of the cells had the same characteristic markings. Cells that looked fresh and unused, yet they had those same markings and if anything was certain it was that those cells had been brand-new and unmarked when Drift Ice Station Zebra had been first set up. A few of the cells were tucked so far away under adjacent floorboards that I had to stretch my hand far in to reach them. I pulled out two and in the space behind I seemed to see something dark and dull and metallic.

It was too dark to distinguish clearly what the object was but after I'd levered up another two floorboards I could see without any trouble at all. It was a cylinder about thirty inches long and six in diameter with brass stopcock and mounted pressure gauge registering 'full': close beside it was a package about eighteen inches square and four thick, stencilled with the words 'RADIO-SONDE BALLOONS''. Hydrogen, batteries, balloons, corned beef and mulligatawny soup. A catholic enough assortment of stores by any standards; but there wouldn't have been anything haphazard about the choice of that assortment.

When I made it back to the bunkhouse, the two patients were still breathing. That was about all I could say for myself, too, I was shaking with the cold and even clamping my teeth together couldn't keep them from chattering. I thawed out under the big electric heaters until I was only half-frozen, picked up my torch and moved out again into the wind and the cold and the dark. I was a sucker for punishment, that was for sure.

In the next twenty minutes I made a dozen complete circuits of the camp, moving a few yards farther out with each circuit. I must have walked over a mile altogether and that was all I had for it, just the walk and a slight touch of frost-bite high up on the cheekbones, the only part of my face, other than the eyes, exposed to that bitter cold. I knew I had frost-bite for the skin had suddenly ceased to feel cold any more and was quite dead to the touch. Enough was enough and I had a hunch that I was wasting my time anyway. I headed back to the camp.

I passed between the meteorological hut and the lab. and was just level with the eastern end of the bunkhouse when I sensed as much as saw something odd out of the corner of my eye. I steadied the torch-beam on the east wall and peered closely at the sheath of ice that had been deposited there over the days by the ice-storm. Most of the encrustation was of a homogeneous greyish-white, very smooth and polished, but it wasn't all grey-white: it was speckled here and there with dozens of black flecks of odd shapes and sizes, none of them more than an inch square. I tried to touch them but they were deeply imbedded in and showing through the gleaming ice. I went to examine the east wall of the meteorological hut, but it was quite innocent of any such black flecking. So was the east wall of the lab.

A short search inside the meteorological hut turned up a hammer and screw-driver. I chipped away a section of the black-flecked ice, brought it into the bunkhouse and laid it on the floor in front of one of the big electrical heaters. Ten minutes later I had a small pool of water and, lying in it, the sodden remains of what had once been fragments of burnt paper. This was very curious indeed. It meant that there were scores of pieces of burnt paper imbedded in the east wall of the bunkhouse. Just there: nowhere else. The explanation, of course, could be completely innocuous: or not, as the case might be.

I had another look at the two unconscious men. They were warm enough and comfortable enough but that was about all you could say for them. I couldn't see them as fit enough to be moved inside the next twenty-four hours. I lifted the phone and asked for someone to relieve me and when two seamen arrived, I made my way back to the *Dolphin*.

There was an unusual atmosphere aboard ship that afternoon, quiet and dull and almost funereal. It was hardly to be wondered at. As far as the crew of the *Dolphin* had been concerned, the men manning Drift Ice Station Zebra had been just so many ciphers, not even names, just unknowns. But now the burnt, frost-bitten, emaciated survivors had come aboard ship, sick and suffering men each with a life and individuality of his own, and the sight of those wasted men still mourning the deaths of their eight comrades had suddenly brought home to every man on the submarine the full horror of what had happened on Zebra. And, of course less than seven hours had elapsed since their own torpedo officer, Lieutenant Mills, had been killed. Now, even although the mission had been successful, there seemed little enough reason for celebration. Down in the crew's mess the hi-fi and the juke-box were stilled. The ship was like a tomb.

I found Hansen in his cabin. He was sitting on the edge of his pullman bunk, still wearing his fur trousers, his face bleak and hard and cold. He watched me in silence as I stripped off my parka, undid the empty holster tied round my chest, hung it up and stuck inside it the automatic I'd pulled from my caribou pants. Then he said suddenly: 'I wouldn't take them off, Doc. Not if you want to come with us, that is.' He looked at his own furs and his mouth was bitter. 'Hardly the rig of the day for a funeral, is it?'

'You mean—'

'Skipper's in his cabin. Boning up on the burial service. George Mills and that assistant radio operator – Grant, wasn't it it – who died out there to-day. A double funeral. Out on the ice. There's some men there already, chipping a place with crowbars and sledges at the base of a hummock.'

'I saw no one.'

'Port side. To the west.'

'I thought Swanson would have taken young Mills back to the States. Or Scotland.'

'Too far. And there's the psychological angle. You could hardly dent the morale of this bunch we have aboard here far less shoot it to pieces, but carrying a dead man as a shipmate is an unhappy thing. He's had permission from Washington ...' He broke off uncertainly, looked quietly up at me and then away again. I didn't have any need of telepathy to know what was in his mind.

'The seven men on Zebra?' I shook my head. 'No, no funeral service for them. How could you? I'll pay my respects some other way.'

His eyes flickered up at the Mannlicher-Schoenauer hanging in its holster, then away again. He said in a quiet savage voice: 'Goddam his black murderous soul. That devil's aboard here, Carpenter. Here. On our ship.' He smacked a bunched fist hard against the palm of his other hand. 'Have you no idea what's behind this, Doc? No idea who's responsible?'

'If I had, I wouldn't be standing here. Any idea how Benson is getting along with the sick and injured?'

'He's all through. I've just left him.'

I nodded, reached up for the automatic and stuck it in the pocket of my caribou pants. Hansen said quietly: 'Even aboard here?'

'Especially aboard here.' I left him and went along to the surgery. Benson was sitting at his table, his back to his art gallery of technicolour cartoons, making entries in a book. He looked up as I closed the door behind me.

'Find anything?' I asked.

'Nothing that I would regard as interesting. Hansen did most of the sorting. You may find something.' He pointed to neatly folded piles of clothing on the deck, several small attache-cases and a few polythene bags, each labelled. 'Look for yourself. How about the two men left out on Zebra?'

'Holding their own. I think they'll be OK, but it's too early to say yet.' I squatted on the floor, went carefully through all the pockets in the clothes and found, as I had expected, nothing. Hansen wasn't the man to miss anything. I felt every square inch of the lining areas and came up with the same results. I went through the small cases and the polythene bags, small items of clothing and personal gear, shaving kits, letters, photographs, two or three cameras. I broke open the cameras and they were all empty. I said to Benson: 'Dr Jolly brought his medical case aboard with him?'

'Wouldn't even trust one of your own colleagues, would you?'

'No.'

'Neither would I.' He smiled with his mouth only. 'You're an evil influence. I went through every item in it. Not a thing. I even measured the thickness of the bottom of the case. Nothing there.'

'Good enough for me. How are the patients?'

'Nine of them,' Benson said. 'The psychological effect of knowing that they're safe has done them more good than any medication ever could.' He consulted cards on his desk. 'Captain Folsom is the worst. No danger, of course, but his facial burns are pretty savage. We've arranged to have a plastic surgeon standing by in Glasgow when we return. The Harrington twins, both met. officers, are rather less badly burnt, but very weak, from both cold and hunger. Food, warmth and rest will have them on their feet in a couple of days again. Hassard, another met. officer, and Jeremy, a lab. technician, moderate burns, moderate frost-bite, fittest of the lot otherwise – it's queer how different people react so differently to hunger and cold. The other four – Kinnaird, the senior radio operator, Dr Jolly, Naseby, the cook, and Hewson, the tractor-driver and and man who was in charge of the generator – are much of a muchness: they're suffering most severely of all from frost-bite, especially Kinnaird, all with moderate burns, weak, of course, but recovering fast. Only Folsom and the Harrington twins have consented to become bed-patients. The rest we've provided with rigouts of one sort or another. They're all lying down, of course, but they won't be lying down long. All of them are young, tough, and basically very fit – they don't pick children or old men to man places like Drift Station Zebra.'

A knock came to the door and Swanson's head appeared. He said, 'Hallo, back again,' to me then turned to Benson. 'A small problem of medical discipline here, Doctor.' He stood aside to let us see Naseby, the Zebra cook, standing close behind him, dressed in a US Navy's petty officer's uniform. 'It seems that your patients have heard about the funeral service. They want to go along – those who are able, that is – to pay their last respects to their colleagues. I understand and sympathize, of course, but their state of health—'

'I would advise against it, sir,' Benson said. 'Strongly.'

'You can advise what you like, mate,' a voice came from behind Naseby. It was Kinnaird, the cockney radio operator, also clad in blue. 'No offence. Don't want to be rude or ungrateful. But I'm going. Jimmy Grant was my mate.'

'I know how you feel,' Benson said. 'I also know how *I* feel about it – your condition, I mean. You're in no fit state to do anything except lie down. You're making things very difficult for me.'

'I'm the captain of this ship,' Swanson put in mildly. 'I can forbid it, you know. I can say "No," and make it stick.'

'And you are making things difficult for us, sir,' Kinnaird said. 'I don't reckon it would advance the cause of Anglo-American unity very much if we started hauling off at our rescuers an hour or two after they'd saved us from certain death.' He smiled faintly. 'Besides, look at what it might do to our wounds and burns.'

Swanson cocked an eyebrow at me. 'Well, they're your countrymen.'

'Dr Benson is perfectly correct,' I said. 'But it's not worth a civil war. If they could survive five or six days on that damned ice-cap, I don't suppose a few minutes more is going to finish them off.'

'Well, if it does,' Swanson said heavily, 'we'll blame you.'

If I ever had any doubt about it I didn't have then, not after ten minutes out in the open. The Arctic ice-cap was no place for a funeral; but I couldn't have imagined a more promising set-up for a funeral director who wanted to drum up some trade. After the warmth of the *Dolphin* the cold seemed intense and within five minutes we were all shivering violently. The darkness was as nearly absolute as it ever becomes on the ice-cap, the wind was lifting again and thin flurries of snow came gusting through the night. The solitary floodlamp served only to emphasize the ghostly unreality of it all, the huddled circle of mourners with bent heads, the two shapeless canvas-wrapped forms lying huddled at the base of an ice-hummock, Commander Swanson bent over his book, the wind and the snow snatching the half-heard mumble from his lips as he hurried through the burial service. I caught barely one word in ten of the committal and then it was all over, no meaningless rifle salutes, no empty blowing of bugles, just the service and the silence and the dark shapes of stumbling men hurriedly placing fragments of broken ice over the canvas-sheeted forms. And within twenty-four hours the eternally drifting spicules and blowing snow would have sealed them for ever in their icy tomb, and there they might remain for ever, drifting in endless circles about the North Pole; or some day, perhaps a thousand years from then, an ice-lead might open up and drop them down to the uncaring floor of the Arctic, their bodies as perfectly preserved as if they had died only that day. It was a macabre thought.

Heads bent against the snow and ice, we hurried back to the shelter of the *Dolphin*. From the ice-cap to the top of the sail it was a climb of over twenty feet up the almost vertically inclined huge slabs of ice that the submarine had pushed upwards and sideways as she had forced her way through. Hand-lines had been rigged from the top of the sail but even then it was a fairly tricky climb. It was a set-up where with the icy slope, the frozen slippery ropes, the darkness and the blinding effect of the snow and ice, an accident could all too easily happen. And happen it did.

I was about six feet up, giving a hand to Jeremy, the lab. technician from Zebra whose burnt hands made it almost impossible for him to climb alone, when I heard a muffled cry above me. I glanced up and had a darkly-blurred impression of someone teetering on top of the sail, fighting for his balance, then jerked Jeremy violently towards me to save him from being swept away as that same someone lost his footing, toppled over backwards and hurtled down past us on to the ice below. I winced at the sound of the impact, two sounds, rather, a heavy muffled thud followed immediately by a sharper, crisper crack. First the body, then the head. I half imagined that I heard another sound afterwards, but couldn't be sure. I handed Jeremy over to the care of someone else and slithered down an ice-coated rope, not looking forward very much to what I must see. The fall had been the equivalent of a twenty-foot drop on to a concrete floor.

Hansen had got there before me and was shining his torch down not on to one prostrate figure as I had expected, but two. Benson and Jolly, both of them out cold.

I said to Hansen: 'Did you see what happened?'

'No. Happened too quickly. All I know is that it was Benson that did the falling and Jolly that did the cushioning. Jolly was beside me only a few seconds before the fall.'

'If that's the case then Jolly probably saved your doctor's life. We'll need to strap them in stretchers and haul them up and inside. We can't leave them out here.'

'Stretchers? Well, yes, if you say so. But they might come round any minute.'

'One of them might. But one of them is not going to come round for a long time. You heard that crack when a head hit the ice, it was like someone being clouted over the head with a fence-post. And I don't know which it is yet.'

Hansen left. I stooped over Benson and eased back the hood of the duffel-coat he was wearing. A fence-post was just about right. The side of his head, an inch above the right ear, was a blood-smeared mess, a three-inch long gash in the purpling flesh with the blood already coagulating in the bitter cold. Two inches farther forward and he'd have been a dead man, the thin bone behind the temple would have shattered under such an impact. For Benson's sake, I hoped the rest of his skull was pretty thick. No question but that this had been the sharp crack I'd heard.

Benson's breathing was very shallow, the movement of his chest barely discernible. Jolly's, on the other hand, was fairly deep and regular. I pulled back his anorak hood, probed carefully over his head and encountered a slight puffiness far back, near the top of the left-hand side. The inference seemed obvious. I hadn't been imagining things when I thought I had heard a second sound after the sharp crack caused by Benson's head striking against the ice. Jolly must have been in the way of the falling Benson, not directly enough beneath him to break his fall in any way but directly enough to be knocked backwards on to the ice and clout the back of his head as he fell.

It took ten minutes to have them strapped in stretchers, taken inside and placed in a couple of temporary cots in the sick-bay. With Swanson waiting anxiously I attended to Benson first, though there was little enough I could do, and had just started on Jolly when his eyes flickered and he slowly came back to consciousness, groaning a bit and trying to hold the back of his head. He made to sit up in his cot but I restrained him.

'Oh, lord, my head.' Several times he squeezed his eyes tightly shut, opened them wide, focused with difficulty on the bulkhead riotous with the colour of Benson's cartoon characters, then looked away as if he didn't believe it. 'Oh, my word, that must have been a dilly. Who did it, old boy?'

'Did what?' Swanson asked.

'Walloped me on the old bean. Who? Eh?'

'You mean to say you don't remember?'

'Remember?' Jolly said irritably. 'How the devil should I . . .' He broke off as his eye caught sight of Benson in the adjacent cot, a huddled figure under the blankets with only the back of his head and a big gauze pack covering his wound showing. 'Of course, of course. Yes, that's it. He fell on top of me, didn't he?'

'He certainly did,' I said. 'Did you try to catch him?'

'Catch him? No, I didn't try to catch him. I didn't try to get out of the way either. It was all over in half a second. I just don't remember a thing about it.' He groaned a bit more then looked across at Benson. 'Came a pretty nasty cropper, eh? Must have done.'

'Looks like it. He's very severely concussed. There's X-ray equipment here and I'll have a look at his head shortly. Damned hard luck on you too, Jolly.'

'I'll get over it,' he grunted. He pushed off my hand and sat up. 'Can I help you?'

'You may not,' Swanson said quietly. 'Early supper then twelve hours solid for you and the eight others, Doctor, and those are *my* doctor's orders. You'll find supper waiting in the wardroom now.'

'Aye, aye, sir.' Jolly gave a ghost of a smile and pushed himself groggily to his feet. 'That bit about the twelve hours sounds good to me.'

After a minute or two, when he was steady enough on his feet, he left. Swanson said: 'What now?'

'You might inquire around to see who was nearest or near to Benson when he slipped climbing over the edge of the bridge. But discreetly. It might do no harm if at the same time you hinted around that maybe Benson had just taken a turn.'

'What are *you* hinting at?' Swanson asked slowly.

'Did he fall or was he pushed? that's what I'm hinting at.'

'Did he fall or . . .' He broke off then went on warily: 'Why should anyone want to push Dr Benson?'

'Why should anyone want to kill seven – eight, now – men in Drift Ice Station Zebra?'

'You have a point,' Swanson acknowledged quietly. He left.

Making X-ray pictures wasn't very much in my line but apparently it hadn't been very much in Dr Benson's line either for he'd written down, for his own benefit and guidance, a detailed list of instructions for the taking and development of X-ray pictures. I wondered how he would have felt if he had known that the first beneficiary of his meticulous thoroughness was to be himself. The two finished negatives I came up with wouldn't have caused any furore in the Royal Photographic Society, but they were enough for my wants.

By and by Commander Swanson returned, closing the door behind him. I said: 'Ten gets one that you got nothing.'

'You won't die a poor man,' he nodded. 'Nothing is what it is. So Chief Torpedoman Patterson tells me, and you know what he's like.'

I knew what he was like. Patterson was the man responsible for all discipline and organization among the enlisted men and Swanson had said to me that he regarded Patterson, and not himself, as the most indispensable man on the ship.

'Patterson was the man who reached the bridge immediately before Benson,' Swanson said. 'He said he heard Benson cry out, swung round and saw him already beginning to topple backwards. He didn't recognize who it was at the time, it was too dark and snowy for that. He said he had the impression that Benson had already had one hand and one knee on the bridge coaming when he fell backwards.'

'A funny position in which to start falling backwards,' I said. 'Most of his body weight must already have been inboard. And even if he did topple outwards he would surely still have had plenty of time to grab the coaming with both hands.'

'Maybe he did take a turn,' Swanson suggested. 'And don't forget that the coaming is glass-slippery with its smooth coating of ice.'

'As soon as Benson disappeared Patterson ran to the side to see what had happened to him?'

'He did,' Swanson said wearily. 'And he said there wasn't a person within ten feet of the top of the bridge when Benson fell.'

'And who *was* ten feet below?'

'He couldn't tell. Don't forget how black it was out there on the ice-cap and that the moment Patterson had dropped into the brightly lit bridge he'd lost whatever night-sight he'd built up. Besides, he didn't wait for more than a glance. He was off for a stretcher even before you or Hansen got to Benson. Patterson is not the sort of man who has to be told what to do.'

'So it's a dead end there?'

'A dead end.'

I nodded, crossed to a cupboard and brought back the two X-rays, still wet, held in their metal clips. I held them up to the light for Swanson's inspection.

'Benson?' he asked, and when I nodded peered at them more closely and finally said: 'That line there – a fracture?'

'A fracture. And not a hair-line one either, as you can see. He really caught a wallop.'

'How bad is it? How long before he comes out of this coma – he *is* in a coma?'

'He's all that. How long? If I were a lad fresh out of medical school I'd let you have a pretty confident estimate. If I were a top-flight brain surgeon I'd say anything from half an hour to a year or two, because people who really know what they are talking about are only too aware that we know next to nothing about the brain. Being neither, I'd guess at two or three days – and my guess could be hopelessly wrong. There may be cerebral bleeding. I don't know. I don't think so. Blood-pressure, respiration and temperature shows no evidence of organic damage. And now you know as much about it as I do.'

'Your colleagues wouldn't like that.' Swanson smiled faintly. 'This cheerful confession of ignorance does nothing to enhance the mystique of your profession. How about your other patients – the two men still out in Zebra?'

'I'll see them after supper. Maybe they'll be fit enough to be brought here to-morrow. Meanwhile, I'd like to ask a favour of you. Could you lend me the services of your Torpedoman Rawlings? And would you have any objections to his being taken into our confidence?'

'Rawlings? I don't know why you want him, but why Rawlings? The officers and petty officers aboard this ship are the pick of the United States Navy. Why not one of them? Besides, I'm not sure that I like the idea of passing on to an enlisted man secrets denied to my officers.'

'They're strictly non-naval secrets. The question of hierarchy doesn't enter into it. Rawlings is the man I want. He's got a quick mind, quick reflexes, and a dead-pan give-away-nothing expression that is invaluable in a game like this. Besides, in the event – the unlikely event, I hope – of the killer suspecting that we're on to him, he wouldn't look for any danger from one of your enlisted men because he'd be certain that we wouldn't let them in on it.'

'What do you want him for?'

'To keep a night guard on Benson here.'

'On Benson?' A fractional narrowing of the eyes, that could have been as imagined as real, was the only change in Swanson's impassive face. 'So you don't think it was an accident, do you?'

'I don't honestly know. But I'm like yourself when you carry out a hundred and one different checks, most of which you know to be unnecessary, before you take your ship to sea – I'm taking no chances. If it wasn't an accident – then someone might have an interest in doing a really permanent job next time.'

'But how can Benson represent a danger to anyone?' Swanson argued. 'I'll wager anything you like, Carpenter, that Benson doesn't – or didn't – know a thing about them that could point a finger at anyone. If he did, he'd have told me straight away. He was like that.'

'Maybe he saw or heard something the significance of which he didn't then realize. Maybe the killer is frightened that if Benson has time enough to think about it the significance will dawn on him. Or maybe it's all a figment of my overheated imagination: maybe he just fell. But I'd still like to have Rawlings.'

'You shall have him.' Swanson rose to his feet and smiled. 'I don't want you quoting that Washington directive at me again.'

Two minutes later Rawlings arrived. He was dressed in a light brown shirt and overall pants, obviously his own conception of what constituted the well-dressed submariner's uniform, and for the first time in our acquaintance he didn't smile a greeting. He didn't even glance at Benson on his cot. His face was still and composed, without any expression.

'You sent for me, sir?' 'Sir,' not 'Doc.'

'Take a seat, Rawlings.' He sat, and as he did I noticed the heavy bulge in the twelve-inch thigh pocket on the side of his overall pants. I nodded and said: 'What have you got there? Doesn't do much for the cut of your natty suiting, does it?'

He didn't smile. He said. 'I always carry one or two tools around with me. That's what the pocket is for.'

'Let's see this particular tool,' I said.

He hesitated briefly, shrugged and, not without some difficulty, pulled a heavy gleaming drop-forged steel pipe-wrench from the pocket. I hefted it in my hand.

'I'm surprised at you, Rawlings,' I said. 'What do you think the average human skull is made of – concrete? One little tap with this thing and you're up on a murder or manslaughter charge.' I picked up a roll of bandage. 'Ten yards of this wrapped round the business end will automatically reduce the charge to one of assault and battery.'

'I don't know what you're talking about,' he said mechanically.

'I'm talking about the fact that when Commander Swanson, Lieutenant Hansen and I were inside the laboratory this afternoon and you and Murphy were outside, you must have kind of leaned your ear against the door and heard more than was good for you. You know there's something far wrong and though you don't know what your motto is "be prepared". Hence the cosh. Correct?'

'Correct.'

'Does Murphy know?'

'No.'

'I'm a naval intelligence officer. Washington know all about me. Want the captain to vouch for me?'

'Well, no.' The first faint signs of a grin. 'I heard you pull a gun on the skipper, but you're still walking about loose. You must be in the clear.'

'You heard me threaten the captain and Lieutenant Hansen with a gun. But then you were sent away. You heard nothing after that?'

'Nothing.'

'Three men have been murdered in Zebra. Two shot, one knifed. Their bodies were burned to conceal traces of the crime. Four others died in the fire. The killer is aboard this ship.'

Rawlings said nothing. His eyes were wide, his face pale and shocked. I told him everything I'd told Swanson and Hansen and emphasized that he was to keep it all to himself. Then I finished: 'Dr Benson here has been seriously hurt. A deliberate attempt for God knows what reason, may have been made on his life. We don't know. But if it was a deliberate attempt, then it's failed – so far.'

Rawlings had brought himself under control. He said, his voice as empty of expression as his face: 'Our little pal might come calling again?'

'He may. No member of the crew except the captain, the executive officer or I will come here. Anyone else – well, you can start asking him questions when he recovers consciousness.'

'You recommended ten yards of this bandage, Doc?'

'It should be enough. And only a gentle tap, for God's sake. Above and behind the ear. You might sit behind that curtain there where no one can see you.'

'I'm feeling lonesome to-night,' Rawlings murmured. He broke open the bandage, started winding it around the head of the wrench and glanced at the cartoon-decorated bulkhead beside him. 'Even old Yogi Bear ain't no fit companion for me to-night. I hope I have some other company calling.'

I left him there. I felt vaguely sorry for anyone who should come calling, killer or not. I felt, too, that I had taken every possible precaution. But when I left Rawlings there guarding Benson I did make one little mistake. Just one. I left him guarding the wrong man.

The second accident of the day happened so quickly, so easily, so inevitably that it might almost have been just that – an accident.

At supper that evening I suggested that, with Commander Swanson's permission, I'd have a surgery at nine next morning; because of enforced neglect most of the burn wounds were suppurating fairly badly, requiring constant cleaning and changing of coverings: I also thought it about time that an X-ray inspection be made of Zabrinski's broken ankle. Medical supplies in the sick-bay were running short. Where did Benson keep his main supplies? Swanson told me and detailed Henry, the steward, to show me where it was.

About ten that night, after I'd returned from seeing the two men out on Zebra, Henry led me through the now deserted control room and down the ladder which led to the inertial navigation room and the electronics space, which abutted on it. He undid the strong-back clamp on the square heavy steel hatch in a corner of the electronics room and with an assist from me – the hatch must have weighed about 150 pounds – swung it up and back until the hatch clicked home on its standing latch.

Three rungs on the inside of the hatch-cover led on to the vertical steel ladder that reached down to the deck below. Henry went down first, snapping on the light as he went, and I followed.

The medical storage room, though tiny, was equipped on the same superbly lavish scale as was everything else on the *Dolphin*. Benson, as thoroughly meticulous in this as he had been in his outlining of X-ray procedure, had everything neatly and logically labelled so that it took me less than three minutes to find everything I wanted. I went up the ladder first, stopped near the top, stretched down and took the bag of supplies from Henry, swung it up on the deck above, then reached up quickly with my free hand to grab the middle of the three rungs welded on the lower side of the hatch cover to haul myself up on to the deck of the electronics space. But I didn't haul myself up. What happened was that I hauled the hatch cover down. The retaining latch had become disengaged, and the 150-pound dead weight of that massive cover was swinging down on top of me before I could even begin to realize what was happening.

I fell half-sideways, half-backwards, pulling the hatch cover with me. My head struck against the hatch coaming. Desperately I ducked my head forward – if it had been crushed between the coaming and the falling cover the two sides of my skull would just about have met in the middle – and tried to snatch my left arm back inside. I was more or less successful with my head – I had it clear of the coaming and was ducking so quickly that the impact of the cover was no more than enough to give me a slight headache afterwards; but my left arm was a different matter altogether. I almost got it clear – but only almost. If my left hand and wrist had been strapped to a steel block and a gorilla had had a go at it with a sledge-hammer, the effect couldn't have been more agonizing. For a moment or two I hung there, trapped, dangling by my left wrist, then the weight of my body tore the mangled wrist and hand through the gap and I crashed down to the deck beneath. Then the gorilla seemed to have another go with the sledge-hammer and consciousness went.

'I won't beat about the bush, old lad,' Jolly said. 'No point in it with a fellow pill-roller. Your wrist is a mess – I had to dig half your watch out of it. The middle and little fingers are broken, the middle in two places. But the permanent damage, I'm afraid, is to the back of your hand – the little and ring finger tendons have been sliced.'

'What does that mean?' Swanson asked.

'It means that in his left hand he'll have to get by with two fingers and a thumb for the rest of his life,' Jolly said bluntly.

Swanson swore softly and turned to Henry. 'How in God's name could you have been so damnably careless? An experienced submariner like you? You know perfectly well that you are required to make a visual check every time a hatch cover engages in a standing latch. Why didn't you?'

'I didn't need to, sir,' Henry was looking more dyspeptic and forlorn than ever. 'I heard it click and I gave a tug. It was fixed, all right. I can swear to it, sir.'

'How could it have been fixed? Look at Dr Carpenter's hand. Just a hair-line engagement and the slightest extra pressure – my God, why can't you people obey regulations?'

Henry stared at the deck in silence. Jolly, who was understandably looking about as washed-out as I felt, packed away the tools of his trade, advised me to take a couple of days off, gave me a handful of pills to take, said a weary good-night and climbed up the ladder leading from the electronics space, where he had been fixing my hand. Swanson said to Henry: 'You can go now, Baker.' It was the first time I'd ever heard anyone address Henry by his surname, a sufficient enough token of what Swanson regarded as the enormity of his crime. 'I'll decide what to do about this in the morning.'

'I don't know about the morning,' I said after Henry was gone. 'Maybe the next morning. Or the one after that. Then you can apologize to him. You and me both. That cover was locked on its standing latch. *I* checked it visually, Commander Swanson.'

Swanson gave me his cool impassive look. After a moment he said quietly: 'Are you suggesting what I think you are suggesting?'

'Someone took a risk,' I said. 'Not all that much of a risk, though – most people are asleep now and the control room was deserted at the moment that mattered. Someone in the wardroom to-night heard me ask your permission to go down to the medical store and heard you giving your okay. Shortly after that nearly everyone turned in. One man didn't – he kept awake and hung around patiently until I came back from the Drift Station. He followed us down below – he was lucky, Lieutenant Sims, your officer on deck, was taking star-sights up on the bridge and the control room was empty – and he unhooked the latch but left the hatch cover in a standing position. There was a slight element of gambling as to whether I would come up first, but not all that much, it would have been a matter of elementary courtesy, he would have thought, for Henry to see me up first. Anyway, he won his gamble, slight though it was. After that our unknown friend wasn't quite so lucky – I think he expected the damage to be a bit more permanent.'

'I'll get inquiries under way immediately,' Swanson said. 'Whoever was responsible, someone must have seen him. Someone must have heard him leaving his cot—'

'Don't waste your time, Commander. We're up against a highly intelligent character who doesn't overlook the obvious. Not only that but word of your inquiries is bound to get around and you'd scare him under cover where I'd never get at him.'

'Then I'll just keep the whole damned lot under lock and key until we get back to Scotland,' Swanson said grimly. '*That* way there'll be no more trouble.'

'That way we'll *never* find out who the murderer of my brother and the six – seven now – others are. Whoever it is has to be given sufficient rope to trip himself up.'

'Good lord, man, we can't just sit back and let things be done to us.' A hint of testiness in the commander's voice and I couldn't blame him. 'What do we – what do *you* propose to do now?'

'Start at the beginning. To-morrow morning we'll hold a court of inquiry among the survivors. Let's find out all we can about that fire. Just an innocent above-board fact-finding inquiry – for the Ministry of Supply, let us say. I've an idea we might turn up something very interesting indeed.'

'You think so?' Swanson shook his head. 'I don't believe it. I don't believe it for a moment. Look what's happened to you. It's obvious, man, that someone knows or suspects that you're on to them. They'll take damned good care to give nothing away.'

'You think that's why I was clouted to-night?'

'What other reason could there be?'

'Was that why Benson was hurt?'

'We don't know that he was. Deliberately, I mean. May have been pure coincidence.'

'Maybe it was,' I agreed. 'And again maybe it wasn't. My guess, for what it's worth, is that the accident or accidents have nothing at all to do with any suspicions the killer may have that we're on to him. Anyway, let's see what to-morrow brings.'

It was midnight when I got back to my cabin. The engineer officer was on watch and Hansen was asleep so I didn't put on any light lest I disturb him. I didn't undress, just removed my shoes, lay down on the cot and pulled a cover over me.

I didn't sleep. I couldn't sleep. My left arm from the elbow downwards still felt as if it were caught in a bear-trap. Twice I pulled from my pocket the pain-killers and sleeping-tablets that Jolly had given me and twice I put them away.

Instead I just lay there and thought and the first and most obvious conclusion I came up with was that there was someone aboard the *Dolphin* who didn't care any too much for the members of the medical profession. Then I got to wondering why the profession was so unpopular and after half an hour of beating my weary brain-cells around I got silently to my feet and made my way on stockinged soles to the sick-bay.

I passed inside and closed the door softly behind me. A red night-light burnt dully in one corner of the bay, just enough to let me see the huddled form of Benson lying on a cot. I switched on the overhead light, blinked in the sudden fierce wash of light and looked at the curtain at the other end of the bay. Nothing stirred behind it. I said: 'Just kind of take your itching fingers away from that pipewrench, Rawlings. It's me, Carpenter.'

The curtain was pulled to one side and Rawlings appeared, the pipe-wrench, with its bandage-wrapped head, dangling from one hand. He had a disappointed look on his face.

'I was expecting someone else,' he said reproachfully. 'I was kinda hoping – my God, Doc, what's happened to your arm?'

'Well may you ask, Rawlings. Our little pal had a go at me to-night. I think he wanted me out of the way. Whether he wanted me out of the way permanently or not I don't know, but he near as a toucher succeeded.' I told him what had happened, then asked him: 'Is there any man aboard you can trust absolutely?' I knew the answer before I had asked the question.

'Zabrinski,' he said unhesitatingly.

'Do you think you could pussy-foot along to wherever it is that he's sleeping and bring him here without waking up anyone?'

He didn't answer my questions. He said: 'He can't walk, Doc, you know that.'

'Carry him. You're big enough.'

He grinned and left. He was back with Zabrinski inside three minutes. Three-quarters of an hour later, after telling Rawlings he could call off his watch, I was back in my cabin.

Hansen was still asleep. He didn't wake even when I switched on a side light. Slowly, clumsily, painfully, I dressed myself in my furs, unlocked my case and drew out the Luger, the two rubber-covered magazines and the broken knife which Commander Swanson had found in the tractor's petrol tank. I put those in my pocket and left. As I passed through the control room I told the officer on deck that I was going out to check on the two patients still left out in the camp. As I had pulled a fur mitten over my injured hand he didn't raise any eyebrows, doctors were a law to themselves and I was just the good healer *en route* to give aid and comfort to the sick.

I did have a good look at the two sick men, both of whom seemed to me to be picking up steadily, then said 'good-night' to the two *Dolphin* crewmen who were watching over them. But I didn't go straight back to the ship. First I went to the tractor shed and replaced the gun, magazines and broken knife in the tractor tank. Then I went back to the ship.

Chapter Nine

'I'm sorry to have to bother you with all these questions,' I said pleasantly. 'But that's the way it is with all government departments. A thousand questions in quadruplicate and each of them more pointlessly irritating than the rest. But I have this job to do and the report to be radioed off as soon as possible and I would appreciate all the information and co-operation you can give me. First off, has anyone any idea at all how this damnable fire started?'

I hoped I sounded like a Ministry of Supply official which was what I'd told them I was – making a Ministry of Supply report. I'd further told them, just to nip any eyebrow-raising in the bud, that it was the Ministry of Supply's policy to send a doctor to report on any accident where loss of life was involved. Maybe this was the case. I didn't know and I didn't care.

'Well, I was the first to discover the fire, I think,' Naseby, the Zebra cook, said hesitantly. His Yorkshire accent was very pronounced. He was still no picture of health and strength but for all that he was a hundred per cent improved on the man I had seen yesterday. Like the other eight survivors of Drift Ice Station Zebra who were present in the wardroom that morning, a long night's warm sleep and good food had brought about a remarkable change for the better. More accurately, like seven others. Captain Folsom's face had been so hideously burnt that it was difficult to say what progress he was making although he had certainly had a good enough breakfast, almost entirely liquid, less than half an hour previously.

'It must have been about two o'clock in the morning,' Naseby went on. 'Well, near enough two. The place was already on fire. Burning like a torch, it was. I—'

'What place?' I interrupted. 'Where were you sleeping?'

'In the cookhouse. That was also our dining-hall. Farthest west hut in the north row.'

'You slept there alone?'

'No. Hewson, here, and Flanders and Bryce slept there also. Flanders and Bryce, they're – they were – lab. technicians. Hewson and I slept at the very back of the hut, then there were two big cupboards, one each side, that held all the food stores, then Flanders and Bryce slept in the dining-hall itself, by a corner of the galley.'

'They were nearest the door?'

'That's right. I got up, coughing and choking with smoke, very groggy, and I could see flames already starting to eat through the east wall of the hut. I shook Hewson then ran for the fire extinguisher – it was kept by the door. It wouldn't work. Jammed solid with the cold, I suppose. I don't know. I ran back in again. I was blind by this time, you never saw smoke like it in your life. I shook Flanders and Bryce and shouted at them to get out then I bumped into Hewson and told him to run and wake Captain Folsom here.'

I looked at Hewson. 'You woke Captain Folsom?'

'I went to wake him. But not straight away. The whole camp was blazing like the biggest Fifth of November bonfire you ever saw and flames twenty feet high were sweeping down the lane between the two rows of huts. The air was full of flying oil, a lot of it burning. I had to make a long swing to the north to get clear of the oil and the flames.'

'The wind was from the east?'

'Not quite. Not that night. South-east, I would say. East-south-east would be more like it, rather. Anyway, I gave a very wide berth to the generator house – that was the one next the dining-hall in the north row – and reached the main bunkhouse. That was the one you found us in.'

'Then you woke Captain Folsom?'

'He was already gone. Shortly after I'd left the dining-hall the fuel drums in the fuel storage hut – that was the one directly south of the main bunkhouse – started exploding. Like bloody great bombs going off they were, the noise they made. They would have waked the dead. Anyway, they woke Captain Folsom. He and Jeremy here' – he nodded at a man sitting across the table from him – 'had taken the fire extinguisher from the bunkhouse and tried to get close to Major Halliwell's hut.'

'That was the one directly west of the fuel store?'

'That's right. It was an inferno. Captain Folsom's extinguisher worked well enough but he couldn't get close enough to do any good. There was so much flying oil in the air that even the extinguisher foam seemed to burn.'

'Hold on a minute,' I said. 'To get back to my original question. How did the fire start?'

'We've discussed that a hundred times among ourselves,' Dr Jolly said wearily. 'The truth is, old boy, we haven't a clue. We know *where* it started all right: match the huts destroyed against the wind direction that night and it could only have been in the fuel store. But how? It's anybody's guess. I don't see that it matters a great deal now.'

'I disagree. It matters very much. If we could find out how it started we might prevent another such tragedy later on. That's why I'm here. Hewson, you were in charge of the fuel store and generator hut. Have you no opinion on this?'

'None. It *must* have been electrical, but how I can't guess. It's possible that there was a leakage from one of the fuel drums and that oil vapour was present in the air. There were two black heaters in the fuel store, designed to keep the temperature up to zero Fahrenheit, so that the oil would always flow freely. Arcing across the make and break of the thermostats might have ignited the gas. But it's only a wild guess, of course.'

'No possibility of any smouldering rags or cigarette ends being the cause?' Hewson's face turned a dusky red.

'Look, mister, I know my job. Burning rags, cigarette ends – I know how to keep a bloody fuel store—'

'Keep your shirt on,' I interrupted. 'No offence. I'm only doing *my* job.' I turned back to Naseby. 'After you'd sent Hewson here to rouse up Captain Folsom, what then?'

'I ran across to the radio room – that's the hut due south of the cookhouse and west of Major Halliwell's—'

'But those two lab. technicians – Flanders and Bryce, wasn't it – surely you checked they were awake and out of it before you left the dining-hall?'

'God help me, I didn't.' Naseby stared down at the deck, his shoulders hunched, his face bleak. 'They're dead. It's my fault they're dead. But you don't know what it was like inside that dining-hall. Flames were breaking through the east wall, the place was full of choking smoke and oil, I couldn't see, I could hardly breathe. I shook them both and shouted at them to get out. I shook them hard and I certainly shouted loud enough.'

'I can bear him out on that,' Hewson said quietly. 'I was right beside him at the time.'

'I didn't wait,' Naseby went on. 'I wasn't thinking of saving my own skin. I thought Flanders and Bryce were all right and that they would be out the door on my heels. I wanted to warn the others. It wasn't – it wasn't until minutes later that I realized that there was no sign of them. And then – well, then it was too late.'

'You ran across to the radio room. That's where you slept, Kinnaird, wasn't it?'

'That's where I slept, yes.' His mouth twisted. 'Me and my mate Grant, the boy that died yesterday. And Dr Jolly slept in the partitioned-off east end of the hut. That's where he had his surgery and the little cubby-hole where he carried out his tests on ice samples.'

'So your end would have started to go on fire first?' I said to Jolly.

'Must have done,' he agreed. 'Quite frankly, old chap, my recollection of the whole thing is just like a dream – a nightmare, rather. I was almost asphyxiated in my sleep, I think. First thing I remember was young Grant bending over me, shaking me and shouting. Can't recall what he was shouting but it must have been that the hut was on fire. I don't know what I said or did, probably nothing, for the next thing I clearly remember was being hit on both sides of the face, and not too gently either. But, by jove, it worked! I got to my feet and he dragged me out of my office into the radio room. I owe my life to young Grant. I'd just enough sense left to grab the emergency medical kit that I always kept packed.'

'What woke Grant?'

'Naseby, here, woke him.' Kinnaird said. 'He woke us both, shouting and hammering on the door. If it hadn't been for him Dr Jolly and I would both have been goners, the air inside that place was like poison gas and I'm sure

if Naseby hadn't shouted on us we would never have woken up. I told Grant
to waken the doctor while I tried to get the outside door open.'
'It was locked?'
'The damned thing was jammed. That was nothing unusual at night.
During the day when the heaters were going full blast to keep the huts at
a decent working temperature the ice around the doors tended to melt: at
night, when we got into our sleeping-bags, we turned our heaters down and
the melted ice froze hard round the door openings, sealing it solid. That
happened most nights in most of the huts – usually had to break our way
out in the morning. But I can tell you that I didn't take too long to burst it
open that night.'
'And then?'
'I ran out,' Kinnaird said. 'I couldn't see a thing for black smoke and
flying oil. I ran maybe twenty yards to the south to get some idea of what
was happening. The whole camp seemed to be on fire. When you're woken
up like that at two in the morning, half-blinded, half-asleep and groggy
with fumes your mind isn't at its best, but thank God I'd enough left of my
mind to realize that an S O S radio message was the one thing that was
going to save our lives. So I went back inside the radio hut.'
'We all owe our lives to Kinnaird.' Speaking for the first time was Jeremy,
a burly red-haired Canadian who had been chief technician on the base.
'And if I'd been a bit quicker with my hands we'd have all been dead.'
'Oh, for Christ's sake, mate, shut up,' Kinnaird growled.
'I won't shut up,' Jeremy said soberly. 'Besides, Dr Carpenter wants a
full report. I was first out of the main bunkhouse after Captain Folsom
here. As Hewson said, we tried the extinguisher on Major Halliwell's hut.
It was hopeless from the beginning but we had to do it – after all, we knew
there were four men trapped in there. But, like I say, it was a waste of time.
Captain Folsom shouted that he was going to get another extinguisher and
told me to see how things were in the radio room.
'The place was ablaze from end to end. As I came round as close as I
could to the door at the west end I saw Naseby here bending over Dr Jolly,
who'd keeled over as soon as he had come out into the fresh air. He shouted
to me to give him a hand to drag Dr Jolly clear and I was just about to
when Kinnaird, here, came running up. I saw he was heading straight for
the door of the radio room.' He smiled without humour. 'I thought he had
gone off his rocker. I jumped in front of him, to stop him. He shouted at me
to get out of the way. I told him not to be crazy and he yelled at me – you
had to yell to make yourself heard above the roar of the flames – that he had
to get the portable radio out, that all the oil was gone and the generator and
the cookhouse with all the food were burning up. He knocked me down and
the next I saw was him disappearing through that door. Smoke and flames
were pouring through the doorway. I don't know how he ever got out alive.'
'Was that how you got your face and hands so badly burnt?' Commander
Swanson asked quietly. He was standing in a far corner of the wardroom,
having taken no part in the discussion up till now, but missing nothing all
the same. That was why I had asked him to be present: just because he was
a man who missed nothing.
'I reckon so, sir.'
'I fancy that should earn a trip to Buckingham Palace,' Swanson
murmured.

'The hell with Buckingham Palace,' Kinnaird said violently. 'How about my mate, eh? How about young Jimmy Grant? Can he make the trip to Buckingham Palace? Not now he can't, the poor bastard. Do you know what he was doing? He was still *inside* the radio room when I went back in, sitting at the main transmitter, sending out an S O S on our regular frequency. His clothes were on fire. I dragged him off his seat and shouted to him to grab some Nife cells and get out. I caught up the portable transmitter and a nearby box of Nife cells and ran through the door. I thought Grant was on my heels but I couldn't hear anything, what with the roar of flames and the bursting of fuel drums the racket was deafening. Unless you'd been there you just can't begin to imagine what it was like. I ran far enough clear to put the radio and cells in a safe place. Then I went back. I asked Naseby, who was still trying to bring Dr Jolly round, if Jimmy Grant had come out. He said he hadn't. I started to run for the door again – and, well, that's all I remember.'

'I clobbered him,' Jeremy said with gloomy satisfaction. 'From behind. I had to.'

'I could have killed you when I came round,' Kinnaird said morosely. 'But I guess you saved my life at that.'

'I certainly did, brother.' Jeremy grimaced. 'That was my big contribution that night. Hitting people. After Naseby, here, had brought Dr Jolly round he suddenly started shouting: 'Where's Flanders and Bryce, where's Flanders and Bryce?' Those were the two who had been sleeping with Hewson and himself in the cookhouse. A few others had come down from the main bunkhouse by that time and the best part of a minute had elapsed before we realized that Flanders and Bryce weren't among them. Naseby, here, started back for the cookhouse at a dead run. He was making for the doorway, only there was no doorway left, just a solid curtain of fire where the doorway used to be. I swung at him as he passed and he fell and hit his head on the ice.' He looked at Naseby. 'Sorry again, Johnny, but you were quite crazy at the moment.'

Naseby rubbed his jaw and grinned wearily. 'I can still feel it. And God knows you were right.'

'Then Captain Folsom arrived, along with Dick Foster, who also slept in the main bunkhouse,' Jeremy went on. 'Captain Folsom said he'd tried every other extinguisher on the base and that all of them were frozen solid. He'd heard about Grant being trapped inside the radio room and he and Foster were carrying a blanket apiece, soaked with water. I tried to stop them but Captain Folsom ordered me to stand aside.' Jeremy smiled faintly. 'When Captain Folsom orders people to stand aside – well, they do just that.'

'He and Foster threw the wet blankets over their heads and ran inside. Captain Folsom was out in a few seconds, carrying Grant. I've never seen anything like it, they were burning like human torches. I don't know what happened to Foster, but he never came out. By that time the roofs of both Major Halliwell's hut and the cookhouse had fallen in. Nobody could get anywhere near either of those buildings. Besides, it was far too late by then, Major Halliwell and the three others inside the major's hut and Flanders and Bryce inside the cookhouse must already have been dead. Dr Jolly, here, doesn't think they would have suffered very much – asphyxiation would have got them, like enough, before the flames did.'

'Well,' I said slowly, 'that's as clear a picture of what must have been a very confusing and terrifying experience as we're ever likely to get. It wasn't possible to get anywhere near Major Halliwell's hut?'

'You couldn't have gone within fifteen feet of it and hoped to live,' Naseby said simply.

'And what happened afterwards?'

'I took charge, old boy,' Jolly said. 'Wasn't much to take charge of, though, and what little there was to be done could be done only by myself – fixing up the injured, I mean. I made 'em all wait out there on the ice-cap until the flames had died down a bit and there didn't seem to be any more likelihood of further fuel drums bursting then we all made our way to the bunkhouse where I did the best I could for the injured men. Kinnaird here, despite pretty bad burns, proved himself a first-class assistant doctor. We bedded down the worst of them. Young Grant was in a shocking condition – 'fraid there never really was very much hope for him. And – well, that was about all there was to it.'

'You had no food for the next few days and nights?'

'Nothing at all, old boy. No heat either, except for the standby Coleman lamps that were in the three remaining huts. We managed to melt a little water from the ice, that was all. By my orders everyone remained lying down and wrapped up in what was available in order to conserve energy and warmth.'

'Bit rough on you,' I said to Kinnaird. 'Having to lose any hard-earned warmth you had every couple of hours in order to make those S O S broadcasts.'

'Not only me,' Kinnaird said. 'I'm no keener on frost-bite than anyone else. Dr Jolly insisted that everyone who could should take turn about at sending out the S O S's. Wasn't hard. There was a pre-set mechanical call-up and all anyone had to do was to send this and listen in on the earphones. If any message came through I was across to the met. office in a flash. It was actually Hewson, here, who contacted the ham operator in Bodo and Jeremy who got through to that trawler in the Barents Sea. I carried on from there, of course. Apart from them there were Dr Jolly and Naseby, here, to give a hand, so it wasn't so bad. Hassard, too, took a turn after the first day – he'd been more or less blinded on the night of the fire.'

'You remained in charge throughout, Dr Jolly?' I asked.

'Bless my soul, no. Captain Folsom, here, was in a pretty shocked condition for the first twenty-four hours, but when he'd recovered from that he took over. I'm only a pill-roller, old boy. As a leader of men and a dashing man of action – well, no, quite frankly, old top, I don't see myself in that light at all.'

'You did damned well, all the same.' I looked round the company. 'That most of you won't be scarred for life is due entirely to the quick and highly efficient treatment Dr Jolly gave you under almost impossible circumstances. Well, that's all. Must be a pretty painful experience for all of you, having to relive that night again. I can't see that we can ever hope to find out how the fire started, just one of those chance in a million accidents, what the insurance companies call an act of God. I'm certain, Hewson, that no shadow of negligence attaches to you and that your theory on the outbreak of fire is probably correct. Anyway, although we've paid a hellishly high cost, we've learnt a lesson – never again to site a main fuel store within a hundred yards of the camp.'

The meeting broke up. Jolly bustled off to the sick-bay, not quite managing to conceal his relish at being the only medical officer aboard who wasn't *hors de combat*. He had a busy couple of hours ahead of him – changing bandages on burns, checking Benson, X-raying Zabrinski's broken ankle and resetting the plaster.

I went to my cabin, unlocked my case, took out a small wallet, relocked my case and went to Swanson's cabin. I noticed that he wasn't smiling quite so often now as when I'd first met him in Scotland. He looked up as I came in answer to his call and said without preamble: 'If those two men still out in the camp are in any way fit to be moved I want them both aboard at once. The sooner we're back in Scotland and have some law in on this the happier I'll be. I warned you that this investigation of yours would turn up nothing. Lord knows how short a time it will be before someone else gets clobbered. God's sake, Carpenter, we have a murderer running loose.'

'Three things,' I said. 'Nobody's going to get clobbered any more, that's almost for certain. Secondly, the law, as you call it, wouldn't be allowed to touch it. And in the third place, the meeting this morning was of some use. It eliminated three potential suspects.'

'I must have missed something that you didn't.'

'Not that. I knew something that you didn't. I knew that under the floor of the laboratory were about forty Nife cells in excellent condition – but cells that had been used.'

'The hell you did,' he said softly. 'Sort of forgot to tell me, didn't you?'

'In this line of business I never tell anyone anything unless I think he can help me by having that knowledge.'

'You must win an awful lot of friends and influence an awful lot of people,' Swanson said dryly.

'It gets embarrassing. Now, who could have used cells? Only those who left the bunkhouse from time to time to send out the S O S's. That cuts out Captain Folsom and the Harrington twins – there's no question of any of the three of them having left the bunkhouse at any time. They weren't fit to. So that leaves Hewson, Naseby, Dr Jolly, Jeremy, Hassard and Kinnaird. Take your choice. One of them is a murderer.'

'Why did they want those extra cells?' Swanson asked. 'And if they had those extra cells why did they risk their lives by relying on those dying cells that they did use. Does it make sense to you?'

'There's sense in everything,' I said. If you want evasion, Carpenter has it. I brought out my wallet, spread cards before him. He picked them up, studied them and returned them to my wallet.

'So now we have it,' he said calmly. 'Took quite a while to get round to it, didn't you? The truth, I mean. Officer of M.I.6. Counter-espionage. Government agent, eh? Well, I won't make any song and dance about it, Carpenter, I've known since yesterday what you must be: you couldn't be anything else.' He looked at me in calm speculation. 'You fellows never disclose your identity unless you have to.' He left the logical question unspoken.

'Three reasons why I'm telling you. You're entitled to some measure of my confidence. I want you on my side. And because of what I'm about to tell you, you'd have known anyway. Have you ever heard of the Perkin-Elmer Roti satellite missile tracker camera?'

'Quite a mouthful,' he murmured. 'No.'

'Heard of Samos? Samos III?'

'Satellite and Missile Observation System?' He nodded. 'I have. And what conceivable connection could that have with a ruthless killer running amok on Drift Station Zebra?'

So I told him what connection it could have. A connection that was not only conceivable, not only possible, not only probable, but absolutely certain. Swanson listened very carefully, very attentively, not interrupting even once and at the end of it he leaned back in his chair and nodded. 'You have the right of it, no doubt about that. The question is, who? I just can't wait to see this fiend under close arrest and armed guard.'

'You'd clap him in irons straight away?'

'Good God!' He stared at me. 'Wouldn't you?'

'I don't know. Yes, I do. I'd leave him be. I think our friend is just a link in a very long chain and if we give him enough rope he'll not only hang himself, he'll lead us to the other members of the chain. Besides, I'm not all that sure that there *is* only one murderer: killers have been known to have accomplices before now, Commander.'

'Two of them? You think there may be two killers aboard my ship?' He pursed his lips and squeezed his chin with a thoughtful hand, Swanson's nearest permissible approach to a state of violent agitation. Then he shook his head definitely. 'There may only be one. If that is so, and I knew who he was, I'd arrest him at once. Don't forget, Carpenter, we've hundreds of miles to go under the ice before we're out in the open sea. We can't watch all six of them all the time and there are a hundred and one things that a man with even only a little knowledge of submarines could do that would put us all in mortal danger. Things that wouldn't matter were we clear of the ice, things that would be fatal under it.'

'Aren't you rather overlooking the fact that if the killer did us in he'd also be doing himself in?'

'I don't necessarily share your belief in his sanity. All killers are a little crazy. No matter how excellent their reasons for killing, the very fact that they do kill makes them a rogue human being, an abnormal. You can't judge them by normal standards.'

He was only half-right, but unfortunately that half might apply in this case. Most murderers kill in a state of extreme emotional once-in-a-lifetime stress and never kill again. But our friend in this case had every appearance of being a stranger to emotional stress of any kind – and, besides, he'd killed a great deal more than once.

'Well,' I said doubtfully. 'Perhaps. Yes, I think I do agree with you.' I refrained from specifying our common ground for agreement. 'Who's your candidate for the high jump, Commander?'

'I'm damned if I know. I listened to every word that was said this morning. I watched the face of each man who spoke – and the faces of the ones who weren't speaking. I've been thinking nonstop about it since and I'm still damned if I have a clue. How about Kinnaird?'

'He's the obvious suspect, isn't he? But only because he's a skilled radio operator. I could train a man in a couple of days to send and receive in morse. Slow, clumsy, he wouldn't know a thing about the instrument he was using, but he could still do it. Any of them may easily have been competent enough to operate a radio. The fact that Kinnaird is a skilled operator may even be a point in his favour.'

'Nife cells were removed from the radio cabin and taken to the laboratory,' Swanson pointed out. 'Kinnaird had the easiest access to them. Apart from Dr Jolly who had his office and sleeping quarters in the same hut.'

'So that would point a finger at Kinnaird or Jolly?'

'Well, wouldn't it?'

'Certainly. Especially if you will agree that the presence of those tinned foods under the lab. floor also points a finger at Hewson and Naseby, both of whom slept in the cookhouse where the food was stored, and that the presence of the radio-sonde balloon and the hydrogen in the lab. also points a finger at Jeremy and Hassard, one a met. officer and the other a technician who would have had the easiest access to those items.'

'That's right, confuse things,' Swanson said irritably. 'As if they weren't confused enough already.'

'I'm not confusing things. All I'm saying is that if you admit a certain possibility for a certain reason then you must admit similar possibilities for similar reasons. Besides, there are points in Kinnaird's favour. He risked his life to go back into the radio room to bring out the portable transmitter. He risked almost certain suicide when he tried to go in the second time to bring out his assistant, Grant, and probably would have died if Jeremy hadn't clobbered him. Look what happened to that man Foster who went in there immediately afterwards with a wet blanket over his head – *he* never came out.

'Again, would Kinnaird have mentioned the Nife cells if he had any guilt complex about them? But he did. That, incidentally, might have been why Grant, the assistant radio operator, collapsed in there and later died – Kinnaird had told him to bring out the other Nife cells and he was overcome because he stayed there too long looking for things that had already been removed from the hut. And there's one final point: we have Naseby's word for it that the door of the radio room was jammed, presumably by ice. Had Kinnaird been playing with matches a few moments previously, that door wouldn't have had time to freeze up.'

'If you let Kinnaird out,' Swanson said slowly, 'you more or less have to let Dr Jolly out too.' He smiled. 'I don't see a member of your profession running round filling people full of holes, Dr Carpenter. Repairing holes is their line of business, not making them. Hippocrates wouldn't have liked it.'

'I'm not letting Kinnaird out,' I said. 'But I'm not going off half-cocked and pinning a murder rap on him either. As for the ethics of my profession – would you like a list of the good healers who have decorated the dock in the Old Bailey? True, we have nothing on Jolly. His part in the proceedings that night seems to have consisted in staggering out from the radio room, falling flat on his face and staying there till pretty near the end of the fire. That, of course, has no bearing upon whatever part he might have taken in the proceedings prior to the fire. Though against that possibility there's the fact of the jammed door, the fact that Kinnaird or Grant would have been almost bound to notice if he had been up to something – Jolly's bunk was at the back of the radio room and he would have had to pass Kinnaird and Grant to get out, not forgetting that he would also have to stop to pick up the Nife cells. And there is one more point in his favour – an apparent point, that is. I still don't think that Benson's fall was an accident and if it was no accident it is difficult to see how Jolly could have arranged it while he was at the foot of the sail and Benson at the top and it's even more difficult to see why he should have stood at the foot of the sail and let Benson fall on top of him.'

'You're putting up a very good defence case for both Jolly and Kinnaird,' Swanson murmured.

'No. I'm only saying what a defence lawyer would say.'

'Hewson,' Swanson said slowly. 'Or Naseby, the cook. Or Hewson *and* Naseby. Don't you think it damned funny that those two, who were sleeping at the back or east side of the cookhouse, which was the first part of the hut to catch fire, should have managed to escape while the other two – Flanders and Bryce, wasn't it – who slept in the middle should have suffocated in there? Naseby said he shouted at them and shook them violently. Maybe he could have shouted and shaken all night without result. Maybe they were already unconscious – or dead. Maybe they had seen Naseby or Hewson or both removing food supplies and had been silenced. Or maybe they had been silenced *before* anything had been removed. And don't forget the gun. It was hidden in the petrol tank of the tractor, a pretty damn' funny place for a man to hide anything. But nothing funny about the idea occurring to Hewson, was there? He was the tractor-driver. And he seems to have taken his time about getting around to warn Captain Folsom. He said he had to make a wide circuit to avoid the flames but apparently Naseby didn't find it so bad when he went to the radio room. Another thing, a pretty telling point, I think, he said that when he was on the way to the bunkhouse the oil drums in the fuel store started exploding. If they only started exploding then how come all the huts – the five that were eventually destroyed, that is – were already uncontrollably on fire. They were uncontrollably on fire because they were saturated by flying oil so the first explosions, must have come a long time before then. And, apart from warning Folsom – who had already been warned – Hewson doesn't seem to have done very much after the fire started.'

'You'd make a pretty good prosecuting counsel yourself, Commander. But wouldn't you think there is just too *much* superficially against Hewson? That a clever man wouldn't have allowed so much superficial evidence to accumulate against him? You would have thought that, at least, he would have indulged in a little fire-fighting heroics to call attention to himself?'

'No. You're overlooking the fact that he would never have had reason to expect that there would be any investigation into the causes of the fire? That the situation would never arise where he – or anyone else, for that matter – would have to justify their actions and behaviour if accusations were to be levelled against them?'

'I've said it before and I say it again. People like that *never* take a chance. They always act on the assumption that they *may* be found out.'

'How could they be found out?' Swanson protested. 'How could they possibly expect to have suspicion aroused?'

'You don't think it possible that they suspect that we are on to them?'

'No, I don't.'

'That wasn't what you were saying last night after that hatch fell on me,' I pointed out. 'You said it was obvious that someone was on to me.'

'Thank the lord that all I have to do is the nice uncomplicated job of running a nuclear submarine,' Swanson said heavily. 'The truth is, I don't know what to think any more. How about this cook fellow – Naseby?'

'You think he was in cahoots with Hewson?'

'If we accept the premise that the men in the cookhouse who were not in on this business had to be silenced, and Naseby wasn't, then he must have been, mustn't he? But, dammit, how then about his attempt to rescue Flanders and Bryce?'

'May just have been a calculated risk. He saw how Jeremy flattened Kinnaird when he tried to go back into the radio-room a second time and perhaps calculated that Jeremy would oblige again if he tried a similar but fake rescue act.'

'Maybe Kinnaird's second attempt was also fake,' Swanson said. 'After all, Jeremy had already tried to stop him once.'

'Maybe it was,' I agreed. 'But Naseby. If he's your man, why should he have said that the radio room door was jammed with ice, and that he had to burst it open. That gives Kinnaird and Jolly an out – and a murderer wouldn't do anything to put any other potential suspect in the clear.'

'It's hopeless,' Swanson said calmly. 'I say let's put the whole damn' crowd of them under lock and key.'

'That would be clever,' I said. 'Yes, let's do just that. That way we'll never find out who the murderer is. Anyway, before you start giving up, remember it's even more complicated than that. Remember you're passing up the two most obvious suspects of all – Jeremy and Hassard, two tough, intelligent birds who, if they were the killers, were clever enough to see that *nothing* pointed the finger against them. Unless, of course, there might have been something about Flanders and Bryce that Jeremy didn't want anyone to see, so he stopped Naseby from going back into the cookhouse. Or not.'

Swanson almost glared at me. Watching his submarine plummeting out of control beyond the 1000-feet mark was something that rated maybe the lift of an eyebrow; but this was something else again. He said: 'Very well, then, we'll let the killer run loose and wreck the *Dolphin* at his leisure. I must have very considerable confidence in you, Dr Carpenter. I feel sure my confidence will not be misplaced. Tell me one last thing. I assume you are a highly skilled investigator. But I was puzzled by one omission in your questioning. A vital question, I should have thought.'

'Who suggested moving the corpses into the lab. knowing that by doing so he would be making his hiding-place for the cached material a hundred per cent foolproof?'

'I apologize.' He smiled faintly. 'You had your reasons, of course.'

'Of course. You're not sure whether or not the killer is on to the fact that we are on to him. I'm sure. I know he's not. But had I asked that question, he'd have known immediately that there could be only one reason for my asking it. Then he would have known I was on to him. Anyway, it's my guess that Captain Folsom gave the order, but the original suggestion, carefully camouflaged so that Folsom may no longer be able to pin it down, would have come from another quarter.'

Had it been a few months earlier with the summer Arctic sun riding in the sky, it would have been a brilliant day. As it was, there was no sun not in that latitude and so late in the year, but for all that the weather was about as perfect as it was possible for it to be. Thirty-six hours – the time that had elapsed since Hansen and I had made that savage trip back to the *Dolphin* – had brought about a change that seemed pretty close to miraculous. The knifing east wind had died, completely. That flying sea of ice-spicules was no more. The temperature had risen at least twenty degrees and the visibility was as perfect as visibility on the winter ice-pack ever is.

Swanson, sharing Benson's viewpoint on the crew's over-sedentary mode of existence and taking advantage of the fine weather, had advised everyone not engaged in actual watch-keeping to take advantage of the opportunity offered to stretch their legs in the fresh air. It said much for Swanson's powers of persuasion that by eleven that morning the *Dolphin* was practically deserted; and of course the crew, to whom Drift Ice Station Zebra was only so many words, were understandably curious to see the place, even the shell of the place, that had brought them to the top of the world.

I took my place at the end of the small queue being treated by Dr Jolly. It was close on noon before he got round to me. He was making light of his own burns and frost-bite and was in tremendous form, bustling happily about the sick-bay as if it had been his own private domain for years.

'Well,' I said, 'the pill-rolling competition wasn't so fierce after all, was it? I'm damned glad there was a third doctor around. How are things on the medical front?'

'Coming along not too badly, old boy,' he said cheerfully. 'Benson's picking up very nicely, pulse, respiration, blood-pressure close to normal, level of unconsciousness very slight now, I should say. Captain Folsom's still in considerable pain, but no actual danger, of course. The rest have improved a hundred per cent, little thanks to the medical fraternity: excellent food, warm beds and the knowledge that they're safe have done them more good than anything we could ever do. Anyway, it's done me a lot of good, by jove!'

'And them,' I agreed. 'All your friends except Folsom and the Harrington twins have followed most of the crew on to the ice and I'll wager that if you had suggested to them forty-eight hours ago that they'd willingly go out there again in so short a time, they'd have called for a strait-jacket.'

'The physical and mental recuperative power of homo sapiens,' Jolly said jovially. 'Beyond belief at times, old lad, beyond belief. Now, let's have a look at that broken wing of yours.'

So he had a look, and because I was a colleague and therefore inured to human suffering he didn't spend any too much time in molly-coddling me, but by hanging on to the arm of my chair and the shreds of my professional pride I kept the roof from falling in on me. When he was finished he said: 'Well, that's the lot, except for Brownell and Bolton, the two lads out on the ice.'

'I'll come with you,' I said. 'Commander Swanson is waiting pretty anxiously to hear what we have to say. He wants to get away from here as soon as possible.'

'Me, too,' Jolly said fervently. 'But what's the commander so anxious about?'

'Ice. You never know the hour or minute it starts to close in. Want to spend the next year or two up here?'

Jolly grinned, thought over it for a bit, then stopped grinning. He said apprehensively: 'How long are we going to be under this damned ice? Before we reach the open sea, I mean?'

'Twenty-four hours, Swanson says. Don't look so worried, Jolly. Believe me, it's far safer under this stuff than among it.'

With a very unconvinced look on his face Jolly picked up his medical kit and led the way from the sick-bay. Swanson was waiting for us in the control room. We climbed up the hatches, dropped down over the side and walked over to the Drift Station.

Most of the crew had already made their way out there. We passed numbers of them on the way back and most of them looked grim or sick or both and didn't even glance up as we passed. I didn't have to guess why they looked as they did, they'd been opening doors that they should have left closed.

With the sharp rise in outside temperature and the effect of the big electric heaters having been burning there for twenty-four hours the bunkhouse hut was now, if anything, overheated, with the last traces of ice long vanished from walls and ceiling. One of the men, Brownell, had recovered consciousness and was sitting up, supported, and drinking soup provided by one of the two men who had been keeping watch over him.

'Well,' I said to Swanson, 'here's one ready to go.'

'No doubt about that,' Jolly said briskly. He bent over the other, Bolton, for some seconds, then straightened and shook his head. 'A very sick man, Commander, very sick. I wouldn't care to take the responsibility of moving him.'

'I might be forced to take the responsibility myself,' Swanson said bluntly. 'Let's have another opinion on this.' His tone and words, I thought, could have been more diplomatic and conciliatory; but if there were a couple of murderers aboard the *Dolphin* there was a thirty-three and a third per cent chance that Jolly was one of them and Swanson wasn't forgetting it for a moment.

I gave Jolly an apologetic half-shrug, bent over Bolton and examined him as best I could with only one hand available for the task. I straightened and said: 'Jolly's right. He is pretty sick. But I think he might just stand the transfer to the ship.'

' "Might just" is not quite the normally accepted basis for deciding the treatment of a patient,' Jolly objected.

'I know it's not. But the circumstances are hardly normal either.'

'I'll take the responsibility,' Swanson said. 'Dr Jolly, I'd be most grateful if you would supervise the transport of those two men back to the ship. I'll let you have as many men as you want straight away.'

Jolly protested some more, then gave in with good grace. He supervised the transfer, and very competent he was about it too. I remained out there a little longer, watching Rawlings and some others dismantling heaters and lights and rolling up cables and, after the last of them was gone and I was alone, I made my way round to the tractor shed.

The broken haft of the knife was still in the tank of the tractor. But not the gun and not the two magazines. Those were gone. And whoever had taken them it hadn't been Dr Jolly, he hadn't been out of my sight for two consecutive seconds between the time he'd left the *Dolphin* and the time of his return to it.

At three o'clock that afternoon we dropped down below the ice and headed south for the open sea.

Chapter Ten

The afternoon and evening passed quickly and pleasantly enough. Closing our hatches and dropping down from our hardly won foothold in that lead had had a symbolic significance at least as important as the actual fact of leaving itself. The thick ceiling of ice closing over the hull of the *Dolphin* was a curtain being drawn across the eye of the mind. We had severed all physical connection with Drift Ice Station Zebra, a home of the dead that might continue to circle slowly about the Pole for mindless centuries to come; and with the severance had come an abrupt diminution of the horror and the shock which had hung pall-like over the ship and its crew for the past twenty-four hours. A dark door had swung to behind us and we had turned our backs on it. Mission accomplished, duty done, we were heading for home again and the sudden upsurge of relief and happiness among the crew to be on their way again, their high anticipation of port and leave, was an almost tangible thing. The mood of the ship was close to that of lighthearted gaiety. But there was no gaiety in my mind, and no peace: I was leaving too much behind. Nor could there be any peace in the minds of Swanson and Hansen, of Rawlings and Zabrinski: they knew we were carrying a killer aboard, a killer who had killed many times. Dr Benson knew also, but for the moment Dr Benson did not count: he still had not regained consciousness and I held the very unprofessional hope that he wouldn't for some time to come. In the twilight world of emergence from coma a man can start babbling and say all too much.

Some of the Zebra survivors had asked if they could see around the ship and Swanson agreed. In light of what I had told him in his cabin that morning, he must have agreed very reluctantly indeed, but no trace of this reluctance showed in his calmly smiling face. To have refused their request would have been rather a churlish gesture, for all the secrets of the *Dolphin* were completely hidden from the eye of the layman. But it wasn't good manners that made Swanson give his consent: refusing a reasonable request could have been responsible for making someone very suspicious indeed.

Hansen took them around the ship and I accompanied them, less for the exercise or interest involved than for the opportunity it gave me to keep a very close eye indeed on their reactions to their tour. We made a complete circuit of the ship, missing out only the reactor room, which no one could visit, anyway, and the inertial navigation-room which had been barred to me also. As we moved around I watched them all, and especially two of them, as closely as it is possible to watch anyone without making him aware of your observation, and I learned precisely what I had expected to learn – nothing. I'd been crazy even to hope I'd learn anything, our pal with the gun was wearing a mask that had been forged into shape and riveted into position. But I'd had to do it, anyway: playing in this senior league I couldn't pass up the one chance in a million.

Supper over, I helped Jolly as best I could with his evening surgery. Whatever else Jolly was, he was a damn' good doctor. Quickly and efficiently he checked and where necessary rebandaged the walking cases, examined and treated Benson and Folsom then asked me to come right aft with him to the nucleonics laboratory in the stern room which had been cleared of deck gear to accommodate the four other bed patients, the Harrington twins, Brownell and Bolton. The sick-bay itself had only two cots for invalids and Benson and Folsom had those.

Bolton, despite Jolly's dire predictions, hadn't suffered a relapse because of his transfer from the hut to the ship – which had been due largely to Jolly's extremely skilful and careful handling of the patient and the stretcher into which he had been lashed. Bolton, in fact, was conscious now and complaining of severe pain in his badly burned right forearm. Jolly removed the burn covering and Bolton's arm was a mess all right, no skin left worth speaking of, showing an angry violent red between areas of suppuration. Different doctors have different ideas as to the treatment of burns: Jolly favoured a salve-coated aluminium foil which he smoothed across the entire burn area then lightly bandaged in place. He then gave him a pain-killing injection and some sleeping tablets, and briskly informed the enlisted man who was keeping watch that he was to be informed immediately of any change or deterioration in Bolton's condition. A brief inspection of the three others, a changed bandage here and there and he was through for the night.

So was I. For two nights now I had had practically no sleep – what little had been left for me the previous night had been ruined by the pain in my left hand. I was exhausted. When I got to my cabin, Hansen was already asleep and the engineer officer gone.

I didn't need any of Jolly's sleeping pills that night.

I awoke at two o'clock. I was sleep-drugged, still exhausted and felt as if I had been in bed about five minutes. But I awoke in an instant and in that instant I was fully awake.

Only a dead man wouldn't have stirred. The racket issuing from the squawk box just above Hansen's bunk was appalling: a high-pitched, shrieking, atonic whistle, two-toned and altering pitch every half-second, it drilled stiletto-like against my cringing ear-drums. A banshee in its death agonies could never have hoped to compete with that lot.

Hansen already had his feet on the deck and was pulling on clothes and shoes in desperate haste. I had never thought to see that slow-speaking laconic Texan in such a tearing hurry, but I was seeing it now.

'What in hell's name is the matter?' I demanded. I had to shout to make myself heard above the shrieking of the alarm whistle.

'Fire!' His face was shocked and grim. 'The ship's on fire. And under this goddamned ice!'

Still buttoning his shirt, he hurdled my cot, crashed the door back on its hinges and was gone.

The atonic screeching of the whistle stopped abruptly and the silence fell like a blow. Then I was conscious of something more than silence – I was conscious of a complete lack of vibration throughout the ship. The great engines had stopped. And then I was conscious of something else again: feathery fingers of ice brushing up and down my spine. Why had the engines stopped? What could make a nuclear engine stop so quickly and what happened once it did? My God, I thought, maybe the fire is coming from the reactor room itself. I'd looked into the heart of the uranium atomic pile through a heavily leaded glass inspection port and seen the indescribable unearthly radiance of it, a nightmarish coalescence of green and violet and blue, the new 'dreadful light' of mankind. What happened when this dreadful light ran amok? I didn't know, but I suspected I didn't want to be around when it happened.

I dressed slowly, not hurrying. My damaged hand didn't help me much but that wasn't why I took my time. Maybe the ship was on fire, maybe the nuclear power plant had gone out of kilter. But if Swanson's superbly trained crew couldn't cope with every emergency that could conceivably arise then matters weren't going to be improved any by Carpenter running around in circles shouting: 'Where's the fire?'

Three minutes after Hansen had gone I walked along to the control room and peered in: if I was going to be in the way then this was as far as I was going to go. Dark acrid smoke billowed past me and a voice – Swanson's – said sharply: 'Inside and close that door.'

I pulled the door to and looked around the control room. At least, I tried to. It wasn't easy. My eyes were already streaming as if someone had thrown a bag of pepper into them and what little sight was left them didn't help me much. The room was filled with black evil-smelling smoke, denser by far and more throat-catching than the worst London fog. Visibility was no more than a few feet, but what little I could see showed me men still at their stations. Some were gasping, some were half-choking, some were cursing softly, all had badly watering eyes, but there was no trace of panic.

'You'd have been better on the other side of that door.' Swanson said dryly. 'Sorry to have barked at you, Doctor, but we want to limit the spread of the smoke as much as possible.'

'Where's the fire?'

'In the engine-room.' Swanson could have been sitting on his front porch at home discussing the weather. 'Where in the engine-room we don't know. It's pretty bad. At least, the smoke is. The extent of the fire we don't know, because we can't locate it. Engineer officer says it's impossible to see your hand in front of your face.'

'The engines,' I said. 'They've stopped. Has anything gone wrong?'

He rubbed his eyes with a handkerchief, spoke to a man who was pulling on a heavy rubber suit and a smoke-mask, then turned back to me.

'We're not going to be vaporized, if that's what you mean.' I could have sworn he was smiling. 'The atomic pile can only fail safe no matter what happens. If anything goes wrong the uranium rods slam down in very quick time indeed – a fraction under a one-thousandth of a second – stopping the whole reaction. In this case, though, we shut it off ourselves. The men in the manoeuvring-room could no longer see either the reactor dials or the governor for the control rods. No option but to shut it down. The engine-room crew have been forced to abandon the engine and manoeuvring-rooms and take shelter in the stern room.'

Well, that was something at least. We weren't going to be blown to pieces, ignobly vaporized on the altar of nuclear advancement; good old-fashioned suffocation, that was to be our lot. 'So what do we do?' I asked.

'What we should do is surface immediately. With fourteen feet of ice overhead that's not easy. Excuse me, will you?'

He spoke to the now completely masked and suited man who was carrying a small dialled box in his hands. They walked together past the navigator's chart desk and ice-machine to the heavy door opening on the passage that led to the engine-room over the top of the reactor compartment. They unclipped the door, pushed it open. A dense blinding cloud of dark smoke rolled into the room as the masked man stepped quickly into the passageway and swung the door to behind him. Swanson clamped the door shut, walked, temporarily blinded, back to the control position and fumbled down a roof microphone.

'Captain speaking.' His voice echoed emptily through the control centre. 'The fire is located in the engine-room. We do not know yet whether it is electrical, chemical or fuel oil: the source of the fire has not been pin-pointed. Acting on the principle of being prepared for the worst, we are now testing for a radiation leak.' So that was what the masked man had been carrying, a Geiger counter. 'If that proves negative, we shall try for a steam leak; and if that is negative we shall carry out an intensive search to locate the fire. It will not be easy as I'm told visibility is almost zero. We have already shut down all electrical circuits in the engine-room, lighting included, to prevent an explosion in the event of atomized fuel being present in the atmosphere. We have closed the oxygen intake valves and isolated the engine-room from the air-cleaning system in the hope that the fire will consume all available oxygen and burn itself out.

'All smoking is prohibited until further notice. Heaters, fans, and all electrical circuits other than communication lines to be switched off – and that includes the juke-box and the ice-cream machine. All lamps to be switched off except those absolutely essential. All movement is to be restricted to a minimum. I shall keep you informed of any progress we may make.'

I became aware of someone standing by my side. It was Dr Jolly, his normally jovial face puckered and woebegone, the tears flowing down his face. Plaintively he said to me: 'This *is* a bit thick, old boy, what? I'm not sure that I'm so happy now about being rescued. And all those prohibitions – no smoking, no power to be used, no moving around – do those mean what I take them to mean?'

'I'm afraid they do indeed.' It was Swanson who answered Jolly's question for him. 'This, I'm afraid, is every nuclear submarine captain's nightmare come true – fire under the ice. At one stroke we're not only reduced to the level of a conventional submarine – we're two stages worse. In the first place, a conventional submarine wouldn't be under the ice, anyway. In the second place, it has huge banks of storage batteries, and even if it were beneath the ice it would have sufficient reserve power to steam far enough south to get clear of the ice. Our reserve battery is so small that it wouldn't take us a fraction of the way.'

'Yes, yes,' Jolly nodded. 'But this no smoking, no moving—'

'That same very small battery, I'm afraid, is the only source left to us for power for the air-purifying machines, for lighting, ventilation, heating – I'm afraid the *Dolphin* is going to get very cold in a short time – so we have to curtail its expenditure of energy on those things. So no smoking, minimum movement – the less carbon dioxide breathed into the atmosphere the better. But the real reason for conserving electric energy is that we need it to power the heaters, pumps and motors that have to be used to start up the reactor again. If that battery exhausts itself before we get the reactor going – well, I don't have to draw a diagram.'

'You're not very encouraging, are you, Commander?' Jolly complained.

'No, not very. I don't see any reason to be,' Swanson said dryly.

'I'll bet you'd trade in your pension for a nice open lead above us just now,' I said.

'I'd trade in the pension of every flag officer in the United States Navy,' he said matter-of-factly. 'If we could find a polynya I'd surface, open the engine-room hatch to let most of the contaminated air escape, start up our diesel – it takes its air direct from the engine-room – and have the rest of the smoke sucked out in nothing flat. As it is, that diesel is about as much use to me as a grand piano.'

'And the compasses?' I asked.

'That's another interesting thought,' Swanson agreed. 'If the power output from our reserve battery falls below a certain level, our three Sperry gyro-compass systems and the N6A – that's the inertial guidance machine – just pack up. After that we're lost, completely. Our magnetic compass is quite useless in these latitudes – it just walks in circles.'

'So we would go around and around in circles, too,' Jolly said thoughtfully. 'For ever and ever under the jolly old ice-cap, what? By jove, Commander, I'm really beginning to wish we'd stayed up at Zebra.'

'We're not dead yet, Doctor . . . Yes, John?' This to Hansen, who had just come up.

'Sanders, sir. On the ice-machine. Can he have a smoke mask. His eyes are watering pretty badly.'

'Give him anything you like in the ship.' Swanson said, 'just so long as he can keep his eyes clear to read that graph. And double the watch on the ice-machine. If there's a lead up there only the size of a hair, I'm going for it. Immediate report if the ice thickness falls below, say, eight or nine feet.'

'Torpedoes?' Hansen asked. 'There hasn't been ice thin enough for that in three hours. And at the speed we're drifting there won't be for three months. I'll go keep the watch myself. I'm not much good for anything else, this hand of mine being the way it is.'

'Thank you. First you might tell Engineman Harrison to turn off the CO_2 scrubber and monoxide burners. Must save every amp of power we have. Besides, it will do this pampered bunch of ours the world of good to sample a little of what the old-time submariners had to experience when they were forced to stay below maybe twenty hours at a time.'

'That's going to be pretty rough on our really sick men,' I said. 'Benson and Folsom in the sick-bay, the Harrington twins, Brownell and Bolton in the nucleonics lab, right aft. They've got enough to contend with without foul air as well.'

'I know,' Swanson admitted. 'I'm damnably sorry about it. Later on, when – and if – the air gets really bad, we'll start up the air-purifying systems again but blank off every place except the lab. and sick-bay.' He broke off and turned round as a fresh wave of dark smoke rolled in from the suddenly opened after door. The man with the smoke mask was back from the engine-room and even with my eyes streaming in that smoke-filled acrid atmosphere I could see he was in a pretty bad way. Swanson and two others rushed to meet him, two of them catching him as he staggered into the control room, the third quickly swinging the heavy door shut against the darkly-evil clouds of smoke.

Swanson pulled off the man's smoke mask. It was Murphy, the man who had accompanied me when we'd closed the torpedo tube door. People like Murphy and Rawlings, I thought, always got picked for jobs like this.

His face was white and he was gasping for air, his eyes upturned in his head. He was hardly more than half-conscious, but even that foul atmosphere in the control centre must have seemed to him like the purest mountain air compared to what he had just been breathing for within thirty seconds his head had begun to clear and he was able to grin up painfully from where he'd been lowered into a chair.

'Sorry, Captain,' he gasped. 'This smoke-mask was never meant to cope with the stuff that's in the engine-room. Pretty hellish in there, I tell you.' He grinned again. 'Good news, Captain. No radiation leak.'

'Where's the Geiger counter?' Swanson asked quietly.

'It's had it, I'm afraid, sir. I couldn't see where I was going in there, honest, sir, you can't see three inches in front of your face. I tripped and damn' near fell down into the machinery space. The counter did fall down. But I'd a clear check before then. Nothing at all.' He reached up to his shoulder and unclipped his film badge. 'This'll show, sir.'

'Have that developed immediately. That was very well done, Murphy,' he said warmly. 'Now nip for'ard to the mess room. You'll find some really clear air there.'

The film badge was developed and brought back in minutes. Swanson took it, glanced at it briefly, smiled and let out his breath in a long slow whistle of relief. 'Murphy was right. No radiation leak. Thank God for that, anyway. If there had been – well, that was that, I'm afraid.'

'The for'ard door of the control room opened, a man passed through, and the door was as quickly closed. I guessed who it was before I could see him properly.'

'Permission from Chief Torpedoman Patterson to approach you, sir,' Rawlings said with brisk formality. 'We've just seen Murphy, pretty groggy he is, and both the Chief and I think that youngsters like that shouldn't be—'

'Am I to understand that you are volunteering to go next, Rawlings?' Swanson asked. The screws of responsibility and tension were turned hard down on him, but I could see that it cost him some effort to keep his face straight.

'Well, not exactly volunteering, sir. But – well, who else is there.'

'The torpedo department aboard this ship,' Swanson observed acidly, 'always did have a phenomenally high opinion of itself.'

'Let him try an underwater oxygen set,' I said. 'Those smoke-masks seem to have their limitations.'

'A steam leak, Captain?' Rawlings asked. 'That what you want me to check on?'

'Well, you seem to have been nominated, voted for and elected by yourself,' Swanson said. 'Yes, a steam leak.'

'That the suit Murphy was wearing?' Rawlings pointed to the clothes on the desk.

'Yes. Why?'

'You'd have thought there would be some signs of moisture or condensation if there had been a steam leak, sir.'

'Maybe. Maybe soot and smoke particles are holding the condensing steam in suspension. Maybe it was hot enough in there to dry off any moisture that did reach his suit. Maybe a lot of things. Don't stay too long in there.'

'Just as long as it takes me to get things fixed up,' Rawlings said confidently. He turned to Hansen and grinned. 'You baulked me once back out there on the ice-cap, Lieutenant, but sure as little apples I'm going to get that little old medal this time. Bring undying credit on the whole ship, I will.'

'If Torpedoman Rawlings will ease up with his ravings for a moment,' Hansen said, 'I have a suggestion to make, Captain. I know he won't be able to take off his mask inside there but if he would give a call-up signal on the engine telephone or ring through on the engine answering telegraph every four or five minutes we'd know he was O.K. If he doesn't, someone can go in after him.'

Swanson nodded. Rawlings pulled on suit and oxygen apparatus and left. That made it the third time the door leading to the engine compartment had been opened in a few minutes and each time fresh clouds of that black and biting smoke had come rolling in. Conditions were now very bad inside the control room, but someone had issued a supply of goggles all round and a few were wearing smoke-masks.

A phone rang. Hansen answered, spoke briefly and hung up.

'That was Jack Cartwright, Skipper.' Lieutenant Cartwright was the main propulsion officer, who'd been on watch in the manoeuvring-room and had been forced to retreat to the stern room. 'Seems he was overcome by the fumes and was carried back into the stern room. Says he's O.K. now and could we send smoke-masks or breathing apparatus for himself and one of his men – they can't get at the ones in the engine-room. I told him yes.'

'I'd certainly feel a lot happier if Jack Cartwright was in there investigating in person,' Swanson admitted. 'Send a man, will you?'

'I thought I'd take them myself. Someone else can double on the ice-machine.'

Swanson glanced at Hansen's injured hand, hesitated then nodded. 'Right. But straight through the engine-room and straight back.'

Hansen was on his way inside a minute. Five minutes later he was back again. He stripped off his breathing equipment. His face was pale and covered in sweat.

'There's fire in the engine-room, all right,' he said grimly. 'Hotter than the hinges of hell. No trace of sparks or flames but that doesn't mean a thing, the smoke in there is so thick that you couldn't see a blast furnace a couple of feet away.'

'See Rawlings?' Swanson asked.

'No. Has he not rung through?'

'Twice, but—' He broke off as the engine-room telegraph rang. 'So. He's still O.K. How about the stern room, John?'

'Damn' sight worse than it is here. The sick men aft there are in a pretty bad way, especially Bolton. Seems the smoke got in before they could get the door shut.'

'Tell Harrison to start up his air scrubbers. But for the lab. only. Blank off the rest of the ship.'

Fifteen minutes passed, fifteen minutes during which the engine-room telegraph rang three times, fifteen minutes during which the air became thicker and fouler and steadily less breathable, fifteen minutes during which a completely equipped fire-fighting team was assembled in the control centre, then another billowing cloud of black smoke announced the opening of the after door.

It was Rawlings. He was very weak and had to be helped out of his breathing equipment and his suit. His face was white and streaming sweat, his hair and clothes so saturated with sweat that he might easily have come straight from an immersion in the sea. But he was grinning triumphantly.

'No steam leak, Captain, that's for certain.' It took him three breaths to get that out. 'But fire down below in the machinery space. Sparks flying all over the shop. Some flame, not much. I located it, sir. Starboard high-pressure turbine. The lagging's on fire.'

'You'll get that medal, Rawlings,' Swanson said, 'even if I have to make the damn' thing myself.' He turned to the waiting firemen. 'You heard. Starboard turbine. Four at a time, fifteen minutes maximum. Lieutenant Raeburn, the first party. Knives, claw-hammers, pliers, crow-bars, CO_2. Saturate the lagging first then rip it off. Watch out for flash flames when you're pulling it off. I don't have to warn you about the steam pipes. Now on your way.'

They left. I said to Swanson: 'Doesn't sound so much. How long will it take. Ten minutes, quarter of an hour?'

He looked at me sombrely. 'A minimum of three or four hours – if we're lucky. It's hell's own maze down in the machinery space there. Valves, tubes, condensers and miles of that damned steam piping that would burn your hands off if you touched it. Working conditions even normally are so cramped as to be almost impossible. Then there's that huge turbine housing with this thick insulation lagging wrapped all round it – and the engineers who fitted it meant it to stay there for keeps. Before they start they have to douse the fire with the CO_2 extinguishers and even that won't help much. Every time they rip off a piece of charred insulation the oil-soaked stuff below will burst into flames again as soon as it comes into contact with the oxygen in the atmosphere.'

'Oil-soaked?'

'That's where the whole trouble must lie,' Swanson exclaimed. 'Wherever you have moving machinery you must have oil for lubrication. There's no shortage of machinery down in the machine space – and no shortage of oil either. And just as certain materials are strongly hygroscopic so that damned insulation has a remarkable affinity for oil. Where there's any around, whether in its normal fluid condition or in fine suspension in the atmosphere that lagging attracts it as a magnet does iron filings. And it's as absorbent as blotting-paper.'

'But what could have caused the fire?'

'Spontaneous combustion. There have been cases before. We've run over 50,000 miles in this ship now and in that time I suppose the lagging has become thoroughly saturated. We've been going at top speed ever since we left Zebra and the excess heat generated has set the damn thing off ... John, no word from Cartwright yet?'

'Nothing.'

'He must have been in there for the best part of twenty minutes now.'

'Maybe. But he was just beginning to put his suit on – himself and Ringman – when I left. That's not to say they went into the engine-room straight away. I'll call the stern room.' He did, spoke then hung up, his face grave. 'Stern room says that they have been gone twenty-five minutes. Shall I investigate, sir?'

'You stay right here. I'm not—'

He broke off as the after door opened with a crash and two men came staggering out – rather, one staggering, the other supporting him. The door was heaved shut and the men's masks removed. One man I recognized as an enlisted man who had accompanied Raeburn: the other was Cartwright, the main propulsion officer.

'Lieutenant Raeburn sent me out with the lieutenant here,' the enlisted man said. 'He's not so good, I think, Captain.'

It was a pretty fair diagnosis. He wasn't so good and that was a fact. He was barely conscious but none the less fighting grimly to hang on to what few shreds of consciousness were left him.

'Ringman,' he jerked out. 'Five minutes – five minutes ago. We were going back—'

'Ringman,' Swanson prompted with a gentle insistence. 'What about Ringman?'

'He fell. Down into the machinery space. I – I went after him, tried to lift him up the ladder. He screamed. God, he screamed. I – he—'

He slumped in his chair, was caught before he fell to the floor. I said: 'Ringman. Either a major fracture or internal injuries.'

'Damn!' Swanson swore softly. 'Damn and blast it all. A fracture. Down there. John, have Cartwright carried through to the crew's mess. A fracture!'

'Please have a mask and suit ready for me,' Jolly said briskly. 'I'll fetch Dr Benson's emergency kit from the sick-bay.'

'You?' Swanson shook his head. 'Damned decent, Jolly. I appreciate it but I can't let you—'

'Just for once, old boy, the hell with your navy regulations,' Jolly said politely. 'The main thing to remember, Commander, is that I'm aboard this ship too. Let us remember that we all – um – sink or swim together. No joke intended.'

'But you don't know how to operate those sets—'

'I can learn, can't I?' Jolly said with some asperity. He turned and left.

Swanson looked at me. He was wearing goggles, but they couldn't hide the concern in his face. He said, curiously hesitant: 'Do you think—'

'Of course Jolly's right. You've no option. If Benson were fit you know very well you'd have him down there in jig-time. Besides, Jolly is a damned fine doctor.'

'You haven't been down there, Carpenter. It's a metal jungle. There isn't room to splint a broken finger far less—'

'I don't think Dr Jolly will try to fix or splint anything. He'll just give Ringman a jab that will lay him out so that he can be brought up here without screaming in agony all the way.'

Swanson nodded, pursed his lips and walked away to examine the ice fathometer. I said to Hansen: 'It's pretty bad, isn't it?'

'You can say that again, friend. It's worse than bad. Normally, there should be enough air in the submarine to last us maybe sixteen hours. But well over half the air in the ship, from here right aft is already practically unbreathable. What we have left can't possibly last us more than a few hours. Skipper's boxed in on three sides. If he doesn't start the air purifiers up the men working down in the machinery space are going to have the devil of a job doing anything. Working in near-zero visibility with breathing apparatus on you're practically as good as blind – the floods will make hardly any difference. If he does start up the purifiers in the engine-room, the fresh oxygen will cause the fire to spread. And, when he starts them up, of course, that means less and less power to get the reactor working again.'

'That's very comforting,' I said. 'How long will it take you to restart the reactor?'

'At least an hour. That's after the fire has been put out and everything checked for safety. At least an hour.'

'And Swanson reckoned three or four hours to put the fire out. Say five, all told. It's a long time. Why doesn't he use some of his reserve power cruising around to find a lead?'

'An even bigger gamble than staying put and trying to put out the fire. I'm with the skipper. Let's fight the devil we know rather than dice with the one we don't.'

Medical case in hand, Jolly came coughing and spluttering his way back into the control centre and started pulling on suit and breathing apparatus. Hansen gave him instructions on how to operate it and Jolly seemed to get the idea pretty quickly. Brown, the enlisted man who'd helped Cartwright into the control centre, was detailed to accompany him. Jolly had no idea of the location of the ladder leading down from the upper engine-room to the machinery space.

'Be as quick as you can,' Swanson said. 'Remember, Jolly, you're not trained for this sort of thing. I'll expect you back inside ten minutes.'

They were back in exactly four minutes. They didn't have an unconscious Ringman with them either. The only unconscious figure was that of Dr Jolly, whom Brown half-carried, half-dragged over the sill into the control room.

'Can't say for sure what happened,' Brown gasped. He was trembling from the effort he had just made, Jolly must have out-weighed him by at least thirty pounds. 'We'd just got into the engine-room and shut the door. I was leading and suddenly Dr Jolly fell against me – I reckon he must have tripped over something. He knocked me down. When I got to my feet he was lying there behind me. I put the torch on him. Out cold, he was. His mask had been torn loose. I put it on as best I could and pulled him out.'

'My word,' Hansen said reflectively. 'The medical profession on the *Dolphin is* having a rough time.' He gloomily surveyed the prone figure of Dr Jolly as it was carried away towards the after door and relatively fresh air. 'All three sawbones out of commission now. That's very handy, isn't it, Skipper?'

Swanson didn't answer. I said to him: 'The injection for Ringman. Would you know what to give, how to give it and where?'

'No.'

'Would any of your crew?'

'I'm in no position to argue, Dr Carpenter.'

I opened Jolly's medical kit, hunted among the bottles on the lid rack until I found what I wanted, dipped a hypodermic and injected it in my left forearm, just where the bandage ended. 'Pain-killer,' I said. 'I'm just a softy. But I want to be able to use the forefinger and thumb of that hand.' I glanced across at Rawlings, as recovered as anyone could get in that foul atmosphere, and said: 'How are you feeling now?'

'Just resting lightly.' He rose from his chair and picked up his breathing equipment. 'Have no fears, Doc. With Torpedoman First-class Rawlings by your side—'

'We have plenty of fresh men still available aft, Dr Carpenter,' Swanson said.

'No. Rawlings. It's for his own sake. Maybe he'll get two medals now for this night's work.'

Rawlings grinned and pulled the mask over his head. Two minutes later we were inside the engine-room.

It was stiflingly hot in there, and visibility, even with powerful torches shining, didn't exceed eighteen inches, but for the rest it wasn't too bad. The breathing apparatus functioned well enough and I was conscious of no discomfort. At first, that was.

Rawlings took my arm and guided me to the head of a ladder that reached down to the deck of the machinery space. I heard the penetrating hiss of a fire-extinguisher and peered around to locate its source.

A pity they had no submarines in the Middle Ages, I thought, the sight of that little lot down there would have given Dante an extra fillip when he'd started in on his *Inferno*. Over on the starboard side two very powerful floodlamps had been slung above the huge turbine: the visibility they gave varied from three to six feet, according to the changing amount of smoke given off by the charred and smouldering insulation. At the moment, one patch of the insulation was deeply covered in a layer of white foam – carbon dioxide released under pressure immediately freezes anything with which it comes in contact. As the man with the extinguisher stepped back, three others moved forward in the swirling gloom and started hacking and tearing away at the insulation. As soon as a sizeable strip was dragged loose the exposed lagging below immediately burst into flames reaching the height of a man's head, throwing into sharp relief weird masked figures leaping backwards to avoid being scorched by the flames. And then the man with the CO_2 would approach again, press his trigger, the blaze would shrink down, flicker and die, and a coat of creamy-white foam would bloom where the fire had been. Then the entire process would be repeated all over again. The whole scene with the repetitively stylized movements of the participants highlit against a smoky oil-veined background of flickering crimson was somehow weirdly suggestive of the priests of a long-dead and alien culture offering up some burnt sacrifice on their bloodstained pagan altar.

It also made me see Swanson's point: at the painfully but necessarily slow rate at which those men were making progress, four hours would be excellent par for the course. I tried not to think what the air inside the *Dolphin* would be like in four hours' time.

The man with the extinguisher – it was Raeburn – caught sight of us, came across and led me through a tangled maze of steam pipes and condensers to where Ringman was lying. He was on his back, very still, but conscious: I could see the movement of the whites of his eyes behind his goggles. I bent down till my mask was touching his.

'Your leg?' I shouted.

He nodded.

'Left?'

He nodded again, reached out gingerly and touched a spot halfway down the shin-bone. I opened the medical case, pulled out scissors, pinched the clothes on his upper arm between finger and thumb and cut a piece of the material away. The hypodermic came next and within two minutes he was asleep. With Rawlings's help I laid splints against his leg and bandaged them roughly in place. Two of the fire-fighters stopped work long enough to help us drag him up the ladder and then Rawlings and I took him through the passage above the reactor room. I became aware that my breathing was now distressed, my legs shaking and my whole body bathed in sweat.

Once in the control centre I took off my mask and immediately began to cough and sneeze uncontrollably, tears streaming down my cheeks. Even in the few minutes we had been gone the air in the control room had deteriorated to a frightening extent.

Swanson said: 'Thank you, Doctor. What's it like in there?'

'Quite bad. Not intolerable, but not nice. Ten minutes is long enough for your fire-fighters at one time.'

'Fire-fighters I have in plenty. Ten minutes it shall be.'

A couple of burly enlisted men carried Ringman through to the sick-bay. Rawlings had been ordered for'ard for rest and recuperation in the comparatively fresh air of the messroom, but elected to stop off at the sick-bay with me. He'd glanced at my bandaged left hand and said: 'Three hands are better than one, even although two of them do happen to belong to Rawlings.'

Benson was restless and occasionally murmuring, but still below the level of consciousness. Captain Folsom was asleep, deeply so, which I found surprising until Rawlings told me that there were no alarm boxes in the sick-bay and that the door was completely soundproofed.

We laid Ringman down on the examination table and Rawlings slit up his left trouser leg with a pair of heavy surgical scissors. It wasn't as bad as I had feared it would be, a clean fracture of the tibia, not compound: with Rawlings doing most of the work we soon had his leg fixed up. I didn't try to put his leg in traction; when Jolly, with his two good hands, had completely recovered he'd be able to make a better job of it than I could.

We'd just finished when a telephone rang. Rawlings lifted it quickly before Folsom could wake, spoke briefly and hung up.

'Control room,' he said. I knew from the wooden expression on his face that whatever news he had for me, it wasn't good. 'It was for you. Bolton, the sick man in the nucleonics lab., the one you brought back from Zebra yesterday afternoon. He's gone. About two minutes ago.' He shook his head despairingly. 'My God, another death.'

'No,' I said. 'Another murder.'

Chapter Eleven

The *Dolphin* was an ice-cold tomb. At half past six that morning, four and a half hours after the outbreak of the fire, there was still only one dead man inside the ship, Bolton. But as I looked with bloodshot and inflamed eyes at the men sitting or lying about the control room – no one was standing any more – I knew that within an hour, two at the most, Bolton would be having company. By ten o'clock, at the latest, under those conditions, the *Dolphin* would be no more than a steel coffin with no life left inside her.

As a ship, the *Dolphin* was already dead. All the sounds we associated with a living vessel, the murmurous pulsation of great engines, the high-pitched whine of generators, the deep hum of the air-conditioning unit, the unmistakable transmission from the sonar, the clickety-clack from the radio room, the soft hiss of air, the brassy jingle from the juke-box, the whirring fans, the rattle of pots from the galley, the movement of men, the talking of men – all those were gone. All those vital sounds, the heart-beats of a living vessel, were gone; but in their place was not silence but something worse than silence, something that bespoke not living but dying, the frighteningly rapid, hoarse, gasping breathing of lung-tortured men fighting for air and for life.

Fighting for air. That was the irony of it. Fighting for air while there were still many days' supply of oxygen in the giant tanks. There were some breathing sets aboard, similar to the British Built-in Breathing System which takes a direct oxy-nitrogen mixture from tanks, but only a few, and all members of the crew had had a turn at those, but only for two minutes at a time. For the rest, for the more than ninety per cent without those systems, there was only the panting straining agony that leads eventually to death. Some portable closed-circuit sets were still left, but those were reserved exclusively for the fire-fighters.

Oxygen was occasionally bled from the tanks directly into the living spaces and it just didn't do any good at all; the only effect it seemed to have was to make breathing even more cruelly difficult by heightening the atmospheric pressure. All the oxygen in the world was going to be of little avail as long as the level of carbon dioxide given off by our anguished breathing mounted steadily with the passing of each minute. Normally, the air in the *Dolphin* was cleaned and circulated throughout the ship every two minutes, but the giant 200-ton air-conditioner responsible for this was a glutton for the electric power that drove it; and the electricians' estimate was that the reserve of power in the stand-by battery, which alone could reactivate the nuclear power-plant, was already dangerously low. So the concentration of carbon dioxide increased steadily towards lethal levels and there was nothing we could do about it.

Increasing, too, in what passed now for air, were the Freon fumes from the refrigerating machinery and the hydrogen fumes from the batteries. Worse still, the smoke was now so thick that visibility, even in the for'ard parts of the ship, was down to a few feet, but that smoke had to remain also, there was no power to operate the electrostatic precipitators and even when those had been briefly tried they had proved totally inadequate to cope with the concentration of billions of carbon particles held in suspension in the air. Each time the door to the engine-room was opened – and that was progressively oftener as the strength of the fire-fighters ebbed – fresh clouds of that evil acrid smoke rolled through the submarine. The fire in the engine-room had stopped burning over two hours previously; but now what remained of the redly-smouldering insulation round the starboard high-pressure turbine gave off far more smoke and fumes than flames could ever have done.

But the greatest enemy of all lay in the mounting count of carbon monoxide, that deadly, insidious, colourless, tasteless, odourless gas with its murderous affinity for the red blood cells – five hundred times that of oxygen. On board the *Dolphin* the normal permissible tolerance of carbon monoxide in the air was thirty parts in a million. Now the reading was somewhere between four and five hundred parts in a million. When it reached a thousand parts, none of us would have more than minutes to live.

And then there was the cold. As Commander Swanson had grimly prophesied, the *Dolphin*, with the steam pipes cooled down and all heaters switched off, had chilled down to the sub-freezing temperature of the sea outside, and was ice-cold. In terms of absolute cold, it was nothing – a mere two degrees below zero on the centigrade scale. But in terms of cold as it reacted on the human body it was very cold indeed. Most of the crew were without warm clothing of any kind – in normal operating conditions the temperature inside the *Dolphin* was maintained at a steady 22° C. regardless of the temperature outside – they were both forbidden to move around and lacked the energy to move around to counteract the effects of the cold, and what little energy was left in their rapidly weakening bodies was so wholly occupied in forcing their labouring chest muscles to gulp in more and ever more of that foul and steadily worsening air that they had none at all left to generate sufficient animal heat to ward off that dank and bitter cold. You could actually *hear* men shivering, could listen to their violently shaking limbs knocking and rat-tat-tatting helplessly against bulkheads and deck, could hear the chattering of their teeth, the sound of some of them, far gone in weakness, whimpering softly with the cold: but always the dominant sound was that harsh strangled moaning, a rasping and frightening sound, as men sought to suck air down into starving lungs.

With the exception of Hansen and myself – both of whom were virtually one-handed – and the sick patients, every man in the *Dolphin* had taken his turn that night in descending into the machinery space and fighting that red demon that threatened to slap us all. The number in each fire-fighting group had been increased from four to eight and the time spent down there shortened to three or four minutes, so that efforts could be concentrated and more energy expended in a given length of time; but because of the increasingly Stygian darkness in the machinery space, the ever-thickening coils of oily black smoke, and the wickedly cramped and confined space in which the men had to work, progress had been frustratingly, maddeningly slow; and entered into it now, of course, was the factor of that dreadful weakness that now assailed us all, so that men with the strength only of little children were tugging and tearing at the smouldering insulation in desperate near-futility and seemingly making no progress at all.

I'd been down again in the machinery space, just once, at 5.30 a.m. to attend to Jolly who had himself slipped, fallen and laid himself out while helping an injured crewman up the ladder, and I knew I would never forget what I had seen there, dark and spectral figures in a dark and spectral and swirling world, lurching and staggering around like zombies in some half-forgotten nightmare, swaying and stumbling and falling to the deck or down into the bilges now deep-covered in great snowdrifts of carbon dioxide foam and huge smoking blackened chunks of torn-off lagging. Men on the rack, men in the last stages of exhaustion. One little spark of fire, one little spark of an element as old as time itself and all the brilliant technological progress of the twentieth century was set at nothing, the frontiers of man's striving translated in a moment from the nuclear age to the dark unknown of pre-history.

Every dark hour brings forth its man and there was no doubt in the minds of the crew of the *Dolphin* that that dark night had produced its own here. Dr Jolly. He had made a swift recovery from the effects of his first disastrous entry into the engine-room that night, appearing back in the control centre only seconds after I had finished setting Ringman's broken leg. He had taken the news of Bolton's death pretty badly, but never either by word or direct look did he indicate to either Swanson or myself that the fault lay with us for insisting against his better judgment on bringing on board the ship a man whose life had been hanging in the balance even under the best of conditions. I think Swanson was pretty grateful for that and might even have got around to apologizing to Jolly had not a fire-fighter come through from the engine-room and told us that one of his team had slipped and either twisted or broken an ankle – the second of many minor accidents and injuries that were to happen down in the machinery space that night. Jolly had reached for the nearest closed-circuit breathing apparatus before we could try to stop him and was gone in a minute.

We eventually lost count of the number of trips he made down there that night. Fifteen at least, perhaps many more, by the time six o'clock had come my mind was beginning to get pretty fuzzy round the edges. He'd certainly no lack of customers for his medical skill. Paradoxically enough, the two main types of injury that night were diametrically opposite in nature: burning and freezing, burning from the red-hot lagging – and, earlier, the steam pipes – and freezing from a carelessly directed jet of carbon dioxide against exposed areas of face or hands. Jolly never failed to answer a call, not even after the time he'd given his own head a pretty nasty crack. He would complain bitterly to the captain, old boy, for rescuing him from the relative safety and comfort of Drift Ice Station Zebra, crack some dry joke, pull on his mask and leave. A dozen speeches to Congress or Parliament couldn't have done what Jolly did that night in cementing Anglo-American friendship.

About 6.45 a.m. Chief Torpedoman Patterson came into the control centre. I suppose he walked through the doorway, but that was only assumption, from where I sat on the deck between Swanson and Hansen you couldn't see half-way to the door; but when he came up to Swanson he was crawling on his hands and knees, head swaying from side to side, whooping painfully, his respiration rate at least fifty to the minute. He was wearing no mask of any kind and was shivering constantly.

'We must do something, Captain,' he said hoarsely. He spoke as much when inhaling as when exhaling, when your breathing is sufficiently distressed one is as easy as the other. 'We've got seven men passed out now between the for'ard torpedo room and the crew's mess. They're pretty sick men, Captain.'

'Thank you, Chief.' Swanson, also without a mask, was in as bad a way as Patterson, his chest heaving, his breath hoarsely rasping, tears and sweat rolling down the greyness of his face. 'We will be as quick as possible.'

'More oxygen,' I said. 'Bleed more oxygen into the ship.'

'Oxygen? More oxygen?' He shook his head. 'The pressure is too high as it is.'

'Pressure won't kill them.' I was dimly aware through my cold and misery and burning chest and eyes that my voice sounded just as strange as did those of Swanson and Patterson. 'Carbon monoxide will kill them. Carbon monoxide is what is killing them now. It's the relative proportion of CO_2 to oxygen that matters. It's too high, it's far too high. That's what's going to finish us all off.'

'More oxygen,' Swanson ordered. 'Even the unnecessary acknowledgment of my words would have cost too much. More oxygen.'

Valves were turned and oxygen hissed into the control room and, I know, into the crew spaces. I could feel my ears pop as the pressure swiftly built up, but that was all I could feel. I certainly couldn't feel any improvement in my breathing, a feeling that was borne out when Patterson, noticeably weaker this time, crawled back and croaked out the bad news that he now had a dozen unconscious men on his hands.

I went for'ard with Patterson and a closed-circuit oxygen apparatus – one of the few unexhausted sets left – and clamped it for a minute or so on to the face of each unconscious man in turn, but I knew it was but a temporary palliative, the oxygen revived them but within a few minutes of the mask being removed most of them slipped back into unconsciousness again. I made my way back to the control room, a dark dungeon of huddled men nearly all lying down, most of them barely conscious. I was barely conscious myself. I wondered vaguely if they felt as I did, if the fire from the lungs had now spread to the remainder of the body, if they could see the first slight changes in colour in their hands and faces, the deadly blush of purple, the first unmistakable signs of a man beginning to die from carbon monoxide poisoning. Jolly, I noticed, still hadn't returned from the engine-room: he was keeping himself permanently on hand, it seemed, to help those men who were in ever increasingly greater danger of hurting themselves and their comrades, as their weakness increased, as their level of care and attention and concentration slid down towards zero.

Swanson was where I'd left him, propped on the deck against the plotting table. He smiled faintly as I sank down beside himself and Hansen.

'How are they, Doctor?' he whispered. A whisper, but a rock-steady whisper. The man's monolithic calm had never cracked and I realized dimly that here was a man who could never crack; you do find people like that, once in a million or once in a lifetime. Swanson was such a man.

'Far gone,' I said. As a medical report it maybe lacked a thought in detail but it contained the gist of what I wanted to say and it saved me energy.

'You will have your first deaths from carbon monoxide poisoning within the hour.'

'So soon?' The surprise was in his red, swollen streaming eyes as well as in his voice. 'Not so soon, Doctor. It's hardly – well, it's hardly started to take effect.'

'So soon,' I said. 'Carbon monoxide poisoning is very rapidly progressive. Five dead within the hour. Within two hours fifty. At least fifty.'

'You take the choice out of my hands,' he murmured. 'For which I am grateful. John, where is our main propulsion officer. His hour has come.'

'I'll get him.' Hansen hauled himself wearily to his feet, an old man making his last struggle to rise from his deathbed, and at that moment the engine-room door opened and blackened exhausted men staggered into the control room. Waiting men filed out to take their place. Swanson said to one of the men who had just entered: 'Is that you, Will?'

'Yes, sir.' Lieutenant Raeburn, the navigating officer, pulled off his mask and began to cough, rackingly, painfully. Swanson waited until he had quieted a little.

'How are things down there, Will?'

'We've stopped making smoke, Skipper.' Raeburn wiped his streaming face, swayed dizzily and lowered himself groggily to the floor. 'I think we've drowned out the lagging completely.'

'How long to get the rest of it off?'

'God knows. Normally, ten minutes. The way we are – an hour. Maybe longer.'

'Thank you. Ah!' He smiled faintly as Hansen and Cartwright appeared out of the smoke-filled gloom. 'Our main propulsion officer. Mr Cartwright, I would be glad if you would put the kettle on to boil. What's the record for activating the plant, getting steam up and spinning the turbo-generators?'

'I couldn't say, Skipper.' Red-eyed, coughing, smoke-blackened and obviously in considerable pain, Cartwright nevertheless straightened his shoulders and smiled slowly. 'But you may consider it broken.'

He left. Swanson heaved himself to his feet with obvious weakness – except for two brief inspection trips to the engine-room he had not once worn any breathing apparatus during those interminable and pain-filled hours. He called for power on the broadcast circuit, unhooked a microphone and spoke in a calm clear strong voice: it was an amazing exhibition in self-control, the triumph of a mind over agonized lungs still starving for air.

'This is your captain speaking,' he said. 'The fire in the engine-room is out. We are already reactivating our power plant. Open all watertight doors throughout the ship. They are to remain open until further orders. You may regard the worst of our troubles as lying behind us. Thank you for all you have done.' He hooked up the microphone, and turned to Hansen. 'The worst *is* behind, John – if we have enough power left to reactivate the plant.'

'Surely the worst is still to come,' I said. 'It'll take you how long, three-quarters of an hour, maybe an hour to get your turbine generators going and your air-purifying equipment working again. How long do you think it will take your air cleaners to make any noticeable effect on this poisonous air?'

'Half an hour. At least that. Perhaps more.'

'There you are then.' My mind was so woolly and doped now that I had difficulty in finding words to frame my thoughts, and I wasn't even sure that my thoughts were worth thinking. 'An hour and a half at least – and you said the worst was over. The worst hasn't even begun.' I shook my head, trying to remember what it was that I had been going to say next, then remembered. 'In an hour and a half one out of every four of your men will be gone.'

Swanson smiled. He actually, incredibly, smiled. He said: 'As Sherlock used to say to Moriarty, I think not, Doctor. Nobody's going to die of monoxide poisoning. In fifteen minutes' time we'll have fresh breathable air throughout the ship.'

Hansen glanced at me just as I glanced at him. The strain had been too much, the old man had gone off his rocker. Swanson caught our interchange of looks and laughed, the laugh changing abruptly to a bout of convulsive coughing as he inhaled too much of that poisoned smoke-laden atmosphere. He coughed for a long time then gradually quietened down.

'Serves me right,' he gasped. 'Your faces . . . Why do you think I ordered the watertight doors opened, Doctor?'

'No idea.'

'John?'

Hansen shook his head. Swanson looked at him quizzically and said: 'Speak to the engine-room. Tell them to light up the diesel.'

'Yes, sir,' Hansen said woodenly. He made no move.

'Lieutenant Hansen is wondering whether he should fetch a strait-jacket,' Swanson said. 'Lieutenant Hansen knows that a diesel engine is never *never* lit up when a submarine is submerged – unless with a snorkel which is useless under ice – for a diesel not only uses air straight from the engine-room atmosphere, it gulps it down in great draughts and would soon clear away all the air in the ship. Which is what I want. We bleed compressed air under fairly high pressure into the forepart of the ship. Nice clean fresh air. We light up the diesel in the after part – it will run rough at first because of the low concentration of oxygen in this poisonous muck – but it will run. It will suck up much of this filthy air, exhausting its gases over the side, and as it does it will lower the atmospheric pressure aft and the fresh air will make its way through from for'ard. To have done this before now would have been suicidal, the fresh air would only have fed the flames until the fire was out of control. But we can do it now. We can run it for a few minutes only, of course, but a few minutes will be ample. You are with me, Lieutenant Hansen?'

Hansen was with him all right, but he didn't answer. He had already left.

Three minutes passed, then we heard, through the now open passageway above the reactor room, the erratic sound of a diesel starting, fading, coughing, then catching again – we learned later that the engineers had had to bleed off several ether bottles in the vicinity of the air intake to get the engine to catch. For a minute or two it ran roughly and erratically and seemed to be making no impression at all on that poisonous air: then, imperceptibly, almost, at first, then with an increasing degree of definition, we could see the smoke in the control room, illuminated by the single lamp still left burning there, begin to drift and eddy towards the reactor passage. Smoke began to stir and eddy in the corners of the control room as the diesel sucked the fumes aft, and more smoke-laden air, a shade lighter in colour, began to move in from the wardroom passageway, pulled in by the decreasing pressure in the control room, pushed in by the gradual build-up of fresh air in the forepart of the submarine as compressed air was bled into the living spaces.

A few more minutes made the miracle. The diesel thudded away in the engine-room, running more sweetly and strongly as air with a higher concentration of oxygen reached its intake, and the smoke in the control room drained steadily away to be replaced by a thin greyish mist from the forepart of the ship that was hardly deserving of the name of smoke at all. And that mist carried with it air, an air with fresh life-giving oxygen, an air with a proportion of carbon dioxide and carbon monoxide that was now almost negligible. Or so it seemed to us.

The effect upon the crew was just within the limits of credibility. It was as if a wizard had passed through the length of the ship and touched them with the wand of life. Unconscious men, men for whom death had been less than half an hour away, began to stir, some to open their eyes: sick, exhausted, nauseated and pain-racked men who had been lying or sitting on the decks in attitudes of huddled despair sat up straight or stood, their faces breaking into expressions of almost comical wonderment and disbelief as they drew great draughts down into their aching lungs and found that it was not poisonous gases they were inhaling but fresh breathable air: men who had made up their minds for death began to wonder how they could ever have thought that way. As air went, I suppose, it was pretty sub-standard stuff and the Factory Acts would have had something to say about it; but, for us, no pine-clad mountain air ever tasted half so sweet.

Swanson kept a careful eye on the gauges recording the air pressure in the submarine. Gradually it sunk down to the fifteen pounds at which the atmosphere was normally kept, then below it; he ordered the compressed air to be released under higher pressure and then when the atmospheric pressure was back to normal ordered the diesel stopped and the compressed air shut off.

'Commander Swanson,' I said. 'If you ever want to make admiral you can apply to me for a reference any time.'

'Thank you.' He smiled. 'We have been very lucky.' Sure we had been lucky, the way men who sailed with Swanson would always be lucky.

We could hear now the sounds of pumps and motors as Cartwright started in on the slow process of bringing the nuclear power plant to life again. Everyone knew that it was touch and go whether there would be enough life left in the batteries for that, but, curiously, no one seemed to doubt that Cartwright would succeed; we had been through too much to entertain even the thought of failure now.

Nor did we fail. At exactly eight o'clock that morning Cartwright phoned to say that he had steam on the turbine blades and that the *Dolphin* was a going proposition again. I was glad to hear it.

For three hours we cruised along at slow speed while the air-conditioning plant worked under maximum pressure to bring the air inside the *Dolphin* back to normal. After that Swanson slowly stepped up our speed until we had reached about fifty per cent of normal cruising speed, which was as fast as the propulsion officer deemed it safe to go. For a variety of technical reasons it was impractical for the *Dolphin* to operate without all turbines in commission, so we were reduced to the speed of the slowest and, without lagging on it, Cartwright didn't want to push the starboard high-pressure turbine above a fraction of its power. This way, it would take us much longer to clear the ice-pack and reach the open sea but the captain, in a broadcast, said that if the limit of the ice-pack was where it had been when we'd first moved under it – and there was no reason to think it should have shifted more than a few miles – we should be moving out into the open sea about four o'clock the following morning.

By four o'clock of that afternoon, members of the crew, working in relays, had managed to clear away from the machinery space all the debris and foam that had accumulated during the long night. After that, Swanson reduced all watches to the barest skeletons required to run the ship so that as many men as possible might sleep as long as possible. Now that the exultation of victory was over, now that the almost intolerable relief of knowing that they were not after all to find their gasping end in a cold iron tomb under the ice-cap had begun to fade, the inevitable reaction, when it did come, was correspondingly severe. A long and sleepless night behind them; hours of cruelly back-breaking toil in the metal jungle of the machinery space; that lifetime of tearing tension when they had not known whether they were going to live or die but had believed they were going to die: the poisonous fumes that had laid them all on the rack: all of those combined had taken cruel toll of their reserves of physical and mental energy and the crew of the *Dolphin* were now sleep-ridden and exhausted as they had never been. When they lay down to sleep they slept at once, like dead men.

I didn't sleep. Not then, not at four o'clock. I couldn't sleep. I had too much to think about, like how it had been primarily my fault, through a mistake, miscalculation or sheer pig-headedness, that the *Dolphin* and her crew had been brought to such desperate straits: like what Commander Swanson was going to say when he found out how much I'd kept from him, how little I'd told him. Still, if I had kept him in the dark so long, I couldn't see that there would be much harm in it if I kept him in the dark just that little time longer. It would be time enough in the morning to tell him all I knew. His reactions would be interesting, to say the least. He might be striking some medals for Rawlings, but I had the feeling that he wouldn't be striking any for me. Not after I'd told him what I'd have to.

Rawlings. That was the man I wanted now. I went to see him, told him what I had in mind and asked him if he would mind sacrificing a few hours' sleep during the night. As always, Rawlings was co-operation itself.

Later that evening I had a look at one or two of the patients. Jolly, exhausted by his Herculean efforts of the previous night, was fathoms deep in slumber, so Swanson had asked if I would deputize for him. So I did, but I didn't try very hard. With only one exception they were sound asleep and none of them was in so urgent need of medical attention that there would have been any justification for waking him up. The sole exception was Dr Benson, who had recovered consciousness late that afternoon. He was obviously on the mend but complained that his head felt like a pumpkin with someone at work on it with a riveting gun so I fed him some pills and that was the extent of the treatment. I asked him if he had any idea as to what had been the cause of his fall from the top of the sail, but he was either too woozy to remember or just didn't know. Not that it mattered now. I already knew the answer.

I slept for nine hours after that, which was pretty selfish of me considering that I had asked Rawlings to keep awake half the night; but then I hadn't

had much option about that, for Rawlings was in the position to perform
for me an essential task that I couldn't perform for myself.

Some time during the night we passed out from under the ice-cap into the
open Arctic Ocean again.

I awoke shortly after seven, washed, shaved and dressed as carefully as
I could with one hand out of commission, for I believe a judge owes it to his
public to be decently turned out when he goes to conduct a trial, then
breakfasted well in the wardroom. Shortly before nine o'clock I walked into
the control room. Hansen had the watch. I went up to him and said quietly;
so that I couldn't be overheard: 'Where is Commander Swanson?'

'In his cabin.'

'I'd like to speak to him and yourself. Privately.'

Hansen looked at me speculatively, nodded, handed over the watch to the
navigator and led the way to Swanson's cabin. We knocked, went in and
closed the door behind us. I didn't waste any time in preamble.

'I know who the killer is,' I said. 'I've no proof but I'm going to get it
now. I would like you to be on hand. If you can spare the time.'

They'd used up all their emotional responses and reactions during the
previous thirty hours so they didn't throw up their hands or do startled
double-takes or make any of the other standard signs of incredulousness.
Instead Swanson just looked thoughtfully at Hansen, rose from his table,
folded the chart he'd been studying and said dryly: 'I think we might spare
the time, Dr Carpenter. I have never met a murderer.' His tone was
impersonal, even light, but the clear grey eyes had gone very cold indeed.
'It will be quite an experience to meet a man with eight deaths on his
conscience.'

'You can count yourself lucky that it is only eight,' I said. 'He almost
brought it up to the hundred mark yesterday morning.'

This time I did get them. Swanson stared at me, then said softly: 'What
do you mean?'

'Our pal with the gun also carries a box of matches around with him,' I
said. 'He was busy with them in the engine-room in the early hours of
yesterday morning.'

'Somebody *deliberately* tried to set the ship on fire?' Hansen looked at me
in open disbelief. 'I don't buy that, Doc.'

'I buy it,' Swanson said. 'I buy anything Dr Carpenter says. We're dealing
with a madman, Doctor. Only a madman would risk losing his life along
with the lives of a hundred others.'

'He miscalculated,' I said mildly. 'Come along.'

They were waiting for us in the wardroom as I'd arranged, eleven of
them in all – Rawlings, Zabrinski, Captain Folsom, Dr Jolly, the two
Harrington twins, who were now just barely well enough to be out of bed,
Naseby, Hewson, Hassard, Kinnaird and Jeremy. Most of them were seated
round the wardroom table except for Rawlings, who opened the door for us,
and Zabrinski, his foot still in the cast, who was sitting in a chair in one
corner of the room, studying an issue of the *Dolphin Daze*, the submarine's
own mimeographed newspaper. Some of them made to get to their feet as
we came in but Swanson waved them down. They sat, silently, all except
Dr Jolly who boomed out a cheerful: 'Good morning, Captain. Well, well,
this is an intriguing summons. Most intriguing. What is it you want to see
us about, Captain?'

I cleared my throat. 'You must forgive a small deception. It is I who wants to see you, not the captain.'

'You?' Jolly pursed his lips and looked at me speculatively. 'I don't get it, old boy. Why you?'

'I have been guilty of another small deception. I am not, as I gave you to understand, attached to the Ministry of Supply. I am an agent of the British Government. An officer of MI6 counter-espionage.'

Well, I got my reaction, all right. They just sat there, mouths wide open like newly-landed fish, staring at me. It was Jolly, always a fast adjuster, who recovered first.

'Counter-espionage, by jove! Counter-espionage! Spies and cloaks and daggers and beautiful blondes tucked away in the wardrobes – or wardroom, should I say. But why – but why are you *here*? What do you – well, what *can* you want to see us about, Dr Carpenter?'

'A small matter of murder,' I said.

'Murder!' Captain Folsom spoke for the first time since coming aboard ship, the voice issuing from that savagely burnt face no more than a strangled croak. 'Murder?'

'Two of the men lying up there now in the Drift Station lab. were dead *before* the fire. They had been shot through the head. A third had been knifed. I would call that murder, wouldn't you?'

Jolly groped for the table and lowered himself shakily into his seat. The rest of them looked as if they were very glad that they were already sitting down.

'It seems so superfluous to add,' I said, adding it all the same, 'that the murderer is in this room now.'

You wouldn't have thought it, not to look at them. You could see at a glance that none of those high-minded citizens could possibly be a killer. They were as innocent as life's young morning, the whole lot of them, pure and white as the driven snow.

Chapter Twelve

It would be an understatement to say that I had the attention of the company. Maybe had I been a two-headed visitor from outer space, or had been about to announce the result of a multi-million pound sweepstake in which they held the only tickets, or was holding straws for them to pick to decide who should go before the firing squad – maybe then they might have given me an even more exclusive degree of concentration. But I doubt it. It wouldn't have been possible.

'If you'll bear with me,' I began, 'first of all I'd like to give you a little lecture in camera optics – and don't ask me what the hell that has to do with murder, it's got everything to do with it, as you'll find out soon enough.

'Film emulsion and lens quality being equal, the clarity of detail in any photograph depends upon the focal length of the lens – that is, the distance between the lens and the film. As recently as fifteen years ago the maximum focal length of any camera outside an observatory was about fifty inches. Those were used in reconnaissance planes in the later stages of the Second World War. A small suitcase lying on the ground would show up on a photograph taken from a height of ten miles, which was pretty good for those days.

'But the American Army and Air Force wanted bigger and better aerial cameras, and the only way this could be done was by increasing the focal length of the lens. There was obviously a superficial limit to this length because the Americans wanted this camera to fit into a plane – or an orbiting satellite – and if you wanted a camera with a focal length of, say, 250 inches, it was obviously going to be quite impossible to install a twenty-foot camera pointing vertically downwards in a plane or small satellite. But scientists came up with a new type of camera using the folded lens principle, where the light, instead of coming down a long straight barrel, is bounced round a series of angled mirrored corners, which permits the focal length to be increased greatly without having to enlarge the camera itself. By 1950 they'd developed a hundred-inch focal length lens. It was quite an improvement on the World War II cameras which could barely pick up a suitcase at ten miles – this one could pick up a cigarette packet at ten miles. Then, ten years later, came what they called the Perkin-Elmer Roti satellite missile tracker, with a focal length of five hundred inches – equivalent to a barrel type camera forty feet long: this one could pick up a cube of sugar at ten miles.'

I looked inquiringly around the audience for signs of inattention. There were no signs of inattention. No lecturer ever had a keener audience than I had there.

'Three years later,' I went on, 'another American firm had developed this missile tracker into a fantastic camera that could be mounted in even a small-size satellite. Three years' non-stop work to create this camera – but they reckoned it worth it. We don't know the focal length, it's never been revealed: we do know that, given the right atmospheric conditions, a white saucer on a dark surface will show up clearly from 300 miles up in space. This on a relatively tiny negative capable of almost infinite enlargement – for the scientists have also come up with a completely new film emulsion, still super-secret and a hundred times as sensitive as the finest films available on the commercial market to-day.

'This was to be fitted to the two-ton satellite the Americans called Samos III – Samos for Satellite and Missile Observation System. It never was. This, the only camera of its kind in the world, vanished, hi-jacked in broad daylight and, as we later learned, dismantled, flown from New York to Havana by a Polish jet-liner which had cleared for Miami and so avoided customs inspection.

'Four months ago this camera was launched in a Soviet satellite on a polar orbit, crossing the American middle west seven times a day. Those satellites can stay up indefinitely, but in just three days, with perfect weather conditions, the Soviets had all the pictures they ever wanted – pictures of every American missile launching base west of the Mississippi. Every time this camera took a picture of a small section of the United States another smaller camera in the satellite, pointing vertically upwards, took a fix on the stars. Then it was only a matter of checking map co-ordinates and they could have a Soviet inter-continental ballistic missile ranged in on every launching-pad in America. But first they had to have the pictures.

'Radio transmission is no good, there's far too much quality and detail lost in the process – and you must remember this was a relatively tiny negative in the first place. So they had to have the actual films. There are two ways of doing this – bring the satellite back to earth or have it eject a capsule with the films. The Americans, with their Discoverer tests, have perfected the art of using planes to snatch falling capsules from the sky. The Russians haven't, although we do know they have a technique for ejecting capsules should a satellite run amok. So they had to bring the satellite down. They planned to bring it down some two hundred miles east of the Caspian. But something went wrong. Precisely what we don't know, but our experts say that it could only have been due to the fact that the retro-rockets on one side of the capsule failed to fire when given the radio signal to do so. You are beginning to understand, gentlemen?'

'We are beginning to understand indeed.' It was Jeremy who spoke, his voice very soft. 'The satellite took up a different orbit.'

'That's what happened. The rockets firing on one side didn't slow her up any that mattered, they just knocked her far off course. A new and wobbly orbit that passed through Alaska, south over the Pacific, across Grahamland in Antarctica and directly south of South America, up over Africa and Western Europe, then round the North Pole in a shallow curve, maybe two hundred miles distant from it at the nearest point.

'Now, the only way the Russians could get the films was by ejecting the capsule, for with retro-rockets firing on one side only they knew that even if they did manage to slow up the satellite sufficiently for it to leave orbit, they had no idea where it would go. But the damnably awkward part of it from the Russian's viewpoint was that nowhere in its orbit of the earth did the satellite pass over the Soviet Union or any sphere of Communist influence whatsoever. Worse, ninety per cent of its travel was over open sea and if they brought it down there they would never see their films again as the capsule is so heavily coated with aluminium and Pyroceram to withstand the heat of re-entry into the atmosphere that it was much heavier than water. And as I said, they had never developed the American know-how of snatching falling capsules out of the air – and you will appreciate that they couldn't very well ask the Americans to do the job for them.

'So they decided to bring it down in the only safe place open to them – either the polar ice-cap in the north or the Antarctic in the south. You will remember Captain, that I told you that I had just returned from the Antarctic. The Russians have a couple of geophysical stations there and, up until a few days ago, we thought that there was a fifty-fifty chance that the capsule might be brought down there. But we were wrong. Their nearest station in the Antarctic was 300 miles from the path of orbit – and no field parties were stirring from home.'

'So they decided to bring it down in the vicinity of Drift Ice Station Zebra?' Jolly asked quietly. It was a sign of his perturbation that he didn't even call me 'old boy.'

'Drift Ice Station Zebra wasn't even in existence at the time the satellite went haywire, although all preparations were complete. We had arranged

for Canada to lend us a St Lawrence ice-breaker to set up the station but
the Russians in a burst of friendly goodwill and international co-operation
offered us the atomic-powered *Lenin*, the finest ice-breaker in the world.
They wanted to make good and sure that Zebra was set up and set up in
good time. It was. The east-west drift of the ice-cap was unusually slow this
year and almost eight weeks elapsed after the setting up of the station until
it was directly beneath the flight trajectory of the satellite.'

'You *knew* what the Russians had in mind?' Hansen asked.

'We knew. But the Russians had no idea whatsoever that we were on to
them. They had no idea that one of the pieces of equipment which was
landed at Zebra was a satellite monitor which would tell Major Halliwell
when the satellite received the radio signal to eject the capsule.' I looked
slowly round the Zebra survivors. 'I'll wager none of you knew that. But
Major Halliwell did – and the three other men who slept in his hut where
this machine was located.

'What we did not know was the identity of the member of Zebra's
company that had been suborned by the Russians. We were certain someone
must have been but had no idea who it was. Every one of you had first-class
security clearances. But someone was suborned – and that someone, when
he arrived back in Britain, would have been a wealthy man for the rest of
his days. In addition to leaving what was in effect an enemy agent planted
in Zebra, the Soviets also left a portable monitor – an electronic device for
tuning in on a particular radio signal which would be activated inside the
capsule at the moment of its ejection from the satellite. A capsule can be so
accurately ejected 300 miles up that it will land within a mile of its target,
but the ice-cap is pretty rough territory and dark most of the time, so this
monitor would enable our friend to locate the capsule which would keep on
emitting its signal for at least, I suppose, twenty-four hours after landing.
Our friend took the monitor and went out looking for the capsule. He found
it, released it from its drogue and brought it back to the station. You are still
with me, gentlemen? Especially one particular gentleman?'

'I think we are all with you, Dr Carpenter,' Commander Swanson said
softly. 'Every last one of us.'

'Fine. Well, unfortunately, Major Halliwell and his three companions
also knew that the satellite had ejected its capsule – don't forget that they
were monitoring this satellite twenty-four hours a day. They knew that
someone was going to go looking for it pretty soon, but who that someone
would be they had no idea. Anyway, Major Halliwell posted one of his men
to keep watch. It was a wild night, bitterly cold, with a gale blowing an ice-
storm before it, but he kept a pretty good watch all the same. He either
bumped into our friend returning with the capsule or, more probably, saw
a light in a cabin, investigated, found our friend stripping the film from the
capsule and, instead of going quietly away and reporting to Major Halliwell,
he went in and challenged this man. If that was the way of it, it was a bad
mistake, the last he ever made. He got a knife between the ribs.' I gazed at
all the Zebra survivors in turn. 'I wonder which one of you did it? Whoever
it was, he wasn't very expert. He broke off the blade inside the chest. I
found it there.' I was looking at Swanson and he didn't bat an eyelid. He
knew I hadn't found the blade there: he had found the haft in the petrol
tank. But there was time enough to tell them that.

'When the man he had posted didn't turn up, Major Halliwell got worried.

It must have been something like that. I don't know and it doesn't matter. Our friend with the broken knife was on the alert now, he knew someone was on to him – it must have come as a pretty severe shock, he'd thought himself completely unsuspected – and when the second man the Major sent turned up he was ready for him. He had to kill him – for the first man was lying dead in his cabin. Apart from his broken knife he'd also a gun. He used it.

'Both those men had come from Halliwell's cabin, the killer knew that Halliwell must have sent them and that he and the other man still in the major's cabin would be around in double quick time if the second watcher didn't report back immediately. He decided not to wait for that – he'd burnt his boats anyway. He took his gun, went into Major Halliwell's cabin and shot him and the other man as they lay on their beds. I know that because the bullets in their heads entered low from the front and emerged high at the back – the angle the bullets would naturally take if the killer was standing at the foot of their beds and fired at them as they were lying down. I suppose this is as good a time as any to say that my name is not really Carpenter. It's Halliwell. Major Halliwell was my elder brother.'

'Good God!' Dr Jolly whispered. 'Good God above!'

'One thing the killer knew it was essential to do right away – to conceal the traces of his crime. There was only one way – burn the bodies out of all recognition. So he dragged a couple of drums of oil out of the fuel store, poured them against the walls of Major Halliwell's hut – he'd already pulled in there the first two men he'd killed – and set fire to it. For good measure he also set fire to the fuel store. A thorough type, my friends, a man who never did anything by halves.'

The men seated around the wardroom table were dazed and shocked, uncomprehending and incredulous. But they were only incredulous because the enormity of the whole thing was beyond them. But not beyond them all.

'I'm a man with a curious turn of mind,' I went on. 'I wondered why sick, burnt, exhausted men had wasted their time and their little strength in shifting the dead men into the lab. Because someone had suggested that it might be a good thing to do, the decent thing to do. The real reason, of course, was to discourage anyone from going there. I looked under the floorboards and what did I find? Forty Nife cells in first-class condition, stores of food, a radio-sonde balloon and a hydrogen cylinder for inflating the balloon. I had expected to find the Nife cells – Kinnaird, here, has told us that there were a good many reserves, but Nife cells won't be destroyed in a fire. Buckled and bent a bit, but not destroyed. I hadn't expected to find the other items of equipment, but they made everything clear.

'The killer had had bad luck on two counts – being found out and with the weather. The weather really put the crimp on all his plans. The idea was that when conditions were favourable he'd send the films up into the sky attached to a radio-sonde balloon which could be swept up by a Russian plane: snatching a falling capsule out of the sky is very tricky indeed; snaring a stationary balloon is dead easy. The relatively unused Nife cells our friend used for keeping in radio touch with his pals to let them know when the weather had cleared and when he was going to send the balloon up. There is no privacy on the air-waves, so he used a special code; when he no longer had any need for it he destroyed the code by the only safe method of destruction in the Arctic – fire. I found scores of pieces of charred paper embedded in the walls of one of the huts where the wind had carried them from the met. office after our friend had thrown the ashes away.

'The killer also made sure that only those few worn-out Nife cells were used to send the S O S's and to contact the *Dolphin*. By losing contact with us so frequently, and by sending such a blurred transmission, he tried to delay our arrival here so as to give the weather a chance to clear up and let him fly off his balloon. Incidentally you may have heard radio reports – it was in all the British newspapers – that Russian as well as American and British planes scoured this area immediately after the fire. The British and Americans were looking for Zebra: the Russians were looking for a radio-sonde balloon. So was the ice-breaker *Dvina* when it tried to smash its way through here a few days ago. But there have been no more Russian planes: our friend radioed *his* friends to say that there was no hope of the weather clearing, that the *Dolphin* had arrived and that they would have to take the films back with them on the submarine.'

'One moment, Dr Carpenter,' Swanson interrupted in a careful sort of voice. 'Are you saying that those films are aboard this ship now?'

'I'll be very much surprised if they aren't, Commander. The other attempt to delay us, of course, was by making a direct attack on the *Dolphin* itself. When it became known that the *Dolphin* was to make an attempt to reach Zebra, orders went through to Scotland to cripple the ship. Red Clydeside is no more red than any other maritime centre in Britain, but you'll find Communists in practically every shipyard in the country – and, more often than not, their mates don't know who they are. There was no intention, of course, of causing any fatal accident – and, as far as whoever was responsible for leaving the tube doors open was concerned, there was no reason why there should be. International espionage in peacetime shuns violence – which is why our friend here is going to be very unpopular with his masters. Like Britain or America, they'll adopt any legitimate or illegitimate tactic to gain their espionage end – but they stop short of murder, just as we do. Murder was no part of the Soviet plan.'

'Who is it, Dr Carpenter?' Jeremy said very quietly. 'For God's sake, who is it? There's nine of us here and – do you *know* who it is?'

'I know. And only six, not nine, can be under suspicion. The ones who kept radio watches after the disaster. Captain Folsom and the two Har-ringtons here were completely immobilized. We have the word of all of you for that. So that, Jeremy, just leaves yourself, Kinnaird, Dr Jolly, Hassard, Naseby and Hewson. Murder for gain, and high treason. There's only one answer for that. The trial will be over the day it begins: three weeks later it will all be over. You're a very clever man, my friend. You're more than that, you're brilliant. But I'm afraid it's the end of the road for you, Dr Jolly.'

They didn't get it. For long seconds they didn't get it. They were too shocked, too stunned. They'd heard my words all right, but the meaning hadn't registered immediately. But it was beginning to register now for like marionettes under the guidance of a master puppeteer they all slowly turned their heads and stared at Jolly. Jolly himself rose slowly to his feet and took two paces towards me, his eyes wide, his mouth working.

'Me?' His voice was low and hoarse and unbelieving. '*Me*? Are you – are you mad, Dr Carpenter? In the name of God, man—'

I hit him. I don't know why I hit him, a crimson haze seemed to blur my vision, and Jolly was staggering back to crash on the deck, holding both hands to smashed lips and nose, before I could realize what I had done. I think if I had had a knife or a gun in my hand then, I would have killed him. I would have killed him the way I would have killed a fer-de-lance, a black widow spider or any other such dark and evil and deadly thing, without thought or compunction or mercy. Gradually the haze cleared from my eyes. No one had stirred. No one had stirred an inch. Jolly pushed himself painfully to his knees and then his feet and collapsed heavily in his seat by the table. He was holding a blood-soaked handkerchief to his face. There was utter silence in the room.

'My brother, Jolly,' I said. 'My brother and all the dead men on Zebra. Do you know what I hope?' I said. 'I hope that something goes wrong with the hangman's rope and that you take a long, long time to die.'

He took the handkerchief from his mouth.

'You're crazy man,' he whispered between smashed and already puffing lips. 'You don't know what you are saying.'

'The jury at the Old Bailey will be the best judge of that. I've been on to you now, Jolly, for almost exactly sixty hours.'

'What did you say?' Swanson demanded. 'You've known for sixty hours!'

'I knew I'd have to face your wrath some time or other, Commander,' I said. Unaccountably, I was beginning to feel very tired, weary and heart-sick of the whole business. 'But if you had known who he was you'd have locked him up straightaway. You said so in so many words. I wanted to see where the trail led to in Britain, who his associates and contacts would be. I had splendid visions of smashing a whole spy ring. But I'm afraid the trail is cold. It ends right here. Please hear me out.

'Tell me, did no one think it strange that when Jolly came staggering out of his hut when it caught fire that he should have collapsed and remained that way? Jolly claimed that he had been asphyxiated. Well, he wasn't asphyxiated inside the hut because he managed to come out under his own steam. Then he collapsed. Curious. Fresh air invariably revives people. But not Jolly. He's a special breed. He wanted to make it clear to everyone that he had nothing to do with the fire. Just to drive home the point, he has repeatedly emphasized that he is not a man of action. If he isn't, then I've never met one.'

'You can hardly call that proof of guilt,' Swanson interrupted.

'I'm not adducing evidence,' I said wearily. 'I'm merely introducing pointers. Pointer number two. You, Naseby, felt pretty bad about your failure to wake up your two friends, Flanders and Bryce. You could have shaken them for an hour and not woken them up. Jolly, here, used either ether or chloroform to lay them out. This was after he had killed Major Halliwell and the three others; but before he started getting busy with matches. He realized that if he burnt the place down there might be a long, long wait before rescue came and he was going to make damned certain that he wasn't going to go hungry. If the rest of you had died from starvation – well, that was just your bad luck. But Flanders and Bryce lay between him and the food. Didn't it strike you as very strange, Naseby, that your shouting and shaking had no effect. The only reason could be that they had been drugged – and only one man had access to drugs. Also, you said that both Hewson and yourself felt pretty groggy. No wonder. It was a pretty small hut and the chloroform or ether fumes had reached and affected Hewson and yourself – normally you'd have smelt it on waking up, but the stink of burning diesel obliterates every other smell. Again, I know this is not proof of any kind.

'Third pointer. I asked Captain Folsom this morning who had given the orders for the dead men to be put in the lab. He said he had. But, he remembered, it was Jolly's suggestion to him. Something learnedly medical about helping the morale of the survivors by putting the charred corpses out of sight.

'Fourth pointer. Jolly said that *how* the fire started was unimportant. A crude attempt to side-track me. Jolly knew as well as I did that it was all-important. I suppose, by the way, Jolly, that you deliberately jammed all the fire-extinguishers you could before you started the fire. About that fire, Commander. Remember you were a bit suspicious of Hewson, here, because he said the fuel drums hadn't started exploding until he was on his way to the main bunkhouse. He was telling the truth. There were no fewer than four drums in the fuel stores that didn't explode – the ones Jolly, here, used to pour against the huts to start the fire. How am I doing, Dr Jolly?'

'It's all a nightmare,' he said very quietly. 'It's a nightmare. Before God. I know nothing of any of this.'

'Pointer number five. For some reason that is unclear to me Jolly wanted to delay the *Dolphin* on its return trip. He could best do this, he reckoned, if Bolton and Brownell, the two very sick men still left out on the station could he judged to be too sick to be transferred to the *Dolphin*. The snag was, there were two other doctors around who might say that they *were* fit to be transferred. So he tried, with a fair measure of success, to eliminate us.

'First Benson. Didn't it strike you as strange, Commander, that the request for the survivors to be allowed to attend the funeral of Grant and Lieutenant Mills should have come from Naseby in the first place, then Kinnaird? Jolly, as the senior man of the party with Captain Folsom, here, temporarily unfit, was the obvious man to make the approach – but he didn't want to go calling too much attention to himself. Doubtless by dropping hints, he engineered it so that someone else should do it for him. Now Jolly had noticed how glass-smooth and slippery the ice-banked sides of the sail were and he made a point of seeing that Benson went up the rope immediately ahead of him. You must remember it was almost pitch dark – just light enough for Jolly to make out the vague outline of Benson's head from the wash of light from the bridge as it cleared the top of the rail. A swift outward tug on the rope and Benson overbalanced. It seemed that he had fallen on top of Jolly. But only seemed. The loud sharp crack I heard a fraction of a second after Benson's body struck was not caused by his head hitting the ice – it was caused by Jolly, here, trying to kick his head off. Did you hurt your toes much, Jolly?'

'You're mad,' he said mechanically. 'This is utter nonsense. Even if it wasn't nonsense, you couldn't prove a word of it.'

'We'll see. Jolly claimed that Benson fell on top of him. He even flung himself on the ice and cracked his head to give some verisimilitude to his story – our pal never misses any of the angles. I felt the slight bump on his head. But he wasn't laid out. He was faking. He recovered just that little bit too quickly and easily when he got back to the sick-bay. And it was then that he made his first mistake, the mistake that put me on to him – and should have put me on guard for an attack against myself. You were there, Commander.'

'I've missed everything else,' Swanson said bitterly. 'Do you want me to spoil a hundred per cent record?'

'When Jolly came to he saw Benson lying there. All he could see of him was a blanket and a big gauze pack covering the back of his head. As far as Jolly was concerned, it could have been anybody – it had been pitch dark when the accident occurred. But what did he say? I remember his exact words. He said: "Of course, of course. Yes, that's it. He fell on top of me, didn't he?" *He never thought to ask who it was* – the natural, the inevitable question in the circumstances. But Jolly didn't have to ask. He knew.'

'He knew.' Swanson stared at Jolly with cold bleak eyes and there was no doubt in his mind now about Jolly. 'You have it to rights, Dr Carpenter. He knew.'

'And then he had a go at me. Can't prove a thing, of course. But he was there when I asked you where the medical store was, and he no doubt nipped down smartly behind Henry and myself and loosened the latch on the hatch-cover. But he didn't achieve quite the same high degree of success this time. Even so, when we went out to the station next morning he still tried to stop Brownell and Bolton from being transferred back to the ship by saying Bolton was too ill. But you overruled him.'

'I was right about Bolton,' Jolly said. He seemed strangely quiet now. 'Bolton died.'

'He died,' I agreed. 'He died because you murdered him and for Bolton alone I can make certain you hang. For a reason I still don't know, Jolly was still determined to stop this ship. Delay it, anyway. I think he wanted only an hour or two's delay. So he proposed to start a small fire, nothing much, just enough to cause a small scare and have the reactor shut down temporarily. As the site of his fire he chose the machinery space – the one place in the ship where he could casually let something drop and where it would lie hidden, for hours if need be, among the maze of pipes down there. In the sick-bay he concocted some type of delayed action chemical fuse which would give off plenty of smoke but very little flame – there are a dozen combinations of acids and chemicals that can bring this about and our friend will be a highly-trained expert well versed in all of them. Now all Jolly wanted was an excuse to pass through the engine-room when it would be nice and quiet and virtually deserted. In the middle of the night. He fixed this too. He can fix anything. He is a very, very clever man indeed is our pal here; he's also an utterly ruthless fiend.

'Late on the evening of the night before the fire the good healer here made a round of his patients. I went with him. One of the men he treated was Bolton in the nucleonics lab. – and, of course, to get to the nucleonics lab. you have to pass through the engine-room. There was an enlisted man watching over the patients and Jolly left special word that he was to be called at any hour if Bolton became any worse. He was called. I checked with the engine-room staff after the fire. The engineer officer was on watch and two others were in the manoeuvring-room but an engine-man carrying out a routine lubrication job saw him passing through the engine-room about 1.30 a.m. in answer to a call from the man watching over the patients. He took the opportunity to drop his little chemical fuse as he was passing by the machinery space. What he didn't know was that his little toy lodged on or near the oil-saturated lagging on the housing of the starboard turbo-generator and that when it went off it would generate sufficient heat to set the lagging on fire.'

Swanson looked at Jolly, bleakly and for a long time, then turned to me and shook his head. 'I can't wear that, Dr Carpenter. This phone call because a patient just happens to turn sick. Jolly is not the man to leave _anything_ to chance.'

'He isn't,' I agreed. 'He didn't. Up in the refrigerator in the sick-bay I have an exhibit for the Old Bailey. A sheet of aluminium foil liberally covered with Jolly's fingerprints. Smeared on this foil is the remains of a salve. That foil was what Jolly had bandaged on to Bolton's burnt forearm that night, just after he had given him pain-killing shots – Bolton was suffering very badly. But before Jolly put the salve on the foil he spread on something else first – a layer of sodium chloride – common or garden household salt. Jolly knew that the drugs he had given Bolton would keep him under for three or four hours; he also knew that by the time Bolton had regained consciousness body heat would have thinned the salve and brought the salt into contact with the raw flesh on the forearm. Bolton, he knew, when he came out from the effects of the drugs, would come out screaming in agony. Can you imagine what it must have been like: the whole forearm a mass of raw flesh – and covered with salt? When he died soon after, he died from shock. Our good healer here – a lovable little lad, isn't he?'

'Well, that's Jolly. Incidentally, you can discount most of the gallant doctor's heroism during the fire – although he was understandably as anxious as any of us that we survive. The first time he went into the engine-room it was too damned hot and uncomfortable for his liking so he just lay down on the floor and let someone carry him for'ard to where the fresh air was. Later—'

'He'd his mask off,' Hansen objected.

'He took it off. _You_ can hold your breath for ten or fifteen seconds – don't you think Jolly can too? Later on, when he was performing his heroics in the engine-room it was because conditions there were better, conditions outside were worse – and because by going into the engine-room he was entitled to a closed-circuit breathing set. Jolly got more clean air last night than any of us. He doesn't mind if he causes someone to die screaming his head off in agony – but he himself isn't going to suffer the slightest degree of hardship. Not if he can help it. Isn't that so, Jolly?'

He didn't answer.

'Where are the films, Jolly?'

'I don't know what you are talking about,' he said in a quiet toneless voice. 'Before God, my hands are clean.'

'How about your fingerprints on that foil with the salt on it?'

'Any doctor can make a mistake.'

'My God! Mistake! Where are they, Jolly – the films?'

'For God's sake leave me alone,' he said tiredly.

'Have it your own way.' I looked at Swanson. 'Got some nice secure place where you can lock this character up?'

'I certainly have,' Swanson said grimly. 'I'll conduct him there in person.'

'No one's conducting anyone anywhere,' Kinnaird said. He was looking at me and I didn't care very much for the way he was looking at me. I didn't care very much either for what he held in his hand, a very nasty-looking

Luger. It was cradled in his fist as if it had grown there and it was pointing straight between my eyes.

Chapter Thirteen

'Clever, clever counter-espionage, Carpenter,' Dr Jolly murmured. 'How swiftly the fortunes of war change, old boy. But you shouldn't be surprised really. You haven't found out anything that actually matters, but surely you should have found out enough to realize that you are operating out of your class. Please don't try anything foolish. Kinnaird is one of the finest pistol shots I have ever known – and you will observe how strategically he's placed so that everyone in the room is covered.'

He delicately patted his still-bleeding mouth with a handkerchief, rose, went behind me and ran his hands quickly down my clothes.

'My word,' he said. 'Not even carrying a gun. You really are unprepared, Carpenter. Turn round, will you, so that your back is to Kinnaird's gun?'

I turned round. He smiled pleasantly then hit me twice across the face with all his strength, first with the back of his right hand and then with the back of the left. I staggered, but didn't fall down. I could taste the salt of blood.

'Can't even call it regrettable loss of temper,' Jolly said with satisfaction. 'Did it deliberately and with malice aforethought. Enjoyed it, too.'

'So Kinnaird was the killer,' I said slowly, thickly. 'He was the man with the gun?'

'Wouldn't want to take all the credit, mate,' Kinnaird said modestly. 'Let's say we sorted them out fifty-fifty.'

'*You* were the one who went out with the monitor to find the capsule,' I nodded. 'That's why you got your face so badly frost-bitten.'

'Got lost,' Kinnaird admitted. 'Thought I'd never find the damned station again.'

'Jolly and Kinnaird,' Jeremy said wonderingly. 'Jolly and Kinnaird. Your own mates. You two filthy murderous—'

'Be quiet,' Jolly ordered. 'Kinnaird, don't bother answering questions. Unlike Carpenter here, I take no pleasure in outlining my *modus operandi* and explaining at length how clever I've been. As you observed, Carpenter, I'm a man of action. Commander Swanson, get on that phone there, call up your control room, order your ship to surface and steam north.'

'You're becoming too ambitious, Jolly,' Swanson said calmly. 'You can't hi-jack a submarine.'

'Kinnaird,' Jolly said. 'Point your gun at Hansen's stomach. When I reach the count of five, pull the trigger. One, two, three—'

Swanson half-raised a hand in acknowledgment of defeat, crossed to the wall-phone, gave the necessary orders, hung up and came back to stand beside me. He looked at me without either respect or admiration. I looked round all the other people in the room. Jolly, Hansen and Rawlings standing, Zabrinski sitting on a chair by himself with the now disregarded copy of the *Dolphin Daze* on his knees, all the others sitting round the table, Kinnaird well clear of them, the gun very steady in his hand. So very steady. No one seemed to be contemplating any heroics. For the most part everyone was too shocked, too dazed, to think of anything.

'Hi-jacking a nuclear submarine is an intriguing prospect – and no doubt would be a highly profitable one, Commander Swanson,' Jolly said. 'But I know my limitations. No, old top, we shall simply be leaving you. Not very many miles from here is a naval vessel with a helicopter on its after deck. In a little while, Commander, you will send a wireless message on a certain frequency giving our position: the helicopter will pick us up. And even if your crippled engine would stand the strain I wouldn't advise you to come chasing after that ship with ideas about torpedoing it or anything of that dramatic ilk. Apart from the fact that you wouldn't like to be responsible for triggering off a nuclear war, you couldn't catch it, anyway. You won't even be able to see the ship, Commander – and if you did it wouldn't matter, anyway. It has no nationality markings.'

'Where are the films?' I asked.

'They're already aboard that naval vessel.'

'They're *what?*' Swanson demanded. 'How in hell's name can they be?'

'Sorry and all that, old boy. I repeat that unlike Carpenter, here, I don't go around shooting off my mouth. A professional, my dear captain, *never* gives information about his methods.'

'So you get off with it,' I said bitterly. My mouth felt thick and swollen.

'Don't see what's to stop us. Crimes don't always come home to roost, you know.'

'Eight men murdered,' I said wonderingly. 'Eight men. You can stand there and cheerfully admit that you are responsible for the deaths of eight men.'

'Cheerfully?' he said consideringly. 'No, not cheerfully. I'm a professional, and a professional never kills unnecessarily. But this time it was necessary. That's all.'

'That's the second time you've used the word "professional",' I said slowly. 'I was wrong on one theory. You weren't just suborned after the Zebra team had been picked. You've been at this game a long time – you're too good not to have been.'

'Fifteen years, old lad,' Jolly said calmly. 'Kinnaird and I – we were the best team in Britain. Our usefulness in that country, unfortunately, is over. I should imagine that our – um – exceptional talents can be employed elsewhere.'

'You admit to all those murders?' I asked.

He looked at me in sudden cold speculation. 'A damned funny question, Carpenter. Of course. I've told you. Why?'

'And do you, Kinnaird?'

He looked at me in bleak suspicion. 'Why ask?'

'You answer my question and I'll answer yours.' At the corner of my range of vision I could see Jolly looking at me with narrowed eyes. He was very sensitive to atmosphere, he knew there was something off-key.

'You know damn' well what I did, mate,' Kinnaird said coldly.

'So there we have it. In the presence of no less than twelve witnesses, you both confess to murder. You shouldn't have done that, you know. I'll answer your question, Kinnaird. I wanted to have an oral confession from you because, apart from the sheet of aluminium foil and something I'll mention in a minute, we have no actual proof at all against either of you. But now we have your confessions. Your great talents are not going to be used in any other sphere, I'm afraid. You'll never see that helicopter or that naval vessel. You'll both die jerking on the end of a rope.'

'What rubbish is this?' Jolly asked contemptuously. But there was worry under the contempt. 'What last-minute despairing bluff are you trying to pull, Carpenter?'

I ignored his question. I said: 'I've been on to Kinnaird, here, for some sixty hours also, Jolly. But I had to play it this way. Without letting you gain what appeared to be the upper hand you would never have admitted to the crimes. But now you have.'

'Don't fall for it, old boy,' Jolly said to Kinnaird. 'It's just some desperate bluff. He never had any idea that you were in on this.'

'When I knew you were one of the killers,' I said to Jolly, 'I was almost certain Kinnaird had to be another. You shared the same cabin and unless Kinnaird had been sapped or drugged he had to be in on it. He was neither. He was in on it. That door wasn't jammed when Naseby ran round to the radio room to warn you – the two of you were leaning all your weight against it to give the impression that it had been closed for hours and that ice had formed.

'By the same token, young Grant, the assistant radio operator, was in cahoots with you – or he wasn't. If he wasn't, he would have to be silenced. He wasn't. So you silenced him. After I'd caught on to the two of you I had a good look at Grant. I went out and dug him up from where we'd buried him. Rawlings and I. I found a great big bruise at the base of his neck. He surprised you in something, or he woke when you knifed or shot one of Major Halliwell's men, and you laid him out. You didn't bother killing him, you were just about to set the hut on fire and incinerate him, so killing would have been pointless. But you didn't reckon on Captain Folsom, here, going in and bringing him out – alive.

'That was most damnably awkward for you, wasn't it, Jolly? He was unconscious but when and if he recovered consciousness he could blow the whole works on you. But you couldn't get at him to finish him off, could you? The bunkhouse was full of people, most of them suffering so severely that sleep was impossible for them. When we arrived on the scene you got desperate. Grant was showing signs of regaining consciousness. You took a chance, but not all that much of a chance. Remember how surprised I was to find that you had used up all my morphine? Well, I *was* surprised then. But not now. I know now where it went. You gave him an injection of morphine – and you made damn' sure the hypodermic had a lethal dose. Am I correct?'

'You're cleverer than I thought you were,' he said calmly. 'Maybe I have misjudged you a little. But it still makes no difference, old boy.'

'I wonder. If I'd known about Kinnaird so long why do you think I allowed a situation to develop where you could apparently turn the tables?'

'Apparently is not the word you want. And the answer to your question is easy. You didn't know Kinnaird *had* a gun.'

'No?' I looked at Kinnaird. 'Are you sure that thing works?'

'Don't come that old stuff with me, mate,' Kinnaird said in contempt.

'I just wondered,' I said mildly. 'I thought perhaps the petrol in the tractor's tank might have removed all the lubricating oil.'

Jolly came close to me, his face tight and cold. 'You *knew* about this? What goes on, Carpenter?'

'It was actually Commander Swanson, here, who found the gun in the tank,' I said. 'You had to leave it there because you knew you'd all be getting a good clean-up and medical examination when we got you on board and it would have been bound to be discovered. But a murderer – a professional, Jolly – will never part with his gun unless he is compelled to. I knew if you got the slightest chance you would go back for it. So I put it back in the tank.'

'The hell you did!' Swanson was as nearly angry as I'd ever seen him. 'Forgot to tell me, didn't you?'

'I must have done. That was after I'd cottoned on to you, Jolly. I wasn't *absolutely* sure you had a partner, but I knew if you had it must be Kinnaird. So I put the gun back there in the middle of the night and I made good and certain that you, Jolly, didn't get the chance to go anywhere near the tractor shed at any time. But the gun vanished that following morning when everyone was out sampling the fresh air. So then I knew you had an accomplice. But the real reason for planting that gun, of course, is that without it you'd never have talked. But now you have talked and it's all finished. Put up that gun, Kinnaird.'

'I'm afraid your bluff's run out mate.' The gun was pointing directly at my face.

'Your last chance, Kinnaird. Please pay attention to what I am saying. Put up that gun or you will be requiring the services of a doctor within twenty seconds.'

He said something, short and unprintable. I said: 'It's on your own head. Rawlings, you know what to do.'

Every head turned towards Rawlings who was standing leaning negligently against a bulkhead, his hands crossed lightly in front of him. Kinnaird looked too, the Luger following the direction of his eyes. A gun barked, the sharp flat crack of a Mannlicher-Schoenauer, Kinnaird screamed and his gun spun from his smashed hand. Zabrinski, holding my automatic in one hand and his copy of the *Dolphin Daze* – now with a neat charred hole through the middle – in the other, regarded his handiwork admiringly then turned to me. 'Was that how you wanted it done, Doc?'

'That was exactly how I wanted it done, Zabrinski. Thank you very much. A first-class job.'

'A first-class job,' Rawlings sniffed. He retrieved the fallen Luger and pointed it in Jolly's general direction. 'At four feet even Zabrinski couldn't miss.' He dug into a pocket, pulled out a roll of bandage and tossed it to Jolly. 'We kinda thought we might be having to use this so we came prepared. Dr Carpenter said your pal here would be requiring the services of a doctor. He is. You're a doctor. Get busy.'

'Do it yourself,' Jolly snarled. No 'old boy,' no 'old top.' The *bonhomie* was gone and gone for ever.

Rawlings looked at Swanson and said woodenly: 'Permission to hit Dr Jolly over the head with this little old gun, sir?'

'Permission granted,' Swanson said grimly. But no further persuasion was necessary. Jolly cursed and started ripping the cover off the bandage.

For almost a minute there was silence in the room while we watched Jolly carry out a rough, ready and far from gentle repair job on Kinnaird's hand. Then Swanson said slowly: 'I still don't understand how in the devil Jolly got rid of the film.'

'It was easy. Ten minutes thinking and you'd get it. They waited until we had cleared the ice-cap then they took the films, shoved them in a waterproof bag, attached a yellow dye marker to the bag then pumped it out through the garbage disposal unit in the galley. Remember, they'd been on a tour of the ship and seen it – although the suggestion was probably radioed them by a naval expert. I had Rawlings posted on watch in the early hours of this morning and he saw Kinnaird go into the galley about half past four. Maybe he just wanted a ham sandwich, I don't know. But Rawlings says he had the bag and marker with him when he sneaked in and empty hands when he came out. The bag would float to the surface and the marker stain thousands of square yards of water. The naval ship up top would have worked out our shortest route from Zebra to Scotland and would be within a few miles of our point of exit from the ice-pack. It could probably have located it without the helicopter: but the chopper made it dead certain.

'Incidentally, I was being rather less than accurate when I said I didn't know the reason for Jolly's attempts to delay us. I knew all along. He'd been told that the ship couldn't reach our exit point until such and such a time and that it was vital to delay us until then. Jolly, here, even had the effrontery to check with me what time we would be emerging from the ice-pack.'

Jolly looked up from Kinnaird's hand and his face was twisted in a mask of malevolence.

'You win, Carpenter. So you win. All along the line. But you lost out in the only thing that really mattered. They got the films – the films showing the location, as you said, of nearly every missile base in America. And that was all that mattered. Ten million pounds couldn't buy that information. But we got it.' He bared his teeth in a savage smile. 'We may have lost out, Carpenter, but we're professionals. We did our job.'

'They got the films, all right,' I acknowledged. 'And I'd give a year's salary to see the faces of the men who develop them. Listen carefully, Jolly. Your main reason in trying to cripple Benson and myself was not so much that you could have the say-so on Bolton's health and so delay us: your main reason, your over-riding reason, was that you wanted to be the only doctor on the ship so that it could only be you who would carry out the X-ray on Zabrinski's ankle here and remove the plaster cast. Literally everything hinged on that: basically, nothing else mattered. That was why you took such a desperate chance in crippling me when you heard me say I intended to X-ray Zabrinski's ankle the following morning. That was the one move you made that lacked the hall-mark of class – of a professional – but then I think you were close to panic. You were lucky.

'Anyway, you removed the plaster cast two mornings ago and also the films which you had hidden there in oilskin paper when you'd fixed the plaster on to Zabrinski's leg the first night we arrived in Zebra. A perfect hiding-place. You could always, of course, have wrapped them in bandages covering survivors' burns, but that would be too dicey. The cast was brilliant.

'Unfortunately for you and your friends I had removed the original plaster during the previous night, extracted the films from the oiled paper and replaced them with others. That, incidentally, is the second piece of evidence I have on you. There are two perfect sets of prints on the leaders of the satellite films – yours and Kinnaird's. Along with the salt-covered aluminium foil and the confession freely made in front of witnesses that guarantees you both the eight o'clock walk to the gallows. The gallows and failure, Jolly. You weren't even a professional. Your friends will never see those films.'

Mouthing soundless words through smashed lips, his face masked in madness and completely oblivious to the two guns, Jolly flung himself at me. He had taken two steps and two only when Rawling's gun caught him, not lightly, on the side of the head. He crashed to the floor as if the Brooklyn bridge had fallen in on top of him. Rawlings surveyed him dispassionately.

'Never did a day's work that gave me profounder satisfaction,' he said conversationally. 'Except, perhaps, those pictures I took with Dr Benson's camera to give Dr Carpenter, here, some negatives to shove inside that oiled paper.'

'Pictures of what?' Swanson asked curiously.

Rawlings grinned happily. 'All those pin-ups in Doc Benson's sick-bay. Yogi Bear, Donald Duck, Pluto, Popeye, Snow-white and the seven dwarfs – you name it, I got it. The lot. Each a guaranteed work of art – and in glorious Technicolor.' He smiled a beatific smile. 'Like Doc Carpenter, here, I'd give a year's pay to see their faces when they get around to developing those negatives.'